POINT
ROAD

Emily on the *Sphinx*.

POINT ROAD

BY

MICHAEL THOMAS BRIMBAU

PearTree Press
SMALL PRESS. JUICY READS.
Fall River, MA

PearTree Press
P.O. Box 9585
Fall River, MA 02720
peartree-press.com

For information, write us at PearTree Press, P.O. Box 9585, Fall River, MA 02720.

LIBRARY OF CONGRESS CONTROL NUMBER: **2017934262**

ISBN-13: 978-0-9908161-4-0

Printed in the United States of America on acid-free paper.

Book design by Stefani Koorey

Cover image: *The Whaling Brig Kate Cory at her Home Port in 1862* by John Stobart. Used with permission of the artist (stobart.com).

For Charlotte White and Paul Cuffe,
legendary citizens of Westport
and residents of color who made their mark in history
against unfavorable odds.

It is the province of knowledge to speak,
and the privilege of wisdom to listen.

Oliver Wendell Holmes Sr.

Chapter 1:

Westport Point Village, early summer, 1861

My best friend has come to visit. Amy Chaloner is a precocious, inquisitive, and compulsive young woman. Though we look somewhat alike, she is my polar opposite—the roar to my tranquility—the wilderness to my desert. I may add flame to our candle but, more importantly, she adds the fuel. In the end, we are the footpath to each other's labyrinth, the compass to each other's soul, and the best of friends.

Where I have sable-colored hair, Amy's is blonde, almost white. Her eyes are a translucent blue-green, like tropical ocean water. At least I think they are, for I have never been to tropical lands. On the other hand, my eyes are mud brown, like the riverbed behind my house. While my nose points to my feet, hers does so to heaven. Her chin I would need to call delicate and handsome, but her lips are always a wet rosy pink, standing up firm, like a proud soldier and daring you to kiss them. Try it. And a slap to the face will be the least of your troubles. We are of contrasting demeanor. After all, contrary flavors compliment one another, and though at times I can be sour, Amy Chaloner is not always sweet—though she is to me. When around her you always know you are alive, for she will find a way of making it so, whether pleasantly or not.

Amy lives in the city. Fall River. That's in Massachusetts. Her family has a summer cottage here at Point Village, at the end of Point Road in the town of Westport, where I live. Her father, Cornelius Chaloner, was a Nantucket whaling captain and one-time sea merchant. He made his fortune harvesting the great mammals and, later, in the transport of cotton from the southern states to New England. With success came a move to the city. Cornelius and his wife have nine children. Amy, a little younger than I, is a mid-child, with four younger and four older siblings. Her temperament and constitution speak to the wisdom of a much older woman, though at times she can be down right juvenile and unruly. You can say her demeanor runs cold or scalding, which to me is what makes her so interesting. My outlook on life is of an orderly tight weave, where hers is of a stitch ripper, splitting the norms of society to discover what it's made of. She is the perfect agent for a person such as myself, whose existence at times is unduly predictable and, dare I say, down right insipid. After all, she does come from the big city. As for Westport, it can be called a tiny hamlet, and Point Village but an unspoken whisper in a shrouded morning fog.

I tried pouring her another cup of tea, but she wouldn't have it.

"Please, Amy, have some more," I said, tipping the teapot over her cup, one finger securing the lid.

"No, I mustn't," she said, her hand hovering over the cup, "Too much tea gives me the jitters."

"Another cookie, perhaps?" I dropped a couple on her saucer.

"Cookies I will never refuse," she said, smiling as she placed a couple in her pocket.

"I am so happy you have dropped by. We haven't spent time together for almost a fortnight now."

"You must forgive me, Emmie. My time has been so occupied."

"Occupied?" I chortled. "You, a damsel of leisure—occupied … with what?"

"Why, riding lessons, fancywork, all sorts of business. Damsels are ladies in waiting. I'll let you know, I wait for no one."

"Perhaps it is a man."

"I wish," she quipped.

"Come now. You can tell me the truth. What is his name?"

She paused, giving my inquiry a thought. "Biscuit," she said, smirking.

"Peculiar name for a suitor."

"You know full well that Biscuit is the name of my Tennessee Walker."

"Oh, that mule?" I said.

"Now, Emmie, if you stop disparaging my foal, I will not venture to chastise your gentleman friend."

"What gentleman friend?" I scoffed.

"Well, you think I don't know about you and Samuel," she remarked, in her reprimanding but playful tone.

"All right, I call for a truce," I said throwing my hands in the air. "I will not mention horses or men if you don't."

"Done," she agreed.

I pulled up a chair and sat. "Will you be staying at the cottage on the Point?"

"No. Father has his schooner here in the harbor."

"Yes, I know."

"We are traveling to Nantucket to visit family. We sail in the morning."

She pulled out a lace handkerchief and wiped the corners of her mouth, folding the cloth neatly before tucking it into her sleeve at her wrist. Amy is particular about the way she looks. Appearance is everything to her. Being alive was a performance and she was always impeccably dressed and prepared for the stage of life.

"Oh, what a shame," I said, getting up to clear the table. "I was hoping we could spend time together. I have so much to talk about, and I get far too few callers. Grandmamma has been ill and I hate to be away from the house, or I would have begged to come along with you to Nantucket."

"Not to worry. We should be back in a week or so. This voyage is a tedious business trip for Father—the signing of papers, land, property, and all that sort of thing. We will lavish some time together when I get back."

"I'm happy you dropped by Amy ... always."

"It is good to see you too, Emmie. I could not leave without inquiring about your health and Charlotte's. I've been concerned about her."

"She is sleeping right now."

With one finger, I pushed back the curtain that separated the kitchen from the small pantry where Grandmamma kept her bed and spied, making certain she was all right.

"Have you read *The Pendulous Demise of Miss Sarah*?" whispered Amy from across the room.

"Yes," I murmured. "Not so loud. She may hear us."

"Well?"

"I finished reading the book earlier this week."

"And?" she begged. Her eyes were inflated and her mouth slack, eager to bite, chew, and swallow every word I fed her. "What do you think? Was it everything I heard it was?"

"My Lord, Amy, it was wicked."

"Upon my return from Nantucket you must steal some time. We will take the book with us somewhere and read it together."

"It even contains a little map of the area where the dead girl was discovered," I said.

"No!" she yelped, a hand over her mouth in astonished disbelief. "We must go and find it. I need to read it for sure now!"

A delicate voice sounded from behind the curtain. "Emily?"

"Shh! Yes, Grandmamma, I'm here." I pulled back the drapes.

Amy stood behind me. "Hello, Miss White."

"Why, girl, I have not seen you for months, now. How is your father?" asked Charlotte, struggling to sit up in bed.

"It's been less than two weeks since you last saw Amy, Grandmamma. Not months."

"Father's fine, Miss White."

"My, my, how time flies." She reached for a glass on a side table and sipped some water. "Why, just the other day you were but a child … still are, I suppose."

"Would you like to get up, Grandmamma?"

"Well, we do have a guest," she said, pulling back the bedsheets.

"No, Miss White. Don't you bother. I was just leaving. I dropped by to see how you were getting on."

"Why thank you, child. But I'm getting on as well as can be expected for someone my age." She let her head and shoulders drop back on the pillow as if a weight had pulled her down. "Just a little tired I'm afraid."

"Now, Grandmamma, you get some rest." I pulled up the sheet just below her chin.

"Just for a while, child," she mumbled, "then I must get up and we will have supper."

"Yes, Grandmamma," I agreed, kissing her. "We will have a wonderful supper."

"It was nice seeing you, Miss White," chimed Amy. "You take care now."

By the time the words left Amy's lips, Grandmamma was fast asleep.

I walked Amy to the door and we bid farewell. I watched as she pranced down the road to the wharf where the schooner *Somerset*, her father's sailing vessel, was berthed. She ambled down Point Road in her lacy white dress of Indian silk, tatting ruffles, and baby pearl piping, flourishing a floppy brim hat with peacock feathers. It was difficult to imagine her on any sort of sailing vessel.

Fishermen jumped aside providing her the ample room her presence demanded. When Amy sauntered along the tiny Westport docks, even good Old Testament Moses could not part a passage as well as she could. Every eye stopped to watch her. Pulleys and winches, lines and cranes, all came to a halt, as if frozen in time. Amy Chaloner was passing. I suppose life was a performance after all, and the world stage was made expressly for her. Yes, she was everything I was not and more. And for that, I am thankful for such a friend.

After Amy left, I sat down and poured myself a cup of tea. Looking out the kitchen window I could plainly see the setting sun melting into the horizon, snail-like, framed by the two sisters. The two sisters, if you don't know, are a pair of large willow trees that stand down by the banks of the Westport River in the field behind our house. The two sisters—at least that is what Grandmamma calls them.

The sun hovered as it descended toward the skyline. Along the shore, yellow zinnias danced to an easterly summer breeze, bowing to a plummeting orange-yellow orb. The horizon is crimson like a blacksmith's glowing iron. I could almost hear the evening hiss away, as the sun sinks and sizzles into a river, red as the ripe Winesap apples that grow by the lane along the shore. Everyday around this time I make myself a heaping cup of black tea and sit by the window, keeping the day company as it retreats in its introduction to dusk. I like holding my porcelain china cup, with its gold hallow rim, up to the piercing rusty light, and allow the glow to filter through the pink roses that decorate the delicate vessel. The backyard is overgrown in a sea of blue and white baby's breath. The numerous posies of the tiny, starlet flowers grow like fixed tumbleweeds in clumps of prickly shades.

Between the house next door and ours, a fence of sunflowers radiates, kept healthy and in fine fettle by Captain Seabury Cory, our next-door neighbor. "Emmie, if one must have fences they should be constructed of flowers," he often proclaims. "Neighbors should be family. No need for partitions of iron or timber, for we are all fish in the same sea, no one man better than his bother." Mr. Cory has called me Emmie since I was a little girl. Everyone does. But my real name is Emily. Emily A. White. Oh! Pay no mind to my middle initial. I really don't have one. It describes how I feel when I get up in the morning, and I change it every day. Today I feel adventurous. So 'A' it will be.

I have lived at the end of Point Road, sometimes called Point Village, with Charlotte White, or Grandmamma, as I call her, ever since I had a memory. I call her Grandmamma, since she is much too old to be my mother. I never knew my real mother.

I was what they call a Christmas basket baby. When I was born, I was delivered in a small straw, toweled hamper, abandoned—left on the back stoop of a family in the village of Troy during the peak of winter. When I was discovered it is said that I was kept warm by the neighborhood cat, which had cuddled in with me, otherwise I would have frozen to death. I have no shame in admitting such things, for I had little say in the matter. Newborns rarely do.

The family I was left with were good people, but they had twelve mouths to feed. So, in short order, I was couriered here to Miss White's in Point Village in the town of Westport. She was known for taking in strays— children who were abandoned or had lost their parents and had nowhere to live. Most of these youngsters were later claimed, or for whatever wisdom, taken away. I was lucky enough to remain. Grandmamma White is as good a mother as any girl can want and she has done right by me in every regard. I am very happy here and cannot imagine living anywhere else.

A fishing community, Point Village is a wonderful charming place, and not because I live here but because it is. Our little home hangs off a gentle grassy rise of earth just above the harbor wharfs. From our sitting room window I can see Fishing Rock, a clump of stone ledge just off the shore in deep water, where young boys sun and frolic and proud seabirds perch and caw at fishing skiffs rowing by.

Down river, throngs of nettlesome seagulls blanket canvassed fishing craft. The winged foragers follow like hovering fog, hoping to share in the day's catch. Between our little, weathered, clapboard bungalow and Fishing Rock lies Cherry Webb Harbor, crammed with whalers and fishing smacks. Battered and beaten, they appear to be held together by miles of rope, supporting ecclesiastical spars and sprits, a maze of cross-treed masts, like church steeples rising to the sky and swaying above their well-worn gray decks. Hemp lariats tie their noses and rumps to the granite seawall. The lines stretch and shiver like silent banjo strings as the ships' hulls creak and groan like cranky old men. At least once a week a caravan of sebaceous wagons carry away leaky casks filled with precious whale oil. These they unloaded from whaling barks, which hunt the majestic creatures in the billowed seas beyond the Elizabeth Islands just off the Massachusetts coast.

Sitting in front of the house, I have met many interesting people—little tanned, smiling sailors from exotic places like the Sandwich Islands, the Azores, and Cape Verde. I cannot tell you where these places are located but I find their inhabitants very friendly. They are cordial and polite, though I don't understand a word they say. In any event, I can see that they are delighted by this new world they have discovered. One of them, a Portuguese named Antonio, is a permanent resident here in Westport. Antonio is employed as a cooper working at Seth Howland's carpentry mill, a place where cherry-scented sawdust and frizzy oak wood chips spill from the band saw and wood plane out onto the dusty road.

I love living in Westport, and summing up my life thus far, I must admit that it has been a happy one … even if my innocent days are well behind me. Aside from the fact that I am aging, and who is not, I will revel that I am almost eighteen years of age. No, I am not married, and though I have no desire of becoming a spinster, it will not be long before people are calling me Grandmamma. I do not mind. Though the ladies in the village make much of it, being an unmarried woman has very little meaning. Not every soul is meant to pair up with another. It can be a messy business …

more trouble than it's worth, really—waking up to the same face day in day out, same drooling voice asking where I have been, where I am going. Thinking thus makes life much easier to manage as a single girl. Then again, Grandmamma has taught me to always be truthful, and, if I must, I need to confess that having someone to hold and keep one warm at night, like that furry feline did when I was an infant, does sound delightful if not wicked. Hmm? Now that you have brought up the subject, I will need to give it more serious consideration.

I am certain that you are aware of the phrase, "the shot heard 'round the world." Well, 1775 was the year Grandmamma was born. I suppose one can remotely declare that Grandmamma helped usher in the American Revolution.

Please be so kind as to allow me to tell you a little about my Grandmamma. She was born on the Island of Martha's Vineyard where she was given the name Cholata. Few could remember it, so most called her Charlotte. Grandmamma's mother was of Wampanoag blood—Indian, and her father, an African. Yes, my matriarchal parent is a multi-colored maiden. That's what I said—colored. At least that is how they officially classify her in town records. She is so much more than that. Charlotte White is a nurse, midwife, a writer of verse—a caretaker of the poor and misplaced. Mostly she is a mother to me. Always, she has placed others first, and first is how I always felt.

I recall many evenings eating supper while she would sit and watch—a pleased and content smile on her sweet face. I would ask why she was not eating. She would insist that she had eaten earlier, when the truth was she had not eaten at all. Enough was at hand for only one. There were too many mouths to pander to and bellies to fill. But with the help of local fishermen—we always had just enough, and the children never went hungry at our house.

The young ones Grandmamma took in became like brothers and sisters to me, short term and long. As I got older, I was taught by example to be a custodian to those less fortunate, curator to the needy, a Christian soldier. For many years now it has been just Grandmamma and me. For all I have been taught, I am proud to call her Grandmamma.

Now I have had my own little room, though guilt has plagued me about it. There is only one bedroom in his tiny Cape Cod style bungalow. A loft bedroom chamber, really. Grandmamma has always slept on a cart in the pantry off the kitchen, behind a large black stove. Seven feet deep and five feet wide—she called the little space her bedroom. I have argued with her on many occasions about trading rooms so she could have more of it, but she will not listen. *I am old. I have always been old*, she proclaims. *You are a young soul in need of your privacy, quiet, a place to store time, so that you may determine your existence, who you are, what you have been placed in this world for. It is important to have your own room when one is young.* Still, I maintained and insisted that she take the proper bedroom for herself. After all, finding one's self is a journey of the mind, not the body, and having more space a matter of metaphysics, not the scope or area under one's feet. But she would not bend. Instead she would insist, *I need to sleep by the fire so my bones will not become rigid and fixed and the stairs have become an arduous climb.* Perchance she is right.

As I have expressed earlier, my innocent days are behind me. Perhaps they will be behind us all. There is talk of war—conflict between the Union and those in the south. They call themselves Confederates. Mr. Cory's son has gone off, to God knows where, to engage in this unholy feud between brothers. News has come that he will have his rank elevated to First Lieutenant and be reassigned to the Massachusetts Sixth Militia Infantry Regiment. This is good news ... I think? At least, it is how his father discerns the news. Mr. Cory senior is very proud of his son, Samuel. After all, shouldn't all fathers be?

Samuel Cory and I have always been very close, though we have no promises between us. Before he left for military service he took my hand, softly kissed it, and uttered the words "wait for me." I said I would and that I had nowhere I needed to go. To this he added, and with a sober and begging tone, "No Emily, wait for me, eternally," to which I replied persuasively, "always." Could he have meant ...? No-o! We were never ... never, well, how can I put it, on intimate terms—just very good friends. I have known Samuel since we were youngsters. Growing up, we were like brother and sister. And though we have kissed in greeting—on the cheek, you see—it has never been anything more.

Now that I give it somber reflection, I must confess that our kisses have been getting longer and our lips closer. The nips he used to offer me have been getting softer, more tender, like moist silky sponges.

Beg me no more, for I will not tell you much. I can confess. Our lips have touched. How do I feel about that, you may ask? I must fall to my knees and beg the Almighty for forgiveness for how I feel about it. Exhilarating, titillating, wicked—like when a puppy dog licks your nose. There! Does that satisfy your curiosity?

I can be so iniquitous at times. God forgive me for my lustful wishes. It is wicked, so wicked. But wicked is far from evil. For it is not how we feel about such matters but how we act on them that determines the latitudes between corporeal license and divinity. For deviant thoughts among the unwed is just a heartbeat away from the seductive passions practiced in conjugality. For sinning with the approval of God is to bathe in his forgiveness. I beg you to forgive me if I sound so sincere about such matters, but I must be true to myself if not to a friend, and in doing so, I must admit that I am keen and inclined to offer my hand to Lieutenant Samuel Cory upon his return, and without reservation—offer much more.

Though, I must acknowledge my fear for Samuel's safety. He has been writing me letters every week. I dread that they will stop coming—that the war will change or swallow him whole. And now that innocence is all but waned in my heart, I have been burdened with more immediate tribulations. What worries I have rehearsed about the well-being of Samuel Cory have been superseded by concerns for Grandmamma's health.

To be 86 years of age is, in itself, a chronologic illness. I'm afraid that her current malady may be much more than old age. You can see it in her eyes, like a candle flame flickering in a strong breeze, and hear it in her voice, hollow and frail like the waning groan of a creaking door. When Grandmamma's father died, she said she could smell it coming, scent filled the house—death had an odor, and though not offensive, it was a miasma to the mind—one that lingered like a consuming vapor, following the stricken in their last days. To avoid such unplesantries, I have picked as many flowers from the field behind the house as I could and placed them all over the house. I have baked bread, spent candles, sprinkled mint herb from the garden along the floor, burnt toast—afraid that I may smell it ... anything to stem the possible scent and anxiety to the redolence of death. Yes, you are right. I am sinfully selfish. Must block all these self-serving sentiments. Grandmamma means so much more to me. I am certain that her affliction is just a touch due to bad weather.

One thing I can thank the heavens for is that she never complains. She sleeps during both sun and moon and awakens for a few hours each day to eat or read. Yes, I said read! Though she never attended school, in our cottage there are books everywhere. She especially loves poetry. Two volumes sit on a kitchen wall shelf between a stack of bowls and the tea tin. Let me pull them down for you.

Let's see ... this little volume is written by Lucy Terry Prince, and the other ... well, it has its covers detached and its title page has been ripped out, but I believe it's by Phillis Wheatley. I can see where Grandmamma has scribbled the author's name along the margin.

Many of the books were gifts. Others Grandmamma found in bookstores in the nearby cities of Fall River and New Bedford, never paying more than a nickel or a dime.

In the sitting room sits a small rickety bookcase with several cloth and chewed leathered volumes, most of the religious persuasion. Many are dog-eared pamphlets, by such authors as George Whitefield and John Barnard, with boards covered in tree calf leather. Most are very well used and in need of mending. It is by no means a wealthy woman's library. But any knowledge that was pressed on paper and covered in fine cloth or leather is still a treasure, despite its condition.

Now, Grandmamma is a faithful disciple of the Holy Scriptures, which is the reason I point out all her religious publications. She often recounts tales of the Great Awakening retreats that she engaged in when she was a much younger woman—telling stories about believers who would gather in the oak forest by the river near Cadman's Neck, in reverent convocation. Devotees would travel by road and river, from near and far, set up tents, camp in the great outdoors, pray in the green woodlands, and preach in fawn-open pastures, where upwards of two hundred enraptured souls assembled to hear the young, handsome preacher Adams deliver his fire and brimstone sermon.

At these spiritual retreats, Grandmamma was known as Nurse White for the selling of her homemade medicines, unique herbal tinctures, made from fish oil, herbs, and vinegar. The vinegar gave it that stinging medicinal bite. The secret ingredient that snared patrons to Grandmamma's elixir, and which contained most if not all the medicinal properties, if you can call it that, was rum. Yes, that's what I said, rum. Manchester's store, down the road in Adamsville, practically sold more rum to Charlotte White than it did to the local public house—at least that is what Grandmamma would boast. At these great awakening observances, believers who complained about feeling poorly could always ease their pain with a bottle of Grandmamma's medicine. After drinking some at bedtime, most would boast about how much better they felt the next day. The truth of the matter was that the rum would help them to sleep and they would get the needed rest to recover from whatever was ailing them. Nonetheless, most swore that Grandmamma's potion contained the cure.

Grandmamma's convictions and canon evolved from countless ecclesiastical volumes that are stashed throughout the house. She states, and does so truthfully, that she is never alone and that the Almighty himself stands, walks, and sleeps by her side, always. She often says to me, *Don't you see him child? He is sitting there, supping with us. Why do you suppose I always pull out a third chair?* I must admit she had me looking over my shoulder at times. Though I am a godly and pious girl, and one who attends Sunday service without fault and strives to keep the faith, it almost brings a tear to my eye to admit that my devotion is not as fervent as she would like it to be.

Many of her well-loved books are rooted in deep ministerial and doctrinal studies, many with a passage or chapter that interests me—especially the poetry. I would rather read a romantic oeuvre by Wordsworth or William Blake, but there is not a volume to be found in the house. And as far as Shelley or Keats ... well, Grandmamma has banned such "sacrilegious poets," as she calls them. All the more reason why I seek them out whenever I get a chance ... like the volume of Shelley hidden between the bedsprings in my room. It is a wicked and mad poetry about ghosts, demons, spirits, and death—wicked! God forgive me, I am drawn to the unknown and the uncharted. After all, is that not what the journey for religion is all about?

Take Percy Bysshe Shelley. He is so bewildered and mystified by the world around him, a world he finds difficult to accept. At times I think he's even mad. But are we not all just a bit so? And why would I read such an author you may ask? Shelley is mad and I am wicked. We were made for one another.

Like Shelley, I aspire to know myself. I know what you are thinking ... selfish, wicked girl. If you really knew anything about me, you would realize that we are not that dissimilar. Look into your own little closet, where there is no window which looks out onto the minds of others but where your innermost secrets are kept, and you will discover that I am right. Yes, I allow you permission to blush.

Be so kind as to allow me the prospect of redeeming myself. Here on the kitchen table is the book Grandmamma was reading the night last. I think she paid a penny for it. It's by an African poet named Jupiter Hammon. I cannot disclose the title since the cover and pages are missing. Much of the poetry she reads is by poets with origins in the Dark Continent. How she unearths and obtains such compositions God only knows.

Grandmamma's father, Zephriah White, was born a slave. I can see why she loves reading Mr. Hammon, who was himself an involuntary servant to the white race, and why she claimed him as her most loved poet. A day does not go by when she does not pull this slim, ragged volume from the shelf and give it a good read.

I'll recite a passage from one of Mr. Hammon's poems for you. This rendering is unique, in that it was revised and rewritten by Grandmamma, Charlotte White. The verse is tidily scrawled onto a sheet of yellow parchment and resting in the book. She loves writing her own account of a poem she has read and written by others. Hammon wrote this verse for Phillis Wheatley, another of Grandmamma's favorite poets. Please pardon me while I work around poor Grandmamma's error in spelling. Now, it goes like this:

O, come you pious youth
Adore the wisdom which you'v heard
N' bringing thee from distant shore
To learn the holy word.

Thou mightst been left behind
Amidst a dark abode
His tender mercy still combin'd
Thou hast his love been show'd.

N' his tender mercy brought thee bare
Tost o'er the raging main
In Christian faith thou hast a share
Worth all the gold of spain.

While thousands tossed by the sea
And others settled down
His tender mercy set thee free
From danger still aroun'.

That we poor sinners may obtain
The pardon of our sin
Dear blessed one now constrain
And bring us flocking in.

Come you, Phillis, now aspire
And seek the living god
So step by step thou mayst go higher
Till perfect is the word.

I preay all living things may be
The light of thy daily soul
The tender mercies still are free
The mysteries to unfold.

Thus, the soul shall waft away
Whene'er we come to die
And leave this cottage made of clay
In the twinkling of an eye.

When thousand muse with earthly toys
And range about the street
Dear Phillis, seek for heven's joy
Where we do hope to meet.

Beautiful, is it not? How can one not love those words? Even if Grandmamma did not write the original herself, still it is her own. I have always loved it and read it at least once a week. As a matter of fact, I can recite it verbatim. To hold the verse in my hand, follow each carefully written word across the paper is a diligent practice, and one which I delight in. Now I pray you … tell me. Do I sound so wicked to you?

Not all the books here are religious text, nor are they all Grandmamma's. I too have my own little pool of books, which I keep up in my room—a little fiction, a few are historical, including a volume of Thomas Church's *History of the Indian Wars*. Grandmamma got me interested in such topics since it was her people who fought in them. She even maintains kinship with the great Wampanoag sachem, Metacom, better known as King Phillip.

Most of my books are along the framework of literature, though my caretaker may see them as secular and vulgar. *The House of Seven Gables* and *Murder in the Rue Morgue* … now I ask you. Do you consider such titles to be vulgar? Well … I suppose to dear Grandmamma they are. They are so different from what she has read. I can't really blame her. She once picked up one of Nathaniel Hawthorne's books, read the subtitle, and because it states that it is a romance, labeled it as ungodly—if she only knew what else I have read!

Many of the books I love address the issue of orphans. You may consider that odd, but then again, I was the quintessential orphan, basket and all, if you remember. Don't get me wrong. I am well-adjusted, well-loved, and optimistic about my prospects for the future, even though the future has already arrived. Still, such reading matter appeals to my peckish curiosity—books such as *Jane Eyre* and *Oliver Twist*. Though I must admit to sitting in a more exalted chair in life than Jane had, or the one that was likened to poor Oliver.

Oh, not all my books are about those who have begun life with coal in their stocking. A couple are adventure tales. One, as a matter of fact, was a Christmas gift from Mr. Cory—Herman Melville's *Moby Dick*. I know, I had a good laugh myself when he gave it to me. I did so adoringly. Even Grandmamma approved of that one. Still others she would not have kind words for. A number of them have been more recent acquisitions by contemporary authors. A good example is a little volume I have borrowed from the Athenaeum, or as they now call it, the library, in Fall River. It was written by a recent author, Wilke Collins. The story is called *The Woman in White*. Shh! I don't want Grandmamma to hear. It is all about adoration, conspiracy, and madness. It contains the utmost scoundrels and illegitimate—scrumptious and wicked discourse. God forgive me for saying so, but that volume is tame compared to another which I keep between the bedsprings, and for which I dare not let see the light of day for fear that Grandmamma will put me out in a laundry hamper and push me into the river. If you promise not to mention it, I will tell you.

The title? *Moll Flanders* by a gentleman named Daniel Defoe—you know, the writer of that famous adventure story, *Robinson Crusoe*—everyone has read *Robinson Crusoe*. My Lord, I am a wicked girl for revealing ownership to such a book as *Moll Flanders*. Even I must lend admission to the actuality that it is a lascivious and lustful story. Shh! I will lend it to you, if you be so inclined.

I have always been interested in puzzles and riddles and much of what I read is entangled in such convoluted scenarios and plots, full of intrigue and collusion. I delight in my attempt to solve the hidden mystery, the enigma, or the obscure resolution behind a story, before its revealing conclusion. Lord knows, there is very little enigmatic mystery to life in Point Village, and one must acquire it from somewhere. Unlike Mr. Seabury Cory, who practices his liaison with the sea, I find mine in books.

Now less you have already concluded that my proclivities in literature are not of virtuous persuasion, let me be so bold, if not somewhat impolite, to remind you that we all have a bit of Moll Flander's sealed in the vault in our hearts—even Charlotte White. I know what you are thinking—that I am being unfair. Even she has hidden books from me. One such volume has fascinated me more than all the titles I've read—even *Moll*. Amy knows the story but I have read the formal account. We dare not let anyone know that we are aware that such a volume exists. It is a true story of an unsolved murder, with local roots, no less. It takes place in Tiverton in the winter of 1832, in what is now called Fall River, on a site of the old Durfee farm, less than twenty miles away from where I live.

The book is titled *The Pendulous Demise of Miss Sarah*, and written by Catherine Williams, but I have dubbed the title Mudfog, after the town where Oliver Twist was born. For it is how Amy and I refer to the bustling city of Fall River.

Catherine Williams' book is about a poor mill girl who is discovered hanged by the neck in a wintry field by a stack pole—murdered by the vile hand of treachery. Yes, murdered! It is a story about villainous misconduct, religious felony, and uncharted mystery. And it is a documented account.

I must admit another fascination, at least for me, greater than the story and the book itself. And that is why Grandmamma keeps this narrative hidden away, or even owns such a book. Could it be that she also thirsts for the knowledge tangled in adventure and peril? As I have insisted earlier on such matters, Grandmamma is no different than you or I. We all search for the hidden ... the essential endeavor to unlock and cut through the seals that may contain that subliminal remedy to life, or to that which we keep imprisoned in our hearts, but cannot find. In the end, we all hope that such mysteries can be encoded in such a volume.

The Pendulous Demise of Miss Sarah is about a girl who aspired to live a spiritual and virtuous life. There have been those who call her wicked. That is just a label which the public has found popular to sear upon her. For we are all branded by social judgment and the opinion of the masses is nothing less than locusts in a plague, both in number and the harm that it brings. After all, if it is written in a book it must be true—if it falls from the tongue of a public official it must be law—and if it is the divine word of a minister it must be holy. Is that what you think? Well ... is it! For, to think for oneself is a lonely occupation—a pursuit which the average individual refuses to practice—or is too lazy or fearful to achieve for him or herself. For if we do not think independently, there are thousands primed to do the thinking for us, and leave us to our own devices, to serve preordained convictions, which we have been trained since childhood to live by. It's much easier that way, you see. And when the wager of blame is doled out, those who let others do the thinking for them only need stand aside and point.

I have rejected that satin folder containing the doctrines, decrees, and instructions written by those that came before me and, instead, exposed my little cerebral bag of pry bars, chisels, and files, in my own cognitive attempt at investigating and removing the obstacles which are accepted as traditional, along with all that is deemed good. After all, who is to say what is good?

And with that cerebral bag I will use those tools to investigate the truth to this hideous crime which was committed in Fall River many years ago. For that is what I have decided to do. To discover what it is that Grandmamma finds so appealing in the story of this killed woman or, at the very least, satisfy my own natural inquisitiveness. Did you know that in this world the only animal more curious than a cat is a woman with time on her hands? Of course, you are welcomed to accompany me on my clandestinely adventure.

Westport has become too uneventful of late. Unlike men and their careers, if a girl is not blessed with the prospect of marriage, life can give her very little profit, tangible or otherwise, unless she struggles to attain it for herself. If we do not hone our analytical faculties and outwit the common majority, we may be destined to become the victim of harsh public opinion, or worse, to wither into obscurity. Though these are bold words, to be wicked for the sake of wickedness is no asset either. I said to *be* wicked, not to think wicked. Remember? Acting wicked may have perilous consequences, whereas thinking wicked is at the very most conjectural conduct, and at the very least circumstantial. If you can live with it and never act on it, you can be as wicked as your little heart desires.

—◊◊◊—

Chapter 2:

Watuppa Lake, Westport, early spring, 1861

The wind off the lake slammed the sawmill door shut as the two men struggled to cut the young girl down. One had his arms bundled around her waist, her feet dangling above the ground, while the other grappled to untie the cord.

"Hurry, lad, hurry. She be heavy," pleaded the man with the tight stocking hat.

"I can't undo it, Josh, I can't undo it ... it is fastened too tightly!" replied the younger man. His hands trembled and his digits quivered. A fingernail broke as he painstakingly toiled to undo the knot in the flat cotton cord. His legs shuddered in a keen endeavor to keep him from falling off the whale oil cask he stood on.

"Cut it, lad, cut it!" ordered the older man.

The excitable boy fumbled through his pockets groping for his knife.

"It's in the sheath, lad, the sheath at your hip," grunted the older man, struggling to lift the girl's dead weight.

Preoccupied by the dire mission at hand, the young man had forgotten that a knife always hung on the rope belt around his waist. He was a deckhand on the steamer *Enterprise* and it was the duty of a good seafarer to keep a blade sharp and ready at all times. He was new to his trade and had forgotten it was there. Taking the rust-speckled, razored tool from its sleeve, he parted the woven line with one slashing stroke.

The sawmill was not very big. It was barely large enough to hold a stack of lumber along with the circular saw that had diced them into furry slabs. The building had barn doors along the back and front. Once these were opened, 40-foot reddish oak and fir logs could be fed in one door and out the other as they traveled through the saw's steel polished blade. Its spiky fangs sat motionless, like a sleeping bear.

A twenty-foot-long leather serpentine belt coiled itself around an iron-spoke wheel attached to the beam assembly along the roof timbers, where it helped the round-toothed disc claw and tear through the hard, virgin trees. Hanging from the beam was a portion of the soiled cord that was once tethered tightly around the young girl's neck.

Mary Sullivan's head, with its tangled long hair covering her face, collapsed and came to rest on the big man's burly shoulder. He embraced her for a few seconds, unsure what he should do next, or perhaps just to provide the lifeless body some comfort and solace. While he held her, he was careful not to let the coarse stubble on his face mar her satiny but cold complexion. He thought of his own three young daughters, each about the same age as the limp body in his arms.

Carefully, he dropped to his knees and lowered her flaccid torso to the sawdust-littered ground. Brushing the girl's coffee-colored hair aside, he lay her head down, adoringly, propping his stocking hat beneath it. He knelt there staring quietly, as if engaged in prayer.

His young companion stood frozen, mutely unsure and afraid. The boy had backed away into the shadows. The murky light in the darkened sawmill hid his face. The only light in the room beamed down through one of two skylight dormer windows up on the roof. The piercing shaft of dusty sunlight illuminated the girl's serene body, as if an angel would soon appear to claim her. But the scene was anything but nirvana, and no ceremony of salvation was about to occur to make the situation less horrific.

The two men had come to the sawmill early that morning to make ready a delivery of some fir logs. Little did they know that terror and dismay lay waiting to greet them.

Joshua carefully removed the cord from around the girl's neck and flung it aside. He studied her waxy white skin. Her sapphire icy eyes, fixed and lifeless, like those of a porcelain doll, glared up at the mill's rafters where the remnants of the hangman's thong hung from an oak beam. The severed cord swayed to the drafty Watuppa Lake breeze that strained through the cracks in the flimsy barnboard walls. At any moment Joshua felt the girl would look over at him—that she would smile and thank him for his help.

He assiduously tugged at the collar of her torn blouse to cover the unsightly rufous ring made by the abrasive cord that haloed her fair slender neck. The girl was dressed in an attractive powder-blue cotton skirt, an ivory cotton blouse, and a sleeveless black woolen waistcoat, laced tightly at the tummy and widening just below the breastbone, where a finely laced tie hung loosely, like clumsily fastened shoes.

"She be just a babe," lamented Joshua.

"Is she, she …"

"Yes, lad … cold as an icy tiller. She has left this world some time ago."

"What must we do, Josh?"

"There is very little we can do, lad, very little."

Abruptly, the door to the sawmill burst opened and a torrent of light flooded the space.

"What is taking so long?" roared Captain Watson.

The man stood there, unsure of what he was witnessing. The scene of his first mate kneeling by the lifeless body of the teenage girl was a sight to observe.

"She is dead, Captain," uttered the young man from across the room. The daylight illuminated his pallid face, registering the fear he felt in his heart. "We, we found …"

"She be hanging by that cord when we walked in, Captain," interrupted Joshua.

The captain wore a heavy, black wool coat with silver dollar sized buttons. On his head sat a droopy brimmed sailor's cap. A gold anchored insignia, a badge of authority, hung above the hat's leather visor. Captain Watson was the master and skipper of the vessel *Enterprise*, a steamship that hauled the logs from Yellow Hill, near the town of Westport, to the city of Fall River.

"In God's name, Josh, what had occurred here, man?"

"The boy and I opened the doors to the mill to prepare a place for the logs when we found the poor dear hanging by the neck." Joshua turned and looked over to his young companion mournfully. "Go up to the main house and see if anyone is there, lad. Summon the master, if possible."

The young deck hand just stood there and stared—his arms crossed taut and tense over his chest, as if it were about to burst.

"Do you hear what I say, lad? Go! Now!"

"Best do what he tells you, boy," ordered the old captain in a slight Scottish accent.

The young man ran out of the small mill and up the grassy knoll that lead to a big house overlooking the lake.

"Do you know who she is?" asked the captain.

"Aye. Her name is Mary … Mary Sullivan. She's the Sanford servant girl."

Captain Watson, with his scraggly bearded chin, bit and chewed the end of a smoking pipe as he studied the girl's placid face. "She cannot be more than sixteen," he said.

"Aye. I have been taken aback by it. She is not much older than my youngest child."

"Can it be possible such a youngster would damn her own soul to the devil like this?"

"Don't know, Captain, don't know. I have had no time to think on it. To look upon the lass has moored my mind in ice. I am frozen for the sight of it."

"Her blouse is torn," the captain pointed out. "Must have caught on a nail or something when she climbed up into that loft."

"I wouldn't know," said Joshua, as if he were expected to.

The tear in the material was a savage parting, starting at the neckline and running down one arm, exposing the girl's shoulder and arm. Joshua noticed three or four bruises along the girl's arms, in the way of long black-red markings. The one on her bicep was oval, egg shaped, and darker than the other three.

"Look at these, Captain."

The skipper knelt on one leg and made a close inspection. With glossy eyes, crowned by grizzly brows, he squinted—a man desperately in need of spectacles.

"Looks like someone gripped her by the arm, wouldn't you say?" Joshua asked.

"Hum!" Captain Watson pushed back the material with the mouthpiece of his pipe. "What are those markings on her chest?"

"Don't know. Looks like a circle of deep scratches. What do you make of it, sir?"

"When she jumped, she must of swung into one of the posts holding up the place, or possibly into the cutting machinery. There are all sorts of blunt and sharp objects in here."

Joshua gently pulled the blouse material back in place.

"Well, my boy, there is very little we can do for her now," said Watson, grunting as he struggled to his feet. "You best make yourself scarce. You don't want to be part of such a sad affair. I will instruct the men to unload the fir timber we promised Hosea Sanford along the shore. Sanford can have his men load it into the mill himself. The less time we spend here the better."

"What of the girl, Captain?"

"I will send a man to Flint Village in Fall River to summon the authorities. Once they arrive my boy, you best not be here."

"We leaving, Captain?"

"I am moving the *Enterprise* down river a ways, out of this cursed place."

The old captain deliberated, his head turned cautiously, left to right, as he examined the dusty mill. Abruptly, the breeze off the lake slammed the barn door shut, stirring a cloud of oaky dust. Once again the only light in the room arrived through the loft dormer windows. It pierced through the thick woody air.

"There be demons here, my boy, demons," uttered the captain. His voice floundered. "Call it captain's intuition, but there's a wheel missing from this dolly and I am not lingering to stumble upon it." He swung open the mill doors. "There be demons," he said, again, his voice bristling as he stood by the mill door. "Not good for business to be associated with this sort of thing. Could bring bad luck to the vessel. You know me well, Joshua. I have no illusory convictions. It's just the law of the sea. I must care for my ship and leave this place. I'll be on the *Enterprise* making an entry in the ship's log, then we sail for Fall River."

"Aye, Captain."

"Are you all right, son?"

"I think so, Captain," replied Joshua, nodding.

The commander of the *Enterprise* walked over and patted the grieving man on the shoulder.

"You're a good man, Joshua. There is nothing you can do here now."

The captain started out the door.

"Captain."

"Yes."

Joshua paused as he wrestled with his thoughts. "If it is of no concern to you, I would like to leave here when I can and make my way home on foot."

The skipper removed his pipe from his mouth and exhaled some smoke. He looked up at the frayed cord that hung from the barn beam and nodded. A chill filtered down his backbone. "I understand. Do what you must. See you tomorrow." The old skipper turned and walked out.

Joshua remained on his knees staring down at the dead girl. It did not seem right that he should depart—leave her alone—alone as anyone could ever be.

He pulled back the torn blouse and studied the deep scratches in Mary's chest. It looked to him like they were drawn there, carved—a convoluted circle with two deep scratches intersecting one another. There was no explanation for why the markings were there. Still there they were. He tucked the blouse back up around her neck and vowed not to linger on it.

Tenderly, he straightened out her hair and placed her fingers, lacing them together, on her tummy, as if he was arranging the body for burial. The hem of her dress was wrinkled up around her knees—one leg skewed and bent beneath the other. With large callused hands, he gently gripped the thigh and shin and made it straight. After he was done he pulled down the hem of her dress where they covered her ankles. She appeared to be resting quietly now, feet together, hands peacefully positioned.

Just then he noticed a pasty warm blotch that stained his fingers. He stood up and walked over to the light. It felt velvety and rusty red. Could be paint, he thought. He rubbed his thumb and fingers together. It was viscid and tacky. Slowly, he brought the tip of one finger to his nose. He could not understand why he did not realize what it was right off—the color, the texture, and the smell. Blood!

In a daze, he stared down at the body as he wiped his hand on his sleeve. The blood must have gotten there when he straightened the girl's legs. He fell to one knee and lifted her dress just above the girl's shoes. He inspected her legs. Though they appeared swollen he could not see any blood. He lifted the garment a little further, stopping just below the knee. He would not dare lift it any higher. Everything appeared as it should.

He wrapped his hand around the back of her legs, just above the knee. It was there he felt a trail of blood. Slowly, he pulled his hand away. As he did, a streak of fresh crimson pigment smeared along her creamy white skin. He looked for cuts or abrasions but there were none. Where did the blood come from, he thought? On closer inspection, he discovered that it came from much higher up on the girl's leg—a godforsaken injury he dare not search for. Quickly, he lowered the dress back over her ankles, jumped to his feet, and moved away.

Mystified, he scrutinized his palm and fingers once more. They were gummed and glutinous with the raw vital fluid that once pumped through poor Mary's heart. He wiped his hand on his sleeve over and over in a futile attempt to erase the horror which he felt. He was beginning to realize that this was more than a simple hanging.

Fear replaced sympathy. Joshua Collins was an uncomplicated man and not completely lacking wit. His mind was not programmed to digest such twisted matters, and he refused to try.

If the sun had split in two, or the night sky suddenly contained two moons, perhaps he could make sense of that. But all the small details he discovered overburdened his mind. Pieces to the puzzle were scattered all around him and he was afraid that he would fit them together. He always knew that life is seldom what it seems. This was unlike anything he ever encountered. He didn't want to know—get involved, should it all be more than what it appeared. Captain Watson was right. "There be demons here."

He wiped his brow with his forearm, languishing in sorrow, as thoughts rushed through his head unrestrained. No matter how much he tried to block them out, they just kept coming. To his unexpected relief, the barn door burst open and someone appeared to shatter his rumination. The thoughts in his head all hid. He was thankful. He would let whoever it was do all the thinking for him now.

"In here, sir, in here!" shouted the young deckhand, as he swung open the mill door. He propped it open with a stick to keep it from slamming shut. "I found the owner of the mill, Josh," he alerted. "In here, sir. In here!"

The young deckhand stood by the entrance, pointing. He stepped aside and let a tall gentleman with a long turned-up mustache and tapered Vandyke enter. The man was impeccably dressed. He wore a white ruffled shirt loose at the collar and a gray suit. A blue paisley cravat was neatly tucked at the neckline and matched the silk lining of his long tail jacket. He stood fixed just inside the doorway.

"What's going on here," he demanded.

"We found her ... hanged by the neck, Mr. Sanford," stammered Joshua.

"Hanged! From where ... who?"

"The girl. By the neck sir ... there, from the beam," replied Joshua, pointing.

Hosea Sanford looked up. His eyes scoured the sawmill as if he had never been there before. He cautiously inspected the saw, the post-and-beam rafters, and the cotton cord, which hung from the center oak lintel, like it was all about to crash in on him. "Who is she?" he asked.

Joshua looked down with sorrow and distress and moved aside as the finely dressed gentleman took a step forward toward the deceased. Stretching his neck, he leaned over and examined the girl, a handkerchief held over his mouth.

"Who cut her down?" he asked, coughing into the embroidered cloth, as if death had burnt his throat. Though he tried sounding unemotional, a worried uneasiness reflected in his faltering voice. He quickly moved away.

"I cut her down, sir," declared Joshua. "I could not bear the sight of her hanging there. I thought she might still be alive. But she is colder than the blade on that cutting saw."

"Who else has set their eyes upon her?"

"The boy and Captain Watson, sir."

"What is it, Father?" came a shout over Sanford's shoulder.

"There has been an accident," said Hosea Sanford to his son who had rushed down from the house.

"Accident?" repeated the younger man, anxiously. David Sanford took a place by his father's side. "What sort of accident?" he asked as he tried getting by the older man.

"No, son, don't go in there!" said Hosea, stretching out his arm and holding him back.

"Why ... it's Mary!" blurted David. "What's wrong with her? What is she doing on the ground?"

"I'm afraid she has gone and hanged herself," declared his father.

"Hanged herself! No, why ... why would she do such a thing?"

"I want you to get back to the house, son ... now!"

"Mary, Mary!" shouted David as he tried to fight his way into the mill.

"Control yourself, boy," ordered the older man, taking him by the arms.

"But, but, Father ... it's Mary!"

"I said, get back to the house and remain there. We don't want this sort of thing to get out of hand. Make certain none of the hands come down here. There is to be no work at the mill today. Tell no one what has occurred. Do I make myself clear, boy?"

David lowered and shook his head. He shut his eyes tightly as he grappled to understand. "Yes, Father."

"Now, listen to me carefully. Before you go up to the house I want you go down to the dock and inform Mr. Watson that I want to see him, immediately. We will not be accepting any delivery of timber today. I want his men away from the place. I don't want any of them on the property. Then go up to the house and stay there until I return. Do you understand, boy?"

"Yes, Father," uttered a shocked David Sanford. As he walked away he kept looking back.

Hosea Sanford watched him closely, making certain the young man obeyed his command. "Who knows of this?" he turned and asked.

"As I said, the captain, myself, and the lad here—that I know of," replied Joshua.

Sanford gave the boy a grave and stern look. Intimidated by the man's scrutiny, the young man took a step back. "Anyone from the crew?" asked Sanford.

"No one else has been here. And the captain would not tell anyone. He's a private man and has little tolerance for gossip. Besides, most of the crew are French Canadians. They speak little or no English."

"Good, good! This sort of thing can send an entire village into panic." Sanford leaned over and took another look at the dead girl. "Mary, Mary! What have you gone and done to us?" he recited in a disgusted and disappointed tone.

The three men stood in silence for a long time, waiting. Sanford paced from one end of the barn to the other, looking at his watch—Joshua, his arms crossed, stared down at the dead girl. Finally, Captain Watson marched in, followed by a policeman and doctor. The young French deckhand who had run into town for help accompanied them.

"Mr. Watson, get that man out of here," demanded Sanford. "This is a dire matter, not a carnival for foreigners."

Watson waived the French sailor back to the ship. Hosea Sanford immediately took the captain by the elbow beyond earshot of the others.

"I need you to do something for me," he whispered.

"Oh yes, and what would that be?" replied a suspicious Watson.

"I don't want this shame to get out. I appreciate if you keep this to yourself and say nothing ... no need to make a report. I will deal with it."

Captain Watson, puffing his pipe, nodded. "You know me, Hosea. I am a solitary man. I don't lend myself to idle talk. It is not the sort of thing a man crows about, if he is any sort of man. I will need to make an entry in my log. I will not mention the girl—only the delivery of the logs."

"Yes, yes, of course."

"Hosea, we have done business going on twenty years now. I suppose we can go on a little longer?" asked Watson.

"Yes, by all means! Do we have an understanding?"

"Unless questioned by authorities I will say nothing of what went on here today," declared Watson, in a perturbed Scottish accent. "I'll speak to Joshua and the lad. Nothing will be said to no one."

"Thank you, Captain. I am beholden to you."

Taking the young deckhand with him, the captain left for the ship, leaving Hosea Sanford alone with the officer and doctor. Joshua remained behind.

Doctor Silas Dwelly threaded his spectacles behind his ears and knelt beside the girl. He reached for her wrist, though he was sure what he would discover. The inquisitive policeman watched over his shoulder as he pulled down the girl's blouse collar and inspected her neck.

Clutching her by the chin he moved her head from side to side, examining the violent abrasive ring that traveled from ear to ear. She was frigid and the hue of her skin colorless and ashen.

"It doesn't appear her neck is broken," the doctor said. "It's a long way down from that loft to the ground. Should have snapped like straw. How did she get up there, anyhow?"

Listening to what the doctor said, Joshua noticed for the first time that there was no ladder and no way of scaling up into the rafters. Another disturbing piece to the puzzle. He was afraid to say anything, though he had countless questions he would like to have asked. Questions such as: Why was there blood dripping down Mary's legs? What are those markings on her chest? And though the flimsy cord could hardly hold her weight, why did it not break when the girl dove from the ten-foot high platform? Joshua Collins said nothing.

"I'm afraid this young lady has been dead a while," declared the doctor. "Four … perhaps five hours."

"That would place it around the early hours of the morning," said Sanford.

"Precisely. I need something to cover the body with," said the doctor.

Sanford handed him an old horse blanket from a dusty shelf. The doctor draped the sawdust-sullied shroud over Mary Sullivan's face.

Joshua watched and shook his head in contempt. *A filthy horse blanket!* He felt insulted for the girl, though anger would have been a more accurate sentiment.

"I must say, there is not much more I can do, Hosea," declared Silas Dwelly. "Of course, I will need to make a formal report for my personal records."

"Yes, yes, of course. I am fortunate that it is you who has come," declared Sanford. He placed his arm around the aging doctor. "Now, Silas, we have known one another for ages. It is comforting to see a man of your ability and many years rendering such vital service."

"Well, yes, I suppose," uttered the doctor, dubious of the man's declaration. He turned his head and scrutinized Sanford's long thin hand, which rested around his shoulder. "Is there something you would like to add to what has gone on here?"

Sanford cleared his throat and removed his arm from the doctor's shoulder. "I think it is best that we go up to the house. I will make my report there. So if you and the good officer …?" Sanford extended his hand to the policeman. "Your name, officer?"

"Fleet sir, Jonathan Fleet," said the young uniformed policeman.

"Well! This is no place to talk. Let us all go up to the house," insisted Sanford. "We will discuss this unfortunate matter over a nip of brandy."

Sanford led the two men up the grassy hill. "Go on ahead to the house, gentlemen," he instructed. "The back door is open. I will be along shortly."

Joshua Collins was still inside the mill when Sanford returned. Hosea Sanford picked up the looped end of the cotton cord that lay on the ground and studied it. Looking up at the other end hanging from the beam above his head he discarded it and focused his attention on the sailor.

"You can leave now. Your ship is making ready," said Sanford.

"With your permission, sir. Can I have five more minutes with her?"

The older man circled Joshua and Mary Sullivan while he entertained his suspicions. He had something to say and it had to be said with persuasion.

"Did you know her?"

"Somewhat, sir. I have spoken to her many times and waved to her from the ship as she hung out the wash on the line behind the house."

"What is your name?"

"Joshua, sir, Joshua Collins."

"I thank you for your assistance Mr. Collins."

"Yes, sir."

"I have seen you around many times … on the steamer. How long have you worked on the *Enterprise*?"

"Going on five years, sir."

"Mr. Collins. I am certain that you understand the gravity and significance of what has occurred here today." Sanford paced the floor while studying his pocket watch.

"I do, sir."

"Then you realize how crucial it is not to spread rumors or indulge in hearsay."

"Rumors, sir? I don't understand."

"Yes. About what you have witnessed here today. There are many who may have their livelihoods and reputations injured by such an incident. My family for instance … your family. We would not want that to happen, now would we?"

"I don't know what you mean, sir."

"Allow me to put it plainly. I will have this matter thoroughly investigated into how and why it occurred. Until then, I want you to say nothing and say it to no one. We will take due diligence in the matter. Everything will be taken care of here and you will continue your employment with the steamer *Enterprise*. The same is true for your companion. Speak sternly to him. Do I make myself clear, Mr. Collins?"

"I have no notion of spreading gossip, sir. As for the lad, he is too frightened to repeat what he has witnessed."

"Good, good." Hosea Sanford reached for a purse in his breast pocket. From it he revealed a Lady Liberty, twenty-dollar note. He folded the crispy bill and cavalierly placed it in Joshua Collin's hand. Joshua looked down on the wrinkled note and stared down at it.

"What is this for?"

"An agreement amongst gentlemen, my good man … and a little something for your valued service you can say. Mary was very dear to us, and you have shown uncommon regard in the matter."

Joshua stood somewhat bemused. He did not believe a word Sanford had said. He looked down at the bill, then over to the blanket covering the body. It was all too much for him. Holding the money in his hand made him feel like he had profited from the poor girl's demise.

"I trust you will not be much longer, Mr. Collins," said Hosea. He turned and walked away, marching up the hill toward the house.

Joshua clutched the bill tightly in his fist, uncertain about what to do about it. He knelt by the girl one last time. Removing the grimy cloak over her face he neatly folded it just below her chin, draping it down to her feet, as if she were sleeping. He was careful to brush any dust and wood chips that littered the old gray blanket.

The stocking hat, which he placed under the girl's head, was still there. He was about to reclaim it. But his heart would not permit him to leave the girl's head resting on the hard, soiled earth. Kissing a finger, he placed it on Mary's forehead. There was not much more he could do—no reason to linger any longer. He stood up, backed away, and gave her one last glance.

Opening his hand, he stared long and hard at the crumbled money, which lay there. By his feet was the discarded cord that once wrapped tightly around the girl's neck. Just before he left he picked up the cord, placed it in his pocket, and pierced the money on a cant hook that hung by the door, leaving it behind. The trek home would be a long one.

He teetered down the road away from the lake and toward the tainted waters of the Quequechan River.

The surging waterway fed a series of cotton mills that suckled and defecated into its cascading flow, and careened through the heart of the city. It was there where he lived between the river's edge and the railway tracks. In the distance, he could make out the belching steam from the paddle-wheeled vessel *Enterprise*, sailing toward its next delivery.

As he stumbled along, he received a sharp poke. Something under his shirt pinched his skin. Reaching down, he clutched his right side, just above his waist, where he felt what he thought was a coin. He pulled the shirt out from inside his trousers, reached out, and caught the object just as it was about to hit the ground. It was a gold and silver pendant. With the pendant was a finely made yellow chain. The jewel must have dislodged itself from around the dead girl's neck and fallen into his shirt when he eased her down.

He held the prized pendant tightly in his hand.

In the distance stood the Sanford estate high on a hill. He mulled over whether he should go back and return the pendant. He thought about it some more. Finally, he decided that there was no one to return it to. Nor was there a single living soul that deserved to have it—not anyone at the Sanford place. Placing the pendant in his pocket, he continued his long walk home.

—◦◦◦—

Chapter 3:

I was on my way to my friend Louisa's. First I had to pay a visit to the Sanford estate. This got me thinking. Across Watuppa Lake in Fall River, large homes are common. In Westport such big buildings are rare. Sure, there are good-sized cottages across the river where I live, at a place known as Acoaxet Village, but nothing like those in the city—not in tiny Westport—with the exception of the Sanford house.

I have always felt uneasy when I visited the Sanford home, though I have known the family all my life. It is an imposing place, with immense shuttered windows, decorative slate mansard gables, and a castle-like widow's watch along its roof. Yes, that's what I said ... a widow's watch. That is what they call them out on Nantucket Island. But instead of waiting for ships returning from sea, Mr. Sanford used his to enjoy magnificent vistas overlooking the lake. It was a place where he could view the entire pond as it flowed into the Quequechan River. At the base of the river, in the city of Fall River, sat the Sanford Textile Mill. The mill tower, with its impressive clock, was clearly visible from the top of his home. Sanford was known to set his watch by the massive timepiece that adorned his factory. Apart from the textile business, Hosea Sanford held substantial interest in several whalers, including the newly built *Nimrod* of Westport. To say the least, Hosea Sanford was a very rich man.

I had been taking piano lessons from Mrs. Sanford, or Mrs. S., as I like to call her, for almost ten years now. Over time our lessons have become more of a music sorority than an actual exercise in instruction. We not only practice piano but talk about music, people, and even world affairs. I dare say, Mrs. S. and I have conjecturally solved many a world conflict in our little talks.

Grandmamma has often said, *Money speaks to affluence, not richness.* She may be right. Now, perhaps I should not spread gossip or spill my mind's thoughts recklessly, but I am afraid that with all her money, Mrs. S. has very little in common with her husband. They both go separate ways when it comes to most of life's flowery activities. Of course, she is expected to attend formal affairs and functions, of which there are many in the Sanford home, but when it comes to the vital facets of life, music, art, conversation—they have little to say to one another. Now, where is the richness there, I ask you? This is one of the reasons why Mrs. S. holds our friendship in such high regard—as do I. We enjoy each other's company. I must add, the situation between Mrs. S. and her husband is sad, since she is such wonderful company. Fortunately, we flourish when we're together and my company helps ease some of the ill relations she has with her husband.

Remember your place when you visit the wealthy, dear. Grandmamma always advises. *They are very influential in high society, you know.* "High society," I am quick to reply! "Huh! Really! You are speaking to high society, Grandmamma … me!" She would just laugh and shake her head.

My sentiments on the matter are that an actual socialite is one who can master intellect and deliver it with conviction and grace. Not how affluent one is. I have never had any trouble competing in a contest of wit and banter with those in so-called high society—at least not with the womenfolk, and I am far from wealthy. The secret is reading books … lots of them. Though I must admit, having fine clothes and plenty of coins in one's purse is no hindrance. Poor Grandmamma is easily intimidated and impressed by those with power and wealth. You see … I am not.

I rotated the little brass lion's head in the center of the door. A bell dinged inside. I waited. The Sanford's two Irish wolfhounds came running across the field and up onto the porch, sniffing and whimpering. Wellington and Montgomery were their names. Now, I ask you, who in their sober minds would name a dog in such a way? I call them Willy and Monty, though I have never heard them called by any other name but their formal ones. When driving down Sanford Lane, one is left to ponder what is more intimidating—the impressive size of the Sanford home or Monty and Willy, who, when standing on their hind legs, are six feet tall, and on all fours can outrun most horses.

Restless, I twisted the lion knob once again. Impatience is proof of social status, if you don't already know. Grandmamma says that it's just an excuse for rudeness. Not an attribute that I'm prepared to admit, you see—at least not in high society.

Through the frosted leaded glass window on the mahogany door I could see someone approaching. To my relief, I could make out the wavy image as it came closer. I could tell that it was a woman and not a man. Mr. Sanford always unhinges me when he comes to the door—so stern and dour. Ever since their maid Mary returned to Ireland months ago, it has been a squabble about whose job it is to answer the door. When it was Mr. Sanford, he was never happy about it. The door swung open and a sunny face was there to greet me.

"We have forgotten something, haven't we?" she said, in a reprimanding but friendly voice.

"Sorry, Mrs. S. It totally slipped my mind. I forgot my satchel with the week's lesson."

"Well, my dear, you left yesterday in such a hurry and without even saying good-bye. Your lesson is still on the piano."

"I know. Sorry!" At first I thought she was upset with me, but a genial smile, one which she reserved just for me, crept onto her face.

"I understand, dear," she said, tapping my wrist. "Say no more. Come in and make yourself comfortable. I'll get your things."

I slid my feet across the wiry mat to clean them and stepped into the marbled foyer. I waited. Somewhere in the house I could hear two men yelling. The same was true the last time I was here, only that time the shouting was between Mr. and Mrs. S. Someone cried out, *'get back here!'* Suddenly the bellowing stopped, followed by footsteps. I tried my best to pretend I wasn't listening. I stared down at my shoes and examined them. The leather was supple and bright, but with deep scuffing along the heels and flaky crazing just up from the toes. The approaching footsteps in the other room became louder. I thought how perhaps it was time to purchase new shoes. The soles showed little wear and, besides, where would the money come from? Suddenly the footsteps stopped. I looked up. David Sanford was standing there.

"Well, well, if it's not Whitie."

"Hello, Davy. How are you?"

"My name is David. And if you must know, I've been out of town on business."

He unfolded a newspaper that lay on a bijou hall table and looked it over. Now that he was older, David, like his father, made me uneasy, though with David, I could scoop and shovel anything he threw at me.

When we were children, the Sanford family lived in a more modest home near the end of Point Road. David and I were much closer then. Most of the other children shunned him and his abrasive nature. I, on the other hand, always felt sorry for him and often looked out for his happiness, even if he did take liberty with my kindness. After the Sanford family moved away and David was sent to school in New Haven, everything changed. I no longer feel the need to nurture or safeguard him—nor does he need it.

In the last few months, things have been getting queer at the Sanford estate. Something doesn't feel right, like when you put the wrong shoe on the wrong foot. But I must stress and make clear—it is not any of my business. Or, as Grandmamma often advised, *Manage what's in your own head instead of paying mind to others. Their heads are not on your shoulders.* Grandmamma is full of peculiar aphorisms. Over the years I have learned that there is more to them than just witty expressions.

"Were you not here just yesterday?" asked David.

"I left my satchel and sheet music. It's down in the studio. Your mother went to get them."

The room fell silent. I could hear Mr. Sanford off in the distance complaining loudly to himself.

"Are you still assistant agent for Troy Manufacturing?" I inquired.

David gave no reply. Instead he just stood there, his aristocratic, barbed nose buried in the newspaper.

I decided to ask a less inquisitive question. "So tell me, Davy, how have you been?"

He peered over the top of the paper. "Concerned for my health, are we?"

"I'm concerned about all my friends and their health."

"We're friends, are we?" he remarked impertinently.

"Why of course! You are mine. Am I not yours?"

"Known you long enough, I suppose." He placed the paper down and examined me from head to foot as if I suddenly appeared out of thin air.

"How is old Charlotte?" His voice was noble and posh, an emblem from his Yale University years. Its inflection was tarnished, if it was sincerity he was trying to convey.

"Under the weather, but getting better," I said.

"That's good." He casually leaned against the doorjamb, legs crossed, one foot resting on its toes, the newspaper tucked under his arm.

"Have you seen much of Amy?"

"I see her all the time."

"She and I will be married some day, you know," he blurted, assuredly.

"I'll make sure to let her know."

"Sure, she doesn't know it now, but we were destined to be together."

"You should give that proposal some contrary thought," I said.

"How old are you now, Whitie?"

"Please, David. Call me by my birth name. It's Emily ... not Whitie. I'm an adult, you know."

"And so you are, so you are." He swept me with a concupiscent eye. So amoral was his stare that if it were anyone else I would have fled the place.

But I knew there was no ill intention behind his wanton expressions. It was his way of intimidation. It never worked on me.

"And that was a silly question," I scoffed. "You know perfectly well how old I am. After all, we have known each other quite a long time."

"We have at that, haven't we?"

Out on the front porch, Willy and Monty barked and scratched at the door.

"Silly animals," he jeered, flinging the newspaper aside.

"Why, they're sweethearts," I said.

"They're dogs," he replied, as if they were vermin.

"So, Davy, where out of town did you go on business?"

"Why would you be interested?"

"I regard all my friends with interest," I spurted, finally a bit annoyed.

"If you must know, I've been in South Carolina looking after father's holdings."

"Oh?"

"Traveling in the South has become perilous, to say the least. I was lucky to secure safe passage home."

"A war is breaking out between states, I hear."

"Looks like," he asserted. "When we sailed into Charleston, there was a battle between locals and a steamer from New York, called *Star of the West*. We were following her into harbor when suddenly they fired upon us from shore. The captain was prepared you see; considering the rumors of war and all that. He raised South Carolina's naval ensign along with a white flag. Clever fellow. Those dreadful Confederates concentrated their fire on the other vessel."

"My Lord, was anyone hurt?"

"Northern pride, I suppose. Things have gotten much worst since I left. In any event, they let us pass—though the captain was fined and arrested for flying what they considered an official naval flag and impersonating a Carolina registered vessel. The captain tried imitating a southern brogue, you see. His intention was to sound like he was a purebred Carolinian. And he made a good go of it, but the ship's papers gave him away. Poor fellow. We were prepared to leave when they boarded the ship and confiscated it."

"The *Cotton Web*?"

"Father's pride and joy. I'm afraid Father has seen the last of that vessel." He removed a silver cigarette case from a pocket in the silk lining of his jacket and struck a match. "Easy come, easy go."

"I'm so sorry to hear that, David. *Cotton Web* was a beautiful ship. Were you taken prisoner?"

"Father was forced to pay a handsome ransom to bail out the captain.

I was questioned and allowed to go my way—after one of the local militia emptied my wallet, you understand. New southern hospitality, I suppose."

"They took all your money?"

"What they could find, my dear. The bulk of my cash I carry in a ... well let's just say it was hidden somewhere on me."

"Where is the *Cotton Web* now?"

"A week later I noticed a cross bar and stars flying from the mizzen mast at its stern. The official Confederate colors. Soon after, all hell broke loose at Fort Sumter. I was on my way to Savannah when I heard rumors that they were arresting all Northern merchants as spies. I fled to Baltimore instead. Of course, Father was very cross." He took a deep puff from his cigarette, threw back his head, and let out a long stream of smoke. "Even in Baltimore I felt unwelcomed. If not for my strong sentiment in favor of slavery, which I made sure to express, I could have had a harder time of it."

When David spoke of his father's losses, he expressed little relevance. David was David and his convictions and notions were nothing new to me. As we talked, I could hear the distant echo of his father wailing throughout the house.

"Mr. Sanford sounds quite upset," I said.

He nodded his head. "The man is always upset about one thing or the other. Getting old. That's what happens to old men. They become whimpering dogs."

"Surely maturity does not make one ill tempered."

"He's lost it all."

"Lost it?"

"Yes. His holdings ... land, plantations, money in southern banks, all of it."

"Oh, my!"

"I advised him it was a risky investment. 'Just worry about your textile mills here in Fall River,' I said. He wouldn't listen ... wanted to control it all ... transport of cotton, the cost of material, delivery of product. For the past decade, he has invested in ships and plantations in the Carolinas and Georgia." A malevolent smile befell his lips. "Excuse the pun, but it's all gone south now."

"What will happen to all of it?"

"Who knows? Who cares?"

"I care, and you should too, Davy. Your father has worked very hard for what he's earned."

He shot me a preposterous smirk.

"All that investment forfeited?"

"Earned! What about me? What about all that I have done for him?

Besides, it's not the fields he is worried about. Land is cheap in the south. It's the capital investment, the holdings he has kept in Southern banks. Now he wants me to go back, become a Southern gentleman, try and retrieve his capital … even going as far as suggesting I join the Confederate cause. Can you believe it?"

"Well, that does sound a little extreme."

"Frankly, I think the old fellow's gone mad."

I stopped prying. It was more than I cared to know. As Grandmamma often said, *Ask for a handful and you may get a brainful.* This was one of those times.

David stood there like he didn't have a worry in the world. He puffed his cigarette and stared up at the gold leaf flowered plasterwork along the ceiling, examining the teardrop chandelier which dripped from above. His handsome looks were only superseded by his vanity. He still had the same wavy golden hair he had as a boy. He was a little older than I, but only by a year or so. When he was little, he was quite the rumbustious tyke, always into mischief. Now he was over six feet tall, thin, with a muscular upper body, strong chin and proud cheeks, all set off by a touch of effeminacy in his cultured lips and long eyelashes, which framed cobalt blue eyes. Still a striking young man and a handsome catch for any girl who wished to go mad.

"Have you read any good authors recently?" I asked.

"Like what?"

"Oh, I don't know, like Jane Austen—Herman Melville has become very popular. Recently I read a poem in the *Fall River Evening News* by an unknown poet making quite a name for herself … called 'No One Knows this Little Rose.' The writer is rumored to be a young lady from western Massachusetts named Emily Dickinson. Emily … the same name as mine. She has a volume of poetry published and I thought …"

"I don't read poetry," he quickly belched. "Let alone women authors. I'm more partial to mysteries. Though, for casual reading I may go to my man, Waldo."

"Oh!"

"I don't suppose you've heard of him."

"If you mean Ralph Waldo Emerson. Of course, I have—the "Concord Hymn"?"

"Can't say I've heard of it."

"No, you wouldn't. It's poetry."

"Did you know that I met Emerson when I was at Yale? Took a class of his at Harvard."

"You met Emerson?" I was astonished.

"Yes, boring fellow."

"You don't say?"

"At class he would go on for hours about the goodness of humanity, man's place in nature, and the relevance of God. Transcendentalism, I think he called it. I can tell you one thing. Living here with father would surely change his mind. No, no, give me a good murder mystery any time of day."

"Murder! My Lord!" Though I sounded shocked, I would never admit to being fascinated by the same genre—of those with the need to kill, with a condition so desperate that they would take human life to satisfy their depraved cravings or misgivings. But it's not what you think. My interest is to interpret these wrongdoers, you understand, investigate what makes their brains ooze such deviant behavior. It had become a compulsion as of late to read such material, one I am ashamed to admit to anyone. Even David Sanford.

"You ever hear of Poe?" he asked, as if he were the only one who had. "Now there is someone whose works you should absorb."

"I have, as a matter of fact."

"And Wilke Collins."

"You have read Mr. Collins?" I said, in disbelief.

"There's a freshly published volume of *The Women in White* on the shelf in the library down the hall if you'd like to borrow it."

"It is rumored to be a most popular book," I added, not wanting to let on that I have read it.

"You see, Whitie. I'm not as untutored as you make me out to be."

"I never insinuated that you were."

"As a matter of fact, I'm thinking of writing a fictional tale myself."

"You are!"

"I even have a title," he announced proudly.

"What's it called?"

"*The Cross and Anchor.*"

"Cross? Is it a religious tale?"

He laughed. "Leave it to your imagination. Little Whitie, always sanctimonious."

I had given up on correcting him about not calling me Whitie. Instead I would continue to call him Davy. And knowing his proclivity for theatrics, I dismissed his claim that he would ever write anything. Still, as Grandmamma always said, *Be nice to the rooster. He can't help but announce his presence.*

"You will lend me a copy once you have written it, won't you, Davy?"

"Why of course. There, you see. We are not that dissimilar after all."

He shot me a slight, warped smirk. "Whitie, we all have our dark side. And you don't fool me."

"Yes, but I try and wash mine in sunlight and hope. That is why I like to read authors like Dickens or the works of Charles Lever. Rising above human frailty. Doing what is right despite mitigating circumstance ... finding one's destiny!"

"Boring! You would make a fine transcendentalist. Dickens! Too lifeless for my taste."

"You think *Oliver Twist* is lifeless?"

"Dreadful little scamp." He put out his cigarette in a silver tray and admired himself in the hall mirror, fiddling with his silk cravat and brushing his hair with the tips of his fingers.

"You mentioned ... well, murder. Have you ever read the account of the mill girl from Fall River who was found dead on the Durfee farm over in Tiverton?"

"Tiverton? When?"

"Oh, about a decade before we were born. They accused a minister, Minister Avery, of murdering her."

"Did you say hanging her?" His voice quaked.

"No, I did not ... but yes, that was what he was accused of ... murder by hanging."

"What was her name again?" he asked, suspiciously.

"I didn't say. It was Sarah, Sarah Cornell. Have you heard of her?"

"No, I haven't."

"How did you know she was found hanged, then?"

He suddenly froze, staring at himself in the mirror as if mesmerized by my question. Like a flung ball on a billiard table, his eyes jounced off every corner of the looking glass as he scrutinized his reflection. His teeth gnashed. His jaw, taught and bony, slid from side to side, and his cheek began to quiver. In the distance, I could hear Mr. Sanford shouting out his name. Just outside Willy and Monty barked, whimpered, and continued to claw at the front door.

"Davy, are you all right?" I asked.

"Of course I'm all right." He swept off his jacket sleeves with the back of his hand. "Why wouldn't I be?"

Hosea Sanford called out again.

"Your father needs you."

"You think I don't hear it!" He barked, loudly. "He has been on my nerves all day. I'm not sure how much more of this I can take."

"I'm sorry, Davy."

"And, no. I can't remember."

"Remember?"

"Any hanging," he said, as he left the room.

Shortly after he was gone everything went silent. All that was heard was a loud dong from the large tall clock clanging in the other room. Outside, the dogs whimpered and clawed the door. I pulled back the curtain on the door and looked out. Monty cocked his head at me and groaned. Finally, to my relief, Mrs. S. walked in with satchel in hand. She clutched her chest as she caught her breath.

"Here you go, dear. Phew! Took me a while to find it. It had fallen behind the sofa. My, my—you would not believe the dust I discovered back there. Well, I just could not leave it. That is why it took so long. It hasn't been the same since Mary returned to Ireland."

"Have you heard from her?"

"Not a word. Suddenly her things were gone and so was she. Never writes."

"Sorry to hear that, Mrs. S."

"People are peculiar creatures, my dear. Now, don't you go vanishing on me."

"Oh, I won't."

She walked me to the door.

"Remember when you are practicing Mozart's twenty-fourth. You need to add more allegro. Your meter signatures are perfect but you need to practice the tempo."

"I will, Mrs. S."

"The old piano I gave you ... have you had it tuned?"

"Ah, no, I haven't the money."

"Say no more. I'll have Franklin down this week to tune it for you. He's been tuning my instruments for years. He'll make certain that those high notes sound crisp and tangy. And it will not cost you anything."

"That's kind of you, Mrs. S."

As she opened the door I could hear Mr. Sanford and his son arguing. Someone shouted out her name. Worried, she looked over her shoulder and then back at me.

"Now you be on your way, dear, and don't forget to practice."

"I won't," I promised as she shut the door.

Willy and Monty wagged their tails and sniffed my feet. In the drive was the old carriage Grandmamma used to get around. If I were to pay you a visit in it, you would hear me squeaking and creaking up the road for miles. Grandmamma has not used the old thing for months now and I have found it very handy on my little jaunts. All that walking I use to do ... how will I ever get use to it again? *This younger generation has been blemished with indulgence and ease of life*, I've been told more than once. Maybe so. But I can take to being indulged every so often. It's good for you, if you don't take it for granted.

As I walked to the wagon, the dogs ran off through an adjacent field and down to the water's edge. There was never a dull moment when a visit was made to the Sanford estate. It was like a tiny town, with all sorts of buildings, barns, and people all around. Poor Mrs. S. She is such a lonely woman, spending most of her time in the studio down by the lake. She calls it a studio. I call it a house, since it was much bigger than the one I lived in. At the studio, Mrs. S. could play up a storm on her grand piano and not disturb the men and their business guests in the main house, for which there were many. At times when she played, workmen, who toiled in the sawmill by the lake, sat on the grassy knoll by the edge of the water, eating their lunch, and enjoying Mrs. S. thumping the ivories of her loved piano.

I was happy to be on my way. It was rare that I ever entered the actual main house and witnessed the grandeur and opulence by which the family lived. Standing in the receiving room was more than enough for my eyes and ears. Once one entered the front door of the Sanford house little Westport was soon left behind. It was another world. If I had the opportunity to trade places with its occupants, I would never consider it. There was a lesson I always walked away with from the Sanford home, and it was that money cannot buy happiness. Happiness was all the wealth I needed and I had plenty of it.

The important mission today was to retrieve my satchel and I had accomplished that. Inside it was a book that was being reviewed by the Drift River Readers Club, a reading group that I belong to. The Drift River Readers Club held its meetings at my friend Louisa's house. It was my original destination when I left home early this morning. Now that I had what I needed, I was on my way.

As I ambled up the Sanford drive I took one last look over my shoulder at the big house. I nervously encouraged the old horse to move a little faster. An apricot sun had broken over the eastern horizon, illuminating the Sanford home's mansard roof and its checkered pattern of gray and burgundy slate roof shingles. Its chromolithographic windows reflected the sun's silky orange light as if they were ablaze. It was a spectacular, almost seraphic scene. So why was I so happy to see it all fade behind me?

—⟋⟍—

Chapter 4:

How can one describe Westport, but as the greatest place in the entire world to live—a bucolic patchwork of bountiful field upon field, of corn, potatoes, beets, and pumpkin—every one of them encircled with a necklace of scenic stone walls, with flowered lanes leading down to delightful cottages, neatly tended gardens, and sinuous, trickling creeks and ample rivers. Unlike the big city, with its tall lumbered structures, clamorous people, and bustling activity, Westport is a carefree pearl, tucked into a happy picturesque clam. Perhaps I am a little partial because I live here, since I have seen very little, if any, of the world at large. So, forgive me if I sound haughty or proud, I'm sure where you live is wonderful—at least for you.

In Westport, you will discover two sorts of folk—those who toil by land and those who work the sea. Myself, I could never imagine living anywhere away from the water—or away from Cherry & Webb Harbor, an uncut jewel whittled by the Atlantic Ocean and nursed by two wonderful waterways—the Westport and Drift Rivers.

The further away I drive from the Sanford home and Watuppa Lake, with its drab cityscape in the distance, the happier I feel. Though the Sanford place is in Westport, it overlooks a lake-shore, containing mills and shacky icehouses. Again, I must be candid and stress that I am being a little disingenuous; since the real reason for my happiness is that I am driving in the direction of Point Village. And when it comes to home, there is no place as cheerful or comforting.

Just before coming to the end of Point Road, I made a turn down the lane between the small white church and Point Cemetery. The detour takes me toward the shores of Westport's Drift River, where I will keep my appointment with the book club crowd, an assembly of girls who get together once a week to discuss literature and poetry. We call it the Drift River Readers Club. Every Tuesday afternoon we meet at Louisa's, who is also known as Lulu, where the gathering usually takes place.

If Amy Chaloner is my best friend, Louisa is more like a younger sister. She can be fragile in temperament and capricious when mystified or criticized … but in a charming way. She has beautiful auburn hair and gentle hazel eyes. Petite, she looks a lot younger than she really is. Lulu, or Louisa Marie Tripp Macomber, lives by the Drift River on Drift Road at "The House of Four Doors"—at least that is what most people call the place. Like the Sanfords, the Macombers lust for nothing and have everything. Whereby the Sanford family is new wealth, the Macombers come from well-earned old money. I mean old, old, money. As it was told to me, Louisa's family, on her mother's side, became affluent shortly after arriving in America on the Mayflower. Her great grandfather, seven times removed, made most of his money in shipbuilding. You are asking me if it is all true? Yes, it is. But don't quote me on it.

The house was not the citadel the Sanford place is. It is much more modest—still a mansion to me. Whereby the Sanford estate overlooks the lake and the smoky stacks and burly mills of the city, "The House of Four Doors" sits on the banks of the tranquil Drift River with a watchful eye over serene tides, voyaging currents, and countless assortment of migrating, colorful river fowl.

You may have asked yourself by now why the Macomber home is called "The House of Four Doors." Well, you will have to ride by and see. It is quite unique. Most would call it a two-story English manor house, American style, or what has become to be known as a colonial variety, covered with white cedar clapboard, clean looking, with no decorative, shuttered windows, or fancy roof, but blessed with large ornately molded front doors, capped with swooping, winged, copper-clad lintels and pineapple finials. Let me finish. You see, the Macomber home has three such doors, each one identical to the other and one on each side of the structure, thus the house has three front entrances. Am I making sense? Why it's called "The House of Four Doors" is beyond me, since it only has three. Ian, Louisa's younger brother, often reminds me that I forget to count the door at the rear of the house, the one that joins the kitchen to the back terrace and which no one sees.

The story is told that Mr. Macomber wanted visitors to feel invited when making a call. No matter what direction the approach, there was always a gracious entrance by which one could enter. One door faced the road, the other the barn and flower gardens, and the third the grove of spindly apple trees by a stone wall covered with moss and briers. Along the rear of the house was a long veranda, or porch as they have become known—placed there quite recently. Mrs. Macomber refers to it as the beam and stick monstrosity—perhaps because her herb garden had to be relocated to build it. With its wonderful umbrella-like cedar roof, held up by looming, Romanist fluted columns, it was the perfect place to retreat from hot sun or drenching rain. Decorative brackets hang from the roofline, and an embellished railing encloses a staircase, which leads down to the river's sandy shore. To anyone who has studied the formality of architecture, the porch did not really look like it belonged there, but to me it looked quite quintessential.

In the summers, the porch was where the Drift River Readers Club held its weekly gatherings. In the hot month of July, we lounged on straw-weaved rockers to the silence of the breezy tributary—a nirvana by the stream, where our thoughts gave birth and ideas flew to whatever story or poem we were reading.

As I drove my carriage down Drift Road, I felt a tinge of bliss as the Macomber home came into view. Butterfly wings fluttered in my belly, sending a groundswell of warmth and anticipated joy up my spine. "The House of Four Doors" had become my home away from home. After all, I spent many overnights there when I was a girl.

Ten-year-old Ian Macomber came running up a green alley of hedgerow leading to the road, screaming out my name. He was always the first to greet me when I visited, since I always made a point to bring him a little gift.

"Emmie, Emmie, I thought you would never get here" he cried.

"Why would you think that, little man, I am not late, am I?"

"I don't know, but I was waiting."

"You were ... were you?" I reached into my satchel and pulled out a wooden carved toy soldier, whittled by one of the fisherman who sat by the Point wharf, frittering and sculpturing little toy figurines, which he sold for pennies. "Here. A little present for a fine little gentleman."

"Oh, Emmie, I knew you would bring me something, I just knew it."

"That should almost complete your regiment of toy soldiers, I would think."

"Wow, he is holding a rifle." His eyes sparkled. "Thank you, Emmie. You are my best."

"Fisherman Moses said he's working on another. That one will be holding a flag."

"Superb!"

"Superb? Where did you learn a word like that?"

"It's the word of the week. Father said that I must learn at least one new word a week and use it when I talk to people."

"Well, that sounds ... superb, Ian."

53

He laughed and ran up the path to the house.

I followed.

"It's about time," said Louisa as I ascended the steps and up onto the porch.

"Look what Emmie brought me!" chirped an excited Ian.

"That's nice," said Louisa, showing little interest. "Now you go and play somewhere. We are having our meeting."

The boy ran off as instructed.

"He's a darling," I said, dropping my satchel onto a chair.

"Hello, Emmie," said Amy. "Sit down and take a load off your feet. You look tired."

"Sorry I'm late. I had to drive out to the Sanford place to get my satchel. It had all the material we need for the meeting today."

"Oh ... did you see David?" asked Louisa with trepidation.

"I did," I said, emptying my leather case on the table beside a tray of cookies.

"Who cares?" pouted Amy.

"Did he ask about me?"

"Oh, Lulu, let it go," trumpeted Amy. "He's nothing but a mean, pampered brat."

"Amy!" I cried. "Louisa's asking a perfectly civil question. No, he did not, Louisa."

She frowned with a pouting grimace.

"Oh, quit with the baby face, Lulu. Father has been an associate of Sanford since the beginning of time. When Hosea Sanford comes calling at our house, he usually has David with him. Every time he does, David goes out of his way to slight me. You don't know how lucky you are he doesn't take interest in you. He's just vain, ill mannered, and indulging."

"We all have opinions, I suppose," peeped Louisa, dismissively.

Amy wasn't finished. "His mother, his friends, they all treat him with silk gloves, you know."

"Oh, come now, Amy," I said. "He's not that bad. Davy is just Davy. You just never tried climbing inside his head and looking around."

"I'd like to climb into more than just his head," chirped Louisa.

"Lulu!" I shouted. "That is a wicked thing to say, wicked!"

"Wicked thoughts for wicked boys," said Amy, brushing cookie crumbs from her lap.

Louisa and I laughed. On a wicker table sat a glass bowl of drink and a tray of treats.

"Think I'll try one of those buttermilk scones," I said, reaching for one.

"Oh, please do," implored Louisa. "And have some punch. It's watermelon ... your favorite."

"It is such a beautiful home," I said as I poured myself a glass. "But there appears to be something foreboding about it."

"What are we talking about?" asked Louisa.

"The Sanford farm," I replied.

"Sanford Plantations," declared Amy, boldly. "That's what he calls it. Farms are for indigents ... plantations are for gentlemen. At least that is the way David puts it."

"He was such a dear when he was a child." Louisa reminisced. "Remember the time we left him on Sandy Island and we rowed away in the boat. He screamed and cried, afraid we were going to leave him there." She looked out toward the tiny one-acre island in the river about three hundred yards away.

"Oh, he was always a baby," grumbled Amy. "Look at that island. You can almost touch it. What did he think we were going to do, never come back? Half the world could hear him whining."

"He really was cute as a button when he was a child," I said. "Crystal blue eyes, rosy cheeks, hair fair as yellow summer squash."

"That description still fits today ... so tall and handsome. What a dream," sighed Louisa.

"Nightmare, if you ask me," barked Amy.

"Oh, he was never that bad," I declared.

"You don't think so, huh?" Amy would not let up on him. "How about later, when he got older. You all forget about later, in school, the Miller's horse ... remember? It was always jumping the wall in the field and we would chase him and ride him all day."

"That was one dumb horse, sweet, but dumb," I declared.

"Well, he killed that horse!"

"Why, Amy, what a mean thing to say," cried Louisa.

"You shouldn't have brought that up, Amy." I warned. "We don't know that!"

"Well, it's true," she said. "That horse kicked him. Nearly broke his leg. Charlotte had to bring him to the city hospital. Remember—couldn't walk for weeks. Lost a whole year of school."

"Yes, I remember now," cried Louisa, her hand to her mouth, as the account pricked her memory.

"Davy did pick on that poor horse," I confessed.

"He tortured that animal," cried Amy. "That horse hated him. David Sanford shot that poor creature right through the head."

"That's an inflammatory accusation, Amy!" cried Louisa, "Now you are just being plain spiteful. There is no proof ..."

"Oh come now, Lulu," reviled Amy. "How about that old yellow cat that slept under the abandoned skiff by the river? David would get a running start before he would kick that poor thing. And remember Mrs. Green's dog he placed under the dory? That defenseless dog had to have been under that dory for three or four days before a fisherman heard it whimpering. You remember, Emmie, don't you?"

"There's no proof Davy did that," Louisa argued.

"He did ill-treat that dog, Louisa … hit it with a stick every chance he got."

"And those were just the animals he abused," said Amy. "Do I need to remind you of the girls? I tell you, that man ties me in knots."

"Just what do you mean, in knots?" inquired Louisa, her head askew like a confused puppy.

"She means Davy angers her," I said.

"Oh! I thought you were accusing him of tying you up with a rope," said a naive Louisa.

"I'd rather not talk about it any longer," I insisted. "Besides, I feel sorry for him. He is forever trying to live up to his father's expectations and failing miserably."

"Why are you all picking on him?" sniveled Louisa.

"I'm not picking on him, Louisa. I feel compassion for the boy."

"Children, children, let's come to order," said Amy, banging her spoon on the punch bowl. "I call to order this meeting of the Drift River Readers Club."

"Yes, Amy is right," I said. "Let's begin."

"Now, as president of the club I need to ask if everyone is finished reading our latest selection and new author?"

"Yes, I have it right here," I said pulling the book out of my little leather case.

"I was first to read it, Lulu read it last week, how about you Emmie?"

"Finished it last night."

"So we have all read it," declared Amy, "*Adam Bede* by George Eliot. Time for discussion."

"I didn't like it," Louisa quickly reported.

"And?" asked Amy.

"And, I didn't like it. That's all," she declared rolling her eyes.

"Well, you just can't say you didn't like it. We need to rank it on the list of books we have read. You need to add an explanation why you did or not like it."

"It was wicked, just wicked," I quickly replied.

"Ah, so you liked it, Emmie. Good!" Amy took out some notes and began to write. "Elaborate, please!"

"Well, it was … wicked."

"Oh, Emmie, you just can't say it was wicked. You must give a better explanation. What's wrong with you two? We went over this again and again. A book is like a sandwich. It has a beginning, a plot, and a conclusion. We agreed to debate all three."

"Well, I think …"

Louisa quickly interrupted me.

"You want a sandwich?" she snapped. "I'll give you a sandwich! How about a slice of indecency, filled with promiscuity, smeared in lewdness, and topped off with a slab of insipid improbability?"

"Just like I said … wicked," I chimed, laughing.

"Oh, you two! I suppose I'll go first," remarked Amy.

"Why don't you," I said. "After all, you're the president. Louisa and I will counterpoint."

"Fine. I will give you a one word description for characters and you tell me if you agree or disagree."

"Go on," said Louisa.

"Ah, let's see! Of the main characters let's take Hetty Sorrel. I would call her selfish and depraved, though she was by far the most interesting person in the story."

"You said one word," lamented Louisa. "You described her using two words. You broke your own rule."

"All right, have it your way," said Amy, rolling her eyes. "Lascivious."

"That's three words now."

"What!"

"You said selfish, depraved, and now you describe her as lascivious. That's three descriptions."

"What is disturbing you anyway, Lulu?"

"I think you insulted her palate for men, earlier," I hinted. I gave Louisa a sympathetic smile.

"All right. I'm sorry," said Louisa, picking up the book and thumbing through it. "I'll pick Captain Donnithorne, and I would call him … noble."

I looked over at Amy and gave her a stern stare, cutting through the mustard before she could express her transparent opinion of Lulu's choice and assessment, or mention how obviously alike David Sanford and Captain Donnithorne really were. "Dinah Morris." I cried out straightaway. "And I would say she was … caring."

"Well, that's thought provoking," said Amy, taking notes. "No one picked the main character, Adam Bede. Why?"

"I found him to be a bit of a dolt," I said. "His dog Gyp is more interesting than he is."

"Hmm, that's interesting," agreed Amy. "Sort of a weak character even though he appeared to practice righteous behavior. What do you think, Lulu?"

"I don't know about that," sounded Lulu. "I thought he was ethical and virtuous, after all, he did get the girl in the end."

"Ah, but not the one he wanted," said Amy. "There's a lesson to be had here."

"Listen, can I be president—just once, and choose a title I may like?" complained Louisa. "After all, most of these club sessions have been held at my house."

"I don't see why not, Louisa," I said.

"You'll get your turn, next month," said Amy. "Right now we are critiquing George Eliot."

"Next month, next month, always next month!" cried Louisa.

"Well, I was the first president," I said, "then it was Maggie, but she stopped coming, and now it's Amy's turn. After all, the Drift River Readers Club has just a three-month history. Amy still has two weeks left."

Amy Chaloner got up from her chair. "You can be president if you like, dear. It's not important to me. I'll step down."

"No, it's all right, I suppose," sighed Louisa, "I'm just being difficult. And you are right. David Sanford can be wearisome at times. It's just that I'm still unmarried and Mother is worried."

"We understand," said Amy. "I'm nearly eighteen. I'm almost a year older than you. I'm not worried about it."

Both girls displayed a sudden timid and fretful frown, first at each other, then at me.

"I know, I know, I'm practically a barren grandmother in your eyes." I said.

We all laughed.

Out in the middle of Drift River a small sailboat glided by Sandy Island, moving south with the tide. Its solitary occupant appeared to be dozing, reclining against the transom and steering with one foot on the tiller. I had seen him before, down on the Westport River. The rim of his hat was low over his eyes and a single mainsail stiff against the breeze ferried him along. On Sandy Island, which was not much larger than the backyard of the Macomber house, sat a tall leafless tree with a huge straw and twig nest at its very top. Two baby osprey, sporting a spatter of downy feathers, cocked their heads one way then the other. With their virgin plume, spiky and whisking in the gentle breeze, they sat quietly and placidly, if not confusingly, scrutinizing a contingent of ducks swimming along and being led by a solitary gray goose. Tiny wavelets were stirred in the southwesterly breeze, as a parade of cumulus clouds maundered along the horizon in a Prussian blue sky.

"You are so lucky, Lulu, to live out in the country," declared Amy.

"Oh, I don't know," wondered Louisa. "At times the comfort becomes monotonous, like eating ice cream for breakfast, lunch, and dinner, day in, day out. Nothing ever happens. On the other hand, in the city where you live …"

"In the city where I live, huh!" crowed Amy, sneeringly. "A couple of days ago a man stabbed another with an ice pick because he looked at him funny, and a mother threw her three babies out the window of her third floor flat, right out onto busy Pleasant Street, of all places."

"Oh, my Lord," exclaimed Louisa, clutching her chest.

Amy continued. "And just last week, down by father's mill, two drunks were having a fistfight on the railroad trestle. Story has it they were arguing about who was a better swimmer. When the train came by they both jumped into the river and drowned. No, Lulu, you are fortunate. Give me ice cream and the Drift River every day, any time. You and Emmie are lucky to be away from the big city."

"You live on the hill, Amy, well away from all the mills and bustle. You are lucky in that respect," I proclaimed.

"Sure, The Hill, they call it," scoffed Amy. "We were the only house on the block when we first moved there. Now houses are springing up all over. One is going up directly across the street. It blocks out the sunsets from my bedroom window, where the river views are obscured. If it were not for the retreats to the family cottage at Point Village, I would go mad."

"I wouldn't move away for the world, but the city isn't that bad if you live in the right neighborhood," I lied.

Amy just shrugged her shoulders. "I suppose."

Like the Sanford and Macomber homes, Amy's abode in Fall River was a tiny city onto itself, with fifteen rooms, five fireplaces, glass pane windows as big as doors, two servants, a cook, and a gardener. The house sat high in an area known as the Highland Hills. On the roof was a sheltered, octagon widow's walk, a miniature sanctuary overlooking Mount Hope Bay, where Amy would escape to read. Along one corner of the house was a circular tower that scaled all three levels of the building, with a party hat-shaped roof, and topped with a copper finial in the likeness of a rooster. When viewed at night, with the moon rising behind it, the darkened silhouette of the Chaloner house was saddled in the sky like a scene right out of Edgar Allan Poe's works. During the day, the distant vistas were spectacular …

for a city, you understand. And when one can use words like *spectacular* to describe a city, it can't be all as bad as Amy claims.

"Oh, I don't know," moaned Amy, boringly. "I don't feel like talking about *Adam Bede* any longer. Lulu is right. I just didn't care for any of the characters."

"I love you, Amy," proclaimed Louisa.

Amy shrugged her shoulders and reached for a snack from the tray on the table.

"You know me so well. You know people so well. I suppose it comes from living in the city."

"Comes from reading books, Louisa," I said. "If you read enough books, eventually, you will discover that every individual you could ever meet has been written into a book one way or another."

"We have reviewed two poets and two novelists," said Amy. "What should we read next?" She pulled out her notes. "Shall we go down my list of authors?"

"I have an idea," I said. "How about reading non-fiction?"

"Oh, Emmie, we agreed only poetry or storytelling," pouted Louisa.

"Well, I have something here that reads like fiction but it's a true story." I reached for my satchel and pulled out my prize. "It's a narrative which takes place in Fall River."

"Oh, Emmie, not another history book! Everyone is writing one these days—history narratives about mills, Indian wars, and on and on. They are so repetitive."

"No, no, hear me out. It occurs on an old farm in a portion of the city known as Tiverton— about a girl that was hung, a city mill girl, killed by someone ... they think a minister."

"Get away!" cried Louisa. The cookie she was eating fractured in her hand. She dusted the crumbs from her lap.

I watched her as she sat there motionless, billowy lips hovering over a slack jaw, a stunned mannequin gripping a crumbled cookie. "The title of the book is ..." I paused.

She flung the fragmented cookie onto the tray. "Yes, yes, go on!"

"*The Pendulous Demise of Miss Sarah!*"

"Let me see!" She shot out of her chair and peered over my shoulder as I held the volume open for her to study.

Amy walked over to one of the windows on the side of the house and used the glass as a mirror and fluffed her hair. "Emmie and I have already read it," she declared. "Reads just like a murder mystery. Why don't you read it this week and we will all discuss it next." Amy removed her floppy sunhat and poked at her wispy blonde bangs—puckering and licking her lips, and making kissy poses at her reflection.

"You say this took place in Fall River?" asked Louisa.

"It all takes place in Mudfog," Amy said.

"Mudfog?" uttered Louisa.

"Yes, that is what Amy and I call Fall River when we talk about the book. We don't want Grandmamma to know I am reading it."

"Mudfog!" Louisa said, once again.

"Yes, Mudfog, you know ... *Oliver Twist*," I reminded her.

Louisa hovered over my shoulder studying the volume in my hand. "Oh look! There's an illustration of the farm."

"It talks about the dead, hanged, wretched body," I said, in a pronounced raspy voice.

Amy smiled and shook her head, trying not to let on that she loved reading it. She poked at the snacks on the tray, swiped a cookie, and walked away.

"You're president of the club now, Lulu," she said. "We need your approval."

"Fine then," said Louisa, sitting back down. "If you can convince me that it holds one ounce of literary equity, I'll consider it."

"Read something, Emmie," said Amy.

"What was this girl's name?" Louisa asked.

"Sarah Cornell," I said.

"Was she anything like Hetty Sorrel in *Adam Bebe*?" she inquired.

"Exactly like Hetty Sorrel," I announced to her surprise.

"Did she have her own Adam Bede ... someone who lusted for her?"

"Lust, yes. Love, no. She had no one. She was all alone in this world," I explained.

"Listen," I said to Amy, "you're the poetry expert. Tell her. It even has poetry in it."

"It does?" marveled Louisa. "Did Sarah write it?"

"No, it was written about her," replied Amy. "And it's very sad."

"Read some," said Louisa, plopping herself back in her chair.

"Let's see. Which part shall I read?" I inquired of myself.

"Read the poem. I want to hear it."

"Yes," begged Amy, "you must read it, now that you have teased her palate."

"All right, let me find it." I thumbed through the small volume. "Ah, here it is. Are you ready?"

"Does it have a title?" asked Louisa. She fell back into her chair.

"If it has a title, Lulu, she will read it. So, stop asking so many questions."

Louisa gave her a stern eye.

Amy laughed.

"Oh, Amy! You always fool with me."

"Here it is. And no, it doesn't have a title," I said. "It first appeared in the *Monitor Weekly*, a big city newspaper. The author of the book must have written it."

"What's the author's name?" Louisa asked.

"Are you going to read the poem," snapped Amy, "or are we going to hold Lulu's hand all day?"

"Just read it, Emmie," said Louisa, crossing her arms in a pout.

"Fine. It goes like this:

"And here thou makest thy lonely bed,
Thou poor forlorn and injured one;
Here rests thy aching head—
Marked by a nameless stone.

"Poor victim of man's lawless passion,
Though e'er so tenderly carest—
Better to trust the raging ocean,
Then to lean upon his stormy breast.

"And thou though frail, wert fair and mild;
Some gentle virtues warmed thy breast.
Poor outcast being! sorrow's child!
Reproach can't break thy rest."

"Oh that poor, poor, girl," wailed Louisa.

Amy became very silent. She walked to the edge of the porch, wrapped one arm around a fluted column and stared out at the river. A pair of swans swooped down and landed in the water by Sandy Island. The sun hid behind billowy clouds, igniting the swollen mass of cotton plumes that hovered high above the horizon, while fanning shafts of streaky light beamed down from the heavens.

"Continue," said Amy, serenely.

I lowered my voice, trying to sound more like a poet than just a reader. Louisa hung off the arm of her chair, sitting at the edge, intensely listening, starry-eyed, her lips parted, as if it made her hear better.

"On thy poor wearied breast the turf
Lies quiet as soft as on the rich:
What now to thee the scorn and mirth,
Of sanctimonious hypocrites.

"That mangled form now finds repose,
And who shall say thy soul does not,
Since he who from the grave arose
Brought immortality to light."

"Oh, that's so sad," lamented Louisa.
"Shh, Lulu," commanded Amy. "Continue, Emmie."
Louisa threw herself back in her chair and grimaced at Amy's reprimand. Amy just stood there, embracing the porch column. As if in a trance, she stroked the fluted wood with the tips of her fingers, her eyes riveted to a dazzling sky. She was engaged by what I read. I continued.

"Poor fated one the day is coming
When sin and sorrow pass away—
I see the light already gleaming
Which ushers in the endless day.

"Where shall the murderer be found?
He calls upon the rocks in vain—
The force of guilt will then confound,
Alas the Judge! no longer man.

"He calls upon the rocks in vain—
The adamantine rocks recoil,
Earth can no longer hide the slain,
And death yields up his spoil.

"Where shall the murderer appear?
My God thy judgments are most deep:
No verdict can the monster clear
Who dies a hypocrite must wake to weep."

After I had finished, I expected some retort or clever remark from Amy. There was nothing but anomalous silence. She stood there, her arm around the porch column, staring toward the river. The breeze had all but gone away and the river shimmered, reflecting a mirror image of Sandy Island and its reclusive tree. The mother osprey fed her chicks, their beaks sprung open, their little heads bobbing up and down, as they chirped and cried, drowning in a desire to be fed. Louisa waited, hesitant to speak, lest she be admonished once again by Amy. No one spoke for what appeared to be a long minute. I waited.

"It was like she was begging from the grave," bemoaned Amy, "begging for, waiting for … justice."

"That was eerie," said Louisa. "I suddenly have a chill." She rubbed her arms. "You say it was a minister who killed her?"

"They think." I said. "No one really knows. He was tried in court and found innocent."

"That is fascinating. It happened in the city, you say?"

"In Mudfog!" wailed Amy. She reached over to the tray and scooped up a cookie.

"Welcome back," I said.

"I know," she replied. "Sad poetry puts me into a state."

"Why have I not heard of this crime?" inquired Louisa.

"It's not talked about, unless you read the book." I said, "Who in civil society would discuss such an event, especially to a young lady? That is the marvelous properties of a book. There is always someone who exposes the truth. And it doesn't matter how old you are. It's there for anyone to read."

"You're right," agreed Amy. "Father would never speak of such a thing in our presence."

"Well, should we take it up at the next meeting?" I asked.

"Give the book to Lulu, Emmie. Let her read it. We know she wants to, now."

"Oh, I don't know," said Louisa. "Sounds so … so disturbing."

"Just pretend it's fiction," declared Amy. "It's sure to offset your sentiments about *Adam Bebe*."

"Here, take it," I said, handing her the volume.

"You sure it's all right?" she asked. "I mean, that I should read such writing?"

"Of course she's sure," echoed Amy. "After all, you are president of the club now."

"I am?" asked Louisa, rhetorically.

"That's what she said, Lulu." I confirmed.

Louisa, sat up in her chair and threw her shoulders back proudly. "Very well," she said, "I will make certain to read it for the next meeting. We will discuss it then."

"Shall we adjourn?" said Amy.

"Wait! That's my job," declared Louisa. "After all, I am president of the Drift River Readers Club, you know."

"Yes, you are," I agreed. "Yes, you are."

Louisa airily tapped the punch bowl with a spoon.

We all laughed.

—◦◦◦—

Chapter 5:

I love foggy summer mornings, especially when a misty cloak of air percolates from the Atlantic Ocean, creating an enigmatic milky vista, where nearby homes are lost, left hovering in a sousing cloud of heavenly mist. Hidden ships in an unseen harbor loiter, waiting for their sea masters to prompt their sweeping bows and pronged sprits through salty breakers to caress and batter their weathered, wooden hulls and sweep across corrugated, gray decks. Above the idle flotilla of slumbering vessels, white-gray gulls emerge and then evaporate into the enveloping fog, with the only proof to their existence whining squeals which pierce the ebbing veil that engulfs them. All part of my somber paradise in this small village, tucked away in a sequestered, New England fishing community.

Today is such a foggy day. I had overslept. I opened my eyes, leaving visions of knights and dragons in sleep, to be continued in future drowsy chapters. The first sound I heard was a creaking of nails tearing from wood. The blackness that was once night is replaced by soft muted light and loud incessant banging. I looked around. I was unsure if the noise was real or residue from a peaceful slumber. Suddenly, there it is again—above my head. Thumping and creaking, followed by the loud striking blows with a hard object. I ran to the window and looked out. On the lawn was a fresh bundle of rufous-colored wood shingles, along with a scattered pile of gray, curled, weathered ones. Abruptly, a shingle tile came flying down from the roof above, followed by another and another.

In the street, someone walked by. They stopped and looked up at the house. Still in my night attire, I backed away so I wouldn't be seen. The image was barely visible, cloaked by the thick, wandering fog. It spoke up to the roof gutter. I listened. Raspy laughter dangled in the muffled air. The image in the street withered and vanished as he or she walked off and up the smoggy, alabaster road. Suddenly there was whistling. *What was going on?* I said to myself. Was I going mad? I scurried down the stairs to the kitchen where I found Grandmamma heating water on the stove.

"Good morning Van Winkle! Sleep well?"

"Morning, Grandmamma. Someone's up on the roof," I said, clutching my chest in dazed confusion.

"Moses Reyals. He's replacing those damaged cedars … remember? I told you he would be here this morning to fix that water leak above your bed."

"Oh, yes. I remember now," I said, groggily.

"Sit, dear, I am making tea. It will help make sense of things."

I threw my languid bones into a chair. "Oh, Grandmamma, I had such a wonderful dream. I was in an Arthurian world, and a Knight from the Round Table came to rescue me. His white horse galloped through a flowered forest as I sat behind him, embracing him tightly." I stroked the side of my face with my hand. "I can still feel the icy steel of his shimmering amour up against my cheek as I rested it onto his shoulder."

"Oh, Emily, where do you find these queer dreams?" she laughed.

"Books, Grandmamma, books."

"Now, what does a nice girl like you need rescuing from?"

"I can't remember. You know, Grandmamma … dreams are like story books, only with pages missing."

"You mean like the one I have missing from under my bed."

I sat down quietly, unsure of what to say. She was talking about the book I took. Not only was my hand in the cookie jar, it was jammed there tightly. I had no way of pulling it out without explaining myself. As in all compromising situations, I found it was best to tell the truth then to wiggle and wag on the end of the fishhook.

"Are you angry?" I asked, sheepishly.

"Angry? What reason would I be angry for, dear?"

"Because I didn't ask to borrow it."

"Borrow what?" She poured hot water into my cup, ignoring my inquiry.

"The book."

"Which book is that?" she asked, pretending not to know and twisting my guilt ever tighter.

I thought on her words while she dropped the silver tea infuser into my cup.

"I packed it tightly," she said, "tea will be nice and strong."

"Thank you." I was prepared to explain why I took the book about the hanging of Sarah Cornell. I waited for her to ask me about it some more. She never did. Instead, she just continued with breakfast. Up on the roof, I could hear Moses singing while he hammered away.

"Now, we have poached eggs with toast and jam … grape jam. You like grape jam, don't you, dear?"

"Oh, yes! I love grape." I stood up and gave her a hug. Her bony shoulders and delicate breastbone pressed against mine. Charlotte White was aging, becoming thinner. It worried me. "I love you, Grandmamma."

"Of course you do, dear. And Grandmamma loves you. We have each other and that is all that matters."

"All that matters, Grandmamma." A happy tear swelled in the corner of my eye.

"Read anything you like," she finally said, pouring some steaming water into my cup.

I waited for the tea to brew. When it was strong enough, I tugged the tiny chain and dropped the infuser into her cup. Bringing the hot drink to my lips, I blew. The steam from the beverage watered my eyes as I sipped.

"The Sarah Cornell book, I see. Well … you can borrow any book you like, dear, as long as you return it," she finished with a compromising smile. "It cost me all of ten cents."

Her declaration caused me to heave and spurt a mouthful of tea in a ruptured spray. The hot liquid stung my nose and poured down my chin. I broke into laugher.

Grandmamma chimed in. "Are you all right, child?" She handed me a towel.

"Fine, Grandmamma," I replied, wiping my face. "I'll return the book as soon as I'm done with it. Honest!"

"Keep it as long as you like. Just don't lose it."

Talking to herself, as she often did, she took the towel and wiped the table of spewed tea. A serene smile and a twinkle in her dark brown eyes always graced her face. Rarely did I ever see her grimace or scowl. It was the peaceful face of an angel. She had taken responsibility of me all my life without protest or regret. A saint who looked after other people's children, lodged them in her tiny home, cramming her bedroom with little, disavowed strangers, giving them a push uphill on this fast-moving cart of life.

The kitchen filled with the raw scent of singed bread, as Grandmamma turned a slice over on the stove. Removing the lid from a clay crock filled with homemade jam, she placed it on the table. It smelled wonderful. Immediately, I discovered my mind wandering to Paul Cuffe's grape orchard, across the road from Louisa Macomber's house on Drift Road. I remember last summer picnicking with Louisa and her family out on their lawn and how the scent of matured grapes filled the air with a tangy sweet fragrance. Not being a creature of privileged society, I suppose that is what a proper lady's toilet water would smell like. It is what Mrs. S. smelled like—a sugary berry—the aroma of honey dripped over tabled-cut flowers. You know the smell. When I go shopping in the big city such scents are everywhere uptown. Though I have never held a precious bottle of perfume in my hand, I have experienced its bouquet at Smith's Everything Store at the corner of Main and Pleasant.

Unfortunately, it is not the redolence of such aromas that linger when I visit the city, but the irritating and decaying scent of horse manure and oppressive mill soot, dawdling to sting the eyes and prick the nose. Then there's the stench of garbage or discarded feculence from city dumps. Along the river that cuts through the center of the big city, dead fish float. The river is a place where toxic dyes and a leaden soup of harmful elements drain from its swampy banks, down to the bay, from mills that siphoned its once crystal waters, returning them tainted and defiled. The Quequechan River, they call it. I often thought about why city folk name their streams and streets after dead Indians. Heaven knows … they've killed enough of them. *Guilt*, Grandmamma would say.

I rarely drive into the city. When I do, it's usually to obtain medicinal compounds for Grandmamma at the druggist, or to visit the bookstore, which there are two—Adam's and the Taste of Honey Book Emporium. That's the big city for you—where even a simple bookstore has a fancy name.

If I entered the city blindfolded, I could still note which street I was on, since each artery has its own particular odor. There's the stinging smell of sulfur and rotten eggs, which spews from the dye factory on Pleasant Street. Why they call it Pleasant Street, I'll never know. Then there's the paper mill on Central, giving off the musty and rancid vapors of moldering, wet rags. To be fair, I must mention Main Street, where the nose may discover agreeable, if not peculiar, fragrances—like those of the fruit market, leather tack and harness store, and of course, the butcher shop. And let's not forget the clothing store. Not everyone makes their own clothes in the city like we do here in Westport, you know.

Human miasma, Grandmamma calls it. *People were not meant to be stacked one upon another,* she often said, *If they were, they would be called sardines, not people.* It always brings a smile to my face when I consider Grandmamma's philosophical or pensive proverbs, for which she has many.

How in God's good earth did I get talking about the city and its odors? Oh, yes, we were talking about perfume. Well, the closest thing to it that I can think of is a Westport country road in summer solstice, when the cool rain falls onto honeysuckle-covered stone walls along Point Road, and the heated rocks begin to steam, sending forth a flowering sweet fragrance which anesthetizes the soul.

After one leaves the city and enters Westport, revolting odors soon fade—replaced by the scent of stacked hay, open pastures, and sweet corn, standing tall like green, open-armed soldiers along horse plowed trenches. I know what you are going to say. How about those repugnant dairy farm odors ... namely, manure. Well! I dare add that Westport manure is not as sour or bitter smelling as the city variety. At least, I don't think it is. And though you may say that there is nothing pleasant about the scent of a dairy farm, I beg to differ. Westport's dairy farms smell as savory as any confectionery shops the city may offer. How can that be, you may ask? Because they are the smells of home.

"What are you going to do with yourself today?" inquired Grandmamma.

"I think I will drive to Fall River and visit the new library."

"You are such a funny girl."

"What do you mean?"

"You and books."

"I love books. After all, I'm just following in your footsteps."

"That you are dear, that you are."

"You know, Grandmamma, I wish I could have gone to college."

She laughed. "Who ever heard of a young girl attending college?"

"Lots of girls do."

"Well then, if I had the money I would send you to the best college ... one in Europe."

"You would?"

"You don't need college. You are a self-learned woman. It may not get you ahead of men, but it won't let you fall far behind."

"You're right, Grandmamma. It's a man's world. They do as they please while the woman is home all day looking after children or catering to husbandly demands."

"Oh, men are not all that bad. Most I've known are good men."

"You mean like grandfather Zephriah White?"

"Oh yes, a better man has yet to live. Why, he and Mother knew their place in marriage, but it never mattered. They still walked in the spirit of the Lord. And though Mother knew her station in marriage, it made little difference. She would insist on chopping wood and Daddy would wash floors and mend curtains. It was all the same to them. 'What better master to mend a curtain than a sailor who once mended sails,' he would always say."

"Do you think I'll ever discover such a man, Grandmamma?"

"Of course you will, dear. Why ask such a silly question? When you are ready and the right one comes along, well … you'll see. You are particular … that's all … and that's good."

"The right one comes along," I echoed, sipping my tea. "What was your mother's name?"

"Libby," she said, smearing some jam onto a warm slice of toasted bread. She gazed down at the floor in thought. Her cocoa eyes sparkled and her high cheekbones reflected light from buff-umber skin, furrowed and puckered by time. She had a gentle proud chin—always smiling—a face revealing inquisitiveness and wisdom. "Libby. Elizabeth White, servant of the Lord." She took a bite from the jellied bread and broke her solemn rule of never speaking with your mouth full. "Servant of the Lord," she mumbled, "that's was her name's meaning. Yes, it was."

"I wonder what meaning Emily holds."

"Beautiful child."

"Does it?"

"It does to me, dear," she said, tapping me on the hand.

"Oh, Grandmamma!"

Just as I took a bite from my jammy bread, there was a knock at the door. I ran up to the window and pushed the curtain aside. My nose rested on the cool glass as I struggled to get a better look.

"Grandmamma, there are two men at the door," I whispered. "I'm not dressed. I am going to step into your room. You see who it is."

I stood behind the curtain in Grandmamma's little bedchamber as she unlatched the door.

"Mornin' to ya, Miss Charlotte," a gruff voice said. "We're done on the ruff. Need ta inspect da leak on da inside fa damage."

"Is it really necessary?" asked Grandmamma, unsure whether she should let the men in.

"I beg ya forgiveness fa da intrusion, but ya would not want it ta happen a-gain, now would ya?" said the voice in a mauled, English Cockney accent. "So if ya let us go upstairs and see, it won't take long at all."

I recognized Moses' guttural, begging speech. When he spoke, he often did so in an overly apologetic tone and for the littlest of things. His approach was one of absurd politeness and inane patronizing—as if he were hiding truth or begging forgiveness. He wore a tattered wool cap, which he was always quick to remove when greeting a woman. His face was unshaven—not quite a beard, his eyes narrow, not quite opened, not quite closed, and his cheeks and nose were red puffed tomatoes. He was ragged, unkempt, and his clothing soiled with whale oil. If you can forgive me for saying so, he smelled of decomposing shellfish.

Though everyone called him Old Moses, he was not that old at all—

forty, perhaps. Though to you that may sound ancient. His occupation was chiefly whaling, but he rarely left shore anymore. Often he was seen going out fishing with the cod fisherman. I never knew where he lived. He appeared to spend most of his days just skulking around the dock, sleeping under old dories, or amusing the neighborhood children with sleight of hand trickery. He could usually be found sitting on a weathered piling by the river whittling on a stick.

Old Moses is well known around Point Village as the tramp whaleman who carved small toy figurines—soldiers or animals—out of driftwood. But the Moses who was here today was a different sort. Perhaps because I never saw him this close up, inside my home, or heard him address Grandmamma so brashly. Why did he insist on coming inside? There was no reason that I know of. The roof leaked from outside not in. There was nothing to see. Unfortunately, the truth is hidden inside Moses Reyals's head.

I peered past a slit in the curtain. Standing there with Moses was another man—a much younger man. I nearly cried out when he looked my way. He appeared quite handsome at first sight, but when he turned his face it gave me a scare. The skin on one side of his face was singed, purple and puckered. One eye drooped and one ear was half the size of the other. It was apparent that the poor fellow was burnt badly at one time. I never saw him around the village before.

"Charlotte, tis me helper," burped Moses. He slapped the burnt-faced man in the back of the head, knocking his cap into his hands. "Take ya hat off, man. Ya in da presence of a lady."

"Nice to make your acquaintance, Miss," said the man. Fidgeting with his tattered hat, he bowed. "Billy Cain, Miss, at your humble service."

Finally, Grandmamma let the men in. Moses practically pushed himself past the door as Grandmamma jumped aside. He walked into the kitchen and toward the front of the house.

"Tis way, is dot not right?" he asked, as he inspected every inch of the place. "Neva been in 'ere before."

"I know you haven't," said Grandmamma, as if to hint that he should count his lucky stars that she let him in. "Up the stairs. The room is on the left. The west corner, right over the bed is where the water was coming in."

"Won't take long, Charlotte," he muttered. He winked at his companion.

The burnt faced man surveyed the house as if he had never been inside one before.

I watched as they disappeared into the sitting room. Grandmamma looked perturbed. I didn't blame her. The house practically shuddered as their lumbering feet climbed the stairs on their way up to my room. I pulled back the curtain.

"They went upstairs to inspect the leak," she whispered.

"Does he need to do that? I don't like it that they're in my room. And that other fellow is frightening. I have never seen him before."

"Nor I," replied Grandmamma.

"I hear them moving up there. What are they doing?"

"I don't know. Do you have any valuables out, dear?"

"Not really. What little money I have is hidden in a sock under my bed."

"I'm going up there and see."

I held her by the elbow. "No, wait, Grandmamma ... I think I hear them coming down the stairs."

"Shh!" she warned, drawing the curtain.

Moses reappeared sounding his apologetic self. "I beg ya forgiveness. Sorry ta tisturb ya, dear lady. Everthin looks n'order, tank da good Lord," he proclaimed as he moved toward the door.

"See Seabury Cory next door," ordered Grandmamma. "He will pay for the repairs."

"He paid us earlier this morning," said Billy Cane, stepping back and looking down sheepishly, as if it were a mistake to acknowledge such a claim. He threw his arms up as Moses turned and whacked the man with his hat.

"Be silent with ya! I do da talking."

Grandmamma shook her head.

"Well, yes, da boy is right ... Seabury has paid us." He skittishly cleared his throat. "I'd still be interested n' da chicken meal ya said ya'd give me."

"That's right. I promised to feed you when you were finished," agreed Grandmamma. She rummaged through the icebox as Moses peered over her shoulder. "I made up a plate with some fried chicken, beets, and potatoes ... and, oh yes, some apple pie. Leftovers, and it's cold, but fresh as the day it was made."

"Tat's fine, Charlotte, fine! Apple!" He uttered to himself, fondly. "Love apple!"

"I didn't know you were bringing a friend. There should be enough there for two."

"Oh, he can 'ave some of da beets n'potada," he was quick to reply. He rubbed his hands together while Grandmamma carefully covered the meal with a towel.

"And I want my plate and towel back," she demanded.

"I'll leave it by da dar," said Moses.

"I thought you went fishing. Don't they feed you on that ship?" she said, handing him the plate.

"I hope ta be shippin' out soon. Da *Marion* is in harba," he added, with a garbled voice. "Da captain promised ta take me along next time they go whalin."

"The *Marion* you say?" said Grandmamma.

I could tell by the tone of her voice that she didn't believe a word the man said.

"Yeah. It arrived yesterday," said Billy Cain. He quickly backed away, expecting Moses to strike him.

"She is gettin' new riggin'. Danny Borden will be workin' on 'er tis mornin'."

"I thought Daniel went off to the military," said Grandmamma.

"He com back yesta'day. He n' young Cory."

"Little Samuel … back home, is he?" Grandmamma sounded surprised, as I did.

My eyes widened and I stiffened when I heard the news. Samuel … back? After being gone almost a year.

"We be shoven-off," said Moses. "Thank ya for da meal Charlotte. God will bless ya for tis. It is good souls like you that keep poor fools like us fed."

"God feeds those who feed others."

The two men walked out the door.

"Don't forget to bring the plate back when you're done, now," she shouted.

Both men marched quickly through the overgrown meadow behind the house down to a clearing by the riverbank. Like two ghosts, their images faded in and out of the hovering fog.

I heard the door slam.

"You can come out now, dear."

"I thought they would never leave."

"That Moses is harmless," said Grandmamma. "I just don't like the men inside the house. Don't like any of those fishermen in here." She watched out the window as the two men trudged through the field. "There is something seriously wrong with that other one."

"Who is he, Grandmamma?" I asked, pulling the window curtain aside and taking a look.

"Don't know. Some whaleman, I suppose." We both spied out the window. Her eyes narrowed as she moved her face closer to the glass. "He's got something in his hand?"

"Who does?"

"Moses. Something red."

"I can't see. It's too foggy."

At that very moment a patch of fogless air moved by the two men.

"There, there!" she cried. "He's waving it in the other man's face."

"Grandmamma. That's my red silk scarf. The one Amy gave me for Christmas. They must have taken it from my room." An icy sting crawled up my spine. "Look!" That Billy Cain fellow is placing it around his neck!"

"Why, that little beggar! I'm going after them," she growled, starting for the door. I reached out and took her by the arm.

"No, let them go. The scarf is torn. It's of little use to me anyway. Besides, he has placed it around his neck. I could never wear it."

"We can sew it … wash it."

"No! Let him have it, Grandmamma."

I fibbed about the scarf being torn. I watched as Moses and Cain wandered into the murky mist.

Moses slapped the other man in the back of the head sending him stumbling forward. He yanked the scarf from around his companion's neck, coiled it around his hand, and shoved it into his pocket.

"Come, Grandmamma," I said moving away from the window. "Let's finish breakfast."

"You should go up and look over your room, dear."

"After I'm done eating," I replied.

Grandmamma removed some hot bread from the stove and placed it on her plate. Dry toasted bread. No jam … no butter, burnt. It's the way she preferred it.

I took one more look out the window. I probably should have not since thinking about having those two men go through my things up in my room made me nauseous.

"Sit down, dear. Your toast is getting cold."

"You will be fortunate if you ever see that plate again," I said.

"Have you heard? Young Samuel is home from the war," she announced.

"Yes, I did!"

"Is that not good news?"

"I'm happy for old Mr. Cory, Grandmamma. To see his son again! I'm afraid the conflict in the South is going to flare and get worse."

"The good Lord knows our desires and he fulfilled them by sending the boy home."

"I read that President Lincoln has called for five hundred thousand troops, and that he expects the war to be a long one."

"Just dreadful. Well, you should know, dear. You read those newspapers. My little world is right here, in this little village. It's all that I care about."

"I wonder why he's come home so soon?" I took a bite from my toast. It was cold. Still, the jam was delicious. "He was supposed to be away for at least two years."

"The Lord only knows," declared Grandmamma. She cut a fresh slice from the loaf of bread and placed it on the stove. "Including the fate of those two turnips that were just here," she added.

"Turnips! That's so funny, Grandmamma."

"Have you ever taken a good look at old Moses ... gotten close up to him? Why you would swear that the good Lord himself just pulled that face right out of his turnip garden. The man lives by the water ... you would think he'd make use of it once in a while to bathe."

"That fellow with him. I never saw him before."

"They come and they go ... whalemen. That one appeared to have been hit in the head once too many times by a boom or something. You can see it in his eyes. A raft—drifting without a paddle."

"Yes, there was something about him. Something appeared absent."

"The good sense the Lord gave him, more than likely," she said.

"Poor fellow. The side of his face ... it was all burnt."

"Boiling fat oil."

"Fat oil?"

"When men try blubber on the whaling ships. He must have angered someone and they threw hot oil into his face."

"Oh, that is terrible."

"A rough bunch, those whalers. They should send the whole lot of them off to the war, I say. They would teach those Rebs a thing or two."

"Oh, Grandmamma. That's a terrible thing to say."

"Well, it's true, you know."

I finished my tea and brushed the breadcrumbs off my nightgown. "I best get ready. It's a long ride into the city."

She walked off to her room without saying a word. I placed my saucer and cup on the counter and rinsed them from a pail of water, taken from the well in the backyard, while standing by the tub sink, my favorite place in the entire house. While most of my friends complained about doing dishes, it was a pensive exercise I enjoyed. The floor by the window above the sink was the sunniest place in the house. Here the evening setting sun would glimmer through the wavy glass, illuminating the room with a warm orange glow. I could wash dishes and delight in the panoramic views of the Westport River, relish the sandy colored hay fields, the flight of the honking Canadian geese as they migrated in autumn, be entertained by parades of clownish mallards skirting the shore and, above all, savor the slothful decent of a falling sun in late afternoon as it dribbled from a smoldering salmon sky with the crimson radiance of a coal-burning fire.

I had just finished drying plates when Grandmamma came out of her bedchamber—a serene smile on her face. She rested a tightly closed fist in my hand and handed me a few coins.

"Now, when you're in the city, buy yourself a new scarf."

"Oh, Grandmamma, you mustn't! Besides, it's summer. I don't need a scarf."

"Then you buy yourself a present. A book, maybe."

"Charlotte White. You are a wonderful mother." I leaned in to kiss her.

She proudly offered me her cheek then quickly returned to her toast burning on the stove. Poor Grandmamma, I thought looking down at the money she gave me. Though I was thrilled with the offer of a gift, it was barely enough to purchase a wool scarf, let alone one made from silk, like the one Amy had gifted me. In the end, it was her thoughtfulness that spoke measures. All the words, in all the dictionaries, in all the world, would not be enough to describe her tender kindness.

Chapter 6:

Not long after Moses and his companion left, I finished breakfast and prepared for my ride into the city. The fog was brightly lit. A veil of muted gleam kindled the morning, while the sun battled to break through a misty day. After harnessing the horse to the carriage, I took a casual stroll down Point Road to the wharf to look around. I must admit a desire to knock upon Captain Cory's door on the way and ask about his son. Ultimately, I decided it was discourteous and unladylike—especially a home where two men lived alone. Does that sound like I'm making excuses? Well, not true. Samuel deserved all the valuable time he could spend with his father. After all, he had just arrived yesterday from the conflict in the South, and I did not want to appear shamelessly brazen or audacious.

I took a short walk down to the docks where there was always something interesting going on—not that much ever does. Before he left for the war a year ago, Samuel would spend most of his time down by the waterfront. Though, I must confess, as you probably have already guessed, the real reason for my little diversion was in hopes of encountering Samuel—by happenstance, you understand.

As I strolled, I noticed the barn door to Seth Howland's Carpentry Shop was swung open as usual. The aroma of damp sawdust mingled with wet fog stimulated the senses. Though I could not see anyone inside, I could hear a hammer doing what hammers do. In the field just behind the woodshop, tiny poppy flowers filled a sloping, green grassy sea with yellow. They leaped and popped, snaring the eye with color all the way to the river below. At the end of Point Road, steam was rising from a vat on one of the whaleboats, where whale blubber cooked until it bled out every ounce of precious oil the whale had to offer. The vat cooled in the brisk morning air from a late night of grimy work.

When I arrived at the wharf I found it surprisingly uneventful—lots of boats—very little people. The fog must have kept the ships in harbor and the fishermen home. Now, when I say uneventful, I am not being completely honest. The mallards were here—little flotilla's zigging and zagging between ship rudders, quaking in complaint to my intrusion. Beneath them, schools of confused and truant mackerel darted and scurried, their blue, zebra-striped backs shimmering and glistening just under the surface of the crystal water. They scattered with the appearance of bigger fish.

A low-flying gull skimmed the glassy sea, adding further drama to the whole affair. His gray and white cousin, poised on an old weathered log piling behind me, cawed in that nettlesome, high-throaty cry—quite annoying—but pleasantly so … if you understand my meaning. Looking out toward the Knubble, an outcrop of rock and ledge at the harbor entrance, the eye travels along a hovering, misty cloud sitting a few feet off the water and not much higher than the hulls of whalers tied to bark-naked trees growing out from the sea. The fog is gradually evaporating beneath a dusky, slate sky, as a brave sun battles to brighten the day.

I decided to pay a visit to Cory's Village Store. The Corys are a well-known and respected family in Westport. Captain Seabury Cory's cousin, Alexander, owned the Point Store where one could purchase everything from candles to a woman's bone skirt hoop. The Cory family is also known for building the sailing vessel *Kate Cory*, one of the whaling ships here in the harbor, and the newest and largest ever build in little Westport. Mary Ann Cory, Alexander's wife, greeted me as I entered the store.

"Morning, Emily!"

"Morning, Mrs. Cory."

"How's Charlotte doing? I hear she has not been well."

"Oh, she's up and around, I'm happy to report. Getting old, I'm afraid."

"Aren't we all?" She folded some dress material and placed it on a shelf. "What can I do for you today, dear, or have you just come to visit?"

"Oh, a little of both. Has the linen for making handkerchiefs come in yet?"

"No, they haven't, but you are in luck." She tapped me on the wrist and retrieved a small box from under the counter. "We have these ready-made store-bought handkerchiefs, direct from Boston." Carefully, she removed a couple from their packets.

"Those are beautiful!"

"Yes, we have rose pink, sky blue, and tulip yellow. Inspect that lacework and the exquisite net embroidery. For two cents, I can even have them initialed, if you like."

"I must admit, they're so pretty. I'd be afraid of using one."

"They were so beautiful that I just had to carry them in the store. They're fifty cents each. If I sell one or two a year, I would be quite fortunate. People here at the Village just don't have that sort of money to throw around on silk handkerchiefs."

"Come now, Mrs. Cory. Some of those whaling captains make hundreds. Entice them to buy a couple for their sweethearts."

"That is what I'm counting on." She carefully wrapped them up and placed them back in their packets. "Now, how about you?"

"I'm afraid they are a little too dear for my purse. I'm accustomed to paying no more than thirty cents for an entire five yards of linen and sewing up my own handkerchiefs. I suppose I'll just have some of those licorice candy sticks, instead. My sweet tooth has been tickling me all morning."

"How many, dear?" She removed the lid from the glass candy jar.

"Three please ... no, make that four."

"Four it is."

"I can be such a child at times."

"When it comes to sweets we are all children." Mary Ann Cory wrapped the candy twigs in a small paper wrapper and tied it with some twine. When I reached over for it she slipped a packet with a pink silk handkerchief into my hand. "That will be four cents, dear."

"Oh, Mrs. Cory, you mustn't," I begged, examining the fine material.

"Must get back to tidying my shelves," she said, quickly returning to her chores.

I placed four cents on the counter. "Thank you, Mrs. Cory."

Mary Ann Cory climbed up a small ladder and moved some stock about on the shelf. I unwrapped the candy sticks and placed one in my mouth. It hung from my lips like a spongy limp cigar. Enjoying the sugary treat, I peered out the window toward the harbor and the forest of masts with their roped branches of booms and spars. Floating close by was the whaler *Kate Cory*, sitting serenely and tethered to the harbor quay. A man hung from a rope in its rigging up near the crow's nest. Standing by the ship were two other men. One flung a ditty bag over his shoulder and shouted up to the monkey above as the aerialist swung from one cable to another.

"Who is that up in the rigging of the *Kate*?" I asked. "He looks quite proficient at what he's doing."

Mary Ann Cory walked to the window and looked out. "Oh, that's my son, Issac ... he's replacing some rope or something, getting *Kate* ready for her next voyage."

"Who's that other fellow standing on the seawall?"

"That's my husband with a coil of rope over his shoulder." She climbed back up the ladder and continued her work.

"No, I mean the man with him, limping?"

"Why, that's young Samuel … home from the military. Have you not heard?"

"Oh … yes, Samuel," I said calmly, pretending it was common knowledge. "Well, I have a busy day, Mrs. Cory. I'm so grateful for your gift of the pink handkerchief. I will cherish it."

"I'm happy you like it, dear." As she climbed down off the ladder she leaned over the counter. "I wouldn't mention anything about it to my husband, Alex, you understand," she whispered. "He's sort of old fashioned. He'd be upset with me if he knew I ordered them in the first place."

"Oh no, I won't." I started to leave. "I'll be going now."

"You do that, dear. Hurry so you don't miss him."

She looked over at me with a comforting smile and winked. I suppose everyone in the village knew of my affection for Samuel. I turned, shamefaced, and walked out the door.

I loitered on the stoop by the store and watched as Alex and Samuel talked. Samuel took the paunchy bag and flung it over his shoulder. A tinge of anxiety came over me as they parted and Samuel began making his approach. I was uncertain whether to run and hide or just throw my arms around him. *How did my hair look? Is my dress tidy? Do I have burnt toast between my teeth?* There was no time to prepare. Why should there be? After all, it's only Samuel. I have never worried about how I looked in the past, or did I ever believe he would even notice. Yet there he was getting closer with every step, and here I am losing all equanimity. I should be happy just to see him home again and place all selfishness aside. After all, Samuel's homecoming is about Samuel and not me. I turned my back to him and pretended to be looking in the store window. I could see his reflection in the wavy glass as he stood behind me, the bulky bag plopped on his shoulder. A gleeful smile was on his face. He cleared his throat.

"Excuse me, Miss. Can you direct me to Captain Seabury Cory's residence," I heard him say.

Turning, I pretended to be surprise. The truth is, I was elated. "Samuel, what are you doing here?"

Dropping the seabag to the ground, he casually gripped me by the arms and offered my cheek a steely kiss. I hurled all self-restraint to the sea and shamefully threw my arms around him. His sturdy limbs wrapped around me like a clawless, friendly bear as I buried my nose between his neck and shoulder. Wickedly, I kissed him behind the ear.

"Oh, Samuel, it's so good to see you!"

"Good to see you, Emily." He held me by the hands, stood back, and looked me over. "You look more beautiful than when I left a year ago."

A flushed smile crept across my face. Such compliments were not common between us. I turned my head with embarrassment, praying he would embarrass me some more. We stood there holding hands and admiring one another. My surroundings all but vanished. The hubbub of birds, the hammering from the carpentry shop, the chill of the damp morning air, even the pungent smell of freshly uncovered seaweed at low tide, paled and waned. All I could discern was the handsome Samuel Cory. I stood there admiring him when suddenly I felt the back of my dress lift and a warm, fleecy sensation fondle the calf of my leg. I shouted, screamed, and jumped away. Samuel laughed.

"Why it's Fuffy!" he said, picking up the candy striped yellow cat. He held the Cory store's resident feline close to his face and stroked its neck. "Do you miss me, Fuffy?" he asked the cat but looking straight at me.

"He startled me," I said, reaching out to scratch it. "Fuffy, you vagabond."

The cat purred, fondly pushing its head against my hand.

"I wonder how he ever got that name?" I said.

"What, Fuffy? One of the neighborhood children named him. I suppose they were trying to call him Fluffy but couldn't articulate themselves very well. So Fuffy it became."

"That's a funny story. Grandmamma always had a cat. But she became allergic to their fur or something—affected her breathing. When the last one passed away she never bothered getting another."

"How is Charlotte?" he asked.

The cat purred and nuzzled his hand as he scratched its ear.

"Fine, but slowing down quite a bit, I'm afraid. It is starting to worry me."

"I see what you mean. Charlotte must be close to ninety."

The cat bit his hand.

"Ouch! You little devilkin." Gently, he tossed the tabby to the ground and sucked his wound.

"Eighty-seven," I replied, laughing. "Frisky, isn't he." I looked down at Samuel's cane. He never carried one before. I was so happy to see him I had forgotten that he was limping. Though concerned, I was somewhat afraid to ask what was wrong. But ask I did. "What happened with your leg?"

"I'm afraid that's the reason why I'm home. My military duty has been cut short—leg injury."

"Oh, my! What sort of injury?"

"Bullet shattered the knee."

"My Lord, Samuel. You said nothing in your letters about it. Why did your father not tell me?"

"Father didn't know until I arrived yesterday. I didn't want to worry him."

"Oh, Samuel! Should you be walking on it?"

"Oh … it's been healing fine. The bone was shattered. I'm afraid it may never be the same. I can still bend it and all, but it hurts like the dickens. Doctors say it may take a year or more before it heals completely. Until then I use this." He held up the black knobby cane.

"You should be home convalescing, not walking about carrying heavy bags."

"Best thing I can do for the leg is walk on it."

"You can't just walk off such an injury. It needs rest."

"You would think. If I rest it too long it stiffens on me." He moved closer and began stroking my face with the back of his hand. "Moreover, looking at you is all the rest I need."

I glanced up at him. I could feel the burn in my cheeks and the surge of a hankering smile. I starved an aspiring hunger to make love to his hand as it caressed my face. Instead, I amorously gazed at him, letting my eyes inflict my craving. At that moment, I saw him in a light like I never had before. I was hoping that I could tenderly wound his heart with my unfulfilled desires. I was stunned by how I felt—my eagerness to surrender, the impulse to indulge in the wicked inclinations of the flesh, to become what Grandmamma would call a hussy. I am ashamed to confess that I could not help myself—to coddle these corporeal yearnings—unbridled enthusiasm that would shock even a salacious drunken sailor.

I continued to study him with an unfretted wanting gaze. He appeared different somehow, taller, older, much more mature. His wavy creamy hair had become darker, his face more angular, his voice deeper. He wore a well-cropped strawberry-blond mustache. He never had one before. This gave him a distinguished and regardful look. There was no doubt about it. Samuel Cory was more of a man and not the boy I once knew.

"Being back home with those who love you will be the best thing for you," I assured him, my eyes like gleaming stars. "Before you know it, you will be as good as new."

"Yes, I'm sure you're right," he replied with a shrug. He pulled his hand away.

I ran mine along my cheek where it had just been caressed. My subliminal advances of the last few seconds melted away. To tell you the truth, I don't think he was even aware that I was sending any. In some respects, that was a good thing. *Wrap your heart with thorns,* Grandmamma often said. *And the right man will suffer injury to reach it.* Instead, I had enfolded my desire with velvety flower petals, offering my womanly aspirations freely and without reservation. Even that had little impression on him. I settled on the comforting opinion that his lack of interest rested on the stealth and strategic approach of a military man. When the time was right he would strike with a passionate bombardment of hugs and kisses—crush my brazen advances in tactical arms and make a wifely prisoner of me. Until then, I will grow those thorns Grandmamma spoke of and give him the courting battle of his life. At least I would like to think that is the way it would go.

"I hear the war is getting bad," I said, quickly regaining composure.

"There's no stopping it now. They forced Lincoln's hand when they fired upon Fort Sumter in Charleston. It's all out war now. And I'm afraid I will not participate in it. I'm certain I will be discharged."

"Discharged?"

"Yes, I'm useless to the military with this injury. At first I was offered a pay clerk's position in Washington, but, at the last minute, I was ordered home. Oh, I'm certain the discharge will be under full honors, you understand. I'm afraid that is of little consolation."

"I'm sorry, Samuel. Look at it this way. Their loss is our fortune. It's wonderful to have you home."

"Let's talk about you," he said, eager to change the topic. "What are you doing with your day?"

"Fall River ... to the library. But that can wait. Why? What do you have in mind?"

"I want to show you a surprise."

"You're here! You mean there's more?"

He plopped his seabag up against the store and we walked down to Lee's Wharf. Between the dark whalers *Janet* and *Mattapoisett* sat a magnificent white schooner. Sleek and gleaming, it was a pearl huddled between two floating mountains of coal.

"Do you like it?" he asked pointing at the double-masted ship with his walking stick.

"Why, it is beautiful. Where did she come from? It's not a fishing vessel, is it?"

"No, it's a gentleman's schooner."

"A gentleman ... here in little Westport?"

"Why yes," he laughed. "Me!"

"I don't understand."

"It's mine, Emily. I purchased her in Baltimore."

"That beautiful vessel is yours?"

"It sure is! This is her new home. The schooner *Sphinx* of Westport."

"Samuel. This is great!" I moved up the wharf, inspecting the ship's graceful sheer.

He hobbled behind me, proud and joyful. "She's ninety-nine feet long. Nineteen-foot bowsprit and eighty feet along the deck. Built as a privateer but never put into service. She has a nineteen-foot beam. Her topsails are gaff rigged and she is very fast."

"What will you use her for, fishing?"

"Come now, none of that. She is a lady built for enjoying the sea."

"You mean … entertaining?"

"That too. Mostly she's for riding the ocean crests and enjoying all the pleasures the sea has to offer—sunsets, moonrise, cool summer breezes, and speed, above all speed."

"Speed, for what reason?"

"Speed for the reward of speed, the essence of swiftness—the thrill of racing. She's a smaller replica of *The America*. You know … the American racing yacht. The ship that won the Royal Yacht Squadron regatta back in fifty-one."

"Racing? What … a ship?" I asked, ignorantly. My lack of knowledge was not totally without merit. I have witnessed horse racing—but ships—unheard of in a working harbor such as Westport.

"Yes, racing! Have you not heard about the big yacht race around the Isle of Wight, between the Americans and the Brits?"

"Isle of Wight?"

"Yes, in England."

"I know how to find the Isle of Wight, Mr. Cory." I pouted, crossing my arms. "I may be an unsophisticated country girl, but it doesn't mean I'm totally lacking wit."

"Of course you're not."

"I may not have been formally educated at college like you have, but after all, I have studied more books then most. I am erudite and well-read, I'll have you know." I tossed my nose up at him and walked away.

He tottered over and whispered in my ear. "Well-read and lovely, I would say."

My arms melted down by my side. I sprinkled him with a forbearing smile. He kindly lobbied for absolution by stroking my cheek and fondling my flyaway hair behind my ear. Fervor flamed. My heart melted in my mouth as I struggled to grow thorns and blunt my spirited impulses.

"So, where is this *America* vessel? Is it still racing?"

"Unfortunately, its at the bottom of the St. John's River in Florida," he added, turning and admiring the schooner.

"Oh my, what happened to it?"

They scuttled her," he replied, glumly.

"Scuttled her! Why?"

"She fell into Confederate hands and the idiots sunk her at the mouth of the river as a blockade to Union war ships trying to enter Jacksonville."

"That's dreadful! If she looked anything like *Sphinx*, she was a beautiful ship, indeed."

"That she was. All the more reason why this little schooner means so much to me. I like to think of it as *America's* younger sister. Sixteen feet shorter but she sails almost as fast. Come. I'd love to show her off to you. I need to make some modifications so she could be more comfortable. Perhaps you can offer me some suggestions."

"Oh, Samuel, I don't know about that," I said, chuckling.

"Come now. Father and I have taught you everything there is to know about ships. I dare say you know more about them than the average fisherman here in the village."

His keen offer was inviting, not to mention flattering.

He took hold of a line tied to the pier and lowered the ship's gangplank onto the granite wharf. Walking half way up the platform he turned and extended his hand. "The *Sphinx* awaits you, my good lady."

I took hold of it as he escorted me on board.

The vessel was unlike any boat I had ever seen. Elegant, sleek, and stately, it was adorned in hand-rubbed brass and buffed bronze. The lacquered deckhouse had raised panel doors in its companionway, which glimmered even under a cloudy sky. Inside, furnishings were sedulously constructed in chestnut and honey locust. One could easily tell that it was not any ordinary vessel. Money had been poured into her—into her burnished brass cowls, and varnished line blocks, studded in ivory. She had a glossy mahogany railing, meticulously carved and circling the entire deck like a fine-polished necklace. In her cabin, hammered beam timbers were true and graceful, like the archways of a fine cathedral.

"She's spectacular, Samuel. I can't see how you can improve on her."

"She does need work. You are accustomed to these befouled whaling ships. That is why *Sphinx* looks so good to you. As I said, this is a gentleman's vessel. And a gentleman would find much that needs to be improved."

"Why, the deck looks like the floors in Louisa's home." I squatted and caressed the hoary scrubbed gray planking. "These are beautiful."

"Cyprian cedar. Only the best of timber was used to build her."

He took me by the hand and we walked her deck.

"She is the fastest vessel that Westport ... or dare I say the entire coast of New England, can offer."

"For all it's worth, that's a bold statement, Mr. Cory. Whom will you race? There's nothing like it anywhere around."

"Who will I race? Why ... the wind my dear girl, the wind."

"Hmm?"

"There are plenty of fast vessels along the New England coast. There's the three-masted barkentine *Nimrod*. It's reported to be quick."

"You mean the new Sanford whaling vessel."

"It's much heavier than my schooner. Built to be the fastest whaler in the fleet. It's an entirely different class of vessel, as far as whalers go. Though the *Sphinx* is smaller, I must admit that the *Nimrod* is no match for it. Once they take the *Nimrod* out on the bay and put her through her paces, I will take the *Sphinx* out and play with her. And if David Sanford is at the helm ... well, I'm certain he will challenge me to a contest."

"Samuel ... that is mischievous."

"Do you know anyone more misbehaved then David Sanford?"

"Oh, he's not that bad. Everyone is so cynical of David. If you were to take the time and become more acquainted with his way of thinking, you would discover a real sad individual under all that misbehavior. Unfortunate, really."

"Don't get me wrong. I don't mind David. But I find nothing unfortunate about the fellow."

"You have really attached yourself to this racing notion, haven't you?"

"Not really. As an end to a means, racing is not my intention. This schooner is meant to be my sanctuary, my refuge, a haven getaway. I will go out into open water and *she* and I will make love to the sea."

I blushed. I walked to the rail along the ship's gunwale and looked over the side at the still waters below. Though it may sound absurd, I was a little jealous of the *Sphinx*. Samuel walked over and stood by me.

"Did I say something wrong, Emily?"

"Why no. It was romantic, if you must know."

"I suppose that is why some men call the sea their mistress."

"I suppose. She is beautiful. The ship, I mean."

"She is to be the remedy for my losses in military service—a triumph to my failures."

"Failures? Why, Samuel, you have just begun living. Ultimately, failure is measured within the scope of a long life, and you have it all ahead of you."

"I had hoped that I could become an officer of some achievement. But with the war starting up and all the ugliness that accompanies it, I am discovering much about myself I didn't know."

"And that is?"

"Man can be cruel to which my tolerance can be small. The slavery issue down South is like nothing I have ever witnessed—the unmitigated brutality and unjust prejudice. Conduct I never knew existed."

"Grandmamma believes that people are the same all over and that those transgressions also happen up North."

Could be. Perhaps I am more sheltered than I realized. I suppose I have never really examined the constitution or the embodiment of my spirit. I have grown up in this tiny heaven of a town and rarely has the good Lord exposed the ugliness that he had reserved for me in this world. Maybe this injury was a godsend after all. I am discovering that I am delicate and thin-skinned.

"Oh, Samuel, you are anything but thin-skinned. You have faced the heartlessness of war and had the courage to express compassion and caring. You must not confuse empathy for your fellow man with weakness. It is just the opposite." I tenderly clutched him by the arm.

He looked down at the water and nodded his head. An aching mien draped his face.

"A penny for your thoughts," I said. I wondered whether my words gave him any comfort.

In the distance the *Emma Clifton*, a small, white hulled, fishing smack sailed through the tapered passage known as the Knubble. Its chalky, stained sails fluttered as it pointed up into a dying headwind. With the wind in its nose, it battled to circle Horseneck Point. It barely made it, drifting past the grassy marshland of Bailey Flats, toward the inner harbor. Along the *Sphinx's* bow, a feathered procession of mallards quietly wafted by. Across the docks, lumbering men stacked weathered casks onto the whaler *Janet* in preparation for a long sea voyage.

"What happened when you were away, Samuel?"

He hesitated in his reply, looking up at the sky as if waiting for some unseen power to allow him consent to speak. When he did, he told a story of tragedy and adversity.

"After my duties in New York were finished, the military's plan was to transfer us to Washington, which took us through Baltimore. Tensions there were unnerving. Baltimore was a cauldron of opposing views and ideals on the subject of slavery. Advocacy for slavery was strong there, though, I dare say, not as much as it was in the deep South." He clutched his hands into angry fists. Eyes became glossy and wet as he bit a trembling lip.

"We don't have to talk about it, Samuel, if you don't want to," I said.

"No. I need to tell someone. You see, many things happened when I was away ... many things." Tears swelled in his eyes.

I pretended not to notice, and instead moved closer to him. I rested my hand over his clenched fist.

He gave up a brave smile and tapped me on the nose with his finger. "You've been a wonderful friend, Emily. Father loves you like a daughter. I've learned that you never really appreciate what is dear to you until you are away from it." He became silent once again.

"Would you still like to tell me what happened, Samuel?" I said, looking into his eyes.

He stared out to sea, with a pensive gaze, collecting what must have been unhappy thoughts. I took a licorice stick from my package and offered him one. He took the ebony sweet and chuckled. "Hmm! Still eating these, I see."

"Need to feed that itchy tooth."

He collected his thoughts, rapping the gunwale railing with the candy stick. "As I said, we were ordered to Washington—Company D, Sixth Regiment. Most were only boys. Unlike myself, for many it was the first time away from their hometown. We traveled by locomotive to Baltimore. The train line did not go all the way through Baltimore and we had to disembark and pick up another rail on the other side of town—one station to another. 'On to Camden Station, men,' came the order. So we exited the train and marched through the city in strict military formation. A crowd soon gathered. They followed, getting larger as we went. Then someone threw a stone. We were instructed by our officers not to react—not to hurt anyone if a scuffle broke out. Even as they pelted us with rocks, we were not to fire our guns. The crowd jeered and taunted us. Police tried to control the situation. Things just got out of hand. All we wanted to do was get to Camden Station without incident. Suddenly the crowd turned into a mob. Someone threw a bottle, then a brick. Before we knew it, we were fired upon … *pow, pow*! We stood there helpless. One of my comrades slumped to the ground, then another."

"You mean …"

"Yes, they shot at us. Of course, we closed rank and fired back. We were ordered to fire only on those who fired at us, but we couldn't' make out where the shots were coming from, so we fired directly into the horde. All hell broke loose as we were commanded to continue our march. A good portion of us were left behind both dead and wounded. I was one of them."

"Oh, Samuel! That's horrible. How did you get away?"

"I lay on the ground, watching my company march off. The police finally moved in and held back the crowd. My friend Luther Ladd lay dead at my feet. I was shot through the leg, but in so much pain I was unsure whether I took a bullet anywhere else. I crawled to the side of the road. I thought for certain I was looking at my last day."

"That is a harrowing story, Samuel!"

"Yes, it was terrible!"

"I'm sorry about your friend, Luther."

"He was only seventeen." He wiped a tear from the corner of his eye with the palm of his hand. "War is an abyss, Emily. I'm afraid that this one will have no bottom. After that day, all I felt was vengeance. The beast within me raged. I had been cut down ... infected by war's infirmity, become part of its vile essence. I became confused. My exasperation played on everything I was taught about how people should be treated—the respect we should show others. That manner of thinking has no place in war. After all, I did enlist in military service. In retrospect, I don't know what it was I was expecting. Now, with this injury, I feel betrayed, broken, and useless."

"Oh, Samuel, you are not useless. You are Samuel Cory. Westport gentleman and mariner. And you will always remain so."

"Thanks, Emily. Now that I am back home, I realize that. Life goes on in sleepy Westport as it is softly left in the past ... the wonderful past. Knowing what I do now, somehow, military service holds little meaning to me. It's just not who I am."

"Samuel! You're thinking too hard about things. All you need is a little time with family and friends. They will help you heal both body and mind." I clutched his hand. "You will see. Everything will work out for the good."

He stared out into the distance. I was uncertain whether he even heard what I had said. He continued with his dreadful tale.

"Not everyone in Baltimore was hostile. Some good people helped us, bandaged us. Luther's body was prepared and sent home to Lowell. I stayed in Baltimore for six more weeks, until I could walk again. The army placed me on sick leave. That was quickly followed by rumor of a discharge."

"You are not certain whether you will be discharged though?"

"Nothing official. For all intents and purposes, I consider myself retired from the military."

Brimming with outrage, he struck the ship's railing with his fist.

Still, I felt strongly that the more he talked about things, the more his discontent was allowed to bleed, the more rapidly healing could begin.

"What happened after the conflict in Baltimore?"

"When I could walk, I strolled the docks and became acquainted with the *Sphinx*. I would walk the waterfront and admire her lines, the sheer of her hull, the graceful sweep of her bow. In time, I discovered she would go up for auction. Rumor had it that a fellow named James Dunwoody Bulloch was interested in purchasing her."

"James Dunwoody Bulloch? His name sounds important."

"A Confederate patriot dedicated to what they called 'the cause'—to relinquish the Union. He owned a plantation, along with sixty-two slaves. When I heard he was interested in the *Sphinx*, I quickly wired home and asked Father to send me every penny I had in the bank and then some. The day the schooner went up for auction I made acquiring it my own private little war. I had heard gossip in Baltimore's taverns that it would ultimately end up in the Confederate States of America and sent directly to Charleston to be outfitted for military service. I was going to make certain that that would not happen—that the Confederation or James Dunwoody Bulloch could not procure her."

"Who was this fellow Bulloch? Was he part of the mob in Baltimore?"

"I have no way of knowing whether he was or not. But his heart was there. Everything I heard about him gives me cause to consider him just as guilty as those who fired on us. He made his doctrine and sentiments plain. He was with the Southern cause, and rumor had it that he would purchase the *Sphinx*, modify her, and press her into Confederate naval service."

"Tell me. What happened?"

"On the day of the auction, Bulloch thought he had the schooner in his pocket. It was understood that no one was to bid for it and that he should have her. When the auction started no one expected that I, a stranger, would bid against him. Every eye on the waterfront was upon me. Time and time again Bulloch would trump my bid. I would up the stakes. The more he bid, the more I was worried that my money would run out. Then it happened."

A smug countenance widened on Samuel's face as he sprouted an air of satisfaction. He turned and leaned against the ship's railing. Looking up into the rigging of the *Sphinx*, he smiled and shook his head.

I was excited to hear what happened next. "What! Tell me!"

"You see, I had a little angel by my side that day. The auctioneer was a local tavern owner and brother to the mayor. I had talked to him at length about the trouble between the North and South at his drinking establishment. It was my belief that the man was a covert abolitionist. In the end, I could very well have been right. As the bidding commenced and it was his turn to bid, Bulloch hesitated for a second or two. It was just enough of a pause. In that moment, and with little warning, the auctioneer struck the hammer. The sale was over. James Dunwoody Bulloch was stunned. The *Sphinx* was mine."

"How exciting, Samuel. I'm happy for you. You see! Not everyone in this world is cruel."

"This fellow Bulloch verified my suspicion later when I discovered that he had commissioned a Confederate war ship to be built in an English port—a steam driven war sloop. Speculation has it that it will be one of the fastest most advanced hunters ever built."

"Hunters?"

"Yes. Meant to prey on Union commerce and whalers like the ones you see here in this harbor."

"That's terrible!"

"I'm going to tell you something. You must never repeat it."

"Oh, I won't."

"Last I heard the Union has sent out spy ships to intercept the Confederate war ship once she is commissioned and tries to leave the British shipyard. It has orders to take command of it or sink it."

"For all you have done, it's a tremendous loss to the Union if they release you from military duty."

"I must confess. While I was convalescing, the Union used me as an intelligencer. My mission was to keep my ear to the Southern cause and see what I could uncover. Due to my obvious accent and my presence at the riot, I became well known in Baltimore and not to be trusted. I practiced all sorts of disguises. But everyone knew me. I could silence a boisterous tavern by simply walking in. I had failed! I unearthed nothing. So you see, it was vital for me to make certain that the schooner *Sphinx* came home with me and to never be used in the Southern cause."

"I cannot think of a more patriotic accomplishment. It was brilliant. Think of the lives you may have saved."

He lowered his head and nodded. "It was not easy getting her out of Baltimore. A strategy by the locals was put in place to confiscate her. They knew I needed a crew, and the local population in Baltimore was unwilling to help me. Even those who sympathized with the Union were afraid to sign on."

He took hold of a loose halyard, pulled out some slack, and tied it off tightly to a belaying pin along the rail. Looking up, he examined his work. Once satisfied it was secured firmly, he took a bite of the licorice stick and munched.

"How did you get the schooner out of Baltimore, Samuel?"

"They were planning on purloining her. They were never going to allow me to take her out of Baltimore. There was no one I could trust. With all the talk along the docks, their plan to usurp her was obvious."

"So, how did you escape?"

"It wasn't easy. They had placed a rotting whaling tub in front of the *Sphinx* and hemmed her in, blocking any egress." He uttered a detested chuckle and took another bite of candy. "The *Curse* was its name—a hunk of a rundown whaler whose better days were well behind her. With some luck and obscure ambiguity, I found a willing crew. I prayed none of them would betray me. We waited for the right night, with the breeze blowing across the harbor. Clandestinely, we boarded the *Jonah Curse* around one in the morning. We ran up a couple of her tattered sails and unfurled her battered mainsail. There was plenty of breeze and it was in our favor. It strongly tugged on her as we made her sheets fast to their cleats. The old girl tugged and leaned as the wind pushed and pulled. Her dock lines were tight as piano strings by the time we cut her free from the sea wall. Quickly, she drifted into harbor and instantly began colliding with other moored vessels."

"Oh, my!"

Samuel smiled and shook his head. "It was pandemonium ... someone yelled and crew sleeping on other ships scurried up on deck. They lowered dories and rowed like the devil to catch the careening *Curse*. They needed to get some men aboard her before she could cause serious damage to other ships in the harbor. This was our plan for escape. Everyone was too occupied to lend any mind to us. Meanwhile, the men and I made the *Sphinx* ready to sail. One by one we hoisted sail. There was a full moon. The brilliant white canvas on the *Sphinx* reflected the moon's light lighting up the docks. I was certain we would be discovered and stopped. But everyone was too busy with the wandering whaler."

"Where did you find the men to help you?"

"My unskilled crew was made up of four African free slaves—men who could not find suitable work. In essence, they were starving, forced to work on plantations, picking cotton, cultivating tobacco. Though they were free black men, they were treated as slaves, nonetheless. I promised them each a year's salary for a week's work to get the ship to New England. Once here, I pledged to supply them with passage anywhere they wanted to go, and help them find employment in the North."

"Fall River is growing," I pointed out. "I'm certain they would find employment there."

"You know Paul Cuffe, don't you?"

"Who doesn't? Grandmamma and Mr. Cuffe both have African and Indian heritage in their blood. They're good friends. The Cuffes own the farm across from Louisa."

"Then you must know that Cuffe is a well-known abolitionist. I saw him this morning and he agreed to help find the crew homes and jobs. My coxswain, a keen, African-Bermudian, will remain caretaker of the *Sphinx* when she's here in harbor and as first mate when I take her out."

"Tell me more about the escape, Samuel. It sounded so dangerous."

"I suppose it was." He stared down at his feet then out at the fishing smack sailing by. The smack rang its bell as it sailed out of the foggy mist and between two other small boats. "Navigating out of Baltimore was the high point of my short military career. Playing captain, watching four greenhorns as they scampered to tug lines and raise canvas … adhere to my bewildering commands. I had rehearsed the escape with them over and over, still, they were very uneasy about what to expect. I can't blame them, I suppose. If captured, they could be put to death. Both their courage and adeptness shone when the time came. Our hasty departure was an ill executed and orchestrated production, fraught with praiseworthy chaos, where everything that was meant to go wrong did not, and those that did, in our favor. It was coordinated disorder, lacking luster or refinement. But oh, what a glorious flight!"

"Oh, Samuel, you make it sound so stirring."

His eyes brightened and his smile became more joyful. He was thrilled with the schooner and spoke of it as a proud father would his child.

"You should have been there, Emily! We waited for the right night— one where the wind was blowing out of the harbor and a full moon lit our way. We didn't have to wait long. While the *Curse* careened through the harbor ramming one ship after another, we made our escape. We raised canvas and a gust snatched the large aft main. The crew quickly raised the fore-jib, then the working jib. I had no idea how the vessel would behave. A couple of bystanders stood on the docks and watched us. I worried about their intentions. But all they did was watch. Once we released the dock lines no one could stop us. The majestic *Sphinx* lifted off the water like a mystical bird. In no time, she was riding her bow wave at cautionary speed. The night wind vibrated through her untuned rigging with whistling acclamation, and her bow sang a bubbly tune as the hull silently glided through the watery chop and out toward open water. We still needed to get past the meandering *Jonah Curse,* which partially blocked our way. Suddenly, it was a contest between the drifting ghost whaler and the well-canvassed, winged *Sphinx.*"

"*Jonah Curse*, what an awful name for a ship," I declared.

"Actually, it was named after the owner's infant son."

"Poor child, with a name like that. What happened next? Please continue!"

"In any event, a couple of the town's men had already boarded the old whaler and were trying to steer her toward us, in an attempt to ram or block our egress. However, the *Sphinx* was accelerating. I had to keep her on course to pick up as much speed as she could muster. We came closer and closer to the ever-evocative *Curse.* When they realized I was not about to veer or drop sail, the small crew on the whaler scurried along its decks to get out of our way. The *Sphinx* bore down on her with remarkable speed. Just as it appeared our bowsprit would spear her broadside, I spun the wheel fast to port and she turned gracefully without a sliver of complaint.

"As she passed through the eye of the wind the sails flapped for a few seconds and the crew hurried to rearrange the sheets. They raised the large fore-main. It was an awful sloppy trim. They only got it half way up the stick before it jammed. The ship caught the wind once again and the vessel ever so slowly fell onto an apposing tack. The canvas stiffened and quickly she picked up speed once again. It was just enough. We passed inches from our adversary's stern, and with a clear view of a brave new sea, watched victoriously as she rushed by us. One brave fellow jumped and boarded us. He brandished his pistol but the men made quick work of him, and over the side he went. The lumbering *Curse* had little maneuverability as her crew rushed to prevent the old girl from hitting other ships. We, on the other hand, continued our trek as the men raised more sail—not very successfully I may add. But, we had enough cloth flying above and were well on our way. They would never catch us.

"I surrendered the helm to my new wheelman, took the stars and stripes from my pocket, and hoisted it on the aft port stay. Up it went in full stately flutter. Everyone aboard cheered and danced. In my enthusiasm, I ran to the front of the ship, limped out onto the bowsprit, almost twenty feet to its tip, and hung on. Caution was thrown to the wind in a defiant feat of victory. This was my little private fray and I had won. As the *Jonah Curse* rounded up, I looked back and gave her a haughty Union salute. Strangely enough the fellow at her helm saluted, giving us the due respect we deserved. We sailed out of Baltimore to a glimmering moonlit night, free men, both black and white."

"What a heroic account, Samuel. I can picture it, and you … out on the bowsprit hanging on triumphantly. A fine figurehead of freedom, I may add."

"In hindsight it was quite a foolish move. Like a cat that has no trouble going up a tree but not down, I began to worry how I would get back on deck. I remember my leg was hurting something terrible, but my heart was singing. With a little effort, I did get down. I would have done it over if given the chance."

"What an amazing tale—the sort of danger and peril you only read in books."

"Come Emily, I will show you the foredeck!" He mumbled as he spoke, the licorice stick hanging from his lip like a droopy cigar.

In the excitement of the moment he rushed forward in a limping stride, tripped and collapsed to the deck. Clutching the capstan's bar, he lifted himself to a seated position. Rushing over, I flung myself by his side.

"Oh Samuel—your leg?" I cried, as he clutched his knee.

A frown crumpled his brow as he massaged the injured limb. "I'm all right," he groaned.

I cradled his face in my hands. "Are you sure?" I asked stupidly. It was obvious he was hurting.

He gave me an implausible, stinging grin while he sat holding his leg. I tried to help by gently rubbing the injured knee.

Doting, he took hold of my hand, brought it up to his face, and lightly caressed it along his warm cheek. The frown he wore faded and a serene smile emerged. His supple lips trembled and his eyes were partially closed as he held firmly onto my fingers. I could tell he was waiting for the pain to pass. His taut angular chin went slack as he opened his mouth to breath, exposing the tips of glimmering white teeth. His slender graceful nose, smooth and level, rested upon a neatly trimmed mustache. He looked over at me with hazel eyes that reflected blue at times, and were now indigo as a tropical sea.

I tried to speak but words failed. Lips begging to be kissed confronted me. Our faces became closer. I rested my nose upon his cheek.

"You smell delightful," he said.

"You dropped your licorice stick," I told him.

"You do, you know."

I picked up the mushy-tipped sugar treat. "Here it is," I murmured.

"Delightful as a posy of freshly-picked flowers."

"What, the licorice?"

"You, Emily, you. You smell heavenly."

"I don't wear any scent."

"I mean your scent, the fragrance of your hair, the smell of your lips, your satiny, soft skin. You are a symphonic bouquet. Only you could smell sweeter than any perfume in a bottle."

"Oh, Samuel, stop it. You're talking silly, now."

He did and I loved it. His whispered voice was arousing. I became intoxicated by his fulsome accolades. Every muscle in my body languished in numbness as I tumbled into an inflamed utopian slumber. Every atom of my being sizzled and a fiery passion smoldered in my tummy—quivering down my legs. The licorice stick in my hand became hot. Gripping it loosely, it slipped through my fingers. The candy treat came to rest in his lap. No one had ever spoken to me in such a manner. I reached down for the licorice. His breath singed my desires while our lips nuzzled—lightly grazing. My heart trembled. A spark of glee gushed down my spine. My hand wandered up and down his leg as I searched for the elusive candy treat. I pulled my hand away. I didn't want to move, I couldn't move—afraid I would betray all respectable and suitable behavior. After all, I was a good girl.

Threading his fingers behind my ears and up into my hair, he amorously caressed the back of my neck. I closed my eyes, threw back my head, and let it wallow in his strong adoring hands. I had one foot in heaven and the other in a hellish, prurient yearning. I felt compelled to snip the moment. I decided to focus on his injured leg.

"Are you still in pain?" I whispered.

He gave no reply. Instead he offered me a tranquil and placid mien. Our faces wrestled. I felt his warm sugary lips sweep across mine. He clenched his eyes tightly, as if in pain, and ever so slowly shook his head.

"I've been so lonely," he sighed.

"What?" I said.

"I want you, Emily," he murmured.

What was he asking me? The words sounded so imaginary—like a wishful yearning hovering in morning slumber. Was it idle desire speaking to me from inside my own wishful brain? Or was he parroting my inner voice—musings of deep-seated impulses that have been sprouting in my heart for long lonesome years.

Before I had the chance to fully interpret his engaging and forbidden request, his lips fell tenderly upon mine. My canvas unfurled, my ship rose above the water, and my heart set sail into ravishing bliss. Who could imagine that two simple wet cushiony lips could inflict such euphoric rapture? A fuzzy warmth pulsated inside me, igniting a tingling thirst from the inner corners of my private cravings. One could never tell that this was the first time our lips ever intimately embraced. I know what you are thinking. I can be so juvenile at times. If so, then call me child. Sure, in the past there was the idle peck on the cheek or the casual affectionate greeting, but I can assure you, this felt altogether different. I did not want the breathtaking moment to end. Suddenly, I understood what Samuel meant when he said he was lonely. I too hungered for the little girl inside me to be set free and the wanton woman longing to be wicked, to breathe. At that very moment chastity and innocence were evaporating. I looked down and reached for the licorice stick that had fallen in his lap.

Before that could happen, a roar of cheers and whistling reverberated from around me. Passion had an audience. Of that you can be sure. I pulled away from Samuel and quickly looked around. It appeared that the crew of the whaler *Janet* had been spying on us. They dangled from rigging and deckhouse as they broke into revelry. Feeling somewhat flustered and naked, I quickly leaped to my feet and pretended like nothing had happened. The embarrassment was unavoidable, as laughter and frolicsome mockery echoed across a muted harbor.

"That's quite the welcome home, Sammy boy," someone yelled.

"Give her another," a gruff voice hooted.

"I'm next, I'm next," a sailor cried out.

"Oh, get back to work," shouted Samuel. He couldn't help himself. A triumphed smile blistered on his face all the same.

Looking back at the whalemen and feeling somewhat humiliated, I helped Samuel struggle to his feet.

Jovial applause broke out from the *Janet*. They could not help themselves, and I was left with little defense or reason to blame them.

We walked down the plank and onto the wharf.

I held out my hand to help him but he waved it away. "Are you sure you're alright?"

"Fine. I'm afraid that at times when the pain shoots up to my knee the muscles yield without warning. My fault for not using the damn cane. I feel so useless with it or without it. There's just no winning."

His frustration was obvious. I rarely ever heard Samuel curse the way he did.

"It's nothing to be ashamed of. I'm certain your leg will heal like new in time. Before you know it, you will not need a cane at all."

"Thanks for saying so. I'm afraid that may be wishful thinking."

"Of course it's not … you'll see."

"Can we talk about something else, please?" he barked, limping off the platform, a stiff arm resting on the walking stick. He quickly moved up the wharf.

"Samuel, wait!" I hastened to keep up.

He stopped and turned. "I'm sorry. I was rude," he confessed. He offered me a kiss on the side of the face.

Shutting my eyes, I instantly drifted away.

"So where to next?" he asked, as I stood immobilized, waiting for another. He continued walking.

"I was on my way to the city, remember?" I replied, climbing down from my stupor. I rushed to keep up. Even with his bad leg, I had to trot to sustain his pace.

"That's right. You had mentioned it." He offered me his arm. "Would you like company, Miss White?"

"I would love company, Mr. Cory." I retorted, gladly cuddling his arm.

We walked up Point Road to his house where he dropped off his belongings. We decided on taking his father's buggy instead of

Grandmamma's old lumpy wagon and aging horse. The sleek three-seat carriage gave a much more satisfying ride.

"It's amazing how much faster and quiet this buggy is from what I'm used to."

"Speed is the key to life these days," he said, as we quickly accelerated. "The faster you get where you're going, the more time you have to experience what's there."

"Grandmamma says that fast people have a wish to reach the end of life and an early grave."

"Charlotte lived in different times. Today speed is money. The faster you work the more of it you can make."

"And owning a fast schooner?"

"Especially on the water. Getting goods to market before they spoil. Swiftness can also be a thing of beauty … meant to be relished along with the sensation and excitement it has to offer. And if your desire is to experience life to its fullest what better place then on a fast sailing vessel. Enough about the ship. Let's talk about you. How has life been for you in the time I've been away?"

"Oh, just fine. Nothing changes around here, and I hold very little complaints. Doesn't take much to keep a girl like me happy—a good book, a cup of tea, an oatmeal cookie, and life is lovely."

"My kind of gal." He chuckled. "Tell me more about what you've been up to."

"Let's see … well, the girls and I have started a book club."

"Book club?"

"Yes. The Drift River Readers Book Club, we call it. We meet once a month to discuss fiction and poetry. We read an assortment of titles then have a discussion about their merits."

"Interesting. What have you read thus far?"

"Oh, some Dickens, Thackeray … William Shakespeare, of course."

"How can one avoid Shakespeare?"

"We just started a new title this week."

"Oh?"

"Are you really interested or just making conversation?"

"Why of course I'm interested. I love reading. You know that. How many times have I accompanied you to the Athenaeum in Fall River?"

"Quite a few. But you usually wait outside or leave on an errand while I go inside."

"You have me there. Well, this time we shall both go in."

"You sure?"

"Miss White, why do you doubt me? Today is about you and spending time together—doing what you enjoy."

I smiled. "Yes, it is," I said, joyfully. "Did you know that the Athenaeum is now called a library? They stock all sorts of titles they never had, including fiction and poetry."

"You don't say!"

"Yes! And you can actually borrow books and take them home."

"It's a changing world. So, what sort of titles has the club reviewed?"

"Well, we have a general rule. Only fiction and poetry. This month we decided to break that rule."

"Oh ... in what way?"

"We have taken up a narrative about the life of a mill girl. A true account."

"Ah, a biographical study!"

"Well, not really. It's a mystery about a murder."

"Murder!"

"Yes. About a girl that was found hanged by a hay stack-pole in 1832 at a place called the Durfee farm in Fall River."

"You mean ... ah, the Cornell girl. Is that right?"

"You have heard of her!" I cried. I turned in my seat in astonishment. "When, how?"

"Like I said. I like to read also."

"You have read the narrative about the case then?"

"Not exactly," he said, his words drooping off his lip. "Father spoke of it."

"My Lord, when?"

"Well, you know how Father mistrusts the clergy."

"I know he no longer attends service, aside from that, your father is one of the most pious men I know."

"Father is a good religious man. One day he was ranting on about how the Reverend Avery had killed the mill girl, and how he remembers when it all happened. He stopped attending church shortly after. The death of the mill girl was all the talk in Fall River when Father was a young seafarer. Since then he just doesn't trust the clergy."

"That was a long time ago. Why would he still feel that way today?"

"Let us just say it's a complicated matter ... at least in his mind. As he often said to me—'Son, I choose to slight ecclesiastic gatherings and expose my soul to the Lord, one on one, and on his own consecrated ground ... at the top of a fifty-foot wave.'"

"Between Seabury Cory and Charlotte White they could easily rival Confucius with their views and precepts," I declared, laughing.

"We probably come to live by those precepts and don't even realize it."

I laughed some more. "What did your father tell you about the mill girl, Sarah Cornell?"

"What do you want to know?"

"Everything!" I said. "I was thinking perhaps I could do some investigating myself ... try and solve the crime."

"Solve what crime?"

"Uncover who really killed Sarah Cornell."

"How are you going to do that?"

"Make my proposal to Amy and Louisa about conducting a formal probe, inquire the facts, interview people. Between the three of us ..."

"Oh, Emily, do you think that is realistic? Besides, Sarah Cornell hanged herself. She had gotten herself with child. She was distressed and desperate. There was no crime."

"That was the conclusion of the court. Like your father, I believe she was murdered. I cannot bring myself to believe it was done by the Reverend, though. There must be more ... something the authorities missed ... someone else."

"It was a long time ago, Emily. People have forgotten. Most witnesses have died. What possible evidence could you uncover? You are just a small-town girl."

"Mr. Cory, that does not mean I am completely without wit." I barked, crossing my arms. "I will read the book and let you know."

"Sure, I know you will, but ..."

"Will you not tell me more?"

"All right. Let's see ... back in the early thirties, Father was assigned to the cargo vessel *Harbinger*. He would sail from Fall River with a load of coal or lumber and deliver it to ports south, such as Bristol, Warren, and Newport. At the time, he frequented the pubs and tavern houses in those towns and Sarah Cornell and the Reverend Avery is all anyone talked about. Father was very sympathetic toward the mill girl. Whether the Reverend Avery was found guilty or innocent of hanging her, the station of clergymen took a battering in Father's eyes."

"It is sad that he should miss fellowship with friends and parishioners because of something that happened so long ago. Everyone at church respects your father."

"Everyone," he affirmed. "I'm afraid that Father's deep-seated convictions exceed the passing of time."

The ride up Point Road, chauffeured by spirited conversation, went quickly. Before I knew it we were on the main byway and entering the city limits of Fall River. As we traveled, most of the talk centered on the mill girl and her demise.

"So, what else do you want to know?" he asked.

"Everything."

"I'll ask Father about it. When is your next book club meeting?"

"This Tuesday. We usually hold them at Louisa's."

"Do you think that I can attend one of your gatherings some time?"

"Seriously!" I said, in disbelief.

"The more activity the better. Help me forget the war—ease me back into the community."

"By all means. Though I'll need to warn the girls."

"Oh, what about?"

"I venture to say, about how handsome you have become."

He smiled, and shook his head. His cheeks reddened while mine went rosy and warm. I can be quite intrepid with my tongue at times, delivering compliments at will. When it came to Samuel, giving adulation and respect was effortless. After all, it was an intrinsic component to who he was. I was just expressing what was already there.

I placed my hand over his clutched fists as he held on tightly to the reins and guided the horse. "I hope I didn't embarrass you. I was just joshing. Though I do think you are very handsome."

"No, no, you have no defense," he quipped. "You said it and you cannot take it back. I'll be man enough to accept the truth."

I laughed, lovingly slapping him on the arm. It was the truth. Looking over at him I could not help admire his ample, rippling hair and the long tapered sideburns, which extended well below his ear lobes. The mid-day sun reflected off noble cheeks and the green of the summer trees played with the brightening, emerald tint in his eyes. His once delicate chin had broadened and was now sculptured and strong, giving him a more chiseled and determined appearance. There's no doubt about it. He had a striking profile. Yet, when one added up all the manly features his face had to offer, it came down to the dimples in his dignified cheeks that revealed the kind and unselfish person he really was.

"All right … you win," I confirmed.

"I was thinking. We can hold the next reader's club meeting on the ship, if you like."

"Why, that's an idea!"

"We can sail out to Cuttyhunk Island, drop anchor, have your meeting, and enjoy a picnic to boot."

"Oh Samuel, that sounds wonderful. Wait until the girls hear about this."

The horse gracefully piloted the buggy through Flint Village, the east district of the city, and down the lumpy, stone-paved byway, which led to Main Street. Everywhere one looked there were lots of people. No one appeared to be strolling or enjoying their walk, instead they scrambled along like their clothing was ablaze. Many were mill hands, foreigners from Europe and Asia—a new breed of proud American. *City folk are like ants running to nowhere,* Grandmamma would say, *until the foot of life drops down upon them and stomps them cold, they don't even know their alive.* I'm not sure I agree with her, for the city appears to be teaming with life.

We approached the busy textile district along the Quequechan River, where heaps of musty cotton are unloaded into bleak granite buildings by unkempt, weary laborers, and where duteous children delivered dinner pails to their hungry parents in the mills. As we neared the center of town, Samuel swerved to avoid a group of running boys, playing sport with a tin can, and kicking the clanging receptacle along the tamped dusty street.

Just as we arrived at Main Street, a somber funeral march of dark coaches crossed our path. The buggy stopped and we sat in silence, providing homage to a grim pendant of endless black carriages. A canter of countless hooves plopped and echoed off tall buildings as it went by, while the grating, steel-rimmed wagon wheels clattered and rattled, grinding over the hard city road, and chaffering forlornness and tears. The coffin car passed carrying a casket covered with Old Glory. Samuel stood up and saluted. Unsure of what to do, I also rose to my feet. I clasped onto his arm to keep my balance as the spirited horse shifted the buggy back-and-forth. We sat back down and watched stone-faced men in stovepipe hats, wearing bewitching expressions, go by. Beside them, veil-shrouded women sat transfixed and wretched, as if they themselves were dead.

Death crossed our path. When one is younger we never think of such things. As Grandmamma often said, *As a soul gets older, death becomes a neighbor and we invite him to sup, whether we want him there or not.*

I tried not to think about such dismal matters. Instead I reflected upon the earlier incident on the foredeck of the *Sphinx*—a simple kiss—a delightful pursuit, and one which gave an entirely new meaning to my relationship with Samuel. I looked over at his lips and reflected on the warmth I felt earlier. The tender moment flared and tingled in my bones once again—fluttering deep in my stomach, like a child on Christmas morning.

Until now the depth of our association had its foundation as children. As we became older we strayed, as various interests drew us away from one another, though we always retained that exceptional bond we had as youngsters. Over the years, our relationship had grown to what I would designate as a sibling alliance. Our wanton behavior on the *Sphinx* today was anything but that of brother and sister. Our actions toward one another had taken a new course, set off on an unknown journey, an uncharted route. I can confess that I am certain about where I would like it to go—but what about Samuel? Perhaps our flirtatious conduct was just one of those peculiar affairs, never to be repeated—like it never happened. Even now, this minute, we seem to be back to normal—brother and sister. I may even have the courage to call it love. After all, is that not what a brother and sister feel for one another? Or am I just beguiling things. Was what happened on his boat forbidden or inappropriate? What is it Grandmamma often said? *What the mind cannot reason the heart will decide.* Perchance it was in fact a misdemeanor of the heart—wicked even. And you must forgive me for saying so. For though it may have been wicked—I say it was wicked good.

Death's last carriage passed and we continued toward the library, further up Main Street. I discovered that I could not help but look back at the mournful promenade as it headed north toward the old burial ground. All I could see was the rear of the flower wagon draped in carnations, wreaths, and dripping with roses. The deceased must have been a well-loved and rich individual. Even so, it was probably more flowers than he ever received in an entire lifetime. Odd why we give flowers to those who can no longer enjoy them.

—⦅∞⦆—

Chapter 7:

I wrestled with the sticky barn door. Once inside, I noticed that the eggs in the chicken bins were piling up. After provisioning for the day's take, I placed the surplus aside. Grandmamma's routine was to put them on a stand out front for sale. Lately her barn visits have been curtailed by her recent ill health and eggs have been piling up.

I placed the extra ones into a basket, walked out front, and set them on a stand by the side of the road with a sign—*Fresh Eggs, One Cent Each*. Once I was finished, I went back into the house and prepared breakfast. I was eating my boiled, poached meal when I noticed how late it was. Grandmamma was still asleep. I pushed aside the linen curtain, which led to the tiny room.

"Grandmamma, it's time to get up."

There was no reply. She lay in the darkened room, looking quite rested. Perhaps too rested.

"Grandmamma," I called again.

Not a stir. I watched her closely. I know that some old people sleep so soundly it is difficult to tell if they are breathing. It appeared like she was not. I clutched my chest and gulped some air. I moved closer, my heart thumping against my hand. My knees weakened as I knelt beside her.

"Grandmamma, it's time to get up," I cried. My voice trembled. I jumped to my feet and pulled back the curtain on the window. The small space flooded with light. I placed my hand tenderly on her delicate shoulder, shook it, and called out for her, loudly. Her name reverberated in my head like a cautionary church bell, reminding its flock of the time of day—the time of life.

The early morning daylight illuminated her waxy, crazed complexion. Her bony, elevated cheekbones jutted out, tired but proud—a dignified and noble face, steeped in interminable Wampanoag majesty. Around her sunken eyes, crow's feet spouted, wrapping around the side of her face and vanishing beneath brittle thin hair, like worn crevices leading to all she had ever witnessed in life. And those slender dry lips—lips that kissed away impending bruises and anguish, while reciting wisdom and counsel, were firmly joined like sealed doors to an ancient temple—refusing disclosure to the reflective secrets within. I studied that placid face. I noticed her corn-silk textured hair was as white as ever. My breathing stuttered, and a solitary, fearful tear dropped to my cheek. I shook her some more.

"Grandmamma, Grandmamma, wake up, please, wake up." I reached under the sheet and clutched her hand. It was warm.

Suddenly, and ever so slightly, her fingers closed tightly around mine. Her tranquil eyelids fluttered, her long bumpy nose twitched, and she took a deep breath. Glistening eyes slowly parted revealing the life that had always stirred inside that tender and serene, delicate frame. She turned toward me, smacked her lips and sighed. "What time is it, dear?" she asked, serenely.

"Oh, Grandmamma, the sun's been up nearly an hour now," I said, sniveling. She sensed the fear and apprehension that lingered in my voice. The tear, which had lounged on my cheek, trickled down my nose and into my mouth.

"Why ... you've been crying? What is it dear? What's wrong?"

"Nothing, Grandmamma," I assured her joyously. I wiped my face with my sleeve. "Nothing at all." It was comforting to see that ancient sweet facade speak to me. "I think I am coming down with a cold or the like. My eyes have been watering all morning."

She reached over and placed her hand on my forehead. "You don't feel like you have a temperature. Must be the season, dear. Hay fever."

"I'll be all right, Grandmamma."

"Sure you will, dear, sure you will." She pulled back the sheets and grunted as she struggled to get out of bed.

I placed my arm under hers and helped. "It's always a blessing when the good Lord grants us another sunrise," she croaked, getting to her feet. "There! Now, what do you want for breakfast?" she asked, as she shuffled into the kitchen.

"I have already eaten. I would have called for you earlier. I didn't want to wake you. You need rest."

"My, my, child. Life is short. One must not spend so much of it resting."

"Rest is good for you."

"There's plenty of time for that. There's a little grassy yard across from the church just made for slumber."

"Oh, Grandmamma, don't say such a thing!"

"The Lord favors them who witness to the truth, you know."

"I know He does, Grandmamma."

She sat at the table while I placed the steaming teapot there. As with most mornings, I listened to her ideologies and credos with a pound of interest and an ounce of humor. Every morning she would preach a new one. Though I always delighted her by offering an inquisitive ear, this morning I delighted myself, knowing that indeed she was still able to do so.

"I have poached some eggs. Tea is nice and hot," I said, pouring some into a cup. "Would you like some toast to go with that, Grandmamma?"

"I'll get it, dear," she said, laboring to her feet.

"Please, Grandmamma, I wish you would sit and rest. I can make breakfast."

"You should find a nice young man to do this for. Move to the city— have a happy and active life. Not waste away in this kitchen or tiny village."

"You don't really mean that, Grandmamma. You don't even like the city. Neither do I. Besides, I feel quite fulfilled in this kitchen and living in this village."

"Just thought I would mention it." She took the remnants of a loaf of bread down from a cupboard shelf.

"Oh, Grandmamma, I forgot to bake some. I'm afraid that bread is days old."

"Old bread for an old body," she recited, taking a knife from the table drawer. "One is made for the other. I'll bake some fresh later."

"Why don't you let me do that?" I said, taking the knife from her hand. I straightened out her chair and invited her to sit.

She gave me one of her satisfying grins and patted me on the arm. "You're a good girl."

"Be comfortable. Sit," I begged.

"Comfort pillages the soul, complacency the spirit of the old. We must stir and move or we wither and decay on this vine called life—become fat, wrinkled … and age before our time." She threw her dainty frame into the chair, sat back, and gave out a weary sigh. "Time eats at the fringe of youth, plunders you of those you love, and laughs at us when we complain. You must not let it happen to you, Emily. I must not become a burden to you."

"You're not, ever," I insisted, kissing her. "What would I ever do without you? You took me in as a newborn babe … fed me, gave me a roof over my head … you are the only mother I ever had."

"When I took you in both our lives changed … and for the better. I am your cloak and you have been my button."

I laughed. "Grandmamma, you say some of the wittiest things."

She got up and moved to the kitchen window. Persuading her to sit was easy; keeping her there was another task altogether. I looked over her shoulder toward the grassy field and the river below. Two of Mr. Davis's horses, a paint and a roan, romped along the sandy river shore. Just beyond the Two Sisters, the large willow trees that stood near the water's edge, a small flock of mallards glided and swooped, dropping out of the air, landing on the undisturbed, glassy tributary.

"Fog's low along the water." she declared. "Must be cool outside."

"Stove's still smoldering. I'll get some wood before it goes out."

I walked out the back door and a few paces to the log pile by the side of the barn. While stacking the split timber in my arms, I saw someone scurry around the side of the house. Placing the wood by the back door, I went to investigate. There was no one there. I circled the house and continued my search. Still, I could find no one. Looking up and down Point Road I discovered Old Moses run and duck behind the carpentry shop. It was then that I noticed the egg basket, which sat on the small stand on the front lawn, was empty. I returned to the woodpile and carried a few logs inside.

"Phew! You're right, Grandmamma. It's cool out there," I dropped the firewood by the stove.

"It will warm up before noon."

"I just saw Moses down the road. I think he was out back. I could smell him."

"Smells like a dried-up fish, does he? He sleeps behind the barn."

"With the chickens? He must be the one who stole the eggs."

"Took some eggs, has he?"

"I had piled a basket full by the side of the road. Now they're all gone. And not a penny in the dish."

"Can't refuse food to the hungry when we have enough, dear."

"I placed almost two dozen eggs out there," I said, stacking some small logs inside the stove. I jabbed the timbers with the steel poker. The fire flared and sputtered. I slammed the hatch to the stove. "He had no right taking all of them."

"In all likelihood, Moses was the culprit."

"What's he going to do with two dozen eggs?"

"Sell 'em'."

"Not sure I am happy knowing that, or having him sleep behind our barn."

"Think of the poor chickens!"

"Ugh! Sends a shiver up my spine!"

"Have you finished your sewing, dear?" she asked, changing topic. Talking about Moses and his boring exploits was always old news for Grandmamma.

"Finished yesterday. I need to deliver it to Mrs. Chase before the weekend and that old wagon is creaking itself apart. I think it has a loose wheel."

"Well, dear, the wagon is aging like you and I. I'll have Old Moses look it over."

"No! I'll have Timothy at the carpentry shop do it. Moses takes privileges—thinks we owe him something, even if he's been paid twice over for it."

"Do what you like, dear. Are you off anywhere special today?"

"Yes, Louisa's."

"Well, you be careful with that wagon."

"I think I'll just walk."

"Why don't you go down into the field and take one of Perry Davis's ponies? I'm sure he'd saddle one for you."

"I suppose I could."

I was not happy with the prospect of depending on Mr. Davis. All he ever does is complain about today's youth and how irresponsible we all are. Of course, he is nice enough, explaining how I was different … but all the same … I best use my own legs to get to where I'm going.

Grandmamma pulled open the lid on the flour bin and sprinkled some flour on a cutting board. I smeared some lard onto a bread tin.

"Let me do it," I said, scooping some flour into a bowl. "Toast is ready. You should have your breakfast." I poured a touch of molasses into the bowl while she measured out the yeast.

"I'll eat later," she insisted. "Leave things, dear. If you do it all, what am I to do with myself today?"

"Oh, there is plenty to do around here, Grandmamma."

I backed away lovingly, watching as she hobbled, carrying that petite frame between the kitchen table and hunky cook stove. To relieve an old person from a daily chore can be just as severe as committing them to it. These were simple labors. It sustained her interest—kept her looking forward to another sunrise—solicitous drudgeries that in many respects propped up tolerance and perseverance. For as long as we walk this wonderful green and blue sphere of ours, when we get old, perseverance is all we are truly left with. I left her to her baking duties and prepared for my walk to Louisa's.

Grandmamma was right. Noon had yet to arrive and already it was warm. I stopped by Cory's store and purchased some embroidery thread and needles for Louisa. On my way back up Point Road I passed the carpentry shop. I peered inside. Young Tim Cadman stood by a table with a wooden mallet, pounding a panel door together.

"Good morning, Timothy!"

He placed the wooden mallet under his arm and immediately came over. "Morn'n Emmie."

"You would look disrobed without a hammer in your hand," I said.

He blushed. Taking a dusty cloth, which hung from his trouser pocket, he wiped the back of his neck. "Sure getting hot today," he declared. "Where you off to this gorgeous morning?"

"To Louisa's."

"Chatty Lulu, huh?"

"Oh, she's not that bad. You're right. She does love to talk." I stood on my toes and looked over his shoulder and into the dimly lit workshop. "What are you building?"

"Oh, a door for the master's quarters on the new whaler *Nimrod*."

"The Sanford ship?"

"Yes, I need to get it installed today. They're going to take her out on sea trials tomorrow."

"Oh, I see."

Tim was not much for small talk. He was gracious enough and would answer any questions you may have, but very inhibited. I stood there waiting for him to extend the conversation, perhaps inform me a little more about the work he was doing. He never did. Uncertain about what to say next, he took to inspecting the hinges on the carpentry barn door and struck them with his mallet. A shy nature was part of the charm exuded by young Tim Cadman. Barely twenty years of age, but looking more like twenty-five, he had the muscle and brawn usually reserved for a blacksmith. Always clean-shaven, what little stubble he had on his chin was trumped by a thick, yellow mane, which always slid down off his head and into his eyes. Tim's family owned a dairy farm on Pine Hill. The Cadmans were one of the first settlers in Westport. His father had wanted him to work the land, as did all previous Cadmans. Tim preferred working with wood instead of soil, much to his father's dismay.

"I was wondering whether you could look at Grandmamma's wagon. I'm afraid that one of the wheels may fly off."

"The fastener at the hub flange must be loose. It's one of the first things to go." He swept his feathery hair away from his eyes back up onto his head. "Where is it? I'll take a look."

"Oh, you don't have to look at it right away ... any time would be fine."

"Later today, then." His wispy hair fell back across his eyes. He jerked his head. The silky bangs flung aside.

"How is the new job going?" I inquired.

"Fine."

"Has your father accepted your new vocation?"

"Not really. In fact, I don't live at home any longer. I live here now, at the shop. I have a small room out back."

"I didn't know that."

"I've only been here for a week. The good thing is that I'm never late for work," he grinned. His amiable smile curled at the corner of his mouth, lifting his cheek and squinting one eye. Few could exhibit such an attractive and genial simper—more of a charming smirk than a smile.

"Have you been down to the Pine Hill farm at all?" I asked.

"To see Mother." The smile faded. "I have made it clear to her that I want nothing to do with working the farm. Father insists that if I don't work there, I don't live there. So, here I am."

"That's so sad, Timothy."

"Just the way it is. Not much I can do about it."

"I thought you were working on the steamer *Enterprise* … going to become a sailor—see the world and all that," I quipped.

He just stood there looking glum. He gnawed at his fingernails and walked away. My question had disturbed him. Tim was an easygoing fellow—modest and demure, and always friendly. Everyone liked him. His reserved nature was more evident around men than women, and around me, not apparent at all. He was often the subject of practical jokes by unmerciful whalers—gruff men looking for an unimpeachable target to harpoon. Though most of the time the joke was on them, since I am certain that Tim knew the resolution to their gags and pranks well before they were delivered. He didn't mind being at the tail end of someone's levity if it made him a new friend.

"I'm sorry, Timothy. Did I say something wrong?"

"Sailor!" He scoffed. "What sort of sailor pilots a broken-down barge up and down a small lake delivering timber all day?"

"A very capable one, I would think."

"Well, I didn't think so. One day, I showed up for work and the captain told me I wasn't needed any longer."

"Oh, I didn't know. I'm sorry!"

"You don't have to apologize, Emmie. It was for the best."

"You think?"

"Yeah, they were afraid that I would talk about what I …" He went silent.

"Talk? Talk about what?"

He scrutinized the mallet in his hand, running his fingers along the blunt mushroomed edge.

"A penny for your thoughts," I said.

He ignored me. Pretending to inspect the screws on the barn door hinge, he whacked them with his mallet once again.

My curiosity had piqued and inquisitiveness began to get the best of me. "You never finished, Timothy ... afraid you would talk about what?" The notion that young gentleman Tim could incite fear or deliver gossip was just not plausible to me.

"You must not repeat this to anyone," he whispered, looking over his shoulder.

"Oh, I won't! Go on."

He paced the stoop of the carpentry shop, while caressing the well-used mallet in his hand. A tepid breeze blew up the road from the harbor and tousled his hair. An early-day sparkling sun broke over the Cory store and reflected off his doughy-white complexion. He looked up at the sky as thoughts raced through his head. He removed the cloth, which hung by his hip, and wiped the perspiration from his brow.

"You can count on me, Timothy. My lips are sealed," I said, running a clutched finger and thumb across my mouth.

"Ah ... I'll tell you some other time. I got to go back to work." He turned and walked back into the carpentry shop.

"You will look at the wagon, won't you?" I hollered.

"Anything for you, Emmie," echoed the reply, as he continued walking.

Something was upsetting him. Though it was apparent that he wanted to share, today was not the day. Or, perhaps, I was not the person to share it with. That was fine with me. We all have a bag of bones that we keep under our bed. I've been known to conceal a rib or two myself. Depraved secrets burn holes in our hearts, like a glowing rivet through a blacksmith's apron. Something was simmering inside Tim. Some secrets are just too hot to contain. We must temper their flare, anneal their heat, and beg others to help put out the fire by simply allowing us to share, lest we go mad. After all, is that not what friends are for? Whatever it was that young Tim suppressed was his business. I fully respected that. If need be, I was prepared to never bring it up again. More importantly, I was predisposed to help him any way I could—when he was ready, of course. Until then, I continued up Point Road on my way to Louisa's.

I approached the church at the bend in the road. It sat amongst a cluster of tidy cottages laced in white picket fences. One was a Gothic looking structure, slate in color, and much larger than its neighbors. It had long, emerald green shuttered windows and dripped in all sorts of artfully-carved wood adornments. The house strategically overlooked the church cemetery across the road. It was once the abode of Captain Seth

Boomer, a prominent, but all-but-forgotten, Westport whaler. Captain Boomer was described as having a leg made from the rib of a whale, which he had crafted, after losing his God-given limb out at sea. Legend has it that during a whale hunt the whaleboat he was piloting was toppled by an angry whale, and once in the water the angry mammal bit off poor Captain Boomer's leg just above the knee. Eventually, his crew hunted and harvested the animal from which Captain Boomer took a rib and fabricated his infirmity. It was rumored that so thankful was the captain that his life was spared that he donated the money and land needed to build the church. That was many years ago, and Captain Seth Boomer has long since died.

Over the front door of his neatly painted Gothic home hovers a solitary window. There the reclusive Mrs. Boomer often sits, knitting. The dormered sanctum is a visage to the small cemetery that stands by the church, and where the bereaved widow spends most of her day keeping a loving eye over the silent grave of her long deceased husband.

Poor Mrs. Boomer. I often contemplate such complexities as death, suffering, and those left behind. Now, I'm not a morbid individual, nor do I dwell on such dark ponderings all the time, but some introspection does emerge sometimes. When it does it always leaves me with more questions than answers.

Case in point … take the universe—now, there's an enigma. In many respects, it displaces notions about life and death with its own conundrum. Thinking of such intricacies gives me a headache. Grandmamma insists that I should just accept things as they are. *Sufferance keeps our feet grounded on content soil,* she would counsel, *for those times when we think we have the right to know. Don't question. Humble yourself and accept what you don't understand. That is what faith is for.*

Walking through life with blinders does not suit me. If I see and cannot explain, I need to ask and investigate. For me, the most important word in the English language is the word "why"—closely followed by where, how, and when.

Today I choose to heed Grandmamma's advice and not be so analytical or allow my innermost misgivings to kidnap this beautiful day, or overshadow this delightful walk. For a walk through the Westport countryside is as pleasant as any that one could experience in all of New England.

Now, do you see what I see? Over a sodded field to my left is a striking, open sky. It fills the scene as a backdrop—a Prussian-blue palette for grazing dairy cows, standing silent and staring at the unseen, waiting for the vegetation they chew to ferment in their paunchy bellies.

Behind them the lazy Drift River, a flow of liquid sapphire, dotted with tiny verduous islands, stands in contrast to the handful of whitewashed, gabled cottages that line a narrow green-flowered lane leading down to the river's edge. It's a scene right from the nib of an artist's brush. Across the road is a viridescent pasture, home to a friendly herd of grazing ponies. A shimmering black stallion gallops up to the stacked boulder wall by the road and calls out to me. He jerks his noble head, snorts, and neighs, beseeching that I hand over the treat he knows I carry. I come prepared. I pull a carrot from my book bag, lean over the moss-covered barrier, and offer it to him. He clutches the orange tidbit from my hand, while nodding his approval. His companions gallop over to investigate. Yes, as I began to say, a walk through Westport is a very pleasant one.

I discovered the front doors to the little white chapel swung wide open. I walked up to the entrance and glimpsed inside. The empty pews, with their satin finish and tiger-oak wood grain, glistened in the mid-morning sunrise. The golden-planked floors and milk-white walls were awash by the building's narrow long windows, drenching the room in heavenly light. The church was all but unoccupied, with the exception of Mrs. Delia Hix. Delia was a fisherman's widow who spent most of her time walking the beach and looking out to sea, waiting for a husband who had gone fishing and never returned. Mr. Hix has been missing for over five years now. Delia was seated off to one corner just by the minister's pulpit. A prayer book was opened in her hand and she recited scripture loudly. Her squeaky voice reflected from the sweeping rafter beams above. Poor Delia. Though I couldn't make out what she was saying, knowing her, she was probably airing grievances and objections to any issue she could think of. Some used prayer to praise their Maker ... others to thank him. Delia ... well, let's just say that complaint and prayer went hand in hand. I suppose in some way she has good cause.

Before I was discovered, I turned and quietly walked away. Don't get me wrong. She's nice enough. God forgive me if I were seen. She would surely enlist me to an endless morning of worship, if not an afternoon of objective grievances about people and life. Understand, I am just as faithful as the next person. I attend service every Sunday, participate in church functions, and pray every night, on my knees, before retiring to bed.

I believe that even the Almighty can become bored and stultified by our never-ending appeals and constant patronizing. I am certain that there is not a husband in the world that would not become tired of his wife's preoccupation with praising his every endeavor, or constantly telling him how wonderful he was, and how much she loved him. Even I would go mad if confronted with such excessive devotion. Though I cannot imagine the Almighty losing his mind, I am certain He knows our mind and hearts even before we try and make them plain.

When I arrived at Louisa's the girls were sitting on the back porch sipping tea. Out front was a luxurious six-passenger buggy, with stuffed red leather benches and polished, brass lanterns. The horse was meticulously groomed and adorned in striking black leather and silver studded harnesses. The wagon wheels, with their white painted spokes and apple-red rims, sparkled.

I discovered Louisa's mother kneeling, sitting on her heels, a small paddle in her hand, and digging in the garden. She looked up as the gate slammed behind me.

"Good morning, Emily!"

"Morning, Mrs. Macomber."

"Best hurry, dear," she yelled, "or the girls will eat all the sweets."

I ran around the back of the house and up onto the porch. Ian Macomber played with his wood toy soldiers on the gray weathered deck of the large veranda. At the far end, Louisa sat lady-like, hands neatly folded on her lap, as if waiting for an audience with the Queen. Amy, on the other hand, slouched, legs folded, one limb jouncing on the knee of the other, looking spiritless but relaxed. Then again, that is the way Amy always looked—like a rambunctious adolescent who is made to sit quietly and wait their turn. Just as I took my last step onto the porch, Ian jumped to his feet and ran over.

"Emmie, you're here, you're here!" he shouted.

"Hello, Ian. Sorry. I didn't bring you anything today."

"Ahh, that's all right. Next time."

I tousled his hair. Slightly annoyed, he recoiled and went back to playing with his toys.

"Well, good afternoon," cried Amy, carrying a smirk. "Her majesty finally arrives."

"It's only half past eight in the morning," I let her know.

"Good morning, Emmie," sung Louisa. "Did you pick up that thread for me?"

"I have it here in my book bag," I pulled out the small package and placed it on the table. "I had to walk to get here. The wagon has a wobbly wheel and I was afraid to use it."

"We would have driven down to get you, if we knew," declared Louisa. She unwrapped the brown parcel containing thread and knitting needles.

"How is everyone?" I asked.

"As you can see, Mother has taken to gardening." She unwound some red thread from its spool.

"Is that the color you wanted?" I asked.

"Oh yes. Mother's going to teach me embroidering."

I looked over to the yard where Mrs. Macomber was digging away. "I love your mother. She's such a busy bee."

"She sure is," agreed Amy. "But gardening?"

"What's wrong with gardening?" asked Louisa.

Amy sighed. "Oh, I don't know. Looks tiring. Besides, its a man's occupation."

"I have a garden," I noted. "And I take care of it myself, every day."

"You don't have a man?"

"I'll thank you for reminding me," I snarled.

"You know what I mean," said Amy, "we have a hired man who does ours."

We walked over to the edge of the porch and watched Louisa's mother burrow in the soil—me with admiration, Amy and Louisa with puzzlement.

"I love the little picket fence around your mother's garden," I said.

"Yes. Father built it to keep the goats in the farm next door from wandering over and eating Mother's tomatoes."

"Eating her tomatoes?" Amy chirped. "I thought she was planting flowers!"

"I can't rightfully say. It may be tomatoes—it may be flowers. I would need to ask her."

"Your mother's always doing something," said Amy.

"That's one thing I can say about Mother. She sure keeps herself occupied."

"Well … I suppose with all the domestics we have taking care of our place, there is little for Mother to do," added Amy.

"She should start a circle like Mother has," suggested Louisa.

"A circle?" I said.

"Yes, you know, a club, like our reading club," explained Louisa. "Only for flora and green things."

Amy broke into chipmunk laughter. "Books about tomatoes. How exciting."

"I don't think it's funny. Since Mother started the club it has been very successful. She has compiled an extensive library on gardening. She even entered a contest at the Westport Farmer's Fair to see who can grow the largest pumpkin."

"Are you serious?" said Amy, suppressing a chuckle.

"Does your mother's club have a name?" I inquired.

"The Westport Women's Garden Circle," replied Louisa. "Father has been encouraging her ... keeping her busy. He says at the end of the day she sleeps like a kitten on her side of the bed."

"I bet he does," needled Amy, breaking into laughter. "Next I'll hear you say he has erected a fence down the middle of the mattress to keep the old goat away."

"Oh Amy, that is wicked!" I declared, my hand to my mouth. A smothered giggle crept past my fingers.

"Oh, you two!"

"Where is your father?" I asked. "He usually comes out to say hello."

"He's gone to New Bedford on business."

"Then whom does that beautiful wagon out front belong to?"

"It's mine," acknowledged Amy. "And it's not a wagon, it's a surrey," she declared sneeringly.

"A surrey, huh?"

"Its a fancy word for carriage," said Louisa.

"It is beautiful," I said.

"Father likes to walk. The only time we use it is on Sunday for church."

"And he lets you take it?" I asked.

"I don't see why not."

"I thought you had a coachman?"

"I gave him the day off."

"You are so lucky, Amy. When Grandmamma and I take our old wagon to church parishioners think we're making a delivery."

"What sort of delivery?"

"She's just trying to be witty, Lulu," said Amy, shaking her head. "There is no delivery."

"How was I to know?" snapped Louisa.

"Look, let's stop our squabbling and begin the meeting," I suggested. "Louisa, you're president. It is your place to call this session to order."

"Very well. Let's all sit down and begin." Louisa opened the club diary and made a note of the date. "I, Louisa Tripp Macomber, bring this, the fourth session of the ... or is this the fifth? Does anyone remember?"

"We don't care, Lulu," grumbled Amy. "Get on with it."

"Living in the city does not become you, Amy Chaloner," muttered Louisa. "You must understand that you are now sitting in the lap of geniality—amongst a benevolent and studious assembly. We are ladies, not surly ruffians."

As she often did, Amy ignored her.

"And Amy is a member in excellent standing in this studious assembly," I added. "Is that not right, Louisa?"

"Why yes! I never meant to … that is to say …"

"Amy knows what you mean. Continue."

"Where was I? Oh, yes, today we start a new book. What shall it be?"

"Well, I was thinking we could talk about the book concerning the girl who was discovered hanged in Fall River over thirty years ago," I proposed. "Sarah Cornell."

"I also," chimed Amy.

"Have you read it yet, Louisa?" I asked.

"The entire thing," she declared, taking the small volume from her canvas book bag and placing it on the table.

"I read mine in one night," proclaimed Amy, pulling another copy from her bag.

"My Lord, Amy!" I said in amazement. "You discovered a second volume for yourself!"

"Father drove us to Providence on a shopping trip. I visited Tyson's Bookshop and found the book there."

"You purchased it yourself?" questioned Louisa, awestruck.

"And why not?"

"A woman … purchasing such a book in the light of day about murder."

"As I said, and why not?"

"Did anyone see you?"

"Why would I care if they did?"

"That's incredible!" I said. "That book is quite rare. How did you find another?"

"Well, I didn't see one anywhere on the store shelf. So I asked Mr. Tyson about it. You should have seen his face when I mentioned the title. He had a used copy behind the counter in a locked case, labeled *erotica and the occult*."

"Oh, my!" bellowed Louisa.

"Did he mention anything to you about it?" I inquired.

"He certainly did. He went on about how he was shocked a young lady would ever ask for such a title."

"Gracious! What did you tell him?" asked Louisa.

"I simply told him that a sale was a sale and he was the richer for it. He shook his head and bagged the book for me. What else could he do?"

"I wish I could have seen that bookman's face." I laughed.

"That makes it unanimous," noted Louisa, "We have all read the book and a discussion on its merits can now begin."

"Yes, let's," I agreed.

"I must say, I was very excited about reading it," said Louisa, "I found the entire account very intriguing ... in a disturbing sort of way, I suppose."

"That's the attraction of the entire affair," Amy surmised, "that a pastor and a lady would engage in such maligning behavior."

"Maligning behavior by who?" I inquired, baiting her for a retort.

"If you believe that the Reverend Avery killed Sarah, and that she gave of herself to him ... well, by both of them, I would say."

"Louisa, why don't you summarize the entire tale," I suggested, "and we will take it from there."

"All right! Let's see. We have this mill girl from the city of Fall River. She's a lost soul, like the lost sheep in the Bible. Her never-ending search to belong brings her to the parish of the Reverend Ephraim Avery. Sarah was a humble girl working as a tailorist and she ..."

"As a what?" interrupted Amy.

"A tailorist, you know ... a woman who sews for her livelihood."

"There's no such word as tailorist, Louisa," I said.

"Well, what would you call a woman whose job is to mend cloth and make dresses?"

"It's what I do for my living," I added, "and I call myself a seamstress."

"A tailor, Lulu," barked Amy. "Sarah was formerly trained as a tailor ... someone who works with needle and thread. It matters not whether they're male or female."

"So what's the difference between a tailor and a seamstress?" inquired Louisa.

"A seamstress wears petticoats!" barked Amy. "Now, can we get on with it?"

"Hmm! A tailor. That reminds me of a story," said Louisa. "*The Valiant Little Tailor*. Remember?"

"What?" exclaimed Amy, incredulously.

"You know ... the tale we read when we were children about the tailor that swats the flies on his jam, and the giant and how he ..."

"Can we get back to the title at hand, Lulu?" demanded Amy.

Louisa yielded a bitter frown. "No need to be rude. I am president, I'll remind you."

"Amy, please, let her continue. Go on with the summary, Louisa."

Louisa composed herself shaking off what she perceived as Amy's contumely. She paused and sighed. "Hmm! Where was I?"

"We established that Sarah worked as a seamstress," I concluded. "Proceed."

"Let's see." Louisa thumbed through the book. "In any event, it appears that Miss Cornell did quite a bit of wandering for a girl all alone, living in

Connecticut, Rhode Island, here in Massachusetts—in places like Lowell, Dorchester, Taunton, Fall River, and even some far away places like New Hampshire. Why that's practically in the arctic."

Amy rolled her eyes.

"A well-traveled lady," I surmised.

"Yes, yes, go on!" barked Amy, trying to rush the story along. "Then she meets the Reverend in Lowell, and?"

"Do you think that was where they ... they."

"They, what?" twitted Amy, weaving a taunting grin.

"Never mind," said Louisa.

"They met again in Thompson, Connecticut," I added, "where they began their ..."

"Stop!" shouted Louisa, her hands over her ears. "Don't say anymore. I can't!"

"Oh really, Lulu?" protested Amy. "Where they copulated. Alright! How do you suppose we all got here, anyway?"

"Tell her to stop, Emmie." Louisa closed her eyes tightly and shook her head.

Amy continued her goading taunt. "They removed their clothing one by one and then they ..."

Louisa placed her hands firmly over her ears. Arms erect, and elbows out, she began to sing loudly. "La, la, la, la!"

Amy rolled in her chair, laughing. I grasped Louisa by the arm and pulled it down. "Where they became more acquainted," I said. "Now let's move on."

"Very acquainted," declared Amy.

"Amy, please, stop!" I commanded. "Continue, Louisa."

"Well, it's a fact," lectured Amy. "Four months later she was dead and with child."

"Poor, poor, Sarah," wailed Louisa, throwing her arms into her lap, "enticed by a married man ... a man of the cloth, no less."

"She should have known better," grumbled Amy, "a married minister. Come now—the daft girl was her own worst demon."

"She didn't deserve to be killed," I replied.

"We don't know that she was," remarked Amy. "What we know is that Sarah left a note that read, 'If I should go missing, enquire of Reverend Avery of Bristol, he will know where I am.' That could mean anything."

"She did travel quite a bit. Perhaps she meant that she was on the road—you know, looking for work or something," suggested Louisa.

"That's a good point," I said. "But she writes, 'if I should go missing.' Now if she said, 'if you should need me,' it could mean she went off on some private business. She did not. She specifically used the term 'missing,' which to me denotes fear or foul play."

"And it was foul play," affirmed Amy.

"This story is so convoluted," said Louisa.

"Continue your summation, Louisa," I said.

"Regardless of what the note meant, poor Sarah was found on a cold December day, hanged in a place called …" She took the book and thumbed through the pages, "Durfee Farm, near Fall River in Tiverton, by a stack-pole like the ones across the street at the Cuffe Farm."

Amy walked over to the corner of the porch and looked out toward the road and the hayfield across the way, where an old haystack left over from the autumn previous stood. The dry grassy pile lay depleted and scattered, its timber framework exposed. "I have a question about that haystack."

Louisa and I walked over to see.

"Is that what they call a stack-pole?" Amy pointed to a tall timber protruding from the center of the mound of hay. "If so, I wonder how Sarah Cornell would get a rope up that high to hang herself?"

I studied the crumbled straw structure. "Yes. That's a haystack like the one where Sarah was found," I noted.

"It must be ten feet to the top of that stick," declared Amy.

"You see them all over Westport," added Louisa.

"Looks like a small Egyptian pyramid made of hay," declared Amy.

"Depends on the farmer. Each one has his own method of stacking hay," I explained. "Some are angular, others rounder. Most are made with a tall center post and more posts resting against it … like a tepee."

"I can't see how she would have hanged herself on such a thing," declared Amy.

"Nevertheless, that's how they found her," I declared.

"Well, I think he killed her," Amy said, walking back to her chair. "He strangled her, then made it look like a hanging-suicide. He got away with it."

"That's terrible," wailed Louisa, as she accompanied Amy back to her chair. "I suppose we will never know."

I studied the heap of collapsed hay and its slumped framework. It appeared an odd place for someone to hang him or herself. Amy made a good point. How would Sarah get a rope to the top of that pole? This crime needed further investigation. Now was as good a time as any to place my proposal forward.

"Let's investigate and root out the truth for ourselves," I said.

"Investigate?" said Amy.

"Yes, discover who killed Sarah Cornell."

"Can we do that?" inquired Louisa. "It happened so many years ago."

"I don't see why not. Mr. Durfee, the owner of the farm where Sarah was found must still be alive … or his son. We can start there."

"Sounds like a half-baked idea and just up my alley, Emmie. Count me in. How about you, Lulu?"

"Three young ladies investigating a murder committed thirty years ago. What would people think?"

"Why concern ourselves with what other's think?" snarled Amy.

"We are not certain that it was murder," I insisted. "And by probing the facts we may be able, at the very least, to shine light on whether it was suicide or murder. We will begin with a clean slate and let the cowpat fall where it may."

"Cowpat! Ewww!" yowled Louisa. "I don't know about that."

"Oh, Lulu!"

"Look! Let's begin by doing a comprehensive and thorough study of the facts in the book," I proposed, "and uncover any hidden facts we may have missed. We'll meet back here in a week and take it from there."

"Yes, let's," conceded Amy.

We looked at Louisa.

She pitched us a puckered glance. "I suppose," she nodded. "Anything for poor Sarah."

—◦◦◦—

Chapter 8:

The Chaloner's posh surrey swung up to Lee's Wharf. The coachman jumped out and unloaded some luggage. A bulky bag and a small steamer trunk were removed from the back and dropped by the side of the dusty road. With an indentured smile, the opulently dressed driver dutifully extended an arm and helped Amy and Louisa step down from the gleaming carriage. Delighted, I left the schooner to greet them.

Louisa waved and jerked at the bag trailing behind her. "Hello, Emmie!" she hollered. She limped as she scurried with the overstuffed floral clothing sack bouncing along the ground.

Amy wrestled with her heavy luggage, tugging, straining, barely lifting one end of the small but heavy steamer trunk off the ground. The clumsy planked and steel-thonged chest moved in spurts. She grunted while she heaved the heavy load along the ground. The sound of metal strapping and wood grating along stony gravel was irksome. Nonetheless, she appeared excited. For short-tempered Amy, it was a good thing.

"Morning, Emmie!" she cried, joyfully.

"Leave it, Amy. I'll have one of the crew take it for you," I suggested.

"I can do it myself," she insisted.

Louisa rushed over to me with a hug. "This trip is going to be jolly fun," she declared.

"I'm happy to see you are using the duffel-cloth bag I sewed up for you."

"Yes! It is first rate," she said. "I especially like the way you used bootlaces as a strap tie along the top. Ingenious!"

"You should carry it up on your shoulder like the sailors do," I told her, flippantly.

"Think so?" she grimaced.

"What in the world does she have there?" I asked. As always, Amy appeared more like she was dressed for a dance or formal function then for a casual weekend on the water.

"I told her to bring the bare minimum. Would she listen? She should have used the bag you made for us … said it was too small."

"Well, she has more clothing than most of us."

Amy released the handle and the trunk thumped to the ground. Louisa and I laughed.

"Well, is anyone going to come over and help?" she cackled, her arms and fists akimbo.

"What in the world do you have in there, anyhow?" I hurried over to lend a hand. "We are only going to be away for a couple of days."

"I told her, I told her," parroted Louisa.

"Oh, be quiet, Lulu, and give me a hand."

"Sorry, can't. I have my own things to carry."

I took hold of the leather strap on the small humped trunk. "Lift your end, Amy. We'll carry it together."

"Some people have no manners whatsoever!" she grumbled, taking hold of the strap at her end.

"What's in here, anyway? It weighs tons."

"Clothes and toiletries, some books in case I get bored. Not much else."

"The woolen bags Emmie made for us would have done splendidly," insisted Louisa. She heaved hers up onto her shoulder and walked ahead.

"Don't carry it that way, Lulu!" shouted Amy. "It's unladylike."

Louisa flung the flowered clothing sack to the ground.

"I'll carry it anyway I darn please!" she growled, crossing her arms. "Besides, I don't see you doing any better."

Taking baby steps, Amy and I shuffled along, precariously. Louisa scurried ahead. "You should have used the woolen bag Emmie made for us," admonished Louisa.

"Yes, why didn't you use the bag I made for you?" I said, struggling with my end of the heavy trunk.

"I did. It's inside the trunk," she replied, grunting. "It's filled with undergarments and other unmentionables."

I shook my head. "Serves me right for asking."

We placed the trunk down at the base of the gangplank and took a breather.

Louisa hobbled up the wide catwalk just as Samuel hurried down to lend a hand. "Hello, Sam!"

"Good morning, Louisa." He took her bag and placed it on deck. "What's happening there?"

"Oh, Amy! She's bringing her entire wardrobe along."

Samuel took the bulky trunk and swung it up onto his shoulder. "Good morning, girls."

"Oh, Samuel, be careful," I cautioned.

"So happy you ladies could make it," he said, limping up the platform.

"Father sends his regards," Amy said.

"How is your father?" replied Samuel. "I see very little of him since you all moved to the city."

"Oh, he's fine. It's so nice to have you back, Sam. The old harbor was just not the same without you."

"You think?"

"Oh, yes! It can get boring here at the Point. There is just nothing to do. I often fall into a desperate state of ennui ... one which at times almost brings me to tears. You understand, don't you, Sam?"

"I suppose I do," he replied, not quite certain when he last witnessed Amy desperate or sobbing.

"You have lived in the city far too long, Amy," I said. "We miss you here in Westport."

"Well, in any event, we are happy she could come along," Samuel added. "Amy brings a pinch of city culture to the village."

"Just a pinch?" she chirped.

"A bucket full of pinches," he reaffirmed.

"Why, thank you, Sam. You're such a gentleman." she requited, hurling me a cocksure smile.

Samuel dropped the trunk onto the deck. A dark-skinned burly sailor took hold of it. Samuel introduced us.

"This is Eli Monroe, my first mate."

Eli placed down the luggage and gently bowed.

"This is Miss Emily White and Miss Amy Chaloner."

"Pleasure to know you, ladies," said Eli, removing his stocking hat.

"And just behind you is Miss Louisa Macomber."

"I have met the charming Miss Louisa when I took her bag below," he confirmed.

"If you don't mind, Lulu and I are going to inspect the cabin, Sam," said Amy.

"By all means. I'll be down soon to show you around."

"Come along, Lulu!" ordered Amy, snatching her hand.

"This is so much fun," chimed Louisa, stumbling along while holding her hat to her head as Amy hauled her away.

The shy, dignified Eli waited quietly.

"Mr. Monroe is a vital cog in the critical workings of the *Sphinx,* Emily."

"I'm happy to hear that."

"It is kind of you to reflect me in such good light, sir."

"Nonsense, Mr. Monroe. Few men can pilot a vessel as splendidly and prepare a hardy meal for a hungry crew with little repose."

"You know how to cook, Mr. Monroe?"

"I do, Miss."

"Tell the lady what we are having for dinner tonight, Mr. Monroe."

Eli's eyes brightened as he rubbed his hands together. "Well, sir, ah! Prawn and cod over peppered rice, with Bermudian fish chowder and American wild cherry pie for desert."

"Bermudian chowder!" I said.

"Yes, Miss … island recipe … cod, lots of pepper, thyme, with carrots, onions, and sweet tomatoes made into a delightful creamy puree. Oh, yes, and hot red peppers and garlic for those who like it spicy."

"Not a clam or potato in the entire dish," chuckled Samuel. "You sure can tell Mr. Monroe is not a New Englander. Strangely enough, it's very good." Samuel glanced at Eli and winked. "In its own right, you understand. Isn't that right, Mr. Monroe?"

"I understand, sir. We all have our traditions and particular tastes," replied Eli.

"I am certain everyone will love your chowder, Mr. Monroe," I said.

It quickly became evident to me that Eli Monroe was not your typical African free slave, if he was ever a slave at all. He appeared refined and educated far beyond the average Westporter. As a matter of fact, he displayed himself as one of the gentlest and most cultured boatman I had ever met. Again, that may not be such an exceptional proclamation, since the only boatmen I have ever been acquainted with were the boorish and unsophisticated fishermen of Point Village. Not only was Eli a man of color, he reveled himself to be unpretentious and a worldly soul—and for lack of any further formal description, an honorable gentleman. He appeared right at home on a sailing vessel. His mannerly approach and aristocratic demeanor fascinated me.

"Where were you educated, Mr. Monroe?" I inquired.

"London, Miss. I am ashamed to admit, not completing my studies."

"You're quite fortunate to even see London," I said. "Most of us are lucky to venture twenty or thirty miles from home, ever."

"If you say so, Miss," said Eli, modestly.

"Do you do much reading, Mr. Monroe?"

"Whenever I can get my hands on a book."

"What sort of reading do you do?"

"The classics, Shakespeare, some Greek."

"You read Greek!"

"No, Miss," he said, rubbing his nose while suppressing a smile.

"Traditional classical Greek ... in English."

"Oh, sorry. I misunderstood." I blushed and continued my query hoping he did not think of me a dolt. "Have you not read any current literature?"

"Some Tennyson ... your American, Melville."

"Now, he's the gentleman who wrote about the white whale. Is that right?"

"Yes. Have you not read it, Miss?"

"No. Can't say I have. Though I own a copy."

"Ah, now there is a brilliant piece of work, Miss. It will give you a newfound appreciation for the men and boats that sit in your little harbor."

"Sorry to cut you short, Eli. I need you to place the lady's things below," said Samuel. "You will have ample time to discuss literature with Miss White once we shove off."

"Of course, sir, my apology."

"None called for. You see, I'm afraid you have touched on one of Miss White's favorite pastimes—books. She will have you here all morning talking about them."

Samuel looked over at me and winked.

"I have the two aft cabins in order, sir, one for Miss Amy and the other for Miss Louisa. Will that be suitable?"

"That's fine," the captain acknowledged.

"What about Miss White's luggage, sir? Will she be staying with one of the other ladies?"

"I'll look after Miss White. She shall have my quarters. Father and I will sleep in the forecastle with the men."

Eli's mouth slackened. "With ... the men, sir?"

"Yes. After all, we are all men, are we not, Mr. Monroe?"

"That is not my meaning, sir. It's just that ..."

"I understand your meaning, sailor. We well get underway as soon as Captain Cory senior arrives. Make certain everything is tied down and shut all hatches and ports."

"Very well, sir," uttered the obedient Bermudian.

Amy appeared on deck just as Eli and another crewman were carrying her ponderous trunk below deck. "Oh, please do be careful with that," she pleaded. "I have my china tea set in there."

Samuel rolled his eyes.

"Sam. Do I have time to do a little shopping over at Cory's store?" she asked. "I'm desperately in need of some ribbon for my hair."

"Sorry Amy. Not if you're coming along on this trip. We will be shoving off at any moment."

"Oh, pussy willows!" she cried. "What's all the hurry, anyhow? Everyone's rushing about."

"We need to take advantage of the tide." I said. "It will help carry us away from the wharf. Is that not right, Captain?"

"Good point," said Samuel. "It's more than that. We must get out to Cuttyhunk Island with no time to spare. There's a ship on the shoals. We are going to lend a hand. So, we must leave immediately."

Amy stomped off pouting.

"What sort of ship?" I asked.

"A whaler. Probably hung up on the shoals during the squalls we had yesterday."

"How exciting," crowed Louisa. "Are we going to catch any whales on this trip, Sam?"

Amused by the question, he lowered his head and gently shook it. "We may see one or two," he acknowledged. "I don't think we will be hunting any."

Preparations continued for the short voyage we were about to take. Everywhere you looked there was a drone of activity. I watched as burly men carried bound coils of line on their backs, dropping them in a heap on deck. A huge iron anchor was heaved and tied to the bow of the ship. Small barrels of blackened chain were hoisted high into the air and swung up off the wharf and onto the ship. When it appeared that no one was looking, Samuel leaned over and gave me a kiss. My heart quivered and my knees tottered. Did I mention there was a drone of activity?

"Happy?" he whispered.

"Yes, and you?"

"Whenever I'm on the *Sphinx*. And having you here makes it all the better."

"Sam! All are aboard as you ordered," signaled a familiar voice. I turned to look. It was Tim Cadman.

"Hello, Timothy. You coming with us?"

"I sure am."

"Mr. Cadman will prove to us if he's as good a sailor as he is a carpenter," declared Samuel.

"I'll do my best, Sam."

"I'm sure you will, Tim. I'm hoping this will be the first of many voyages for Tim and me. I'm certain he will prove his worth on this trip."

"We are only going to a tiny spit of land just outside the harbor," replied Tim. "Little distance to prove one's nautical abilities."

"Twelve miles out is distant enough," said Samuel, patting the carpenter on the back. "It's not easy piloting a ship this size. If a storm hits, we may all have to prove our worth once we get out to Cuttyhunk."

Tim nodded in agreement and walked away.

Amy and Louisa appeared back up on deck.

"Samuel, your ship is beautiful," said Louisa.

Samuel just smiled. Amy scrutinized Tim as he coiled some line.

"He's very handsome," she whispered, gleefully, tugging at my sleeve.

"Well, hurry. Go and introduce yourself," I remarked.

"No! It's not lady-like."

"Tim!"

"Yes, Emily?"

"Can you show Louisa and Amy the ship?"

"Glad to! This way, ladies. What would you like to see first?"

Amy turned up her nose and followed as Tim escorted her and Louisa down the deck. He looked back and offered Samuel and me a bashful smile. I winked and nodded.

"Well, perhaps you will see a change in him after this trip. A few minutes behind the schooner's wheel should be enough to cheer any man."

"I thought Eli was wheelman."

"He is. I want Tim to learn how to sail. Though, Eli's the best wheelman a captain can have. After all, he's an experienced seaman. A twenty-year veteran. He can do any job on a ship. Not only that, but the crew respects him."

"He sounds very intelligent."

"He is. Why, the man can speak several languages ... French, Portuguese ... a couple African dialects. He moved to Baltimore from Bermuda. Then the troubles began in the South. When I found him he was looking to board a ship for England and having trouble finding one that would take him. In a way he was fortunate I came along. He taught himself how to sail when he was just a child. Sheer insight and astute observation are traits that are needed on the *Sphinx* and Eli is awash in them."

"He sure moves around the ship like he knows what he's doing."

"Served in the Royal Navy, so he's familiar with nautical protocol. I was lucky our paths crossed. I could never have gotten the *Sphinx* out of Baltimore without him."

As Samuel and I discussed the merits of his first mate, a grave utterance blared from shore.

"Ready to shove off?" blustered the deep commanding voice.

It was Seabury Cory, looking licensed and qualified in captain's jacket, trimmed with polished brass buttons and anchor insignia cufflinks. He sported a briny sea cap with polished leather visor.

"Captain Cory!" remarked Samuel.

"Permission to come aboard!"

"Permission granted, sir."

Captain Seabury Cory tossed his seabag up to one of the crewmen and shuffled up the gangplank. He greeted me with a snug bear hug and a kiss, as he often did. Unlike his son, who was discreet and introspective, Seabury was thunderous and gregarious. Like Grandmamma, he was a spiritual man, always ready to counsel youth with a clever epigram or astute witticism. And although he no longer attended Sunday service, he is always ready to express his respect and fear for the Almighty. He had not been on deck more than a minute before inexorably serving orders.

"Don't let that halyard swing over the side, lad," he yelled. "Take up the slack on that boom, sailor! Mustn't let it slam around that way. Ya want someone to get hurt? You. Yes, you! Get that anchor tied off and get that chain down below and secured!"

"Its all right, Father," assured Samuel resting his hand on the old salt's shoulder. "They're still a little green. But they get it done in the end."

"This isn't the fourteen-foot yawl I build for ya when you were five, ya know."

"And I'm no longer five, Father."

"Nevertheless, if ya ever expect to set sail in a vessel like this, ya can't afford greenhorns," he barked.

"We will be ready to leave when the time comes, Father. I promise."

"Time is passing, my boy. Look at them. They move about like spilled molasses!"

"Relax, Father. We're going out for pleasure. This is not one of your whaling expeditions."

"Never ya mind. Ya still need to run a tight ship. Everyone needs to be kept busy and alert. What are ya going to do, son, when all hell breaks loose, heh? Ya must keep their feet to the coals, boy ... feet to the coals!"

"Remember, I am captain here," reminded Samuel.

"Bagh!" Seabury Cory walked off toward the foredeck, shouting. "You, there! That's not the way ya tie off a line."

"I'm afraid he's going to cause a mutiny," said Samuel, with somewhat content pride.

"Two captains are better than one," I said. He gave me an objectionable glance. "I suppose that's what first mates are for, huh?" I croaked, meekly.

Just then, Eli Monroe appeared, saving me from any further embarrassment. "All is in order below, sir, but I'm afraid Miss Amy is unhappy with her bunk. Apparently, the cushion does not have sufficient feathers."

Samuel laughed. "Very well, Mr. Monroe. Objection noted. Prepare to cast off."

"Aye, sir," said the mate with a spirited salute.

"Going out to sea! This is so exciting," I declared.

"I suppose it is," said Samuel. "So long as you don't have to do it every day just to put food on the table."

He placed his hand on mine and tenderly stroked it. A lost and sad grin adorned his face. I reached up and stroked it. I tried making eye contact with him. He just stared down and away, appearing to be elsewhere. Abruptly, he let go of my hand as quickly as he took hold of it and walked off giving orders to the crew. I looked down at my abandoned limb, dumbfounded, as if it were not mine.

There was a sorrow about Samuel—a melancholy presence I had never noticed before. He just wasn't his normal self. Perhaps it was due to the war. Again, it could just be my imagination. I was lost in thought, pondering the issue when I was jarred from my stupor by Tim as he ran by.

"Are you all right, Emmie?" he asked, noticing my silly expression.

"Yes, yes, I'm fine." He gave me a thumbs-up and scurried off.

Preparations were made to leave. Gathered sails were untied and the gaff spars were prepared to be hoisted. At the foredeck, sailors were busy tugging halyards. Heavy jibs heaved and bloomed as they shimmied up their stays. The pendulous cloth rippled and stirred while untethered sheets, long ropes tied to the end of the sail and made to tame them, meandered and whipped in the playful, belching gusts. Tim boldly stepped out onto the bowsprit and made ready the tall Yankee jib. While I watched, Samuel suddenly emerged amongst all that was going on.

"Tim's my aerialist," he declared proudly, "a lynx amongst dancing spars and fluttering canvas. Always in more than one place at a time, that boy is."

"He sure looks like he knows what he's doing," I said.

"Far cry from the farm boy he once was."

"Oh, oh … here comes the other captain," I warned.

Seabury Cory came marching up the deck loaded with advice. "Women should be down below and out of the way while we move'er out," advised Seabury. He gave me a friendly wink.

"Father, I don't think …"

"No, ya don't! Ya should have more crew, boy!"

"I was going to say that I don't think Emily staying on deck can do any harm. Besides, I have plenty of crew."

"Bagh, greenhorns, everyone of them!"

"Say what you must, Father. I'll soon show you their worth."

"Think ya'll have any trouble getting her away from the wharf? It's pretty tight in here with all these ships."

"I don't see why I should. The wind is with us. Besides, once in the open I can sail this baby alone."

Squinting, Seabury Cory poked his son with an accusatory finger. "Aye, but ya must consider what can happen before ya get out in the open, boy. The Knubble is a narrow channel. What do ya do if the wind suddenly vanishes or changes direction a hundred and eighty degrees, eh?"

"That's what the crew is for," replied Samuel. "They would simply row us out or I would drop a series of kedge anchors and pull us along until we fell upon deep water."

"We'll see, we'll see," said Seabury. He nodded with uncertainty.

"In any event, I've arranged to have the crew of the whaler *Janet* row us away from the wharf, just to make you happy, Father. Pulling her off the wharf in this panting breeze will be child's play. It's not akin to maneuvering one of those heavy whalers you have been use to. Compared to them, the *Sphinx* is but a feather."

"Does she do well off the wind ... say, once we approach the Knubble?"

"She's at her best off the wind. We should glide through the gut with little affair."

"She be yar vessel, son." Seabury patted his son on the back. "Ya must know how she behaves."

"That I do, Father, that I do."

"Come, Emmie," beckoned the old captain. "We shall wait below ... make us some coffee."

I was about to follow when Samuel reached over and took hold of my arm.

"Stay, Emily, please. I want you to experience the *Sphinx* in all her glory as the boys dress and drive her. Sit behind the steering station. You'll be out of the way there."

Six men from the whaler *Janet* approached in a small whaleboat. A taut manila line was stretched from the bow of the schooner to the loggerhead on the small thirty-foot craft.

"Ready anytime you are," yelled the man in the small boat as his companions all took to their oars.

Samuel shouted orders while a neophyte crew of the schooner scurried to their stations. Shirtless sailors, their obsidian toned muscles glistening in the late dawn light, pushed heavy spars and pulled on dangling ropes as more sail was hoisted. Brawny, ebony-fleshed men blazed pasty white smiles and twinkling eyes, an enthusiastic endorsement to the jubilation and pride they felt as members of the sailing schooner *Sphinx* of Westport.

The thirty-foot-long main boom, fastened to the deck, was unleashed. The long lacquered pole and gathered sail slid listlessly to port. Once the main sheet was trimmed and the sail partially raised, the ship lurched. We moved ever so slightly away from the wharf.

"Cast off all lines," cried the captain. "Raise the main to the mast head and prepare to make fast all sheets."

Samuel took his station behind the ship's wheel.

Taut ropes, securing the ship to terra firma, were set free and quickly hoisted aboard. A jumbled assemblage of villagers and fishermen gathered along the granite wharf to watch us depart. Town folk pointed with marveled curiosity, along with loitering fishermen, who quickly lost interest and walked away.

High in the rigging, the schooner's unattended jibs fluttered and swelled, shivering like stray billowing bladders. They filled and then spilled their wind, crumbling under slack sheets, only to fill again. The men on the *Janet's* whaleboat rowed fiercely while pulling the bow of the ninety-nine-foot *Sphinx* away from its berth and into the open harbor. The *Sphinx's* protuberant sprit delicately cleared the hulking whaling vessels tethered like sleeping bulldogs to weathered oak pillars along the shore. Once the forward portion of the ship was away from the granite wall, Tim Cadman untied the whaleboat's towline from the schooner's bow and flung the slack cable overboard. Hand over hand, one of the men on the flailing whaleboat pulled in the manila umbilical aboard. The majestic *Sphinx* slowly migrated into the unseen channel.

The jibs on the schooner were quickly trimmed and their sheets promptly made fast to belaying pins along the rail. The shivering white canvas congealed, flourishing like air-like potbelly gentlemen, in dangling salute to a commanding but gentle wind. The towering masts lazily dipped to port as the surging schooner slowly moved under its own power. The enormous mainsail swung hard to port and stiffened, as it harvested a freshening breeze. Mainsheets were made true and slack booms were hauled in and made secure to their anchoring cleats. The ship lazily listed to leeward and picked up speed, accelerating expeditiously. It was as if the hand of God himself had slipped beneath the stern and given us a nudge.

Samuel handed the wheel over to Eli and scurried forward to inspect the ship's sails and trim. It was blowing about six knots and *Sphinx* appeared to be sprinting along at seven. At the wharf, townsfolk extended a polite applause as the men of the whaler *Janet* shattered the thin morning air with cheer and ovation.

A meek flushed sun advanced just behind us, warming our backs. My spirit soared as the ambiance of the moment became an elixir to my enthusiasm. We were finally on our way. Samuel's floating mistress ran west towing my heart and yearnings. An overture of adventure lay at my feet—the sort of adventure I have only read in books. Yes, I understand what you are telling me. We are not barreling into battle, fighting a punishing storm, or exploring some distant land. The trip is only a short one—a mere twelve miles in distance, and nothing but a casual, seafaring jaunt on a pleasant sunny day. To a land-bound maiden who has lived by the ocean, and able to go out on it, this trip could just as well have been a journey around the world.

At the very end of the nineteen-foot-long bowsprit Tim Cadman clung onto the forestay while the schooner punched along—its bow lifted—plowing—parting a path through swishy spray. Barefoot, and with toes wrapped tightly around the wooden spar, he bravely straddled the tip of the protracted timber. Samuel stood proudly on the foredeck, legs apart, and hands resting on his cane, amused by his young deckhand's antics. He admired Tim's courage and fortitude, wishing his leg was healed so he could celebrate by the young man's side. With his eyes shut, palms up, and arms outstretched, as if waiting to be anointed by a higher power, Tim puffed out his chest, and threw back his head, drinking in the splendor of the moment. He devoured as much courage as the daring exploit allowed. I sat comfortably by the aft rail—a somewhat fortuitous observer, amused by the young carpenter's antics. I had the best seat in the house.

With his large tenebrous hands gripping the polished wheel, Eli Monroe effortlessly piloted the majestic ship. The schooner's razor-flared bow cut through the crystal wavelets on its way up the wrinkled river, in route to the mouth of the tight channel and the Knubble. Below deck, Captain Seabury Cory rang the ship's bell and the girls cheered the *Sphinx's* progress. Louisa gave out a resounding "Yay." Amy's chipmunk laughter filled the cabin. We had only just left Point Village and already it was turning out to be the most exciting journey I had ever taken.

Samuel limped up the deck, gave me a wink, and took control of the helm, as we got closer to the treacherous Knubble. But today the tide was favorable and the seas were kind. Making our way through the impressive rock cliff and adjoining sand aperture was nothing short of routine. On stormy days, taking a ship through the Knubble was like threading a sewing needle while riding a carriage over a lumpy road with a runaway horse. Today, the pass through the Knubble was an easy one.

Samuel did not feel adequately at rest unless he was at the wheel steering his baby past the large rock bluff. As we approached, he looked up, studied the sails, and gave the command to prepare to come about—seaman's vernacular for changing direction. He swung the wheel hard to port and the vessel made a momentous course change from a downwind run to a port tack—from west to south. The wind, which had been somewhat behind us, pushing us along, was now off the nose and giving the illusion that it was blowing much harder and the ship driving a great deal faster.

Illuminated by an orange morning sun, two boys in tattered rompers and frayed straw hats stood high on the Knubble's elevated craggy precipice, fishing. In their hands they held textile weaving shuttles wrapped with twine. With its acre of canvas hung high, the schooner blotted out the bleak, early sunlight as it sailed by the adolescent anglers. The boys waved then quickly retrieved their lines before they were swept beneath the ship's keel. Before we knew it, we were by the Knubble and approaching the next obstacle—a large boulder that sat just outside the mouth of the fading channel. Half Mile Stone, as it was known, loomed ominously but innocuously as the ship headed right for it.

Down in the cabin the spawning scent of cooked coffee bean permeated the atmosphere as the breeze changed direction to the vessel's new compass heading. While the brew simmered on the stove, its aroma mingled with the acrid, stale seaweed air to formulate a strange but inviting thirsty fragrance. Louisa stuck her head out from the hatch above the deckhouse and Amy climbed up on deck.

"Hold on girls, wind's picking up," warned Samuel. "Grip the ship with both hands now."

"Oh, Emmie, this is delightful," Louisa said, stepping out in the breeze. It tossed her wavy locks across her face and blew her plaid tam-o'-shanter cap off her head. She quickly reached out to catch it. Over the side it went. "Oh, no, my hat!" she cried, pointing as it floated away.

"Sorry! Not much we can do about it now," declared Samuel.

All heads turned aft to the wafting bonnet.

Knowing how much the hat meant to Louisa, I lobbied for Samuel to do something. "Can't we just turn around and …"

He stopped me with an upbraided frown. "Sorry Louisa," I said. "We just can't maneuver a ship this large easily."

"No, we can't," confirmed the captain. "Besides, we are in a narrow channel. There is nowhere to go but forward. Sorry."

"Oh, shoot! Amy gave me that hat. It came all the way from Ireland."

"I'll get you another, Lulu," promised Amy. "Besides, I have a trunk full of hats below."

Seabury Cory appeared, a steaming cup of coffee was in his hand. "Aye, lass. It will wash up on the beach. Someone will find it. That's if it doesn't make its way all the way back to Ireland," he declared, chuckling.

Like grieving school girls, we stood on the aft deck and watched the natatorial cap loop wave over wave and finally disappear.

"Good-bye, faithful hat," muttered Louisa.

"There goes Westport," said Amy. "Good-bye, Westport."

"I have lived in that little village all my life and have never journeyed this far out to sea," I confessed. "Yet, there it is … just yards away. I feel like I can reach out and touch it."

"Oh, this is nothing," replied Amy, "I've been way out to sea many times."

"It's different for me," I said. "I ask you! Do I live a sheltered life or what?"

"I'm a little scared," wailed Louisa, suddenly. "Why does the ship keep leaning over so much?"

"It's meant to do that," I said.

"It's what ships do, Lulu," added Amy. "Nothing to worry about."

"Look!" yelled Louisa, alarmingly. "We are going to hit that rock, Samuel, Samuel! We're going to hit that rock!"

Samuel smiled. "Everything's fine. That's Half Mile Stone. We need to stay close to it so we can remain in the channel, that's all. We are not going to hit it."

"Are you sure?" She peered down into the water. "Are there any others we can't see?"

"Oh, Lulu! You're acting like an infant," declared Amy. "I'm going to sit at the bow so I don't have to listen to it."

As she left, Amy looked back at me with a pleased smile and walked off to the front of the ship where Tim sat, keeping watch. Her decision to do so had more to do with wanting to sit by Tim than not wanting to listen to Louisa fret. She sauntered down the deck while her large brimmed straw hat flapped in the breeze, draping her arm over it to hold it in place. Sitting by Tim, she briefed him on Louisa's fears. Tim looked back at us and laughed.

"Help, we're going to hit that rock, we're going to hit that rock!" he yapped, facetiously. He slapped his knee in laughter.

The shrieking din of Amy's stuttering guffaw filled the air. "Hide, Lulu, hide!" yelled Amy.

"I don't think its funny," cried Louisa.

I put my arm around her. "They're just funning you," I said. "Pay them no mind."

The imperial Knubble bluff and Half Mile Stone were now well behind us. Just off Horseneck sandy beach a solitary fisherman, wearing a hat laced with a silk ribbon, sat motionless in a gleaming white dory. The planking on the Bristol skiff glimmered, reflecting and softening the hard morning light, while its sugar-white sail gently fluttered in a playful offshore breeze. The foamy sea percolated in the sandy shoals around him as the man reclined comfortably, smoking. I did not recognize him. By the way he was dressed—wearing a cream-colored suit, white shirt, and red bow tie—it was a sure bet he resided in the village of Acoaxet, and that fishing was not a fundamental occupation.

Acoaxet Village was a small village across the river from where I lived and where a handful of wealthy mill owners kept their summer homes. Most people could not pronounce or remember the village name, thus the place was simply referred to as The Harbor. Grandmamma claims that its residents are city folk, narrow minded and intolerant in their way of thinking, and feeling themselves superior to the average Westporter. I wouldn't know. I've never been to Acoaxet or had reason to visit there. Seabury Cory mentioned that a rumor is circulating that Acoaxet Village wants to start its only little town, and secede from the proper town of Westport. I must admit that is a provincial way of thinking. To tell you the truth, such lofty matters do not concern me. Nor do I care one way or the other—as long as my little world at the Point remains a happy place to live.

The man in the dory glanced over at us with indifference as we passed—a bent bamboo rod in one hand and a stubby cigarette resting on his lower lip. I waved. He hesitated. Then without even looking over, reluctantly raised a limp hand and waved back. How rude. I wanted to holler to him, "Our boat is bigger than yours." Instead, I chuckled. I didn't care. It is funny how what others think and the critical convections they posses, whether valid or prejudicial, influence our sentiments and mold our analytical perceptions of others. He was probably a nice fellow. Or perhaps just having a bad day. I must always remember what Grandmamma often said, *Animals do not allow people to think for them. So why would you allow others to think for you.*

We were now placing some good distance between our vessel and the Westport shore. Louisa continued studying the sea around her for peril.

"How do we know where the channel is?" she asked.

"Local knowledge and experience," replied Samuel. "Sometimes it's trial and error. Especially after a storm carries the sandy beach into the channel filling it in and moving it over. We are well into deep water now. No need to worry, Louisa."

"Two Mile Rock, coming up on the right," hooted Amy.

"Not another!" yowled Louisa.

Samuel handed the helm over to Eli Monroe. "Look out for Cock Shoals off our port beam. Keep well clear of them," he warned, pointing out a nearby dangerous reef. "There you can see the Hen and Chickens to the east. Once they are spotted Cock Shoals are just southwest of them. Just keep the course at 160 degrees and we'll be fine."

"Aye, aye, Captain," replied Eli, gripping the wheel and studying the compass.

"And never try to shortcut between the shoals like some of the old seadogs do. They're familiar with every submerged stone there. We are not."

"I don't see any hens and chickens, out here," chimed Louisa, peering over the rail.

Samuel laughed. The charm and innocence that Louisa often exhibited never failed to amuse him. "That's what we call the shoals to the south of Gooseberry Island," he explained. "The Hen and Chickens Reef."

Louisa looked over at Samuel and gave him a dour look. Looking over the rail, she just had to ask. "Where are these hens and chickens? We're not in any danger, are we?"

"Don't worry. We are going nowhere near them," assured Samuel.

Eli Monroe piloted the ship beautifully. To own and skipper such a vessel was a dream he held all his life. To act as second mate was the next best thing. As second mate one could enjoy all the pleasures of sailing the ship and none of the headaches of upkeep. Eli appreciated that and was happy for it. Samuel knew how he felt and handed Eli the helm anytime he could.

We soared by Gooseberry Island where a colony of orbicular, woolly sheep wandered the brush-cropped landscape. Grandmamma said she remembered Gooseberry when it was thick forest. With the timber all but removed to build and heat homes, it was now a shrub island, home for roving sheep. At high tide the rolling surf would break between the mainland and the Island, covering the sandy, shallow land bridge that connected the two, and stranding the fleecy animals, leaving them to graze its sandy soil.

Though there was fog well offshore, it was a beautiful day, with a bright rising sun and cloudless blue sky. The breathtaking spectacle of the *Sphinx* fully draped in voluminous canvas and cutting through the bay chop must have been a glorious sight from Horseneck Inlet. Samuel stood vigilant and observant to every move the vessel made, not unlike a father watching a toddler frolicking along the surf. Though we all assured Louisa that we were in deep water, she continued peering over the rail for any unseen danger. At the bow, Amy and Tim laughed every time a cloud of misty spray from a fractured wave washed over them. Unlike Louisa and I, Amy was a seasoned traveler, having sailed this way many times on her father's sloop.

As the shoreline receded I was happy to just sit by the wheel and listen to Eli hum his haunting canticle of despair and woe.

"That's a lovely melody, Mr. Monroe. Does it have a name?"

"It does, Miss Emily. It's a ballad whose lyrics are as beautiful as its harmony."

"What's it called?"

"'Upon the Shield of Freedom,' I suppose. Some folk have different titles for it."

"Can you sing the words for me?"

"If you like, Miss. Let's see … it goes something like this." He began to sing.

"I was once in his pocket
In an awful place of hurt
And the harder I did toil
Got me deeper in the dirt.

"Then along came Lady Freedom
With an apron she did tow
I will lie upon its fabric
Underground up north I'll go."

His voice boomed in perfect operatic baritone bluster. Like celebrant cannon fire it thundered across the bay bringing a smile to all on our happy floating community.

Crewmen Tabeu and Admon sang along.

"Away from fields of cruelty
From cotton and from sweat
I will follow the northern twilight
To where I never need to fret.

"And to freedom I will follow
On a righteous shield I'll ride

With the badge of emancipation
On a doting caring tide.

"And from the shroud of virtue
I no longer need to hide
On my journey up to heaven
I will take with me my pride.

"Upon the shield of freedom
Upon the shield of freedom
Where my bonds will be untied
Upon the shield of freedom
I will gladly take my ride."

Eli finished singing and went back to humming.

"That was wonderful, Mr. Monroe!" I applauded.

"Oh, it was lovely!" praised Louisa.

An enthusiastic ovation was offered by Tim and peppered by Amy's delinquent laughter. Eli just smiled and continued to hum.

Seabury Cory appeared at the companionway holding two tins of coffee. "Sounds like I'm back on River Street in old Savannah," he remarked. "Now, any of you ladies up for a fresh cup of coffee?" He held up the two cups of hot drinks.

I took one and handed it to Eli.

"No, thank you, Miss," he said, politely waving it away.

"Mr. Monroe does not drink coffee," said Samuel.

Seabury handed his son the other cup. "Tea will be ready shortly, ladies," announced Seabury as he returned to the galley.

"I'll have Eli's coffee," I decided. "Do you not like coffee, Mr. Monroe?"

"Unfortunately, I have ill memories of the sin trade."

"Sin trade?" I said.

"Yes, Miss, coffee plantations. Sending African brothers to the farmsteads of Cuba to work the fields. It is kidnapping, I tell you."

I looked down at my steamy cup with conflictive discretion.

"Eli befriended a family who was eventually separated and sold to a coffee plantation owner in Cuba," explained Samuel.

"I'm sorry, Mr. Monroe. I didn't know."

"You were not expected to, Miss. Please! Have your coffee," he pleaded. "It would injure me if I should be the impetus for any discomfort. It is my personal protest, not yours. Besides, I was raised around the English. I prefer tea."

"I can't drink coffee," chimed Louisa. "Father forbids any strong drink around the house."

"Last call for coffee," bellowed Seabury from the galley below.

Tim came over for a cup and took one back for Amy, sitting on the foredeck.

"This tastes marvelous!" I declared. "I never had such tasty coffee."

"Ya have never been around the world, Lassie," remarked Seabury. He emerged holding a cup, took a sip, and smacked his lips. "Ahh! It's a special brew ... all the way from the other side of the globe."

"Where?" I asked.

"Ceylon?"

"Ceylon?" I echoed.

"An island near India," said Samuel. "Father loves his coffee. He is always experimenting with different varieties. When he was whaling, he would bring coffee home from all over the world. Now he has to depend on the other whaling captains to do so, for which he pays handsomely."

"Aye, but I need to ask ... is it not worth it?"

"Yes, it is," I confirmed.

Seabury Cory sat and whispered into my ear. "Makes little difference where the coffee is from, dear," he confessed. "As long as ya use a dash of Dutch cocoa and lots of brown sugar."

"Food and drink always taste better when you're out on the water," said Samuel.

"When will we arrive at Cuttyhunk?" inquired Louisa.

"If the wind holds up, about an hour," replied Seabury. "I dare say, at this speed we'll be there in less than that."

"Look, I can see some ships in the distance!" I said, pointing.

Samuel moved forward with the spyglass.

"What do ya see, son?" inquired Seabury.

"Looks like the *Nimrod!* And she's listing to port just north of Cuttyhunk, between Penikese and Gull Island."

"Gull Island!" sounded Seabury, taking the scope and bringing it up to his eye. "What in the world is it doing there? It's nothing but shoals." He braced himself against the rail and studied the scene through the tunneled glass. "There are two other ships along side, just off. Looks like the *Acushnet* and the *Morgan.* Who is captain on the *Nimrod*?"

"I suppose David Sanford is," replied Samuel. "From what I hear he took her out for a shakedown yesterday with a short crew and she blew onto the rocks. John Horan went out in the *Sea Fox* yesterday to drop off Hosea Sanford and appraise the situation."

"Gull Island!" I said. "I never heard of it."

"It's the tip of some shoals on the east side of Penikese Island overlooking Cuttyhunk Island," explained Samuel. "Just a big rock, really."

"Hosea Sanford is going to give that boy a thrashing when he gets him ashore," declared Seabury. "On the rocks, hmm! Maiden voyage, no less."

"Head up 120 degrees, Mr. Monroe" ordered Samuel. "We will approach her on the east side of the Island."

"Aye, aye, sir," confirmed Eli.

"*Nimrod* up on the rocks," I said. "Why, it's a new ship!"

"Ya said it, Lassie. Hosea Sanford will have that boy's hide," said Seabury.

"She looks hard on the bottom," reported Tim, as he came walking up the deck.

"How much line did we take aboard, Tim?"

"Eight hundred feet, Sam. Most of it inch and a half."

"Fine. We should have another eight hundred or more in the hold below. We'll need plenty of it if we are to help the *Nimrod* off the rocks."

"They just finished putting her together. I installed the master cabin door just this week."

"Your labors may have been for naught, Tim, if they don't get her off. For now I need you to go forward and make certain four hundred feet of line is true and ready to dispatch."

"Will do, Sam."

Tim set off for the bow as Amy came strolling up the deck. She paused, turned, and watched him go. "What's going on?" she asked.

"We're in for a wicked adventure," I said.

She shrugged and sighed. "Sometimes these trips can turn so boring."

"Tea ready in two minutes, ladies" cried Seabury.

"Oh, I'll have some!" begged Louisa.

"Here's your chance, Mr. Monroe," I said.

"By all means, a tin for me, Captain," he bellowed.

We continued our drive toward Cuttyhunk Island. At that very moment there was nowhere else in the world I wanted to be. I perched myself by my two girlfriends at the starboard rail, where we huddled in delightful shade behind the schooner's towering canvas. Amy lifted the rim of her floppy hat and covertly feasted on the image of the handsome Tim Cadman as he worked the foredeck. Barefoot, and with the legs of his trousers rolled up to his knees, Tim pulled his shirt up over his head and tossed it aside, exposing his Michelangelo sculptured torso. Standing on his toes, he reached up and pulled on some line. Buttery muscles heaved and undulated in the glistening morning sun. Flinging caution to fire,

Amy made no attempt to conceal her somewhat lecherous inquisitiveness. With a libelous raised eyebrow and flirtatious smile, she displayed proof beyond reproach that even the fairer sex can be shamefully entertained. Fortuitously, none of the men had noticed her wicked behavior, nor would I condemn her for it. By contrast, Louisa stood quietly and innocently, looking down into the water—her head resting on my shoulder. She was much too occupied looking for rocks to notice what Amy was enjoying. *Oh, Amy, you are so wicked*, I thought to myself. *Wicked but good.*

In the galley below, Captain Seabury Cory whistled a tune, while Samuel stood by the wheel with Eli; two maritime sentinels paying duty to a splendid day. Underneath us, the sea rushed, tickling the hull's planking, while the effervescent, rushing wake from the ship's bow caressed the stern and rudder in a foamy kite tale of turquoise splendor. Our eyes watered to the arid salty breeze. Like an imaginary swain, it kissed our lips and playfully tousled our hair as the schooner gently pitched and plunged, cutting through the rolling swell. The rocking motion made my eyelids heavy, leaving them to beg for slumber as it lobbied to steal this magical and intoxicating moment. With my two best friends in the world, a crew of capable, handsome gentlemen, and a magical, swooping lady called *Sphinx*, the journey improved by the minute.

Chapter 9:

The *Sphinx* fell onto a port tack as Eli spun the wheel and steered the ship in the direction of Penikese Island, a small spit of land slightly north of, and overlooking, Cuttyhunk Island.

"Has the tide begun to flow, Father?" inquired Samuel. He studied the shore through the spyglass, trying to gauge the ebb or flow by the level of water along the shore.

Seabury grimaced. "A good captain would not have left the dock without noting such a vital fact."

"I'd say it's approaching slack tide, Captain … starting to turn." informed Eli.

"Thank you for the input, Mr. Monroe," replied Samuel, in a somewhat articulated tone. He lowered his head and shook it. "Of course you are right, Father. I suppose I'm a little out of practice. In my excitement to leave the wharf I …"

"Out of practice!" he quickly scoffed. "Ya should have made an entry into the logbook before this vessel was ever moved. There are shoals all over this world just waiting for those who are … out of practice." Seabury tore the spyglass from his son's hand and moved down to the foredeck.

Eli looked over at Samuel, waiting for him to pitch his father a more definitive defense.

"There's no excuse, Mr. Monroe," admitted Samuel. "Its my fault. I was so busy I didn't take notice to the level of the water." He brought his fist down hard on the cabin roof. I walked over to him offering comfort and rested my hand on his arm. "Damn it, I should have made a departure entry in the log this morning. I swear the old fellow has salt running through his veins."

"More like jelled brine," I chuckled.

"Forty-five years at sea … I suppose I can't blame him for being so critical," Samuel said.

"His reprimand was not criticism, Samuel," I said. "It's nurturing."

"I'm not a child, Emily, who needs tending. Especially in front of the men."

"I don't think there's any need to worry. The men love you. They would think nothing of it. Besides it makes your father feel useful."

Samuel's dour expression soon softened. He bit his lip and shook his head. A trifling smile emerged. "Yes. You're right, I suppose. In our parent's eyes, we are forever in need of looking after. And if it makes him feel useful, I can take a little criticism."

"There, you see!"

"I expect I'm more upset with myself than anyone else."

"And you must manage that. To be upset with yourself ... you know what they say about a house divided."

"Thanks, Emily. I knew it was a great idea to have you along on this trip."

I thanked him and the issue was soon forgotten.

As the day unfolded, the late morning breeze freshened. The ship pounced the water, cutting through the bay swell and parting the waves with ease. At times the starboard deck became submerged as a churning deluge of rushing water fizzed up and over the deck. Louisa went below to seek refuge while Amy hung onto my arm in sporadic, fitful laughter as the flooding surge of seawater crept ever closer. Seabury Cory stood tall and sure-footed as the eighty-foot masts that grew out of the schooner's deck. He gave very little notice to the cascading water crashing at his feet. Holding the spyglass to one eye he studied the lump of land on the horizon.

"Get a reef into the main!" commanded Samuel. "Lower the Yankee and slacken the mainsheets! Spill some air! Let's get the rail out of the water!"

The main topsail was taken down along with the high-footed jib. The vessel sat up and took notice. We now sailed along at an amicable pace and the ride became more manageable. It was not long before the midday sun had dried the decks and our dampened clothing.

Louisa crawled out of the companionway wearing a new hat that she had rummaged from Amy's trunk—with Amy's blessing, of course. This time she wore a silk scarf over it, tied tightly under her chin.

As she sat beside me, Seabury came marching up the deck in his usual complaining form. "I was wondering when ya were going to shorten sail," he said.

"I was just trying to record her maximum speed in a fresh breeze," replied Samuel.

"Makes no difference," barked Seabury. "Once she's over on her ear, ya should know yar losing speed, not gaining. That's the time to shorten sail. That's how ya keep her moving in a blow. Otherwise, all the energy used to drive the ship forward is spent laying her over on her side."

In truth no one knew this better than Samuel. He had been sailing small boats all his life. "I'll make a note of that, Father."

"Bagh, greenhorns!"

Samuel shook his head and geared the conversation another way. "Can you make out the ships on the horizon, Father?"

"Four whalers," said Seabury, peering through the monocular. "The *Acushnet*, and I think the *Morgan*. Can't make out the other two. Lots of longboats in the water, though."

"The wind has died down," announced Louisa, happy to be back up on deck.

"It only seems that way. We took down sail," said Samuel.

"*Nimrod* to starboard!" yelled Tim from the bow.

We all hurried forward for a better look.

"Where, where?" cried Louisa.

"The small Island to the left," I said.

"Will you set your eyes on that!" marveled Samuel.

We were all lined up along the starboard rail gazing in the direction of tiny Penikese Island. Seabury chewed the end of his pipe in casual contemplation, a demeanor that said, *I've seen it all before.* I must admit. Cory senior looked quite distinguished. I had never met a ship's captain who did not nurse his pipe. Though a pipe seemed to suit Seabury, I was happy Samuel did not contract the fetid custom—smelly, smoky things. Oddly enough, I did not mind the scent on Seabury when he smoked. Strange the allowances the human heart will permit for those we love.

"She's on the rocks," came the cry from a watchman halfway up the mast.

"I see her," hollered Samuel. "Down with the aft main—remove the staysail. We will drift in close and survey the situation."

"Where is Gull Island?" I asked. "I only see Penikese and the stranded ship."

"It's difficult to see from here," said Samuel. "It's just a rock, really, but imposing and dangerous enough to command a name."

"Looks like she's in the center of it all," reported Seabury.

"Between Gull and Penikese," confirmed Samuel.

"And there's where she be moored ... the *Charles Morgan*," announced Seabury, pointing with the mouthpiece of his pipe.

The three-masted black ship sat motionless. Its crew of thirty men lined up along the rail. They watched our approach with enchanted interest.

"Now that's what a whaler should look like," he declared.

The closer we got to activities in the harbor the longer it seemed to get there. Since shorting sail, the *Sphinx* crawled along at a little over two knots. I leaned on the rail along the gunwale looking out to sea. Samuel and Eli were standing just the other side of me, while Tim was still keeping watch off the bow. Seabury paced the deck. I had to ask myself. Who was steering the ship?

Looking aft, I was completely amazed to discover Amy at the helm, appearing quite capable. With feet wide apart and arms outstretched, she clutched the massive wheel with a bold embrace, communicating a staunched constitution. Her cheeks were made rosy by the open sea air, lips were parted with teeth pinching a jutting tongue, and her long silky hair danced on her shoulders. Her white ruffled dress ballooned and swooned in the midday breeze. The stylish garment contained tiny sewn-in pearls along its lacework, which twinkled in the glimmering sunlight. She almost looked comical, with the wind-blown brim of her floppy straw hat slapping at her face—nose in the air, and wearing a determined squinch. It was a sight to be witnessed.

"Amy's steering the ship!" I cried.

Eli nudged Samuel on the elbow and pointed toward the helm. A smile broke out on both their faces.

"She's doing very well steering," declared Samuel.

"She does no such thing, Captain," replied Eli. "I have tied the wheel down. The ship steers itself."

They laughed.

We quickly approached the small flotilla of whaling vessels.

"Look! There! The bark *Sacramento* and the *Governor Carver.* They're preparing to assist," declared Seabury. "I'd be surprised if Captain Hamilton of the *Morgan* lends a hand. He is not the sort of man to suffer dogs or fools."

"I dare say, David Sanford may have tried to sail between Gull Rock and Penikese Island. If so, it may be my fault," confessed Samuel.

"Yar fault? How do ya figure it?"

"I made a wager with David long ago that I would sail a vessel through Gull Channel before he ever did."

"Are ya serious, boy?"

"We often talked about who would be the first to take a large vessel up through that narrow channel between Penikese and Gull. You know David. He always wanted to be the first at everything."

"Only a nitwit would attempt such a maneuver, especially with a newly commissioned ship," declared Seabury.

"I've been through it," said Samuel.

"Through what?"

"Through Gull Channel."

"When?"

"Abe, the captain of the old whaler *Hero*. He took David and me through on his family sloop. The vessel was only thirty feet long, but it had a very deep draft. We never hit bottom. Then he came about and sailed through it a second time. He said the secret of sailing through Gull Channel is to study your bearings at low tide when all the rocks are exposed, and sail across at low water."

"That's what he said, did he?" sneered Seabury.

"Simple, really. Just a matter of knowing where you are."

"That simple ya think, heh?"

"Sure! There is plenty of deep water in Gull Channel. You just have to know where it is and weave your way around the dangers to find it."

"Ya do, do ya?"

"I told David that I would christen the *Sphinx* by taking her through Gull Channel first chance I got. He must have tried to beat me to it."

Seabury stared out to sea puffing his pipe and shaking his head.

"Come now, Father," said Samuel, draping his arm over the old sailor's shoulder. "I had no plans of taking this gracious lady through Gull Channel. I love this schooner too dearly to place her in harm's way. Not even to spite David Sanford."

"Well, son, it is apparent that young Sanford is a worm in need of a hook and ya hooked him good, if in fact what ya say is true."

"I never meant to bait the man, Father."

"No, ya did not. A fool's actions are his own. Now, let's get the anchor down and the longboat in the water. The girls will want to disembark and explore Cuttyhunk."

The *Sphinx* drifted slowly as all sail was taken down. Samuel gave the order to drop anchor and to place the sixteen-foot whaleboat over the side. Amy, Louisa, and I sat on the aft deck sipping the sun and taking in the activities in the harbor. The whalers *Sacramento* and *Governor Carver* had tied lines to the *Nimrod's* stern and were trying to pull her off the reef. After nearly two hours of work, the stranded whaler had not moved an inch. Samuel and crew made preparations to lend a hand while the girls and I made certain to stay out of the way. On the *Nimrod*, there was shouting. David Sanford followed his father along the deck as the older man screamed at him. Poor David.

We lay anchored along with the whalers *Charles Morgan* and *Acushnet,* as the bark *Sacramento* and the *Governor Carver* worked with effort to pull *Nimrod* off the rocks. A line from each ship led back to the stern of the stranded vessel. The whalers stood motionless, sails in full bloom, pulling—tugging. At times the cumbersome whale ships swung to and fro, heaving and hauling—their lines, iron rods just feet above the water. The grounded *Nimrod* listed violently, rocking from side to side. The copper-clad keel, torn and crated, glistened in the turbulent swell. No matter how hard and how long the whale ships toiled, the *Nimrod* would not budge. Off our bow, the clunking rattle of chain over timber resonated as the *Charles Morgan* pulled up anchor, unfurled sail, and prepared to leave.

"She be going!" cried Seabury.

"Are they not going to stay and help?" I asked.

"There's not much they can do," said Samuel. "In any event, the *Morgan* was on its way to the Pacific. They'll be gone two years or more. I'm certain they are eager to be on their way."

"If they could help they would," said Seabury. "No captain will compromise his vessel or valuable time for a buffoon."

"You know, Father, we don't know for certain whether David tried to cut between Gull and Penikese or if he was just blown there in yesterday's squall."

"Bagh! Either way, the boy is reckless."

Tim stacked coils of line on deck and made them ready in case our help was needed. Once done, he came over and stood by Eli and me and examined the scene.

"When I think about the time that went into building that vessel," said Tim. "What if it should be lost?"

"Would be a shame," bewailed Eli.

"Hosea Sanford has set all his bridges ablaze," declared Seabury. "Many of the whalers want nothing to do with him. Those clothing mills he owns in Fall River—he's purchased tons of baleen and oil for his factories, unfairly chiseled down the price, and is always late to pay."

"He has resorted to doing business up in the North Shore ... Gloucester area," said Samuel, "where they don't know him as well."

"Until they discover what he's like," said Seabury. "Believe me, I know how everyone feels. Many whalers are struggling. Whales are vanishing and whale oil has almost doubled in price in less than a year."

"Yes, I noticed that the price of whale oil has been very dear, as of late," I added.

"Bagh! I never thought I would see the day. We are killing off the whale," growled Seabury. "Soon there will not be any. It is getting to be that a man cannot make a living working the oceans any longer."

"Whaling captains in Westport complain that there are very little sperm and right whales to speak of along the east coast," added Samuel.

"Ship's owners will go broke unless they move to the more fertile arctic grounds," said Seabury. "Many are heading for the Pacific, well above the South Sandwich Isles."

"Then there's the war in the South to complicate things," said Samuel. "Afraid the price of oil will only go up."

"Longboat off the port bow!" alerted Tim.

The *Acushnet's* whaleboat with four men approached. Samuel and his father were there to greet them.

"Seabury, you old harpooner. How's retirement treating you?" yelled one of the men in the small vessel. It was the working vessel from the whaler *Acushnet*.

"Saul, ya lobster devil!" blustered Seabury.

The whaleboat slammed into the hull of the schooner as one of its crew reached up for the gunwale and tied a frayed line to the rail.

"Eh, careful with the topside," grumbled Seabury. "Yar suckling up to a lady, ya know."

"And a fine vessel she be," replied the sailor.

"What's the story with Sanford's vessel?" asked Seabury.

"We tried getting her off earlier this morning. Wind wasn't strong enough or we would have her off by now. It's up to the *Carver* and *Sacramento*, now. We've had it."

Though of pure Anglo-Saxon heritage, Saul's sun-tanned skin was darker than Eli's. He was a gruff fellow, with part of one ear maimed and fingers missing on both hands. He wore a red bandanna tightly around his neck. Upon close inspection one could make out a crimson, jagged scar just beneath the tainted cloth where a rope, unintentionally or otherwise, wrapped around his neck and grated the skin. Even with all his infirmities, Saul seemed a jolly sort.

"Her keel is nipped to the rock," he said. "If she is not taken off today, who knows what sort of weather will greet it tomorrow."

"Only the good Lord can tell that, I'm afraid," replied Seabury.

"She's been taking a pounding sitting on that rock," said Saul. "I can tell you that."

"Is she holed?" asked Samuel.

"No. Old man Sanford had her built well. But it's only a matter of time."

"Her copper is torn to bits," said one of Saul's companions. The man was much older than Saul but just as untidy looking, with one glassy eye, leathery complexion, and teeth the color of sea moss. He had a tricorn hat, worn low over mad, bristly eyebrows. He spoke with a chafed voice that sounded like a rasping file over hard oak. "We've moved her a bit. She could come off at any time."

"Who's to know?" bemoaned Saul. "A sad state of affairs."

"Aye! Have ya tried tying to her sprit and concentrate yaur effort on twisting her off the bottom?" asked Seabury.

"Sanford's afraid the spar will snap away," said the man with the chafed voice. "Old man Sanford likes giving orders. You know how he is. We're just about done with the old coot."

"We'll be leaving right after we're done here," added Saul.

"You should lay her on her side then use the sprit as a fulcrum to spin her off," suggested Samuel.

"Lay her on her side?" scoffed Saul.

The men in the long boat all laughed.

"And how do you propose we do that, lad?" asked the man with the three-sided hat.

"Have one ship tie a line to her masthead and pull her over and another ship with a line to her snout." explained Samuel.

"Boy's right," said Seabury. "One cable to the top of the mast and another to her sprit may just do the trick. And with two whaling vessels doing the job should make it a piece of cake."

"You would need the correct angle for that. The only way to get it is to sail on her other side, through Gull Channel," declared Saul's companion. "And what sort of mad man would try that?"

"I would!" shouted Samuel—a battle cry of conviction in his voice.

"What! With this Carolina wineglass?" sneered Saul, his words frolicking off his tongue.

The four men on the longboat laughed. Furious, Samuel lunged forward. Seabury took his son by the arm.

"She'll do better than those arctic tubs you have floundering out there!" roared Samuel.

The men laughed some more.

"Think it's funny?" he growled, pecking his cane toward them. "Is that what you think?"

"Calm boy, calm," urged Seabury.

"Your boy's got spunk, Seabury," said Saul. "I like that."

"What would they know, Father, about fulcrums and levers ... physics for that matter? They're just whalers."

"No need to hurl insults boy!" grunted Saul's companion.

"They know more than ya think, son," said Seabury, "more than ya think." Samuel stormed off.

"Emily, get the girls together," he instructed. "I'll have one of the men place you on Cuttyhunk. We have work to do."

I had never witnessed Samuel so angry. His request sounded more like a command and one we were prepared to heed.

The men on the longboat talked and laughed. Samuel stormed over.

"You want the *Nimrod* off that rock?" he shouted. "If the *Sacramento* and *Carver* can't get the job done, the *Sphinx* will."

Abruptly, the laughing stopped. The glassy eyed man looked up. "Seriously lad, with this lacquered lady? It just doesn't have the tonnage to complete such a task."

"She doesn't need tonnage. She has speed," said Samuel. "And just like a six-ounce musket ball can knock a two-hundred-pound man off his feet, so can this vessel move a ship twice its weight."

"It's not the rate of the blow but the weight of the fist," said the man with the unsightly teeth. "Takes a strong heavy vessel, boy."

Seabury Cory listened quietly while he nursed his pipe. The dried leaf glowed and smoldered in the pipe's throat as he slurped from the embers within. A cloud of blue smoke hovered and swiftly dissipated as it was carried away in the fresh bay breeze.

"Boy may be right," said Seabury, looking out to sea and ignoring the men in the whaleboat, "a swift running start and one good tug may make all the difference."

"Retirement's waterlogged your brain, you old seagoat," sneered Saul.

Laughter broke out amongst the whalers.

"Maybe so," replied Seabury, "maybe so, but for now ya best cast off boys. We have work to do."

The longboat pulled away, its oars waving over the side like muddled seagull wings over a lumpy sea. With time, they found their rhythm and flapped away over the rolling swell and back to the mother ship. Not long after, the whaler *Acushnet* set sail and moved in the direction of the mainland.

"Arrogant fools," tweeted Samuel.

"Ya take them too serious, son. They're not a bad sort once ya get to know them."

"The *Acushnet* is leaving," announced Tim. "Think they've lost the stomach for it?"

"That's their problem," said Samuel. "They use their stomachs when they should have used their brains."

Amy, Louisa, and I collected a blanket and picnic basket and made ready for our visit to the Island. We would lounge on the beach or pick berries while the crew made plans in case they were needed to help the stranded ship.

"Doesn't look like the *Sacramento* and *Carver* have made much headway," reported Seabury. "They're severing the tow lines. They would need a gale to pull her off that rock. It may very well be up to us, son."

"They are too heavy, Father," said Samuel. "A whaler's canvas has all it can do to move its own weight, let alone tow another. What they need is a flying start. They don't seem to understand that."

Father and son leaned over the railing, watching in silence as the *Sacramento* and *Carver* sailed away. Seabury chewed on the bit of his pipe. It had gone out. He taped the bowl on the railing, emptying the chamber of charred tobacco.

"Ya know, son, Saul is right. The only way to free her is to cross in front of her, pull her forward and twist her off."

"You're right, Father. If she could be pulled forward and twisted a little it could be enough to free her."

Seabury stared out toward the stranded whaler in muted contemplation. He ran the mouthpiece of his unlit pipe along his lip as he appraised the situation. "Think ya can take'a through, boy?" he blurted.

"Not sure."

"It must be done now while the tide is up."

Samuel hesitated, not quite certain in what way his father was asking. Perhaps he was testing his good judgment, in an attempt to bait him into revealing that indeed he was a captain who aired on the side of recklessness—just another David Sanford ready to sacrifice a worthy vessel. Or perhaps he was scrutinizing his courage, to discover what he was made of, whether he lived up to the esteemed title of captain. Knowing his father well, Samuel knew it was just a simple inquiry. "Tide's just about high, Father. Rocks used as markers are completely covered."

"That's not an answer, son."

Samuel reflected some more on his father's words. He stared out toward the prostrated *Nimrod,* then off at the two whale ships as they sailed away.

Seabury patiently waited for his son's retort. He dug in his pocket and pulled out a worn leather pouch filled with tobacco. Carefully, he packed his pipe, stuffed the purse back in his jacket, and struck a match. The flickering flame leaped over the tiny polished furnace and newborn smoke swirled by his bristly eyebrows. His face tightened to reveal a momentary grimaced smile, one of fulfillment, as the pipe maintained its fiery slag.

He studied developments in the distance and the marooned whaler, which slammed from side to side in the churning surf. On the horizon at the western end of Penikese Island, the cloddish giants *Sacramento* and *Carver* sailed off in a fresh blow, vanishing behind the island's low hilly landscape. It was now left up to the *Sphinx* to ferry the crew of the *Nimrod* home, or try and free her.

"The whalers are all but gone," declared Samuel.

"We are the *Nimrod's* only hope now, son."

Samuel paused, stared at his father, then out to the stranded ship. He had bragged that he would pull the marooned whaler off the rocks. He had a new dilemma now—saving face. "I'm willing, Father."

Seabury smiled as he leaned over the gunwale sucking his pipe. He toked and puffed as annular plumes of smoke clouded his face. Finally, he looked over to his son and lovingly rested his hand on his shoulder.

"Heaven and Hades are full of those who were once willing ... the exulted and the dammed. Once ya decided on a course of action, advocate on the side of discreetness ... keep ya failures deep in your heart, and yar accomplishments deeper. Then go on with life. Measure it not by endeavor, but by a job well done. In the end, whatever ya do, the choice is yars and yars alone to make ... to bury or bear."

Samuel nodded.

"Come, my boy!" persuaded Seabury. "We have work to do."

The preparations took all of an hour. Seabury and another crew member rowed to the *Nimrod* with instructions of how they would attempt to free them. Though Hosea Sanford objected to the methods, he was left with little choice, since all the other ships had given up and sailed away.

"Is all in place?" asked Seabury, as he climbed out of the longboat onto *Sphinx's* deck.

"As you instructed, Father."

"My job is to free the whaler. Yars boy is to steer us through Gull Channel. Now, I can do my job, can ya do yars?"

"I can!"

"Ya ready, then?"

"Let's get to it!"

"Now listen up," shouted Seabury to the crew. "We are going to sail through Gull Channel and free that ship. I need everyone alert and able. There is no room for error. Make a mistake and our vessel may end up on the bottom. I will be in command. Anyone without the courage or fear to the task at hand may leave on the longboat and wait on shore ... with the women."

"With the women? That may not be a bad thing," said Tim.

A whoop of laughter was had by the crew.

Samuel stepped forward. "We've been called to assist a fellow seaman. What say you, gentlemen!"

The men silently looked at one another.

Eli Monroe stepped forward. "I'm with you, Captain!"

"You can count on me!" said another.

Instantaneous cheers broke out as the crew swore their consummate support.

"Then let us show them what the *Sphinx* can do, shall we, gentlemen!" declared Seabury, in gruff acknowledgment.

The ebullient crew set off to their stations, trimming lines and making the ship ready for its perilous mission. Samuel stood amidship studying the prostrated *Nimrod*. Fear of failure and doubt seized him by the throat, while the acrid tang of uncertainty smoldered at the back of his tongue. He thought about that fateful night when he had eluded Confederate conformists and sailed the *Sphinx* down the dark Patapsco River and out into the placid Chesapeake—of his friend Luther Ladd, whose life was unjustly taken during the riot in Baltimore—and of the first time he heard news of impending war and how he was not to be a part of it. A tear of anguish glazed his eye. He bit his lip. It was not that he wished war or had the desire to fight, let alone the stomach—it was the betrayal he felt. Perhaps it was misplaced betrayal, an argument lacking logic and without good reason or legitimacy, but as he saw it, betrayal no less. He just didn't understand it all. He had to ask why he was any different a man before and after he was hurt. There were many positions he could have held in military life, even with a bad leg. Ultimately, it was just not in his nature to understand such matters, or maybe it had to do with the fact that he came from a small New England town, and all the conflict and aggression he had encountered was in a contrasting world far, far away. Even so, he had to ask himself. Was this country not speckled with small towns—towns just like his—or had Westport made him different somehow?

The sea was the best place to face your demons when they prodded at your soul. No one knew that more than Seabury Cory. He had been well aware that his son was haunted by what he witnessed while away on military service, and he knew that an adventure such as this one was what was needed to quell the storms. Success was vital, and Seabury was prepared to do everything in his power to make the rescue of the whaler a victorious undertaking for his son.

He placed his hand lovingly on Samuel's shoulder, sensing his uneasiness, then discreetly walked away. Samuel was left with the task of skirmishing with his monsters, while summoning the courage he needed to face dismay and inner fear. No one could do it for him. It was up to the task at hand to derail and banish any distress or foreboding that ate away at him.

Chapter 10:

Admon jumped into the surf and pulled the open boat up on shore. With the bow up onto the sandy beach, I did my best to get out of the boat without suffering wet feet. Walking around in sopping shoes and socks would be like having morning tea with sour milk and a ruptured infuser—pretty much ruin the day. I had worn high-laced boots and didn't want to remove them. It would take me the greater part of the day to lace the leather footwear up again. The smart one amongst us was Louisa. She just slipped off her simple clogs and jumped into the calf-deep water. Besides, who needs shoes along a sandy beach?

"Take your boots off, Emmie," she cried. "Let the soupy sand ooze through your toes."

"I don't know about that."

"Oh, come now. It feels wondrous."

"I should have removed these things when I was on the ship," I said, hurrying to unfasten them. It didn't take as long as I thought, and before I knew it my boots were off. I would store them away for the remainder of the trip. Though I could not help the queer feeling that being barefoot was not considered very lady-like. "Here I come," I announced, clutching the hem of my dress up around my knees. I plunged one foot into the water. Louisa was right. It felt wonderful. Once in the surf, I lingered along the shore, letting the wavelets fondle my toes. My feet were gulped by the boggy sand as the tidewater advanced and receded. I felt like a little girl.

Louisa and I waited by the edge of the shore for Amy to disembark. Patiently, Admon held the bow of the boat steady as the stern lifted up and down with the placid breakers. Amy remained seated, her nose high in the air, and with an expression that cried out, "Waiting!" There was no way she would chance getting her silk dress slippers wet—or would she ever remove them. With an outrageously embellished outfit, she looked like the Queen of the Nile sitting there.

She extended one limp limb, as if begging to have her fingers kissed, and blithely summoned the boatman. I cupped my hand to my mouth and giggled in expected amazement. Admon patiently held the boat in place and ignored her.

Louisa wiped the clinging sand from her feet. "Come on, Amy! We haven't all day," she hollered.

"Not until someone comes over to assist me," replied Amy, audaciously.

"Why she wore those shoes I'll never know," I marveled. "She will ruin them walking along this beach."

"Will no one come and help me?" she beseeched.

Finally, Admon waded through knee-deep water to where she was sitting. Reaching over, he scooped her up, and cradled her ashore. With her arms loosely around the brawny sailor, Amy cast us a smug smile, making certain we knew she was privileged. It was wicked.

Admon deposited her gently on the ground. He removed his cap, and with a sweeping hand, bowed, offering her a willing if not saucy smile.

"Thank you, Mister, ah ... What is your name?"

"Admon, ma-lady," he replied, looking over at me and affably rolling his eyes.

I giggled.

"Yes, of course," she said, ignoring him and beating at her dress as if she just exited a dusty cellar. "That will be all, Mr. Admon," she said.

The good-natured sailor shook his head and pushed the longboat out into the bay.

We had brought a hamper with us filled with fruit, bread, and cheese. I also made sure to bring along a bottle of Grandmamma's grape punch. It was a wonderful day and a picnic was in order. I spread the blanket out on a sand dune beneath a shady tree. Amy quickly staked a corner, sprung open her parasol, and made herself comfortable. She sat there staring out to sea and looking somewhat weary and bored.

"I'm going rock hunting," declared Louisa. "Anyone want to come?"

"I'm tired, Lulu," lamented Amy. "It's been an exhausting trip. Think I'll sit a while," never alluding to the fact that all we did on the entire trip was rest.

Louisa and I walked along the shore, exploring and watching the rescue of the *Nimrod* in the distance. Admon rowed back to the ship. Louisa and I waved. He waved back. We could not ask for better weather. I gathered a couple of wild daisies that grew between some beach stones. Louisa picked up a rock, examined it, and tossed it into the surf. Walking with a friend along the shore is one of the most fulfilling activities two people can share.

It knits souls into an alliance of unity and appreciation for nature and one another. And though I reflect no disparity on this intimate time Louisa and I are sharing, I must confess, I wish she were Samuel instead.

Back on the ship, preparations were made to rescue the stranded whaler. The outline was actually an ingenious one and the hallmark of a seasoned ship's captain. Of course, Seabury would claim that it was "straightforward and elementary." I suppose the details are somewhat technical. I will endeavor to explain.

A long rope was tied at the top of the *Nimrod's* mast. I call them ropes or lines. A proper sailor would call them cables. Another rope, this one fifty feet longer than the first, was tied to the whaler's massive bowsprit. Knotted eyelets were fastened to the bitter end of the two lines. These were loops with fancy knots in them. The two coils of rope were taken overboard and handed to a man in the longboat docked to the side of the mother ship.

On the *Sphinx*, a similar operation was orchestrated. One long, stout line was fastened to the schooner's hefty Samson post at the bow and led aft through a fairlead in the stern and coiled on the deck, where it sat ready for deployment. It, in turn, would be tethered to the two on the *Nimrod's* longboat to become as one very long towline. The ship was now primed and ready for duty.

The *Sphinx* hauled anchor and set sail. Orders were given to take her southwest, around Penikese and to approach the stranded whaler from the northeast. The plan was to move the ship away from the blanketing effects of the Island's hill and give it enough room to build momentum and gain speed. When the ship was in line with the required course, the orders were given to drive down onto Gull Channel.

The crew migrated toward Seabury as he gave instructions to how they would attempt to drag the *Nimrod* off the rocks. Samuel and Tim listened keenly as Eli piloted the vessel under full sail. Samuel sat on the deckhouse behind his father, happy to allow the elderly sailor to take command.

"Gather here, men!" barked Seabury. "Listen up. We get only one chance to make this work. You there, what's yar name?"

"Tabeu Washington, Captain," replied the slim lanky dark-skinned man.

"Very well, Mr. Washington. On my orders, I want ya to take the end of the cable and walk it along the deck outside all the rigging and over to Mr. Cadman who will be standing by the rail. Ya must be quick. Think ya can do that?"

"Aye, aye, Captain."

"And you, sailor. What is yar name?"

"Admon, Captain," replied the big man. "They call me Razor."

Admon was a monstrous burly fellow, well over six feet. His most prized possession was a six-inch straight razor that he used to shave his head, for which endowed him with the pet epithet, Razor. He wore a slipover shirt that appeared much too small for him, with crinkled sleeves rolled high above large hummocky shoulders. He had arms the width of a common man's leg with cannonball biceps and steely forearms. He displayed a broad friendly smile that exposed a mouth full of snowy, picket-fence teeth. His eyes were two large cocoa truffles and his head clean-shaven and glimmering as a ripe, oversized eggplant. Though his impressive image could appear intimidating, his menacing size was curtailed by a humble smile and the perpetual twinkle in his eyes.

"Well, sailor, we use proper surnames on this vessel. What is yar father's given name?"

The gentle giant lowered his head shamefully. With his back to the midmorning light, his large gauche frame blotted out the sun, casting a shadow over Seabury. "I haven't one, Captain. Just Admon. I never knew my mother and father." When he spoke, he revealed an unexpected, sonorous tone, which rumbled off puffy lips like the distant sound of whispering thunder.

"Not to worry, Mr. Admon. We'll find a proper surname for ya later. For now, ya job will be as line keeper. After we tie our cable to those on the *Nimrod,* ya will stand by the aft fairlead as the line pays out ready with axe in hand. If it should tangle or jam at the hawsepipe, ya will sort it out by giving it several rapid blows with the blunt end of the axe until the cable runs free again. Do ya understand, son?"

"I think I do, Captain."

"I do the thinking, sailor! Ya just get the job done. Understood?"

The gentle giant stood up straight and saluted.

"Aye, aye, Captain."

"Mr. Cadman, you are the latchkey."

"Latchkey, Captain?"

"The nucleus to our little operation. Tying the cables from both vessels together as one. Are ya primed for it, lad?"

"Yes. How do you want it done, Captain?"

"Listen carefully. Ya will take yar place by the main shrouds on the port side as we sail on through Gull Channel. We shall slide along the whaler's starboard beam ... by the longboat tied alongside her. A man in the longboat will hand ya two cables with eyes tied to the end. You will take the whale gaff, hook and retrieve the two cables, and pull them up on deck. Do I make myself clear?"

"Yes, Captain," replied Tim.

"Remember! We will be moving as speed. You must be quick before the lines run out and go taut."

"Got it!"

"No fancy knot work, lad … just simple overhand knots, tight and sure. It has to be quick. Once ya have the cables tied ya will fling the entire bundle overboard, well away from the rail. Is that clear?"

"Yes, sir!"

"Fine. Once done, all that is needed is to hold course, hold fast, and hold yar breath."

"What do I do if I should drop one of the lines overboard, Captain?" inquired Tim.

"Ya will do no such thing!" growled Seabury. "We get one opportunity, here! It will be a miracle if we do not hit bottom and sink this vessel."

"I'll do my best, Captain."

The wind whisked by the yacht's lacework of ropes and riggings leaving them to quiver and shriek like a screaming choir of angry bees. With every stitch of canvas in service, the schooner bore down on the stranded whaler with astonishing speed.

Along this modest New England coastline of small sailing craft and lumbering whalers, a vessel with a refined pedigree such as *Sphinx*, one made not for cargo, passenger, or fishing, but for pleasure, agility, and speed, was a rare animal. And, with its acre of sails hanging aloft, it was a spectacle of wonder to behold.

Louisa and I sat on the blanket and watched from shore as the *Sphinx* made its approach. *Nimrod's* sails fluctuated violently while the prostrated ship was tossed to-and-fro, like a wilted reed in a rude tempest. No ship could stand such a battering and remain together for very long.

It was almost high tide and for Samuel not a very advantageous time to attempt passage through Gull channel. All the rocks he needed as markers to help navigate through the slotted corridor were submerged, hidden below betraying waters. He would need to maneuver the ship intuitively. Odds were against him.

In any event, the wind was blowing in the ship's favor, which for Samuel was one less worry. The two enormously long main booms hung outside the rails—one to port the other to starboard, or as it was known, wing on wing, and left to the thrust of a following wind. To some on the grounded whaler the schooner must have appeared as an approaching angel, with colossal, canvassed wings spread broadly, ready to sweep them into deliverance. To Hosea Sanford, who scurried along the whaler's deck like a muddled and confused sand plover, the attempt by the advancing schooner was nothing short of a reckless undertaking, by a vessel of deranged madmen. The way Sanford looked at it, it left him with little choice. To be saved by a lunatic or destroyed by a deviled sea.

The *Sphinx* was well into the channel. Eli voiced concern, as the schooner got closer to the helpless vessel. He was afraid that the *Sphinx's* bellowing sails would tangle in the *Nimrod's* rigging as they sailed by it. While Samuel was at the wheel, in truth, it was Captain Seabury Cory who would ultimately guide the ship through the narrow and alarming passage.

"No time for unfavorable concern, Mr. Monroe," exhorted Seabury.

"Rock! Five feet off starboard," shouted Tabeu. The man stood on the bowsprit looking out for submerged danger. The vigilant bowman pointed down at the turquoise water with uneasy anxiety, as moss-covered boulders materialized just below the shallow, hyaline surface, like craggy demons reaching up from a watery grave. "Rock, Captain! Twenty feet off the port bow," alerted an overwrought Tabeu.

"Let me know when ya come upon the Nuns, Mr. Washington," shouted Seabury. "It will be three white boulders in an orderly fashion, just to port."

"Aye, aye, Captain," replied Tabeu.

"We are getting closer, Father," said Samuel. "We should take in the main over the port rail."

"In with the port boom, lest it smashes into the whaler's rigging!" ordered Seabury.

"We are traveling fast," wailed Samuel with a nervous grin. "Gull Reef will be at our bow before we even see it."

"The Three Nuns, Captain ... twenty feet off the port bow," yelled the bowman.

"Stand ready with that gaff, Mr. Cadman!" shouted the old captain. He walked to the rail, calmly emptied his smoking pipe over the gunwale, and shoved it into his pocket. Surveying the channel, he peered down into the water and up at Penikese Island and back down into the water, attempting to get a bearing.

"The Nuns, Captain ... passing on the port side," trumpeted Tabeu.

"Carry on, sailor," shouted Seabury. He looked down at the three granite stones and verified his location. "Make ready, Mr. Cadman. We can't get too close to her. You'll need to reach well overboard for those cables."

Tim gave an affirmative salute. Samuel appeared uneasy, stretching his body over the rail, and sorting out his bearings. The old captain knew just where they were.

"Keep her on course, helmsman!" warned Seabury. "Mr. Admon! Take your station at the rear of the ship."

The big man lumbered over the coil of line with the axe in his hand. "Ready, Captain."

"Blunt end of the axe, Mr. Admon, the blunt end!" shouted Seabury, reminding the sailor of his duty.

Everyone was ready and prepared, each man to his post. Like a confident impala running from a charging lion, the schooner sprinted along. Instead of running from the lion, the *Sphinx* ran toward it.

Ever since Samuel could remember, Gull Channel was a right of passage for apprentice seafarers. Many were bright and capable, while others were carefree and foolish. A small number of these seadogs would go on to become capable and successful commanders of their own vessels, even though they had attempted and failed to make passage through the jeopardous channel. These forbidden waters had become a proving ground for new seamen, teaching them prudence and wisdom—but not in the way one would expect. A green captain could demonstrate his abilities by safely transiting this narrow passageway—notably, displaying a hunger for enterprise and fortitude. More importantly, he could illustrate wisdom and prudence by simply not attempting the passage in the first place. On the other hand, if he tried and failed, he would need to accept failure as a measure of wisdom made naked and learn from it—having the foresight to deal with and secure an understanding of his somewhat foolish actions. After all, we should learn from our blunders and carry them in the purse of maturity for future reference. A good captain must realize that failure within the context of foolishness is but a defeat in perception and not one of competence. After all, how else does one get ahead or gain experience if he or she does not consort with contingency or challenge regulation and criteria, while nipping off a pinch of daring and defiance?

Seabury Cory was no exception. Danger had become a sixth sense for him. This was not the first time he had been through parlous Gull Channel. As a young sailor, he had successfully transited it more than once—an admission he would never let shine on his son. Though it had been over thirty years since he had practiced foolish seamanship, he was about to do it again.

The old captain made note of a cucumber-shaped boulder along the shore of Penikese Island, waiting for it to fall in line with an old oak tree on a hill just behind it. As it did he gave his command. "Twenty degrees to starboard, helmsman, and hurry!"

"No, Father. I'm nearly certain I am on the right course," declared Samuel.

"Do it, now, boy. Now!" demanded Seabury.

Samuel ignored his father's command. Instead, he tried to reason with him. "Father, I think …"

Seabury scrambled over to the wheel, pushed his son aside, and quickly turned the schooner hard to starboard. Suddenly there was a harsh grating and grinding followed by a jarring crash. The vessel quivered and quaked. At the bow, Tabeu was flung onto the sprit and nearly tossed off the ship. Dazed and clinging on for dear life, he reached for the port whisker stay and pulled himself back up onto the heavy timbered spar. Had he fallen in the water, he would have been drawn under the ship and crushed between the ledge and the ship's keel.

As it scraped the bottom the schooner surged and faulted. Masts flexed and palpitated, and the rigging thrashed about like nautical bullwhips. Halyards tore free, ripping their cleats from the deck.

"Sailor! Tie off that loose halyard," shouted Seabury calmly, in the face of danger. "Get that flogging jib trimmed and back up its stay before it shakes itself to hell."

The vessel kept moving as the crewmen scurried to secure the loose rigging. The noise made by the keel's copper sheathing being wrenched off on the granite ledge made a ghastly and petrifying sound. Suddenly the ship dipped. Its stern rose high out of the water as it rode over the massive ledge losing all blistering impetus.

"We hit, we hit!" came a fearsome yell from one of the crew.

"Mr. Monroe, get below and inspect the bilges," hollered Samuel.

Eli rushed below to inspect the bowels of the ship for incoming water. Admon dropped the axe and rushed to look over the rail for damage. Samuel hurried to his side. With terror, the gentle giant pointed down at the shimmering granite cliff just below the shallow water. His eyes were the size of twenty-dollar coins and his mouth had succumbed to a permanent yawn. Both men gazed in horror at the ominous, stony shoal.

Though the *Sphinx* had lost most of its speed, and its stern hung high above the surface of the water, it kept moving forward. The submerged cliff migrated by like the stony vertebra of an enormous blue whale. The wheel in Seabury's hand shuddered and danced as he wrestled to hold it in place. A terrible baritone groan wailed and the ship cried out, as the submerged ledge clawed at its belly. Abraded planking splintered, sounding like breaking fingernails across a cultured-slate blackboard. Suddenly the stern of the ship slid back down into the sea and as quick as the assault on the ship was made, it was over. Where once there was a bottom carpeted in stone, there was only smooth, khaki sand. Seabury Cory had done his best to carefully and judiciously pilot the ship away from Gull Channel's crystalline, igneous ledge.

Samuel looked over at his father with the look of relief. "Do we still have steerage?" he asked.

"It's a miracle we do," grunted Seabury. "How she scaled that rock and sailed away with her rudder is a mystery to me."

With peril behind her, the *Sphinx* accelerated once again. In no time, she was sailing at hull speed. Though the danger was behind them, there was little time for repose. A new danger awaited them as Seabury steered the schooner toward the whaler. The ships were on a collision course. To those on the *Nimrod*, it must have appeared that an impact was unavoidable. The old captain stood on his toes and looked over the side for the longboat and the lines they were to take aboard.

"Stand in," he ordered, handing Samuel the wheel. "Keep her true and heed my command this time."

"Aye, aye, Captain," agreed Samuel taking the wheel.

"Any water?" yelled Seabury down the companionway.

"Just a trickle from the starboard aft quarter planking, Captain," came the reply from below. "Otherwise, no breach."

"Stay and make certain it stays that way, Mr. Monroe," ordered Seabury.

"Were getting close, Father," declared Samuel, expressing concern.

"I have eyes," jeered Seabury.

"Everything looks different at high tide. I can't tell where we are in the channel."

"Just follow my instruction," replied Seabury. "The worst has passed."

The schooner quickly bore down on the stranded whaler. The *Sphinx* had to sail close to retrieve the tow lines, but not so close as to hit the shoals which kept the whaler pinched to the bottom. The longboat moved out into open water and closer to the schooner's path. Samuel stared over at his father. His worried face begged for the order to turn the ship away from the impending danger. Seabury finally gave it.

"Now, son! New heading, 130 degrees!"

Samuel swiftly veered the *Sphinx* onto the new course. The crew scurried to trim the sails for the new downwind heading. Though they may have been greenhorns, as Seabury described them, they were winning over the old sea captain with their agility and spirit.

The long spruce poles supporting the mainsails hung well over the side, making the majestic *Sphinx* almost as wide as she was long. It was a magnificent sight to witness from shore as the courageous schooner blasted through a cauldron of confused seas—an aquatic floating train barreling down a rock littered valley, while flying enormous bed sheets. As they got closer, Seabury gave the order to trim in the main boom over the port side before it could collide with the whaler's rigging.

The two ships were now almost beam-to-beam, as their bows quickly passed one another. Tim Cadman hung the lengthy gaff over the side. The man in the longboat flung the two ropes over the hook while Tim quickly pulled them up on deck.

"Hang tight to those cables, Mr. Cadman," yelled Seabury. "Get them tied, quickly."

The twisted line, fed from a barrel on the longboat, uncoiled franticly as the schooner pulled away. The rope heaved and jerked as the coarse twisted lines tried to tear themselves from Tim's hands. He had to be quick. Time was running out and so was the rope.

While the *Sphinx* continued to pass the stranded whaler, Hosea Sanford and his son leaned over the gunwale, awestruck. Suddenly they jumped back, as the schooner's boom nearly grazed their heads. The long-drawn-out spar raked along the whaler's shroud rigging, slamming the deadeyes and plucking the stays like a nautical troubadour strumming a thalassic banjo. Seabury Cory gave out a long belly laugh.

"Watch yar heads," he roared, with little concern, "we're coming on through."

The schooner's canvas bellowed in the fresh breeze. Samuel puffed out his chest, glanced over at David Sanford, and shot him a supercilious smile. David glanced over then away, biting his nails, like he had not a worry in the world. Samuel noted that amongst the crew of the *Nimrod* were Old Moses and his companion with the burnt face, cowering behind Hosea Sanford.

"Hurry with those cables, Mr. Cadman," shouted Seabury.

"Doing my best, Captain," came the quivering reply.

Tim Cadman struggled to fasten the lines. In a panic, Seabury rushed over. He snatched the twisted hemp from his hands, tossing Tim onto the deck. With a quick turn here and a nimble twist there, the old whaling master fastened the lines together. Making certain they were secure, he pulled on them tightly then flung the knotted bundle overboard. Tim just lay there feeling beaten and defeated.

"On your feet, Mr. Cadman," ordered Seabury, unreservedly. "No time to be resting on your backside when there's work to do." The coil of rope on deck began to rapidly unravel. Seabury marched away. "Everyone, out of the way, out of the way. Keep clear of that cable," he beckoned. The crew watched with consternation as the rope launched itself over the side.

"Cable's running out. Make yourself fast to the vessel," yelled Samuel.

The ropes on the deck continued to uncoil and feed out quickly. Admon watched as the lines whipped by him and out through the hawse aperture. With axe ready, he made certain the ropes did not tangle or jam. Finally, the last few feet of the rope ran out. It suddenly burst out of the water and snapped taut in midair between the two vessels. Immediately the schooner lost most of its speed. Samuel was violently thrust into the ship's wheel. The line fastened to the top of *Nimrod's* mast was the first to run out. The stiffened line steadily yanked at the whaler's mast, pulling the enormous ship instantly onto its side. With its port deck nearly submerged, Sanford and crew hung on precariously as a torrent of salty sea swamped the deck. At that very moment, the second line, the one tied to *Nimrod's* extended bowsprit, burst out of the water and tightened. The jarring force sent Admon to the deck.

Seabury indulged in a hardy laughter as he watched those on the *Nimrod* scramble along its deck. "Hang on, you stone lovers," he roared. "The forces of the Almighty command you!"

Straightaway, the *Sphinx* came to a complete stop. Both vessels were now umbilically linked. One cord pulled the whaler over on her ear while the other tugged at her snout. With her sails in the water, she lay helplessly on her side. Crewmen slid along its deck, dangling precariously, reaching out for anything they could to prevent from being tossed over the rail. The towropes creaked and wailed within the silence that commanded those crucial moments. With full sails blooming, the schooner continued to tug as the whaler continued to list on its gunwales. Its white glimmering hull twisted and squirmed as the *Sphinx* heaved and charged like an eager pup on the end of a leash.

"Come on! Come on!" murmured Samuel, looking back at the prostrated vessel. "Move, move!"

With its naked timbers raking along the jagged bottom, the shipwrecked *Nimrod* roared and rumbled in defiance. The frightening sound echoed off Cuttyhunk Island's hilly landscape like ominous, distant thunder. The whaler slowly began to shift. Suddenly, the helpless ship twisted on its keel with an ominous roar, spun around, and surged ahead. Eli ran up on deck to watch. The cables went slack and the *Sphinx* began to move once again. Instantly, *Nimrod* violently sprung up onto its feet and, like a wet seadog, shook itself off. The sea-filled jib sails shredded as they lifted out of the water, flapping in the wind like torn flags of surrender. Buckets rained onto *Nimrod's* deck. With seawater everywhere, the scuppers vomited the torrent flood into the sea.

With its beam now to the wind, the whaler's sails filled, and it slowly moved ahead. The *Nimrod* was free. The schooner tried to move away. At that very moment Captain Seabury Cory took the axe from Admon's hand. With one quick blow, he severed the towline, sinking the rusted blade deep into the burnished deck.

Cheers of ovations blared from the *Sphinx* as the whaler maneuvered under its own power. With a jubilant jig, Eli and his companions kicked up their feet, waved their hands, and jumped about in elated celebration. Samuel smiled joyfully. He had felt the same gratification on that fateful day in Baltimore, when he freed the nimble *Sphinx* from Confederate hands. He looked over at his father with revitalized pride and respect. The old seasoned captain winked.

"What do you think of my greenhorns now, Father?"

Seabury smiled and nodded, casually stuffing his rooster tail pipe with fresh tobacco. "Wind is picking up," he reported. "If old man Sanford has one brain cell in his head he will follow us out of this channel. Keep her on course, son. Get us out of here."

The old captain lit his pipe, kissing it until he drew a mouthful of freshly burnt leaf. He let out a modest sigh of victory with a random puff of smoke. Flicking the spent match overboard, he leaned on the rail, looking out onto the bay as if the entire affair never occurred. "Ya've done well, son, ya've done well," he muttered to himself.

Samuel was listening. "Thank you, Father. It means a lot to me to hear you say that."

"Keep in mind, boy. Old man Sanford owes us for seven-hundred-and-fifty feet of grade A cable."

"He owes us a lot more than that, Father."

"Aye! That he does, that he does."

Samuel looked back at the precarious channel and the slow-moving whaler. The *Sphinx* was doing what it was built for. Running at speed, free and unmoored. It was all behind him now. Samuel had met the challenge on his own terms and proved his worth—worth of self, only to one's self. That's how it had to be. As his father cautioned, he would place it all behind him—never speak of it—advocate on the side of discreetness and keep his accomplishment deep in his heart. Even so, he had to admit that if not for his father's help he may have failed. That, too, he would bury deep in the confines of pretentiousness and propriety, a cryptic place deep between mind and heart, a hole where he would entomb it all, and where modesty and vanity could be tempered and tamed, and the need to ring one's own bell quenched.

"How could you have known?"

"Known what, my boy?"

"Our location, Father, in that channel—that we were heading straight for that ledge. If you hadn't taken the wheel and turned us away, the *Sphinx* would have surely been sunk."

Seabury puffed on his pipe and grinned. "Son, there are many skilled seafarers on these waters—sailors and mariners, fishermen and explorers, romantics, even. Then there are whalers, my boy, whalers!"

Chapter 11:

The *Sphinx* anchored off Cuttyhunk Island just east of Pease Ledge. Tim made certain the anchor was doing its work and that the *Sphinx* was secure, while Samuel and his father watched as the *Nimrod* hove-to and drifted off the western end of the island.

"What's he doing?" asked Samuel.

"Inspecting for damage, I expect," replied Seabury.

"Longboat rowing away from the whaler, Captain," announced Eli. He stepped onto the cabin doghouse for a better look. "They are rowing up to shore, sir."

"Well, it is no concern of ours," said Seabury. "We've done our part."

Samuel sprung open the collapsible spyglass and scrutinized events along the far end of the island.

"It's looks like David Sanford," said Samuel. "They placed him ashore … the longboat's rowing back to the ship."

"Hosea Sanford probably banished the boy," declared Seabury. "Repudiation. It's what most captains would have done when a crewmember proved a danger to the ship, refused orders, or became unruly. After all, the boy put the ship up on the rocks."

"Sounds rather harsh," declared Samuel.

"Sometimes captains are left with little choice. It's either rid oneself of the rabble-rouser or gamble insurrection. Some captains were known to have stranded delinquent crew on deserted islands, never to be seen again."

"Boy is very lucky that the captain was his father," chuckled Eli.

"Nevertheless, in a day or two the lad will secure passage back to the mainland," said Seabury. "Old man Sanford is just making an example of him. It's no business of ours."

Samuel swept the island with the telescope.

"Do ya see the girls? Are they enjoying themselves?" his father asked.

"Don't see them. They could have gone to the Flint retreat up the hill behind the pond."

"Well, we best get someone in the water and inspect for damage," proposed Seabury.

"Yes, we should," agreed Samuel.

The crew of the schooner spent a good part of the day inspecting for damage and making repairs to the keel. Remarkably, there was none that would endanger the vessel. After they were done, the ship was made clean and comfortable for the long stay, including placing out deck chairs and hanging canvas tarpaulins to supply shade. The crew engaged in a friendly diving competition, jumping from the fifty-foot-high crow's nest and into the opaque green-blue water. Seabury used the spyglass and inspected the island and its towering hill. On the west summit, he could make out the roof of the large Flint estate. Something or someone caught his eye. He cleaned the glass with the cuff of his jacket and took a better look.

"See something, Father?"

"Don't know. Here take this." He handed his son the glass.

"Hard to tell with all those trees," said Samuel. "Something white flapping. Looks like it's moving quickly down the lane from the top of the hill."

"What do you make of it?"

"Looks like one of the girls. Waving her arms."

"I see her," said Eli.

"You must have eagle eyes, Mr. Monroe, if you can see that," proclaimed Seabury.

"Mr. Monroe, get the small longboat ready," ordered Samuel. "We're going ashore."

"Aye, aye, Captain!"

With Tim and Eli at the oars, the small skiff rose and plunged through the choppy swell. Samuel stood fixed at the bow, one foot on the gunwale, as would George Washington crossing the Delaware. As they got closer to the island, they could see Louisa standing along the shore. The young girl had her face in her hands. She was sobbing. Samuel ordered the men to row faster.

The boat rode up onto the spongy sand. Tim was the first to jump into the surf and run over to a tearful Louisa.

"What is it? What's wrong, Lulu? Where's Emily and Amy?" he asked, frantically.

Louisa stood there sobbing, unable to speak. She mumbled some words as tears ran down her face.

"What is it?" asked Samuel, hobbling over on his cane.

"She's not making any sense, Sam."

"Louisa! What's happened?" Samuel asked.

With her hands over her face, Louisa tried telling. She was so distraught they could not understand a word. Samuel removed the hands from her face.

"Louisa, where's Emily!"

Before she could reply, Amy and I came running over the bluffs. Though I was not as upset as Louisa, after what we just witnessed, I, too, had trouble speaking.

"What has happened here, Emily?" begged Samuel.

I paused, breathing heavily after the long run down the hill. Amy was still waving the white towel that she used to signal the ship.

"Oh, Samuel, it is terrible," I said. Amy leaned on me and placed her head on my shoulder. Tears dampened her long, wavy eyelashes.

"Was it true, Emily?" she asked. "Was it all real?"

I gave no reply. Instead, I ran over and threw my arms around Samuel. Amy did the same with Tim.

"She was hanging there, Samuel, just hanging there," I said.

"Who, Emily, who was hanging, where?" queried Samuel.

Though the image was singed in my mind, simple words could not describe the horrible spectacle we had just seen. I turned my back to Samuel and walked down to the water's edge. He tried to follow, but an insightful Eli held him by the arm and shook his head.

"I would give her a minute, Captain," he said.

I looked around trying to ascertain what was real and what was a dream. For a moment, I needed to feel the sand shift under my feet, see the surf roll over the weedy grass, call on the warmth of a God-given sun, and sniff the crisp harbor air—but instead all I could smell was the residuum of dead dry seaweed decaying under a chilly, overcast sky.

Suddenly, visions of Sarah Cornell hanging by the neck from a weathered stack pole reflected in my head. It complicated matters. No matter how hard I tried to be strong a tear escaped and trickled down my face.

Louisa continued crying while Timothy held Amy in his arms. Someone had to speak and describe the entire horrid affair. I took a deep breath. Death was not an easy ordeal to describe.

"Are you all right, Emily?" asked Samuel, as I walked up to him.

I placed my head on his shoulder, drawing in his comfort. He wrapped his arms around me. I looked over at Amy and she at me. Our eyes said that everything would be all right—at least for us.

Eli stood on the bluff looking up the narrow lane that lead up the hillside. He sensed that we would need to go back up the hill and was ready to lead the way.

Samuel ran the back of his hand lovingly up and down my cheek. "Are you ready to tell me, Emily?"

I wiped my face with the heel of my hand. "We ... we trekked up to the Flint house to see if Phoebe Flint was there ... to pay her a visit. There was no one home. So, we went looking for Annie, their maid who lives in the small cottage behind the house. The door to the dwelling was open, but Annie wasn't there."

"Perhaps she's on the mainland," said Tim.

"No, you don't understand," I said. "The house was vandalized. Everything was toppled, table, chairs, as if some sort of scuffle occurred. So we searched around the place. Our attention was drawn to the barn across from the cottage—its doors flapped open in the wind." As I spoke a surge of tears filled my eyes.

"It's all right, Emily. Say no more," said Samuel. "We'll go up and look. You and the girls wait here."

"No!" shouted Louisa. "I don't want to wait here. I want to stay with the men."

"We want to come," insisted Amy, displaying a stiff upper lip. With newfound courage, she ran up the small bluff and stood by Eli. "I'm ready!"

"Emily, how about you?" Samuel asked.

I looked over at Louisa.

She nodded her head. "Yes, let's all go."

Cuttyhunk was populated by a handful of fishermen and their families, along with a few cottages kept by mainlanders who wished to escape the summer heat. The Flint estate was one of them. It sat on a prominence a hundred and fifty feet above the sea. The house overlooked the entire island and enjoyed marvelous views of the mainland and open water. The hill around the Flint property was mostly brushland. Man, being an animal of want and need, had taken down most of the large trees, which once occupied this diminutive spit of land. From the top of the lane, the path, which led up to the main house, was a corridor of small fruit trees. Privacy was a benefit of the small Flint estate.

Cuttyhunk Island had always been a mysterious place to me. Though I could plainly see it from shore, I had never been here. First impressions are often lasting ones. And with the horrid events I just witnessed, I'm afraid that I have been left with sullied memories of Cuttyhunk—memories that will occupy the deepest reaches of my being for as long as I live.

What should have been a delightful stopover has turned into a knot of haunting recollections. Once I leave here, will I ever come back? If I know Louisa—she will not. I would not blame her. I must be strong. I will not allow despicable events to patronize my torment, or like an unforeseen plague, poison my aspirations to explore new places. Yes, I will be back.

Now that I think of it, how was I to investigate the murder of Sarah Cornell and not think that I would unearth distasteful or alarming revelations? I did not. Neither did I expect to cut my teeth as an investigator by such a dreadful day as this. Even the death of Sarah Cornell could not rival the horrors that we witnessed up on that hill.

We all arrived at the property. Toward the back of the main house, and up a slight slope, was the servant's cottage, along with the barn. As we carefully approached the weathered outbuilding, Amy clutched Louisa by the arm.

"We'll remain here, Lulu," said Amy.

"Hold my hand!" pleaded Louisa.

"I'm going up with the men," I said.

"Oh, Emmie, don't go!" cried Louisa.

"It's all right," I said, giving her a kiss. Amy stuck out her cheek and begged for one of her own.

"You be careful, Emily White," she declared.

I rushed up to keep pace with the three men.

"Go stand with your friends, Emily," said Samuel. "We're going to look in the barn."

"No! I want to come."

Samuel and Eli looked at one another. I suppose they were asking themselves how I could have been so distraught and now so brave. Instead of being ambushed by what I discovered earlier in the day, this encounter was on my own accord. I knew what to expect and I was no longer afraid—just disheartened and sad. Courage and grit were qualities which I needed to master if I was to tame and challenge death throughout life—natural or otherwise. After all, are death and life not attributes on a single coin? Yet, as I entered that dreadful place I could not make a pledge or assurances that I would not tear up.

Samuel looked over at me—wide eyed. I nodded.

"I'll be alright. I promise."

I noticed that the doors to the unkempt barn were no longer swung open. Samuel walked over and pulled on one of them. Strangely, they appeared to be locked. He pulled again, but they would not open. He banged on them with his fist. He listened.

"Hello! Is anyone in there?" No reply. He rapped on the door once again. "Hello!" He looked back at me. "Are you sure this is the place, Emily?"

I walked over and tried the door. It was firmly secured.

"She's in there, Samuel," I insisted.

"Emily, this door is fastened with a timber from inside."

"How does one secure a door from inside and leave?" I asked.

"She's got you there, Sam," said Tim. "Someone is in there, whether alive, sleeping or …"

Samuel gave the door a forceful tug. It was of no use. He stepped back and inspected the small building, specifically a loft window above the doors. "Eli, do you think if I lift you on my shoulders you can climb in that window up there?"

"I think I can, sir."

Samuel stooped down while Eli climbed onto his shoulders. As he lifted the man to the window, his knee gave way and they fell to the ground.

"Samuel!" I cried.

"I'm all right," he said, clutching his knee. "I'm afraid my leg's still not strong enough."

Tim helped Samuel to his feet. "I can," he said. "A bowl of pudding." He stooped down on one knee with his shoulder into the door. "Try again, Eli. Climb up."

Eli stepped up onto Tim's shoulders. With little affair or effort, he stood up and lifted Eli high into the air. The windowsill was now just level with the top of Eli's head.

He reached up and pushed on the small attic window. It swung open.

"Not sure I can pull myself up that high, Mr. Cadman. I need a little more height."

"Hold on." Tim reached up and clutched Eli by the ankles. Lifting his arms well above his head he heaved the helmsman the rest of the way, where he disappeared into the barn.

We waited for Eli to open the barn doors.

A long time went by. I began to fear that something was wrong. "Why is he taking so long?" I asked, nervously.

"I can hear him moving inside," said Tim, his ear to the door. "Eli!" he shouted.

Samuel tried looking through a crack in the barn siding.

We waited. Two or three minutes had passed, and Eli had yet to unfasten the door.

"Something must be wrong, Samuel." I said.

Tim listened more carefully.

"It sounds … it sounds like he's praying."

"What!" said Samuel, moving Tim aside. He listened then pounded on the door.

174

"Eli, Eli! Are you all right!" He clutched the tarnished wrought iron handle and shook it vigorously. Suddenly, the door splintered and wobbled free. Samuel held back and listened. Eli Monroe could be heard clearly reciting a passage from the Old Testament. We held our breath. Samuel flung the door wide open.

"Even though I walk through the darkest valley, I will fear no evil. You are with me …"

Light flooded the place. Tim pushed by us and rushed inside. Suddenly he stopped, as if running into an unseen wall. He stood frozen his mouth plummeted open.

"Your rod and your staff, they comfort me, Though preparest a table before me …"

I shuffled inside holding my head down, fearful of looking up. Samuel stood in horrid reverence if not in shocked silence. Eli continued to pray. I slowly lifted my head, then my eyes, and there she was.

We all stared up at the young woman hanging from the beam. Her broken body spun to and fro, like a heinous weather vane twisting in an evil breeze. Images vomited in my head—of the time I wandered into Perry Davis's barn when I was a little girl and stumbled upon the slaughtering of a deer, which dangled from the ceiling in his barn. This was a nightmare altogether different.

Samuel meandered around the kneeling Eli and stared up at the stiff hanging body. He was lost for words. The girl's naked feet swayed in the air just inches from Eli's head as the Bermudian slumped and prayed.

"Thou anointest my head with oil, my cup runneth over …"

A twisted face with ebony pearl complexion and tumescent eyes, she just hung there, with a cord strangling her neck. Her teeth lay behind parted lips, white and orderly as the petals on a spring daisy. Was this real? I recognized her—Annie Slocum—and indeed she was real. Now I know how Sarah Cornell must have looked on her last day.

"Surely goodness and mercy shall follow me all the days of my life. And I will dwell in the house of the Lord for ever and ever."

"Amen," said Samuel placing a hand on Eli's shoulder. He dropped his cane, and carefully wrapped his arms around the dead girl's legs.

"Take your knife, Tim," ordered Samuel. "Cut her down while I hold her. Hurry, she's heavy."

Tim just stood there. A look of terror and horror was inscribed onto his face.

"Hurry, Tim. Take your knife and cut her down, man!"

Tim stood chilled by what he saw.

"My knee! Tim … hurry!"

Tim Cadman lifted his hands and looked down on them as if they had committed the crime. He looked up at the pendulous body and went into a tremor. His face took on a contorted mien.

"No, no!" he wailed, staring down at his hands. Suddenly, he ran out of the barn and bolted down the hill toward the shore, as if the devil himself was giving chase.

Clutching one another, Amy and Louisa jumped out of the way as Tim sprinted by. Instantly, they began to scream and run down the lane behind the terrorized boy.

"Eli, help me," pleaded Samuel.

Eli reached up above the dead girl's body and severed the cord with his knife. I rushed over and wrapped my arms around Annie and helped lower the flaccid corpse to the ground. Her listless head fell onto my shoulder. Embracing her felt like wrapping one's arms around a pine tree, firm and rigid, but still emitting the sweet anthropomorphic scent that we humans all emanate. Poor Annie Slocum, resting at our feet in eternal slumber.

What a terrible place this was. Mr. Flint had rented the old weathered barn to a whaler. Here was stored all sort of whaling implements—rope, harpoons, pole saws, sickles. On the rafters off to one corner hung an elongated whale skull. The old stable reeked of rotting fish. Casks of raw, tainted salt, along with crates of aged cod lay piled against one wall. A fungal heap of decomposing whale blubber was stacked along another. The sullied floor was laminated in a layer of discarded, parched, and putrid fish scales and oily, crumbled hay. The stagnant air was infused with a choking, briny dust. Persistent flies kept striking us in the face. This was the least of our discomfort when compared to their incessant, deafening murmur. It was an undertone of torment and death—the extinction of human life, in a space saturated with the pervading stench of gloom and slaughter.

"Can we take her out of this awful place?" I pleaded.

"Eli, take hold of her feet and let's move her out of here," said Samuel.

"Ashanti," said Eli, shockingly. He stood there, studying the dark-skinned girl.

"Her name is Annie," I said.

Samuel stood, his hands under the dead girl's arms. "Come, Eli. Take her legs."

"She is Ashanti," he said in a splintered hypnotic stupor.

"Eli!" shouted Samuel. "Are you listening to me?"

Taking the girl by the ankles Eli helped carry her limp body out into the open air. What was once Annie Slocum, the Flint family maid, now lay motionless in the open light of day. Though it had started sunny, the heavens had turned menacing, with plumes of fast moving black clouds. In spite of the fact that it was mid-afternoon, there was darkness—a lack of illumination that spoke to the shadow and death. And indeed, death lay at my feet.

It is strange to think, in all my years I have never witnessed it or had I given it much serious consideration. Sure, I have heard of wakes, though I have never been to one, and have been a spectator to funeral processions. When I did, all I could observe was a pine box riding on the shoulders of men dressed in their Sunday best—just a box. Here there was no box—just poor Annie lying lifeless on overgrown green grass. Though she could not speak I thought I heard the reflection of a woman's voice blowing in the wind. Was it distant thunder—or the utterance of death introducing itself to me for the first time? If it was, death spoke in tongues. The words were gruff and grumbled. Yet I understood its meaning, its cautionary warning. *I am always with you. And as you get older we shall see more of each other.*

The temperature began to drop. Eli removed his coat and covered Annie's cold body. It was emblematic of Eli to do so, but nothing would ever make her warm again. A shattered vein of lightning shot across black, smudged clouds. Samuel fell to one knee, looked down on the dead girl, then up to a foreboding sky. A light rain sprinkled and a strange gelid breeze blew up from the shadowy lane that led down to Cuttyhunk Pond and the harbor, where the schooner was anchored. We stared down at Annie Slocum through the rainy mist uncertain of what to do next.

"A squall is brewing from the north, Captain," declared Eli.

"What should we do?" I asked, rubbing my upper arms in an attempt to fend off a chill.

"We have to get her to the ship," declared Samuel.

In a nearby meadow, a sudden gust swept up some withered vegetation and parched soil and managed it into an ominous dust devil. The whirlwind quickly gyrated across the lane and into a sloping field like an imperceptible spirit making its escape. As quick as it stirred, it died. An eerie silence became a vacuum around us. The temperature continued to drop. Soundless lighting cracked the sky. On the horizon, whitecaps speckled the waves along Cuttyhunk Harbor. The wind swept the swell, curling them into an aqueous war dance. At its moorage below, the *Sphinx* tugged at its anchor cable as it hobby-horsed to the building sea. Yet, where we stood, the air was tranquil and untroubled. A gentle drizzle fell. There was no wind to speak of.

"Look how stormy it looks over the water," I said. "Why is it so calm here?"

"It's a black squall," Samuel said looking up. "Look how dark the sky is. It will hit us any time now."

"She is so petite," said Eli. "We can't just leave her out here for the rain, Captain."

"No we can't. Emily, run over to the cottage and get something we can cover her with."

"You mean like a sheet?"

"Yes. A sheet, a blanket. Anything you can find."

While I searched inside the small house, Samuel examined the body of Annie Slocum. Her dress was torn just below her neckline exposing an injury beneath the girl's shoulder blade. He inspected it carefully. It had symmetry and order—as if intentionally carved into the girl's skin. Samuel folded the material away to expose the entire wound.

"What do you make of this?" he asked.

Eli peered down and quickly moved away. "I wouldn't know, sir."

"Come here. I need you to see this, Mr. Monroe. It may be of some importance. Is this some sort of seal or crest? It appears to have been whittled into the skin right over her heart?"

Though at first reluctant, Eli leaned over for a better look. A humble man, his wavering had just as much to do with fear as it did with embarrassment. He gave a painful squint, his cheeks bulged and his eyes widened. He moved back. "I don't know what it is, sir."

"It looks like some sort of symbol. Look here. It has blistered. And there, under her shoulder, dried blood. Is it a religious crest of some kind?"

"I wouldn't know, sir. It looks like it was done quite recently. It's not anything I have ever witnessed."

"Odd."

"Perhaps the sign of spirits—Vodun, sir. Evil Vodun!"

"Vodun?"

"Of the spirit world, sir. The Ewe people of Africa call it vodon. I have never seen it practiced for evil until my arrival in the Americas."

"I understand. I have heard of this voodoo, or Vodun, as you call it. Father spoke of it. They practice such cults in the gulf states and along the Caribbean chain of islands."

"It is a belief of the god that presides over us all. You discover your way through life and put forward your requests through Vodun. It is the truth of life for many. It can also be the death of them."

"Well, Mr. Monroe, what we have here appears as evil as it can get."

"Yes, Captain."

Do you worship this voodoo, Mr. Monroe?"

"I am Christian, sir."

"But of course. Someone who knows the 'twenty-third Psalm' would be."

"My allegiance is to the Almighty, though, I have spent some time in Haiti where Vodun is commonly practiced and have witnessed its evil sway."

I returned, carrying a bundle of sheets and blankets—all the covering I could find. In the short time I was gone, the wind had kicked up and the heavens wailed petulant thunder.

"Will this do, Samuel?" I asked, my voice quaking while the sky did the same.

"Yes. We must hurry," he said, looking up. "The squall may hit at any moment." He placed a sheet over Annie's body.

"The cord is still around her neck. Shouldn't we remove it?" I asked.

"No. Leave it for the authorities," replied Samuel. "Mr. Monroe, get some rope from the barn. Let's cloak and tie the body."

Eli rushed to the barn and returned with a bundle of heavy twine. "Will this do, sir?"

"Yes, that's fine."

"May I make a suggestion, sir?" He handed Samuel the rope.

"Yes, go on."

"That you cover her well, Captain … her face. Some of the men may … well, they may become alarmed if they see her … especially an African girl. I would make certain they do not see those markings on her chest or her face."

"Understood, Mr. Monroe."

"What markings?" I asked.

Samuel folded back Annie's collar.

"What … what is it?"

"We don't know."

"Vodun!" cried Eli.

"What does he mean, Samuel? Vodun!"

"Never mind. I'll tell you later. Let's wrap the body. We need to get down to the ship before it's too late."

Eli struggled as he carried Annie over his shoulder. With his bad knee, Samuel was of little help and there was not much I could do. When we arrived at shore we discovered that Amy and Louisa had been taken out to the *Sphinx*. Tim sat by the rocking lifeboat with vanquished courage, feeling trounced and defeated. He rushed over to help Eli with Annie's body, taking the bundled corpse from the exhausted man. He easily lifted the shrouded body in his powerful arms and placed it gently inside the boat. It was as if Annie were asleep. I noticed he was in control of his wits and did not appear frantic or alarmed as he did earlier.

"I took the girls back to the ship," he said. "This weather looks dangerous."

"It was the right move," said Samuel. "We don't want to overload the boat in the storm."

"Look, Sam, about the incident in the barn ... I'm sorry, but you see ..."

"Say no more." Samuel placed a sympathetic hand on the young man's shoulder, "I too have been startled by death and this was the most injurious sort of demise. Seeing her hang there was enough to test any man's nerve."

"It was. And more than you know, Sam."

I can fully appreciate the fear and horror Tim must have felt. I also understand that he is a man, and for this, a more tangible reason for his fear could have been veiled by a compassionate perception of what he had witnessed—which speaks to emotion and sensitivity. And there are few men as sensitive and gentle as Tim. I was prepared to accept that, though he was a tall muscular young man, there was no reason for him not to feel the same vulnerabilities and consciousness as a strong but delicate woman. After all, it was an unexplained miracle why I did not panic when I first saw Annie Slocum hanging from that beam. Though I must admit what I have witnessed has aged me. For the termination of a young life first hand is a terrible lesson. It is a teaching which none of us can escape. Death makes us aware of these eggshells we display, as we breathe, eat, drink, age, and in the end ... all for dying. With this in mind, there is a twisted perversion to think that Annie provoked death and challenged it on its own grounds, by rushing time along and taking her own life. It is a distorted travesty that I cannot accept. Not Annie—not anyone.

Tim shoved the longboat out into the harbor in a steady rain and hopped in. The furious sky was now cloaked black and stamping its feet in a sonorous rumble. Crazed lightening fractured the horizon to the north and, in the distance, thunderous streaks of light struck the earth like the falling, jagged branches of a lifeless tree. Eli and Tim rowed as fast as they could. I sat by the stern of the boat with Samuel, while Annie Slocum, unknowingly, rested at the bow. The seas were dangerously humped and confused as the squall closed in. The longboat slammed through the fluttering waves as they curled and battered us with scourging spray from short-tempered spumes. The wind blew from all directions trying its best to stop us from getting to the ship.

Suddenly, it began to pour so hard that sight of the *Sphinx* was lost. Tim looked over his shoulder as he rowed, trying to fix his bearings. Samuel kept watch and pointed the way. Raindrops the size of Indian pennies battered our faces. I have seen the skies open up many times, but never plunging rain, horizontally, as if shot from the barrel of a gun. The moment appeared surreal. It was a good time to cry. And in this pelting rain no one would ever notice. I released all manner of grit and boldness, gave up the stiff upper lip, and, with a forsaken smile, allowed the tears to flow and flow. I can't tell you how comforting it felt, shedding the anguish that I felt for poor Annie—for myself.

Through the deluge, the constant ringing of the ship's bell called out for us. I found myself drawn to Annie's body and could not help peering over the rower's shoulders to the front of the boat where she lay, wrapped like some sort of Egyptian mummy. I must admit being a bit fearful as we headed out into deeper water. What if we could not find the ship and were blown out to sea? What if a wave toppled the boat and washed us away never to be seen again? Although we made slow progress, Samuel looked confident. Eli appeared unafraid, and Tim, well, Tim just smiled and winked, assuring me that all would be fine. Very little ruffled him. He was shy but confident. But in that barn today, something terrified him. Whatever it was went beyond witnessing Annie Slocum. We all have our demons. In Tim's case the demon had him deep in his pocket. His actions at the Flint estate puzzled me.

Though his demeanor was gentle and kind, and in many respects, ladylike, truthfully, very few men were as manly as Tim. All one needed to do was look. Through his wet shirt you would plainly see the muscular ladder of brawn climb his tummy, accompanied by sturdy powerful arms and broad shoulders. He was tall and propped with pectoral burliness that would make any overbearing male proud or virtuous woman blush. Yet, I never have—blushed, you understand. Forgive me. I know, I know, I am being wicked in my portrayal of Timothy. I suppose what I'm trying to say is that the most attractive aspect to masculinity is sensitivity—without a doubt.

I was happy to be back on the ship. After changing out of my wet clothes, the girls and I sat around the salon table discussing the terrible events of the day, a day like no other. It was late—almost dusk. The sky had all but cleared while the setting sun sunk below the western horizon like a languishing, fiery grapefruit. Dun bands of streaky clouds, left over from the earlier storm, slashed the sky like plums of ink-dipped cotton on a fuchsia canvas. The evening became muggy and hot. Up on deck the crew passed their time telling tales of bondage and long, brutal days of fettered obedience and forced labor. But it was not all talk of despair and glumness. There was an abundance of laughter and song.

With arms crossed and resting on the table, Louisa sat slumped, her chin propped on her forearm and staring at nothing in particular. Amy plunked herself in a chair against a bulkhead and brushed her hair. They appeared quiet and withdrawn. Who could blame them after the day we had all experienced. We were exhausted, mentally weary, and emotionally crippled.

Eli sat just outside the companionway ladder enjoying his cheroot, while Samuel broke open the liquor locker and poured himself a brandy. Mr. Cory senior had retired to his quarters over an hour previous. "Early to bed, asleep by nine keeps a man healthy and fine," he often recites. After completing his duties up on deck, Tim came down to join us. Samuel poured him a drink.

"There's no way the men will sleep below with a body in the forecastle, Sam," declared Tim.

"Well, we can't just tie the girl up on deck like she was cargo."

"Where did you … you place her? I mean, where in the forecastle?" I inquired, hesitantly.

"The line locker," said Samuel.

"Oh no, Samuel!"

"It's all right, Emily," he assured. "It's also sleeping quarters. It's freshly painted and there's a small bunk in there. It's quite comfortable. Slept in there myself, many times."

"Eli covered her with a blanket," said Tim. "She looks like she's sleeping."

"All quiet, Captain," announced Eli as he came down below. The three men sat and drank. Tim had two drinks for every glass Samuel poured for himself.

"Boy, we were lucky to get the *Nimrod* off the reef when we did," said Tim. "That storm would have surely sunk her."

"You mean the *Nimrod* was lucky," I added.

"Aye! It was quite the undertaking. Thanks to Father."

"Samuel. How long will we be staying?" I asked.

"Well, I was hoping to stay at least three days. I'm afraid we need to deliver the body to the authorities as soon as possible. In the morning Tim and I will go back to the island and see if anyone is around … possibly question some of the islanders. Perhaps someone may know something. Then we'll shove off."

"Can I come with you?" I asked.

"If you like."

"What do you suppose happened to her?" asked Louisa. Her voice quaked, somewhat afraid someone might reply.

"I would imagine she locked the door and hanged herself," said Samuel.

"But why?" begged Louisa. "Why would someone do that?"

"No, Samuel, no!" I argued. "The door was open when we arrived and she was already dead."

"Emily's right," said Amy. "I saw it too."

"When we arrived at the cottage the wind was blowing," said Louisa. "Maybe it slammed the door shut and it locked."

"Yes, that's it. It was the wind," said Amy.

"The door was barricaded from the inside with a large timber. The plank would need to be lifted and put into place. How do you explain that?" asked Samuel.

"The loft window," interrupted Eli.

"What about it?" I asked.

Eli put out his cheroot and stuffed the stub it in his shirt pocket. "Someone could have been there after you and your friends left. Discovering the body, they could have gone in, placed the brace on the inside of the door, and left ... through the loft window."

"Why?" I asked.

Eli shrugged his shoulders.

"What do you think, Tim?" I asked.

Tim was tight-lipped. It was obvious the talk about Annie disturbed him. He pushed his drinking glass toward Samuel and pointed at it with his nose.

"Better go easy there, Tim," cautioned Samuel, pouring him another drink. "This stuff will creep up on a man and knock him on his posterior."

Tim winked, held up his glass, and took a swallow.

"What is this Vodun you talk about, Mr. Monroe?" I asked.

"This woman you call Annie. Her people are from West Africa—the Akan. To be more precise, the Ashanti clan. They are a very religious sect and are known to practice Vodun. It is their creed."

"But what is it?" Amy asked.

"Vodun are their gods, supreme beings that watch over nature and humanity."

"You never saw Annie before. How do you know where her people were from?" I asked.

"The headdress that was lying by her feet when I first saw her—the material, the weave, and the color of her clothing. She came from an influential family. Only a woman of position would wear such fine attire."

"Are you sure?" asked Louisa.

"Yes. You see, I am also from the Akan region. Father called it the Costa do Marfim, or Ivory Coast. When they were very young, my grandparents were seized from their native land by Portuguese slave merchants and taken across the sea to Bermuda where they were sold as slaves and made to work tobacco fields. It was there where I was born."

"You were a slave, Mr. Monroe?" asked Amy, with astonishment.

"An infant slave," he said, laughing.

"That's so sad!" said Louisa, making a doleful baby face.

"I remember very little of it, Miss Louisa. You see, I was seven years of age at the time my parents were made free. The summer of 1834. It is a date I shall never forget."

"You must have had a kind owner to allow you your freedom," said Amy.

"There are no kind owners, Miss Amy—only determined ones. Kindness had very little to do with our liberation. It took formal emancipation by the government. You see, Bermuda ended slavery twenty-seven years ago. The reaction was very different to what we are experiencing in the South here in the Americas. We in Bermuda are a civilized people."

"You must have fond memories of Bermuda?" I asked.

"Yes, of course. It is my home. I have tried securing passage back to Bermuda several times. Due to the war and the naval blockade by the northern states, I have had very little success finding a ship that would give me transit. I had to get myself out of the south and if not Bermuda, then New England is the next best place."

"Mr. Monroe. About those markings we discovered on the girl. You don't think she did them herself?" inquired Samuel.

"No, I do not. Captain. Those marks were freshly made. And if you lobby my opinion, I would tell you that they were placed there by someone other than the girl placed there just after or before she died."

"By the killer!" echoed a woozy Tim.

"Did you say killer!" cried Amy.

"Oh, my!" squealed Louisa, leaping to her feet.

"Ladies, ladies! No one knows that anyone was actually murdered," declared Samuel. "Chances are Miss Slocum and she alone is responsible for her own fate."

"I'm going to my cabin and lock my door," declared Amy.

Tim gave out an evil, snort. "If you only knew," he scowled.

"What do you mean, Timothy?" I asked.

"Nothing! Nothing at all."

"Oh, Emmie, I'm frightened," whimpered Louisa.

"Come, Lulu," touted Amy, taking her hand. "We'll bunk together."

Louisa looked back at us, franticly, as Amy dragged her off by the hand.

Shortly after the girls retired to their cabin, Eli went up on deck to bed down with the crew. By now, Tim was filling his own glass with liquor. Samuel seized the crystal decanter from his hand before he could fill the glass to the brim.

"Tim, my good man, easy there." Samuel capped the bottle and stored it away. "Must save some for medicinal purposes."

"I can handle it," he proclaimed, wobbling his words. "And I can handle murder as well!" Samuel looked over at me and shook his head. "Furthermore ..."

"Tim, Tim! No one has been murdered."

"I know murder when I see it," slurred Tim. He stood up and walked away—spilling his drink as he went. "And it's not the first time." He pointed at me with the glass in his hand. "As a matter of fact, I saw it just last ... year." His speech faded away as he climbed the companionway ladder and started for the deck.

"Whoa there," said Samuel, clutching him by the arm. "You know the rules. No drinking on deck."

Tim brandished a smirk. Throwing back his head, he emptied his glass.

It dropped to the floor as he started up the ladder. Samuel threw an arm around him. "Why not stay here with us, Tim. We don't want anyone falling off the ship."

"I'm fine ... Mr. Captain," he mumbled, puffing out his chest. He closed his eyes tightly and shook his head. "I have no desire of leaving the ship, unintentionally or otherwise."

"As a friend, Tim. Please, stay below," I begged.

Tim looked at me, then out at the moon—then back at me. "If you insist, Emily. Just for you ... and the moon." He snickered. Plopping himself at the table, he reached for Samuel's glass but it was empty.

"Tim, you said you have seen murder before?" I asked. "What did you mean?"

"Mean, mean what?" he muttered.

Samuel made a face, warning me not to press the issue. I thought that it was something he needed to share, get off his shoulders.

"When you said you have seen it before."

"Seen? What have I seen?" He stared at me with one open eye. "Ah, you know, don't you?"

"Come, Tim," said Samuel, helping him to his feet. He led his friend to a corner in the cabin. "Rest here on this bunk."

"Don't I get a private cabin, Captain, sir?" He asked with a contorted smile.

"Yes, later. For now, just rest here."

Samuel had barely finished escorting Tim to the bunk before the young man was snoring away. We sat quietly. Everyone had retired for the night. It was just Samuel and I. I counted on my fingers.

"There are twelve people on this ship, Samuel. Only eleven are alive," I said.

"Try not to think about it."

"I can't help it."

"Did you know Annie Slocum very well?"

"She would shop at the Cory store. I spoke with her perhaps no more than three or four times. She was sweet."

"I'm sorry you had to see her this way."

"Nothing to be sorry about. It's just sad. Do you think she was really murdered?"

"I don't know."

Samuel offered to make some tea. It was late. I just wanted to sit quietly and wait for sleep to come. He took out the bottle of liquor and shook out an inch of brandy. We sat quietly looking at the moon out the companionway entrance. The dimpled, white ball swayed to the boat's movements. In one corner in the cabin Tim snored loudly. Every once in a while, he would talk in his sleep and yell—gibberish, really. Every time he did, Amy and Louisa giggled from their cabin like juvenile girls.

"I almost forgot," said Samuel. "With all that's happened today."

"Forgot what?" I said.

"David Sanford."

"What about him?"

"Did you happen to see him on the island?"

"No. David was on the *Nimrod* with his father."

"He was. Before they set sail, they left him off on the island."

"What, and sailed off?"

"I think his father meant to punish him—set an example. In any event, the Sanford and the Flint families are good friends. I would think he would have gone up to the estate."

"No, we didn't see him at all, I'm sure. One of us would have mentioned it."

"Well, he's on that island until the next ship leaves for the mainland."

"Perhaps we can find him and take him home with us."

"I don't think he would come. He's too proud."

"Poor David. Always has to win. Such childish and primitive behavior."

"Oh he'll be all right. Believe me. There's nothing poor about David Sanford. Nonetheless, we will look out for him in the morning when we return to the island. The least we can do is offer him passage."

"Thank you, Samuel."

"Don't mention it."

"Eli talked about this thing called Vodun."

"It's a religion along Western Africa. Their connection to the Almighty."

"About the markings found on Annie. You think this Vodun had anything to do with it?"

"They appeared to be freshly made. Eli was right about that. It was a peculiar shape, like a circle or a strawberry with the letter X over it." He took a sheet of paper and pencil and drew the image.

"Hmm, doesn't look much like anything … the scribbling of a child at most," I said.

"The more I think about it, the more I come to believe that it was placed there by someone other than Annie."

"Oh, Samuel, what does it mean?"

"I thought nothing of it at first, but she did have some bruising on her arms and wrists. Not the sort of thing a maid may be exposed to doing chores. And the torn dress disturbs me. How did that happen? I doubt she did it herself."

"Why do you say that?"

"Well, to me it almost looked as if it was intentionally ripped … like someone was trying to get at her."

I picked up the paper and studied the drawing. "What could this symbol mean?"

"Don't know if it is a symbol at all or why it was placed there. It was freshly made and bleeding. Her heart had to still been beating since the dead don't bleed."

"Oh, how terrible."

"We best try and get some sleep, Emily. It's almost midnight."

"Where do I sleep?"

"The captain's quarters?" I shot him a wary smile.

"Without the captain," he said, smiling. "I'll sleep out here and keep an eye on Tim."

He prepared the bunk that we were sitting on and turned it into a bed. I started for my cabin.

"Emily, wait!"

"Yes?"

"I'm sorry this trip didn't go as planned."

"It's not your fault."

He reached over and took my hand. "It's regretful that you should be left with such a bad impression of this little island. It's really a wonderful retreat … like you are for me."

I looked at him and he at me. And like one of those new-fangled inventions they call cameras, the moment was captured in my mind. I held it in my heart as long as I could. He pulled me closer; our bodies fixed as he gently stroked my cheek with the back of his hand. Timidly, I kissed it. Inside I quivered. Amorously, he embraced me, tucking me in, and languidly gazed into my eyes. I looked over at Tim. He was sound asleep. Samuel held me firmly in his arms, I couldn't move—or did I want to. My affections were instantly, if not gladly taken hostage. I was pleasantly trapped. Oh, what a delightful snare it was. I wanted to tow him with me into the captain's quarters, close the door, and eat him up. I know. Call me wicked!

"I'll make it up to you," he said. "We'll sail out to Nantucket some time soon. You will love it there. It's just like Cuttyhunk Island but with a lot more people."

"Sounds wonderful," I whispered, resting my head on his shoulder.

He took my face and cradled it in both hands, jailing my lips to his. I was hoping to be issued a sentence that would last a lifetime, to be taken away—incarcerated in his embrace forever. Liberation came much too soon and he pulled himself away.

"Goodnight," he said, softly.

I tried to say the same. Words would not flow. In fact, it was a good night and I didn't want it to end. After I closed my cabin door it all came tumbling down, like a basket of eggs on a two-legged table. Samuel's charm was enough to burn all unpleasant thoughts from my mind for just a short moment. Now that he no longer held me in his arms, all I could dwell on was the dreadful events of the day and poor Annie Slocum.

Chapter 12:

Perhaps I should be ashamed to admit that the sail home was enjoyable. You could possibly defend the argument that I am being insensitive and disrespectful, and that I should be mourning a lost life. Allow me to speak the truth, for it is how I feel. The sail back to the mainland was uplifting and exhilarating. It helped me to forget the dreadful events of the previous day, though the mournful body of Annie Slocum still lay in the forecastle.

And you must understand that how I lament is my affair. We must all grieve in our own exceptional or uncommon way. So, I persuaded myself that I should enjoy the sail home. There was little I could do for poor Annie. Dwelling on her demise was a morbid practice I wanted to avoid—a rehearsal in unhappiness and self-pity and one that did very little to help the dead girl or me. I am certain that if Annie were looking down on me from heaven, she would want to see me untroubled.

Questioning those on Cuttyhunk Island about Annie's ultimate fate yielded no clues, only fear and apprehension. And although we spent several hours knocking on doors and searching lanes and fields for witnesses to question, we never once crossed paths with David Sanford. On such a tiny island, it was a small wonder to where he could have hidden.

After leaving Cuttyhunk, the *Sphinx* sailed nonstop under slabs of swollen canvas. Samuel thought it best that we sail straight for Fall River, where we could report the incident to the authorities. Formality and protocol are vital in such matters, along with immediate accessibility of the facts, if they are to uncover what really happened to Annie Slocum. These matters were well beyond the authority of small town folk, such as those who live at Point Village, or even well traveled captains like Samuel and Seabury Cory. You may think it imprudent to get involved in such an unsavory circumstance, but what were we to do? Samuel said that if we left matters to the islanders, the benighted fishermen on that distant spit of land would have crudely salted down the delicate body of poor Annie, to preserve it, until the next vessel could deliver it to the mainland, like cod to market. And it could have easily been a week before the next ship visited the island. Samuel was not about to allow such a thing to occur. Though you may think of such behavior by the islanders cruel, these were good people, hard-working, most were poor, preoccupied with making a living, and with little time to consider a lowly African girl who may have hanged herself—to say nothing of the fear and shame it could bring them.

We prepared to round Brenton Reef and turned north, up through Newport, between Conanicut and Aquidneck Islands, where rich merchants, traders, and prophets of wealth and fortune benefited from the China trade, and built magnificent large homes by the sea—elegant sanctuaries away from big cities like Boston, Providence, and New York, where they lived.

The fog began to burn away. The smell of vegetation warned us that land was close. I asked Captain Seabury how he knew where we were in such thick fog as we rounded Brenton Point. He played on my credulous nature informing me that he navigated by dog, claiming that a dog on the point just by the reef was trained to bark when it was foggy, and that he, Seabury, could tell how far away we were from danger by the woofing. I am embarrassed to say that I did not know what to think when I first heard this facetious declaration—or how silly the look on my face when I actually heard a dog barking in the distance.

Tim had been at the wheel during the entire trip home. Good thing too, since he needed the sterile salt air, or any air, to cleanse his mind and body of the intoxicating spirits, which he had abused. Poor Tim! He was confused and hurting. Why did he not just beat himself about the head with Samuel's cane, instead of drinking himself blind? One foolish practice was just as harmful as the other.

You can tell a lot about a man when he drinks strong spirit. Some become genuine and sincere, others, callous and mean, and some will even spill their convictions and release their demons with every worded slur. Of all these type of men, Tim Cadman was all three.

The wise Eli Monroe sat by the wheel making love to his cheroot and allowing the burnt tobacco to embrace him with its satisfying redolence—that is … to Mr. Monroe. Cheroots are smelly, smoky things!

Captain Seabury sat on the cabin deck, weaving cord into something he called a monkey fist. Samuel sat at the chart table below, studying the ship's position after taking soundings with the lead and line. I enjoyed this interesting amalgamation of sailors, a fraternity made up of a Westport farmer, Bermudian gentleman, and African crewman, mariners of various age, color, and place. A better floating diverse crew could not be had, anywhere.

Amy and Louisa hung over the rail at the bow, waiting for land to appear. It did not take long before the white, needled steeple of Trinity Church in Newport became visible as it protruded from the hovering fog up into a brightening sky. The girls talked and laughed, unaware or forgetful that less than five feet directly below their feet lay poor Annie Slocum. In the main salon, the black crew sat on the floor, cross-legged, playing their little game of Crown and Anchor, tossing colorful dice with card playing symbols onto a felt covered board. It looked like an entertaining pastime, though Captain Seabury called it gambling and declared it would never be allowed on any ship under his command. Soon they were all summoned on deck as land came into view.

The approach to the city was a revelation. I must admit this entire voyage has been a surprise—especially the reason why we needed to come here in the first place. As we sailed into Fall River Harbor, Tim maneuvered the schooner by the steamer *Bay State* which blew its horn as it left the city pier. The echo it made rudely bounced off the mills along the shore and slapped me in the ears. The smells of the city were repulsive. The abhorrent factory smoke, the odor of spent coal, along with the stench of mucous water, singed my sense of smell and scalded my eyes. *How can people live in the city?* I thought.

I was amazed by how many church steeples I could see resting on the hill. Along the shore there were three times as many brick chimneys, rising from the waterside and depositing their black talc directly onto rooftops and city streets. Nothing stood still. Everywhere you looked people were moving, walking, running. I had often heard how exciting the city can be and wondered what was wrong with me—why I did not feel the same as those who expounded its perceived virtues.

Amy pointed to the hill above the waterfront and showed Louisa where she lived. Samuel interrupted and ordered them below since the unpleasant errand of carrying Annie to the longboat would surely disturb them. I preferred to stay on deck and say goodbye.

Tim circled the harbor, turning the gracious schooner around just south of the Slade's Ferry Landing. The lazy sails wafted from port to starboard, and the long heavy booms slothfully swung in the gentle breeze. With help from the captain, Tim did his best to stay out of the way of the incoming steamer *Empire State* as it pulled up to the city pier. Sails came down, and the crew scrambled to drop anchor in the middle of the river. After the schooner was secure, the longboat was quickly deployed and the carefully wrapped body of Annie Slocum was lowered into it. Unexpectedly, I began to cry. I had elected to stay on deck and observe the transfer. I never anticipated the tears. The more I tried to stop crying the faster they were delivered to my cheek.

I woefully watched as Eli and Tim rowed ashore. The two men braided the longboat carefully around ship traffic in the busy harbor, while Samuel somberly sat with Annie. Passengers on the steamer *Empire State* leaned over the railing and watched with a spirit of inquiry, as the longboat ghosted by with the mummy-like bundle. It was one of the saddest sights I had ever laid eyes on.

Seabury Cory startled me when he came up from behind and placed his arm around me. It felt like a wool blanket over my shoulders on a cold winter night. The needed warmth only made me feel more mournful. I knew it was a melancholy that needed to be bled. His services were appreciated. And what better way to ration grief than in the arms of a man I could easily call father.

"I have seen it many times," he said. "The war in 1812 ... the first time ... I was barely thirteen. I had witnessed a soldier die. I could have looked much older if I just didn't cry. I was found out and sent home by the military captain—told to come back when I was sixteen. Later death would visit many times while I was out at sea. The most haunting was when it came for my Martha, Samuel's mother. Its first appearance is not always the most injurious. Although, as ya grow older the bruise it leaves will heal with less and less time, until acceptance and resilience are fused."

He tucked me in closer, prompting the tears that needed to flow.

"You really think that in time it gets easier, Mr. Cory?" I asked.

"No, dear, not really. It never does. But yar reaction to it will not be so bewildering."

"It's so sad. She was so young," I said, choking on fresh tears.

"It is always a sorrowful and unhappy time. Make the best of this day and learn from it. There are worthwhile lessons in death. Lessons ya can utilize in life, Emily."

"How ... what can one ever learn from death, Mr. Cory?"

"How to live, child ... learn how to live," he recited, "and live life to its fullest. It's a big world and very few get to see it. I have and ya should also."

He cloaked me with his arms as I cried, tenderly rocking me like a baby as we watched the longboat disappear behind a ship traffic.

Later in the day, some of the crew abandoned ship. Though Eli had stayed on, some of his companions were too shaken by the lifeless body, which had been stored in their sleeping quarters. They had asked to be put ashore since superstitions and Vodun had condemned the ship as cursed. Though they felt obligated and thankful for all the opportunities given them, there was nothing that could convince them to stay. As for Eli, he was an educated gentleman and had converted to Christianity when a child. Even his dress was unlike his compatriots, with his brass button coat, paisley neckerchief, and leather shoes. Yet, when he agreed to stay, his voice stammered. Though Eli could rationalize the truth, he had difficulty quelling the fear of tradition and ritual custom. In the end, reason won out.

For the trip home, Samuel was left little choice but to wait for favorable winds. This could take upwards of a week. It looked like the girls and I would be taking a coach home. First we would stop at the Chaloner residence. Seabury Cory had been more than kind and had given me some money to hire a carriage with a little left over for shopping. There was no way we would ride past Main Street without feeding Amy's inclination to buy a new hat or another pair of shoes. The four pair she owned were just not enough, she argued. One pair was for everyday wear, one for church, and ... I couldn't tell you what the other two pair were used for. "You can never have too many shoes," she would maintain.

Amy lived on the corner of Rock and Maple Streets in Fall River. The house was not like anything I had ever seen. A stately home, it was three stories high and painted in bright colors.

"See that window up there in the round tower?" she said, proudly. "That's the sitting area in my bedroom."

The Chaloner house was not as dignified as the Sanford place. It had an almost playful look, with fancy pastel painted corbels and multi-colored trim work. It had the look of a rainbow carnival. Once inside, Amy led us to the widow's walk, high atop the roof, a small room with windows for walls.

"This is a marvelous place!" proclaimed Louisa.

"All the houses on Nantucket have them," said Amy. "They call them roof walks. They are open to the air, platforms with a railing, just a porch, really. Father had this one turned into a small room with windows, roof and all."

"Look at those spectacular views!" I said.

"A captain's wife would come up to a place like this to wait their husband's return from sea," said Amy. "Father said that sometimes they never did. You live by the water, Emmie. Have you never been up in one?"

"Oh, yes, on the Sanford house," I replied.

"You're right, I had forgotten. David took us up there when we were children."

As we sat talking and enjoying the vistas, a servant soon appeared with refreshments. We made ourselves comfortable and Louisa and I settled in for a pleasant visit. A well-earned one, I might add.

"Oh look! Is that not the *Sphinx* in the distance?" said Louisa.

"Yes, it is," I said.

We looked out toward the river, all three of us, quietly.

"That poor Annie," lamented Amy.

"Where do you suppose they will take her?" asked Louisa.

"I would imagine to the North Burial Ground down a way on Main Street," said Amy.

"Do you think she really, really..."

"It's all right to say it, Lulu. Hanged herself? Unlikely."

"I agree," I added. "Very unlikely."

"Only those with money hang themselves," said Amy.

"What makes you say that?" Louisa asked.

"Father is always saying, someone-or-other will hang himself, every time they lose money on a business proposal," she explained.

"Interesting," I replied.

"I've got an idea," said Louisa. "Let's have a special meeting of the Readers Club while we're here."

"Yes, let's," I said.

"Everyone come to order," said Louisa, knocking on the table. As President of the Drift River Readers Club, I would like..." She stopped mid-sentence.

"Yes, go on," I said, sipping my tea.

"I still am president of the club," she said, uncertain. She looked over at Amy and bit her lip.

"You sure are, Lulu," declared Amy. "Now what were you about to say?"

"I was thinking about Sarah Cornell and how we were planning to investigate the ... the..."

"Hanging, Lulu, hanging! Just say it!" yowled Amy.

"Yes, that. Well, I regret to say that I lost the stomach for it," said Louisa, taking a scone from the tray on the small table.

"If you don't feel like you want to, we won't. I fully understand," I said. "Is that not right, Amy?"

194

"Well, it was so long ago. If there was something to uncover, I'm certain someone would have," said Amy.

"I suppose you're right," I said.

"Instead, let's investigate Annie's," she said.

"Say that again," cried Louisa.

"Let's investigate the hanging at Cuttyhunk Island," Amy said.

"No, Amy, no!" wailed Louisa.

"Why not? After all, Emmie and Annie were friends."

"We were acquainted," I said, "Besides, we can't be seen to hinder or obstruct the authority's investigation."

"Oh, pooh the authorities!" said Amy.

"Well, I don't think it's a good idea," decided Louisa

"All those wishing to impeach President Lulu, please raise your hands," declared Amy, holding one up.

"Let's agree to table the idea," I suggested.

"Amy's deranged idea is tabled," declared Louisa, rapping her knuckles on the table.

She expelled an intense, miffed sigh and threw herself back in her chair.

"May I ask the chair for permission to put forward an idea?" I begged.

"Go ahead," said Amy. "The chair is pouting at the moment."

"Go ahead, Emmie. You may as well," grimaced Louisa. "No one listens to me."

I reached into my purse and retrieved a tiny sheet of notepaper.

"These are some books I looked through at the old Athenaeum the last time I was there," I said. "New titles the library just got in. I was thinking that perhaps we can choose from one of these three titles as the next book for the club to read."

"Let's hear them," said Amy.

"The first is one you all heard of, *The Scarlet Letter* by Hawthorne. The next is Elizabeth Browning's *Poems*. And finally, *The Romance of the Forest* by Ann Radcliffe. I think she's English."

"You should know which one my vote is for," said Amy.

"Browning?"

"Yep."

"And you, Louisa?"

"*The Romance in the Forest* sounds interesting," she replied.

"I know you want it to be *In the Forest,* Lulu, but she said *Of the Forest—of the Forest*," Amy whined.

"Will you tell Miss Chaloner that the president is not talking to her at the moment?"

I ignored the quarrel. "I was hoping to break a tie, but I thought we would read *The Scarlet Letter*," I added.

"Oh, I don't want to do this any longer," whimpered Louisa. "The death of that poor girl is wearing on me."

"I'm afraid it is wearing on all of us," I concluded.

"So what do we do about our next assignment?" asked Louisa.

"I vote we table it," said Amy, rapping the table.

"I'll second that," I replied.

"Can we go home now, Emily? I'm tired."

We concluded our visit to the Chaloner residence and Amy made arrangements with the chauffeur to drive Louisa and me home.

The journey to Westport was both long and jarring. The polarity of sailing by sea and riding along a gravel road could not be more dissimilar. If I could sail anywhere instead of riding, I would. On the drive, Louisa and I mulled over the events of the traumatic journey now well behind us—the freeing of the *Nimrod*, the death of Annie, and Louisa's wantoned complaint about how rude Amy was. When we were done, all we were left with were churning questions. Why did Annie hang herself—or did she? Why was the shed door open when we were there and locked when we returned? And why was Tim acting so erratically? We concluded that it was just too much for us to think about. For now, our minds were weary and hearts in need of mending.

We traveled quietly for the last couple of miles. The carriage turned down County Road towards Westport Village, better known as the Head of Westport, and not to be confused with Point Village where I lived. This was the head of the Drift River and the place where most Westportians did their shopping. Here one could find a butcher, grocer, cobbler, and even a lady's haberdashery. This was the true center of the town of Westport. A very busy place, which even included several mills—a gristmill, saw mill, and a paint mill. My fear was that the village would continue to grow and before I knew it, little Westport would be a city.

We rode by Lawton's sawmill and the three-story obelisk-shaped windmill that powered the Davol Paint Works. Just as we approached Winslow's shipyard, the carriage turned down Drift Road. It would not be ten minutes before Louisa was home—ten more after that, so would I.

Chapter 13:

It had been almost a week since the hanging on Cuttyhunk Island and no news has been circulated. I had projected my inquiry toward the whale masters and crew of the whaling fleet. Most had not even heard of a hanging. It was almost as if Annie Slocum never existed.

I strolled down Point Road to the wharf where the *Sphinx* had just tied up the night before. I found Samuel sitting on deck, a pile of line at his feet.

"Permission to come aboard, Captain," I shouted.

With a splicer's awl between his teeth and thread and needle in hand, he mumbled for me to come on up.

"I see you got home in one piece. How was the trip?" I asked.

"Fine. And how was yours?"

"I wish we could have stayed on board, but Fall River harbor is so noisy and sooty." I sat by his side. "What are you doing?"

"Whipping and trimming the end of some line. How about you?"

"I have been asking around about Annie."

"You will need to go to Fall River if you want to discover any news and ask the police. Most people at the Point have not even heard about it. And since Father and I don't gossip—no one probably will."

"Oh, Samuel, I don't want to gossip. I'm just concerned about what happened."

"I know," he mumbled pulling some thread with his teeth.

"Are you not inquisitive?"

"It's human nature to be curious about such matters." He stuck his finger with the needle and placed the pricked digit between his lips and nursed. "I don't see that we can do anything about it." He shook his hand trying to alleviate the sting. "We did our part."

"What happened to Annie in Fall River after the girls and I left?"

"The steamboat company allowed us to keep her in a rope shed until we could send a boy to call for the police."

"Oh, no, Samuel! Could they not put her somewhere more appropriate?"

"We had her lying on the ground on the docks. A crowd began to assemble. We had to move her somewhere. We had little choice."

"A rope shed! It just sounds so distasteful."

"A couple of officers came down, they inspected the body, and commandeered a granite stone wagon from a mason who was driving by. She was placed in the wagon and transported down to the cemetery at the end of Main Street."

"Did the police say anything about the markings on her body?"

"Nothing. The entire affair appeared routine to them. I told them everything I knew, including her employer's name. Mr. Flint will need to come down and identify her and a physician will examine her. After they are certain who she is, the doctor must pronounce her dead—give the time of death, and the cause. All for the record."

"Then?"

"Then they put her in the ground."

"Don't they notify the family?"

"It's unlikely that someone like Annie has a family; at least not anywhere nearby. In any event, that would be up to the Flint family to take care of."

"Did the police not quiz you about how you found her?"

"We told him how she was discovered, he took my name and address, and that was it, I suppose."

"What if she was murdered?"

"I told them about how we found her, the locked barn door, and the symbol engraved on her chest. They pretty much didn't make anything of it."

"Why not, Samuel? There could be so much more to Annie's death."

"She was a common domestic, on an island off the mainland, and she was once a slave."

"But, Samuel?"

"What can we do, Emily?" He put away his awl and thread into a small bag and dropped the line down a hatch in the deck. He held me by the arms.

"Look! It was a terrible thing. I too had dreams about it. If I dwell on it, it will only play on all the other bad memories I have of when I was down South. I'm trying to heal, Emily. There is nothing we can do for Annie."

He picked up his sewing bag full of twine and needle and took it down below. I waited and looked out toward the Knubble—the doorway to the open sea and route to sleepy Cuttyhunk Island. In my mind, I planned an escape—to break away from the terrible memory of Annie's hanging and even of Sarah Cornell; that dreadful book I wish I had never read. Even if I could plan a journey away from it all, far, far away, I knew these ill memories would accompany me. Samuel stood on the companionway ladder watching me.

"Are you all right, Emily?"

"Yes, of course," I said, as if it were none of his business. "Where are Eli and Tim?"

"Eli is down at the Cuffe Farm with the other men, and Tim stayed behind in Fall River."

"Why?"

"Said he wanted to visit a friend in the city who was very ill. Father, Eli, and I sailed the schooner home alone with no crew. I steered her all the way, I'll let you know, with little pain in my knee. I think you were right. My leg has been feeling better each day. Still unpredictable, though." He leaned over and rubbed his knee.

"I am happy for you, Samuel," I said.

"So am I," he said, reaching for my hand. I was jolted by his touch. I felt my fingers and my heart evaporate into his. "What are your plans for today?"

"Today …"

"Yes, you must have something you were planning to do."

As he held my hand, the spirit of Annie slapped it away, pleading for my help.

"I am going to Fall River to try and see what I can discover about Annie."

"Oh, Emily, let it go." He placed his arm around me. His embrace has always been a harbor of refuge, to be warmly held, released from the ache that pressed heavily on my heart, a haven where I could drop anchors of trouble—but this time the winds of misfortune and quandary were blowing and those anchors began to drag. How could I live with myself if I didn't help discover what happened to Annie? What of the nights when Samuel is not there, when I'm alone, and visions of an indigent body hanging from the rafters of a vulgar fishing shed, pleading for a solution to why it had died, lingers and haunts me? Samuel removed his hand from my shoulder. I walked off the ship.

"Wait, Emily!" he shouted. Clutching his cane, he followed. "Where are you going?"

"I told you. If you weren't listening, Fall River!" I announced, walking faster.

He hobbled behind me, a stiff knee supported by a walking stick. I could hear him trawling his injured leg along the ground as he hurried to keep up. I walked at a more leisurely pace and allow him a chance to catch up.

"Can I come with you?"

"If you like."

"I'll get the buggy," he said, limping away.

"Samuel! You don't have to do this for me," I cried as he continued on his way.

"I'm not," he yelled, with a doting smile. "I'm doing it for Annie."

Our visit to the Fall River police uncovered very little, except for the name of the doctor and place of burial. When I told the officer at the station that I was the one who discovered Annie's body, he just handed me a self-congratulatory, smug expression. I almost expected him to tell me that they were all out of medals. When I pressed him for more information he informed me that there was none. I stormed out, short of giving him an irksome piece of mind.

"That was rude," I said, as we left the police station.

"They have a tough job," replied Samuel.

A policeman walked by towing a ten-year-old boy by the ear.

"They could have fooled me," I said, climbing into the buggy. "I believe they just couldn't be bothered."

"Where next?"

"We have the doctor's name and address. We may as well go there."

"Hopefully, we will have better luck."

We pulled the buggy up to the curb in front of the First Congregational Church and tied the horse to a lamp post. Across from the stately house of worship was the doctor's residence. A quaint little white building with emerald green shutters, it had a large black door with a brass knocker in the shape of a lion's head with a ring in its mouth. Hanging above the door was a small sign—*Dr. Silas Dwelly, Internal Medicine.* I took the ring in the lion's mouth and rapped it on the door. We waited. No one answered. I knocked again—waited—still, no one. We were just about to leave when we heard someone inside fiddle with the lock.

A dapper young man, not more than twenty-two years of age, opened the door. With white shirtsleeves rolled up to his elbows and held in place by tightly gripped armbands, he wiped his delicate fingers with a towel streaked with blood. He was handsome and dashing. So much so that I hardly noticed the red soiled towel he used to wipe his hands.

"Good day, we are la-looking for Doctor Dwelly," I quickly inquired, nearly stumbling over my words.

"I am *Docteur* Marcus Theroux," he replied, with a slight exotic accent.

"I'm Samuel Cory and this is Emily White."

"Ah oui, Monsieur Cory," declared Theroux, singing Samuel's name in a French intonation. He extended his hand. "I remember you from the dock ... the dead girl."

"Why yes, you are Doctor Dwelly's helper," confirmed Samuel, shaking his hand. "Is that not right?"

"Assistant," said the young man.

"You examined the body."

"Oh, Samuel, must you say it that way. She has a name," I insisted.

"Forgive me ... Annie," he said, grimacing. "We would like to speak with Doctor Dwelly," said Samuel, pointing up at the small sign above the door.

"Escort them in," shouted a mature voice from inside the house.

"Yes, yes, *s'il vous plait,*" said the young assistant, moving out of the way so we could enter.

Samuel ushered me by the elbow and I hesitatingly stepped into the darkened, musty space. Once inside, an elderly gentleman in a wrinkled suit raised the window shades and illuminated the room.

"I'm Silas Dwelly," he said plopping his weight into a desk chair. "What can I do for you young people?"

"We are here to ..."

The doctor interrupted before Samuel had a chance to explain. "If you are looking any medical assistance you best see the new man in town, Dr. Peckham, around the corner on Cherry Street. I don't have a formal practice, you understand."

"We are not here for any medical care," I quickly added.

"You're not?" He deliberated and carefully looked us over with a watery, glassy stare. His lower lip, shiny, wet, and drooping, trembled under a bulbous, crimson-cratered nose. Doctor Silas Dwelly was an elderly man of about seventy-five. He was stout, overweight, and balding, with straggly long white hair hanging over cauliflower ears. With well-worn, iron-rimmed glasses and fuzzy eyebrows looking like woolly angel wings, he resembled an elderly Benjamin Franklin.

"No, sir, we are not in need of any medical assistance," insisted Samuel. "We are here about the black girl, Annie Slocum."

The aging doctor thought for a second, shot to his feet, and hobbled to the front door. He opened it, looked up and down Main Street, slammed it shut and fastened the lock. "The city didn't send you, did they?" he asked, sprouting a dubious raised eyebrow.

"Why, no!" I said. "We have come of our own accord."

He rubbed his chin and studied the floor. Marcus Theroux leaned against the side of the desk, continuing to wipe his hands with the sloppy towel. His ordinary but gentle expression was in sharp contrast to Silas Dwelly's queer behavior.

"Our lesson is done for the day, Marcus," said Dwelly. "Store the liver back in the jar along with the heart and kidneys and place them in the ice box. Make certain you sterilize your hands when you're done."

"Yes *Docteur*," said Marcus, rushing off.

"You must excuse my young assistant. At the moment, we are performing an autopsy, you see." Silas Dwelly pulled up two chairs, invited us to sit, and sat himself back down at his writing desk. He dropped down the hinged writing surface and rummaged through some papers in the pigeon slots inside the secretarial desk. "All right, what can I do for you then?"

"We just came back from the police station," said Samuel.

Silas Dwelly paused and then folded close the desk lid. "I knew some authoritative weasel was involved," he said. "All right let's get on with it. What is it this time?"

"No, you have us all wrong doctor. My name is Samuel Cory and this is Miss Emily White. You remember me. Down on the docks."

"Annie was a friend of ours," I said.

"You're the captain of the ship that brought the body ashore," confirmed Dwelly.

"Yes that's right."

"Ah! Now I recognize you!"

"We are on a mission for some personal information about a ... well, about our friend, Annie Slocum," I said.

"Slocum, yes, the African girl from Cuttyhunk," said Dwelly.

"Miss White is the person who first found Annie's body," said Samuel.

"Found her?"

"In a barn ... on Cuttyhunk ... hanged," Samuel said.

Doctor Dwelly retrieved a small notebook from his desk and began to write. "And what do you want from me?"

"We were hoping you could help us," I said, somewhat annoyed by his indifference.

"I don't know about that, young lady," he said. "I don't have a formal practice, you see. Haven't done so in years. Yet I am always called upon. The city uses my services because I have the credentials and I never ask for a fee."

"We would be more than happy to pay for a consultation," I said.

"Why now? The police haven't paid for my services since 1845," barked the doctor.

"We are not with the police," I protested.

"You're not?"

I was beginning to think that the good doctor's confusion had less to do with misunderstanding and more with irrational thinking. "We were hoping you could supply us with general information," I said.

"I see," said the doctor. He scratched the stubble on his sandpaper chin and with bulging, sodden eyes, examined me over the rim of his tarnished glasses. A qualmish bloodshot stare spoke of uncertainty.

"We would be more than appreciative if you can tell us something about Annie's death and how she died."

"I see, I see."

"And?" tweeted Samuel.

"Self inflicted execution!" he concluded.

"I think what Miss White is asking, Doctor, is what was the medical cause of death?"

"Didn't you read the death certificate at the police station?"

"We think there is more to Annie's death than what was entered into law, Doctor. As a matter of fact, I am sure of it," I said.

"You do, do you?" Dwelly peered over the rim of his spectacles.

"Yes, we do!" said Samuel, sternly. "I believe there was foul play in Annie's departure from this life."

The doctor sat staring at us and collecting his thoughts. I had hit an ancient and exposed nerve, a doctor's creed to tell the truth and do no harm. He wrestled with his conscience.

"What do you know about it?" he asked.

"Emily found Annie hanging from the rafters in a small barn," explained Samuel, "and when we cut her down I inspected the body and discovered some bruising and other injuries."

"Hmm, I see. Anything else?" the doctor asked.

"There were some scratches on her chest which I found strange."

"You did, did you?" uttered Dwelly. He sat there in silence, looking introspective—tapping his pencil on the desk. "Well, I have no proof to how those things occurred. Perhaps her employer beat her."

"Oh no!" I cried. "I have never witnessed any distress or anxiety when Annie and I spoke. She was a happy soul who often mentioned how lucky she was to work for the Flint family. Besides, if she was beaten, as you put it, would that not be a crime in itself?"

"Well young lady, her injuries were not what killed her," said the doctor, "now were they?"

"Surely, you must have some opinion—a splinter of doubt about the girl's suicide," said Samuel.

The doctor rummaged through his desk and retrieved a folded piece of paper. "I'm getting too old for this," he groaned. "I'm tired, you see, tired of it all. I tried to retire ten years ago but they just keep knocking at that door. Should take down that damn sign. Well, you want to know what I think, do you?" He tossed the paper onto the desk as if it held little worth. "I don't know what is going on in this world," he said. Whipping off his glasses he pulled out a handkerchief and wiped them. "This is the third hanging I have investigated this year."

"Oh, my! Sounds very upsetting to be a doctor," I said.

"I don't know about that young lady, but it sure has become convoluted. Health care today is all about parchment and lead."

"Parchment and lead?" I said.

"That's right. I have gone through more pencils and paper then I have bandages and sutures. You need to bloody write everything down these days, everything! There is always a certain someone who will have questions, want to know why, how, and when. Sometimes it's not that simple." He picked up the document laying on the desk and looked it over. "Jumaane Slucrumb, alias Annie Slocum. Place of residence, Gosnold, Cuttyhunk Island, mother, unknown, father unknown, place of birth, unknown, place of rest, North Burial Ground." He peered through the top of his spectacles. "Cause of death, suicide by hanging."

"What about …?"

"What about what, my dear man?" barked, Silas Dwelly. "The police are satisfied with the cause of death. If they feel no need to investigate, who am I to stir the pot?"

"I see," said Samuel.

"I wish I could help, but matters like these are bigger than you or I."

"Perhaps bigger than you, Doctor. Not me," I shrieked, leaping to my feet. Outraged, I started for the door. "Come, Samuel, we must look elsewhere. It is obvious we will receive no assistance here."

"Hold it there before you go," said Dwelly. "Miss White, is it?"

"Yes."

"Miss White, I'm a tired old man. I no longer practice medicine. The city insists that I examine corpses, and when I give them my medical evaluation they demand that I simplify. Omit the details, cut down the paperwork. Well I have simplified. I have done what they asked. It all culminated with the police. And very few of them are sympathetic to a black servant girl. And there is very little I can do about it."

"Sorry, Doctor. I don't subscribe to such rash and delinquent practice. Come, Samuel. We have work to do."

"Before you go, I must inquire. Did Annie have a gentleman friend?"

"I don't think she did," said Samuel, looking at me for a clue.

"No, she did not. Why do you ask?"

"A sweetheart, perhaps," said the doctor.

"Not that I know of … no," I said.

The doctor hobbled over and whispered, as if the walls had ears.

"Well, she did," he nodded, with a wink.

"Did what, Doctor?" inquired Samuel.

"Had a lover, of course." With a sinister smile, the old physician shook a reprimanding finger. "And just like the other servant, he was not a gentle man."

"What other servant?" I growled.

He became silent. "I have said enough." He escorted us to the door. "You must go now, please leave." He opened the door and nearly pushed us out. Samuel, the gentleman that he was, took the stormy doctor's hand. "Good to see you again, Doctor, and thank you for your time."

Silas Dwelly nodded, humbly. The glum look of guilt sagged on his aging face. "Wait. You look like nice young folk. Now listen. You say that the dead girl was your friend. Judging by the tint of her skin and the tone of yours, I would have to guess she was not that close of a friend. And to go poking around, asking questions … well, at times it is just not worth it. We live in a closed society … a black-and-white one, you see. You will not find the answer you are looking for … certainly not from the police. She was just a servant. As far as the police are concerned, Annie Slocum hanged herself. That was good enough for them and they made it good enough for me, no matter what else I think."

"What sort of man are you!" I shouted.

"A careful man, my dear, a careful man."

"She may be just a servant to you sir, but Annie Slocum was my friend," I wailed. "Come along, Samuel," I said, clutching him by the arm.

The doctor reached up and took down the small sign that hung above the front stoop and slammed the door.

Appalled, I walked away, arms tightly crossed in front of me. Samuel rushed over and took me by the arm.

"Something is wrong with that man," I proclaimed.

"He's just an old fellow. He's afraid of something."

"It's an awful way to go through life, being afraid. Afraid of what?"

"Something's askew."

"You're right about that. And it's in that doctor's head."

"You weren't that close to Annie, were you?"

I wrinkled my face and shrugged my shoulders. "Not really, I suppose. I stretched the truth a little by calling her a friend. But we spoke every time she came to town, talked about all sort of things."

"Dr. Dwelly sure did speak in riddles."

"What did he mean when he said just like the other servant … and not a gentle man?"

"I'm not sure. Come on, it's getting late, we'll talk about things on the way home."

Samuel was helping me onto the carriage when a hissing sound snagged our ear.

"Psst! Monsieur, one moment, *s'il vous plait.*"

"It's the doctor's assistant," I cried.

He stood by a door at the side of the house.

"Wait in the carriage, Emily. I'll go see what he wants."

The young assistant looked over his shoulder and made certain no one was listening. "Monsieur Cory. I must speak with you," he gruffly whispered.

"Yes, go on."

"Not here, Monsieur. We must not be seen."

"Choose the place."

"Somewhere out of town."

"I'll tell you what, Mr. Thoreau. Here is my card. There will be a festival in Westport this Saturday evening … at the fishing village at the end of Point Road. We can meet there and no one will know. Is that acceptable to you?"

"Yes, yes."

Thoreau studied the card and slipped it into his shirt pocket. In the house Silas Dwelly could be heard calling out for his young assistant. "I must go," said Theroux.

"See you soon," reminded Samuel.

An indulging smile graced Samuel's face as he climbed up onto the carriage.

"What did he want?"

"I think he wants to open doors."

"Doors?"

"It's getting late. I'll tell you later. Now it's time for shopping."

"For real?"

"You did say you wanted to look for a new hat."

"I did! A sun hat."

"Let's go find one."

Chapter 14:

Louisa rapped her spoon on the small tray and prepared a pencil and paper. "I call to order this session of the Drift River Readers Club, everyone come to order."

Amy walked along the porch admiring the tidy garden in the backyard.

"Amy you have to sit down," indicated Louisa, "the meeting has started."

"Go on, Lulu, I'm listening."

"Oh, Amy," moaned Louisa. "You need to sit. That's the rule."

I patted her wrist and solaced her with a smile. "It's fine, Louisa. It's not that important. Move ahead."

"Very well, let us begin. You have the floor, Emmie. First, tell us! What have you discovered about poor Annie?" An intense look gripped her face.

Amy finally took to her chair.

"I must make you both aware. This is a heavy load on the heart. I have not been able to sleep. But let me say that it looks like … ah, like …"

"Yes, go on! Looks like what?" pleaded Amy.

I was uncertain to what I should disclose. This was a delicate if not parlous case—if I can use such a term. I did not want to cater to rumor or frighten the girls. But it couldn't be helped.

"Give her a chance to speak, Amy! Go on, Emmie."

"Annie Slocum … was violated!" I finally whispered.

"Oh … my … God!" yelped Louisa. She twisted in the chair, her hands to her face.

"What was that you said?" cried Amy.

"Well, if you had been paying attention, you would have heard," chided Louisa. "Emmie went to Fall River to see what she could uncover about Annie and she was violated."

"That's not what I said, Louisa."

"I thought that you said …"

"Quiet, Lulu, I want to hear what Emmie has to say!"

Perturbed, Louisa sat up straight, threw back her shoulders, and let out a sniveling sigh.

"You must hold this in utmost confidence," I advised. "It is privileged information and I cannot disclose the source."

"Oh, we don't care where it came from," declared Amy. "Just tell us what it is."

"Samuel said the bruises that were found on Annie were probably placed there by someone."

"Oh, my!" cried Louisa.

"Poor girl," said Amy. "Tell us more."

"Well, I believe that Annie did not die of the hanging. In fact, I think she was strangled to death."

"How do you know all this?" Amy asked.

"From a series of bruises Samuel found around Annie's neck. Like someone had wrapped their fingers around it. Its my personal sentiment you understand."

"How do you explain the fact that we found her hanging?" Louisa asked.

"It's my guess that whoever killed her hung her there to make it look like a suicide. And whoever it was went back after we discovered her and locked that door, probably so no one would find her."

"My Lord! The killer could have come for us while we were there!"

"Not with the three of us, Lulu," snarled Amy.

"Oh, Emmie. How do you sort these things out? Your brain works so different from mine."

"That's a fact," muttered Amy. "What else can you tell us?"

"It appears that Annie had some sort of motif or symbol carved into her chest. It was deep enough to break the skin."

"That's dreadful! What sort of symbol?" asked Louisa.

"Well, from what I can remember, it looked like this." I took the paper and pencil lying on the table and sketched the shape.

The girls eagerly spied over my shoulder.

"What do you mean, from what you remember?" Amy asked.

"I saw it on her the day we were on the island, when you and Louisa went back to the ship. It was incised in her skin, just below her breastbone under her left arm."

"Over her heart!" shrieked Louisa.

"A circle with an X over it," said Amy. She examined the paper in her hand, turning it upside down and back again.

"Let me see," Louisa said, trying to clutch the drawing.

"Wait, Lulu," shouted Amy, holding it up and away, "Then again, it looks like a heart with a cross in it." She handed Louisa the sketch.

"Hmm! Something familiar about it. I've seen something like it somewhere," said Louisa. "Where did I see it?"

"Odd, don't you think," I added.

"To say the least," Amy said. "Do you think it was done by the … the murderer?"

"I doubt she would have done it to herself," declared Louisa.

"Any more?" asked Amy.

"That's about it," I said, holding back the hint Doctor Dwelly relayed about a possible boyfriend. Not certain of the facts, I did not want to diffuse any gossip. "Now we are left with even a bigger dilemma," I added.

"What's that?" asked Amy.

"Who it was that killed Annie and why?"

"What can we do about it?" Louisa inquired.

"Yes, what's next?"

"I don't know, Amy. This murder business is more complicated than I thought. I suppose the thing to do is go to the police, but I'm afraid that they just won't believe us—or even care."

"What do you mean they won't care?" said Louisa. "They're the police. It's their job to care!"

"That is what my source implied. They don't care. And he should know. He more or less hinted that Annie was an African girl. Her demise holds little concern to some. People just don't care about … well, you know, servants—you see what's happening down South don't you?"

"People are strange," said Amy.

"No, I haven't," replied Louisa, "What's happening down South?"

Amy and I gave her an admonishing glance.

"Did I say something wrong?"

"Reading a newspaper every once in a while wouldn't hurt, Lulu," proposed Amy.

"I believe that the police just have no interest, and who are we to push them," I said.

"You are probably right, Emmie," assessed Amy. "Father claims the police are just a boy's club and that crime solves itself. When we reported that someone was stealing apples from the backyard, they sent an officer down to investigate. He was of no help at all. Before he left he picked himself an armful from our tree without even asking."

"I must say, apples and murder are not the same," said Louisa.

"When it comes to a servant girl, living in a far-off island, apparently it makes little difference," I said with some dismay.

"So let's look at the situation and weigh our options," suggested Amy.

"We will come to order and consider options," announced Louisa, rapping her spoon.

"Will you stop banging that thing!" growled Amy.

"Now, now, girls. Let us focus. I think one of the first things we must discover is who was Annie Slocum, who are her friends, and so on."

"How do we do that?" asked Louisa.

"I suppose we could ask some of the islanders about her," I said.

"How about asking Mr. Flint? He would probably be the most likely source," declared Amy. "My father knows him well. He knows most of the mill owners in town from the days when he trafficked cotton up and down the east coast."

"Not sure if that's a good idea, Amy. You can try. Don't let on to what you heard here today or to any particulars."

"What can I do?" Asked Louisa.

"Be president of the Readers Club and keep the tea and cookies coming," I said.

"And reading a newspaper wouldn't hurt," said Amy.

"Well, let's get down to why we are here," I suggested. "Our next selection, Louisa's choice."

Before the Readers Club meeting adjourned we agreed to read Ann Radcliffe's *The Romance of the Forest* and review it in the next session. I had changed my vote and decided to read Mrs. Radcliffe's story as to appease Louisa, since it was her choice, though I had hoped for something a little more wickedly, like the *Scarlet Letter*. Amy thought Nathaniel Hawthorne's narrative haughty and distasteful, especially in its portrayal of women, even though she never read it or knew anything about it.

When we left Louisa's, Amy was picked up by her family coach. She had offered to take me home, but it was such a nice day that I decided to walk. My legs and brain worked very well together, and I do much thinking when using my feet. And considering everything the girls and I had just discussed, my feet and legs had a lot of thinking to do.

It was evident that I needed to discover a little more about Annie. I am crossing my fingers that Samuel will take me out to Cuttyhunk Island, where I can speak to Annie's neighbors or possibly someone from the Flint family about the incident.

When I arrived at Point Village, I strolled down to the wharf to look for Samuel. It was a windy and hot, blustery day. The purging scent of salt and withered seaweed spoke to a falling tide. Cool gusts blew from the north as heat pushed up from the south. It was not unlike sitting by a squally, radiant fireplace and an open window in winter. A close-knit, lazy swell rolled up the gusty river. Ships in harbor bounced and swayed like bucking bulls, their masts scribbling across fast moving clouds. The *Sphinx* lay tied to the wharf, silent and waiting—a floating hobbyhorse, begging to be ridden. But Samuel was nowhere to be found. I started for home.

You don't know how happy I felt to see Tim Cadman sitting by the back of the old carpentry shop where he lived. I peered over. He turned his head and looked away. It was not like him to ignore me.

"Hello, Timothy," I yelled.

He turned his back to me without a reply. Walking over, I stopped short, noticing right off that something was wrong. He wiped the corner of his eye with his sleeve.

"Are you all right, Timothy?"

"Hi, Emmie," he said, wiping his other eye.

"Lord, it is windy today, is it not?" I asked, pretending I had not noticed him crying.

"Yes, it is."

"You didn't sail home with the *Sphinx*."

"I had to visit my sick friend, Josh," he said, his voice creaking, amidst broken words.

"Oh, how is he?"

He turned away. I watched as his body heave as he fought back tears. "He's dead."

"I'm sorry, Timothy." I moved closer to him. He walked away holding up his hand and waving me off. He wiped his face with his sleeve. Having no desire to shame him I turned to go.

"Wait, Emmie." He shot me a counterfeit smile. "How's Amy?"

"Fine. I was just with her this morning."

His smile suddenly became sincere, curling over to one side of his face as it always did. "She's a good girl," he declared.

"You love her, don't you?"

He chuckled. The embarrassment of my proclamation annexed a twinkle in wet eyes. "Like I said, she's a good girl."

"And a good friend."

"So, where are you going off to?"

"I was looking for Samuel but I couldn't find him. I guess I'm on my way home."

"Come. I'll walk with you. I need to talk to him myself. Perhaps we'll run into him on the way."

I waited as he closed the door to the carpentry shop. The wind blew harder than ever. A harbor zephyr sent a whirlwind of sawdust funneling up Point Road. I was always amused by some of God's little nature games. Grandmamma often talked about the wind funnel of 1838, which spun down from the sky like an enormous black mushroom and traveled along the river, and like the draft of a powerful chimney sucked water and fish right out of the sea, dropping cod and flounder all along the fields of Point Road. Yep, the man upstairs must have had Himself a good laugh that day.

"Did you enjoy your stay in the city?"

"What can I say," I grumbled, "it's a city."

"Yeah, I know what you mean." He snickered.

"Timothy, what happened to your friend?"

"Consumption."

"That is a terrible way to die."

"He was only thirty-two."

"That is too young. How long had you known him?"

"About two years. I worked with him on the lake steamer. He was a good friend, but a lonely man. Estranged from his wife. He told me some things before he died, awful things."

"What sort of things?" I asked, not really expecting to be told.

"Have you ever seen anyone die, Emmie?"

"I, I can't say I have."

"I was there when Josh passed. Just him and I. I didn't realize he was that sick. I had gone to visit him hoping to see him up and about. If I hadn't visited, he would have died alone."

"That's just awful, Timothy. At least you were there to comfort him."

"Yes, I sat with him. Josh was afraid of dying. Who's not! Big man, over six-foot-tall, huge muscular arms, yet, he wanted me to hold his hand, and I did. As he lay dying I could feel a surge fizzle up my arm from his, like a gentle breaking wave along the beach. I heard him whisper my name and grip my hand ever so tightly. Then all his strength was gone. The outpouring I felt left his hand—it stopped, he went limp. At that moment, he mumbled his last words—*hello mother*. Strange. Then he was gone."

"I'm so sorry for you and your friend, Timothy."

"I could no longer stay with him. I called his landlady and left him there, alone."

"That was alright. He was that much richer in having you with him."

"Don't you understand, Emmie. I left him there. I abandoned him. I could no longer see him in that state. Just like I abandoned Sam and Eli that day on Cuttyhunk."

"No, Timothy, no. It's nothing to be ashamed of. Death is frightening."

Tim's encounter with death and his friend Josh was so much more intimate than my discovery of Annie. He actually held death in his hand, felt the spirit of another enter and leave his body and, ultimately, his friend's. What a gruesome sensation and despairing experience it must had been. A tear tickled and fell from the corner of my eye.

"Before Josh died we had a long talk. He opened my eyes to many things. Including the reason why he and I were fired from the steamboat company."

"Do you want to talk about it?"

He stopped walking and looked down, kicking the soil in the road. "I need to talk about it, Emmie."

"I'm more than happy to, if you like."

"No, you don't understand. What Josh told me involves us. Before he died, he tied up some loose ends—ends I wish I never knew existed. What I know is not pleasant. Its tentacles are long and ominous, and one of them leads right to us."

"What do you mean?" At first I was eager to help him with whatever ailed him. Now he had me concerned.

"It has to do with Annie."

"What about Annie? Tell me."

"I spoke to Sam last night when I got back from Fall River. He was closing up the *Sphinx*. After I informed him of what Josh had told me he explained that you two had a visit to Doc Dwelly."

"Yes we did."

"It all makes sense now."

"Please Timothy, you're scaring me."

"You still take piano lessons from David Sanford's mother, don't you?"

"Yes. What does that have to do with anything?"

"You must have known Mary Sullivan."

"Quite well. She's a gentle and kind soul."

"Does she still work for the Sanfords?"

"Well, no. She went back to Ireland, why?"

"Mary Sullivan did not go back to Ireland, Emmie."

He faced me and looked me in the eyes. His jaw moved from side to side as he ground the words between his teeth, preparing to spit them out. "We must find Sam," he said. "We need to talk."

"No! You're frightening me. Tell me what it is you know."

He turned and walked away.

I gave chase, clutched him by the arm, and spun him around. "Timothy, talk to me! What do you know about Mary?"

He gave me a serene and bewildered look. His face melted back to sadness. It was not the look of grief, which he displayed earlier, but one of regret and sorrow. I yelled at him. My voice bounced off the small cottages lined along Point Road.

"Timothy, tell me!"

His words were hushed and bleached of all sentiment and warmth. "Mary is dead, Emmie."

"What did you say?"

"She's dead," he mumbled, voice cracking.

"No, she can't be. How would you know? Why would I not have heard?"

"I was there. I saw her."

"There, where, Timothy, where?"

He paused and peered down Point Road to the dozing whaling vessels, their masts swaying to the stormy tide like topsy-turvy clock pendulums up into a cloudy sky. He turned and looked at me. "Josh and I found Mary Sullivan."

I froze unable to move. When I tried to walk, my legs became gelatin. Timothy looked at me with as much dolefulness as a heart could hold.

"Find Sam, Emmie. We need to talk."

"No, it can't be true," I said staggering back, dazed and speechless. I anchored my tearful eyes on his face.

He struggled with a mournful squint.

I opened my mouth, uncertain what to say. Finally, I mustered some words—an inquiry swathed in dread. A one-word question dropped from my lips. "How?"

He looked down at his feet and then at me. "Hanged!"

Chapter 15:

It was 7:30 in the morning when I heard Grandmamma calling up to me. Bearing in mind that I am usually up by six a.m., there was a trace of consternation to her voice. Perhaps she heard me weeping in the night. I confess to crying myself to sleep after receiving the news from Tim that Mary Sullivan was dead. In this tiny house, grieving would not have gone unheard.

In truth, I have been awake since daylight. I just felt too emotionally drained to get my tired bones up and out of bed, battered by the demise of two women, one who I was well-acquainted with. After giving it some critical reflection, I have concluded that I must harden my outlook on things ... especially the unexpected passing of a friend or someone I felt close to. After all, that's life, past, present, and future tense.

How does one arrive at such unharmonious reasoning? Our feelings and hearts are not steel latches we can fasten and loosen at will. Attempting to contain the affliction of sorrow, the misery in sadness, or the torment of the soul is like trying to suppress a kettle from boiling without removing it from a roaring fire.

Seabury Cory appeared to imply that such a resolution is accomplished through time and time alone, and that the older we become the more accepting we are of our fragile existence, thus the easier it is to endure the death of another. If true, it would take the average flesh and blood girl a lifetime to hone such a stout and vigorous resolution. I have told myself that I should be prepared and more aware and not see death as an unnatural occurrence. How do I accept such permanent circumstances when someone close takes their own life, or it is taken from them. There is nothing natural about such an outcome. What would I do, how would I conduct myself, if in fact it was someone I loved, someone very dear to me ... like Grandmamma? No! I cannot think such terrible things. I will not think such terrible things! Still I must be strong and not let Grandmamma notice that I had been crying. Though the weeping is long over, I can still taste the tears deep in my throat, feel the puffiness under my eyes, and the river that still flows from my runny nose.

"I have toast on, dear," she yelled from the foot of the stairs.

"Coming, Grandmamma!"

I wiped my cheeks with the sleeve of my nightdress, tousled my hair down around my face, and started the sheepish trek down the creaky stairs to the kitchen.

"Good morning, sleepy-head."

"Morning, Grandmamma. I didn't realize what time it was."

"The old rooster called on you well over an hour ago," she said. "You must have seen the sun. It shines right in your window by seven."

"I know. I was tired, I suppose."

I sat myself at the table. Bread was toasting. The smell of preserved strawberry filled the kitchen, while the hissing water in the kettle came to a boil.

"That's quite alright, dear. I've been tired most of my life."

"It gets really hot in that attic bedroom," I said. "I had trouble getting to sleep last night."

"I know it does, dear. Enjoy your breakfast. I just opened a fresh bottle of jam made from the strawberries we picked at Gooseberry Island." She unlocked the kitchen window above the sink and swung it out. An ambrosial gust of brisk air swept across my face. "How's that?" she asked.

"Lovely, Grandmamma."

"God knows, there can't be any berries left on that spit of land after Mr. Atkins let his sheep wander it."

"Remember last year when the sheep all became sick from eating the unripe berries—lay down and wouldn't get up?" I said, chuckling.

"Took old Atkins a week to move the woolly things."

"Poor animals. They are adorable, though," I said.

"Adorable yes, but as mindless as a grassy dune."

I sat, silently, eating my toast and jam. Watching Grandmamma eat breakfast was a lesson in repose. *Simplicity is a precondition to contentment,* she often said during a morning meal, *quantity and abundance just misery in fancy dress, where the sun always rises but supplies no warmth.* And though we have no money to speak of, I suppose in many respects she is right. Simple toast and jam is all a body needs in the morning to get one started through the day. In other respects, I do enjoy a new dress, trinkets, and a good book occasionally.

"Where are you off to today?" she inquired.

"I may go uptown to the library in Fall River to pick up a new title for the Readers Club."

"That's nice dear. What's it called?"

"*The Romance of the Forest* by an author named Ann Radcliffe. Have you heard of her, Grandmamma?"

"Can't say I have. I hope it is not one of those wayward, sinful writings."

"Oh no, it' a book about ... forests, trees, and nature." A tinge of guilt poked at me for telling a white lie.

She smiled. "That's nice, dear. Most young people today can't tell the difference between a maple, elm, or oak."

I finished my breakfast and cleaned off my plate. Grandmamma's routine of having her meal, washing dishes, and daily prayer was no different today than any other. As for me, I got dressed and hurried out the door, off on a mission.

On my way down to the wharf, I stopped and glimpsed into the carpentry shop. I could hear the sawing of wood inside. I called out for Tim and was greeted by Mr. Howland instead.

"Good morning, young lady!"

"Oh, morning, Mr. Howland."

He held a barbed-tooth saw. "How's Charlotte ... haven't seen her in a while?"

"As well as can be expected. She's almost eighty-seven now, you know."

"We all have a little catching up to do now, don't we?" The old carpenter smiled. He pulled a rag from his pocket and wiped the sharky teeth on his saw.

"Is Timothy working today?"

"He's down by the wharf taking measurements on the *Sphinx* for a new bulkhead."

"A bulkhead?"

"A partition to strengthen the hull ... you know, a wall."

"Oh yes! You have such an interesting job Mr. Howland—furniture, casks, boats, is there anything you don't build?"

"If it's made of wood we will construct it, young lady."

"Well, I best be on my way. It was nice talking."

"Same for me. You take care now."

"Goodbye, Mr. Howland."

With the commissioning of the *Nimrod* a couple of days off, activities along the harbor were busy as ever. With a hoisting boom dangling from the whale ship, men lifted a large iron flensing tub or try pot used for the cooking of whale blubber, up onto the deck. Lined along the dock, waiting to be loaded, were countless oak casts, standing in a row like potbelly soldiers, their freshly painted iron strapping gleamed to dawn's dilated sunlight. Stony, the village mason, along with two boy helpers, hauled bricks from a carriage onto the ship, where they would build the furnace, which cooked blubber and helped extract the oil from those behemoth gentle giants of the sea. Two men pulled a line, tethered to a block at the top of the mast as a pallet of barrels rose from the wharf and swung onto the bustling vessel. Repairs had been made to the copper clad bottom of *Nimrod* and she was ready to marry the sea.

I walked along the wharf and noticed Amy chatting with Hosea Sanford, the owner of *Nimrod*. He kept a busy eye on his new investment. Feeling uneasy, I made certain to keep my distance, not quite sure what to say to the man. I must confess, I have never felt comfortable in the company of Hosea Sanford, especially now since learning about poor Mary Sullivan. I waved to Amy when he wasn't looking.

As always, Amy was overly dressed and exquisitely so. You may pay her a compliment on her flushing attire if you must, but you would only be relaying knowledge that she was already quite acquainted with, and may be insulted when she hands your accolade back, and imply that you should pitch the patronizing praise to someone else. From a distance, she looked conservatively dressed, in a chestnut-colored moire' fabric, and matching shawl. The silk lace throughout the weave and the *passementerie* braid woven into the shawl, with matching parasol, spoke to a more formal decorum, one which clashed with the grubby oil veneered ships, and primordial whalemen around her. Should we ever encounter the President of the United States or the dignitary of a foreign country in our idle travels, Amy would be the only person not ashamed of what she was wearing.

"Emmie, how delightful," she said, in her own classical style, greeting me as if we hadn't seen each other for years.

"Hello, Amy. That is Mr. Sanford you were talking with."

"I was trying to uncover what he knew. Men's brains are constructed like string instruments. You just have to know how to pluck them. Unfortunately, old man Sanford's brain is out of tune. Makes no sense when he speaks ... never gave me a sensible reply to my questions."

"Probably feels guilty about what he knows."

"In any event, Samuel was right. David was left on Cuttyhunk Island after the ship was freed."

"Wonder whether he went up to the Flint estate," I said.

"Well, the Sanfords and Flints are good friends."

"Did he mention anything about Annie?"

"Said he knew all about it. Became quite unhinged when I mentioned the incident."

"He did, did he?"

"Yes. Told me that a cultured young lady shouldn't be alluding to such distasteful matters or loitering about a whaling wharf. I found him quite rude."

"Well you have to expect such a remark from Hosea Sanford."

Looking offended, she threw back her head and turned her back to me, spinning the parasol between her fingers. "I was about to give him a piece of my mind!"

"Mr. Sanford's always been dour and unfriendly," I reminded her. "He's like that with everyone."

"I suppose. I got the impression he was trying to brush me off. Oh, he was polite enough, but every time I brought up Annie Slocum he became annoyed. I suppose it disturbs him like it does all of us."

I could only presume that Hosea Sanford's exasperation had more to do with what he knew and didn't want to tell. Questions in my head snowballed. Why would Sanford spread the rumor that Mary had returned to Ireland? How did he hear about Annie Slocum's death, when most in Westport hadn't? Had he spoken with Mr. Flint? More importantly, how was Annie's death connected to Mary Sullivan? There had to be a link.

"So, have you seen ... ah, Tim?" asked Amy.

"I'm hoping he's on the *Sphinx*. I'm going there now. Want to come?"

We walked down the wharf to Samuel's schooner, which was tied at the end of the long stone pier. The elegant ship had taken on the appearance of a busy carpentry shop with timber, tools, and woodchips littering its deck. Its copper bottom had been replaced and its hull had received a pearly coat of white paint.

We boarded the ship unannounced and moved to the forward portion of the cabin roof where we sat basking in the warmth of a low rising sun. Amy kept looking around, eagerly waiting to be noticed.

"I hear him whistling down below," she whispered, with a little girl Christmas face.

"Who?"

"Tim, silly. Who do you think?"

"Call out to him."

"No! You do it."

While we jabbered, Tim appeared from the aft portion of the ship with a pencil in his mouth and hammer in hand. "Morning, ladies," he mumbled, "thought I heard someone out here."

"Oh, you startled us," said Amy, clutching her chest. "We didn't realize anyone was aboard."

I looked at the tools scattered all over the deck and frowned. A bashful smile was on her face. It was more manipulation then shyness. "Sam down below, Timothy?" I asked.

"He's gone to Fall River for some bronze fasteners."

"Oh?"

"We're finishing up the new bulkhead. He's been gone a couple of hours. Due to arrive at any moment, I would guess. Good time for us to talk."

Amy ignored him, pretending she had no interest. Instead she sat looking out at the harbor, playing with her hair, wrapping loose golden strands around her finger. If I knew Amy, she was contemplating how she would do the same with Tim. Funny thing. You notice life more closely when you're on the water. Your smell is keener—drink is more quenching—food more flavorsome—and Amy Chaloner more radiant. Her sky-blue eyes blossomed even in the low morning light, and the skin on her rosy cheeks was like polished cherries. Louisa's father called her Strawberry, for the shape and color of her ruby lips. Yes, Amy had artillery and she knew how to use it.

She elbowed me, hinting that I should push over and have Tim sit between us. "Here, Tim, sit," I said, moving myself over.

Tim placed down the hammer and plopped himself between us. He was the perfect unsuspecting prey and Amy the quintessential huntswoman. "I'm sorry about yesterday, Emmie," he said.

"All forgotten," I assured him.

"You look very nice today," he remarked.

"Thank you, Tim. That's a sweet thing to say."

Amy shot me a glaring stare.

"Don't you like Amy's new hat?"

He looked over at it and grimaced. "Yes ... well, it's lovely ... I suppose."

I kicked him in the shin.

"No ... I mean, yes! Difficult to improve on perfection!"

"Why, thank you, Timothy. Now, you were apologizing about yesterday. Tell me what happened yesterday?"

Tim lowered his head and nodded. A few seconds passed in silence.

"Mary Sullivan, the Sanford's domestic, died," I finally said.

"Died?" Amy looked at me disparagingly.

Tim remained silent.

"What do you mean died? She was so young!"

"Yes, it's terrible news," I remarked, "I just recently found out."

"You knew her well, Emmie," said Amy.

"Yes. We often talked for hours, sat by the lake, watching boats go by."

"How did she die?"

I tried to speak. The words clung in my throat. The preoccupation of controlling my emotions precluded any reply I could give. Tim sat with his head in his hands, his fingers kneading his brow. No one spoke.

"Can no one tell me how she died?" implored Amy.

"She was found hanged in a barn!" shouted Tim, unable to contain his silence.

"What!" Amy's dismay mutated into horror. The image of Annie Slocum flickered in her head. "What do you mean! We're talking about Mary Sullivan, not Annie Slocum."

"Like I said," repeated Tim, "she was found hanged, by her neck, in a barn."

"My Lord! What are the chances of two local girls hanging themselves," declared a shocked Amy.

Tim rose to his feet. He moved to the ship's rail and gazed down at the water. A lone horseshoe crab crawled along the river's grassy seabed. The shelled scorpion slithered through the crystal-clear water in pursuit of a wriggly sea worm. On the wharf men worked, carrying coils of line on their shoulders. A spanking new longboat lifted off the wharf and onto one of the whaling ships. In the distance, along the sandy beach on Horseneck Point, Delia Hicks stood forlorn, staring out to sea, anticipating a husband who would never return.

"Remember when I ran down the hill on Cuttyhunk Island?"

"Yes, but you had good reason, Tim," I reminded him.

"When I saw Annie hanging there I couldn't believe it ... that it was happening all over again."

"What's he talking about? What happened all over again?" inquired Amy.

"Let him finish," I said.

"Josh and I had prepared to make a timber shipment to the Sanford estate. There's a sawmill on the property. We saw the door to it ajar and went looking for the mill tender to let him know we were making a delivery. That's when we found her. I was shaken. I couldn't believe what I was looking at. Josh took hold of her legs and I cut her down. Josh believed that Mary Sullivan was murdered."

"My Lord," said Amy.

"You say she was found in the sawmill down by the lake?" I asked, my words sputtering. The hair on my arms stood up as a chill splintered my spine. Tim's account along with the motion of the ship made me woozy. I held my stomach, hoping I would not become sick.

"I can't believe it!" cried Amy. "Hanged?"

"Yes, with this." Tim pulled a flat, ropey cord from his pocket. He handed the five-foot line to Amy. She hesitated. Then took the cord from his hand.

"Looks like some sort of strapping," she said.

"Does it look familiar?" he asked.

I reached over, my hand shaking, and inspected the thick ragged cord. "Not sure. Should I?" I asked.

He reached into his pocket and pulled out another shorter piece of the same line. "How about this?" he asked.

Amy reached out and examined it, turning it over—entwining it in her fingers. "Same cord, only shorter."

"What are you trying to tell us, Tim?" I asked.

"That longer cord was around Mary Sullivan's neck. I found it at Josh's apartment. He had it hanging on his bedpost. I took it with me after he died. I asked him what he was doing with it. He said it spoke to him, so he took it from around Mary's neck."

"Two pieces?" Amy said.

"The smaller length came from Cuttyhunk Island," said Tim.

A gyrating fright heaved in the pit of my stomach—churned, and erupted up into my throat. A chill tingled through my body. My knees quivered. The fear of what it was became ominous, if not unthinkable. My breathing labored. I attempted to speak. Before I could, my words belched from Amy's mouth.

"This is part of the cord that was around Annie's neck," she said.

Tim nodded.

I reached over and clutched the cord from her hand. I studied it.

"Samuel left it tied around Annie's neck. He thought it was important that police should have it. I recognized it right off. Just before they took her away, I cut a piece off it and slipped it into my pocket. Like Josh said … it spoke to me."

"How can this be?" I asked.

"That's not all. There is this."

Tim pulled a pendant and gold chain from his pocket. It dangled from his hand. The bulbous, gold amulet was the shape of a heart. Attached to the surface of the amulet was a silver cross. On the back, engraved in fancy script, were the initials MS. The chain was made of fine yellow links. You could tell by the rich dark color that it was constructed of high-grade European gold. There was no doubt. I was becoming sick to my stomach.

"Why, it's beautiful!" proclaimed Amy.

"What do you make of it?" asked Tim, handing it to her.

"MS is that …"

"Yes. Mary Sullivan!" he said.

"Where did you get it?" Amy asked, enthralled by the charm as she held it up to the light and examined it.

"Lovely trinket," boomed a voice from the wharf. It startled me. It was Old Moses and his companion, Billy Cain. He appeared dazzled by the gold piece in Amy's hands.

"Moses … what can I do for you?" asked Tim, sternly.

"I was just admiring da lady's choker. Given to ya by yar sweetheart my darlin', was it?" He grinned.

Amy shunned him. Uncomfortable by the man's presence, she nervously draped the charm around her neck and pretended he wasn't there.

"What is it you want, Moses?" bellowed Tim.

"Yes, Tim me-lad. Yar gotta come ova' and look at da door to da master's cabin on the *Nimrod*, da one ya put up. It sticks along da frame." Moses elbowed his companion. "Isn't that right, Billy boy?"

"Yes, it sticks, it does … somewhere …" said a spellbound Billy Cain. He stared up at Amy.

"I'll be over later. I'm busy right now," said Tim.

"Tank ya, sir," grunted the old sailor. "Mr. Sanford will be grateful."

The old fisherman walked off leaving Billy behind still gawking, an obtuse banana smirk across his face.

"Don't you think you should be going, Billy?" remarked Tim.

"Billy! Get ova' hey'a … now!" commanded Moses.

The burned-face boy bowed, backed away, and scurried off.

"Skunk," grumbled Amy.

"Cheeky, to say the least. Did you see the way he looked at Amy?" I said. "What do you suppose they really wanted?"

"Nothing, absolutely nothing," declared Tim. "Just sticking their nose in other people's business."

Amy removed the pendant from around her neck and handed it to Tim.

"Why don't you hold on to it for safe keeping?" he said.

"Poor, poor, Mary," wailed Amy. "It is beautiful, isn't it?"

"How did you acquire it, Timothy?" I inquired.

"Josh had it in his hand when he died. He showed it to me just before clutching his fingers tightly around it. I asked him what he was going to do with it. Just before he passed he said, *I'm taking it home to Mary Sullivan.* Minutes later he was gone."

"I'm so sorry, Tim," said Amy, throwing her arms around his neck. They embraced. When she tried to pull away, Tim held her tighter. They looked at one another, their eyes wandering and darting, scouring each other's face. Amy placed her hands flatly on his chest and gently pushed herself away. Tim slowly dropped his arms like he had awakened from a dream.

They made such a charming couple—the rich city girl and the modest country carpenter—the impetuous worldly woman and the arrested country gentleman. Perhaps I am making more of it than it was—or can ever be.

"Ah, well, yes. That was, ah, ah, nice," stammered Amy. "How did your friend Josh find this pendant?" she asked.

"By accident. It came loose from around Mary Sullivan's neck. It must have slipped down into his shirt when we cut her down from the rafters. He didn't notice he had it until he was almost home. He was afraid to return to the Sanford property and give it back, so he held onto it."

"And he mentioned to you that Mary was murdered, did he?" I sputtered.

"That's what he felt, and I do too."

"How would he know?" asked Amy.

"He saw bruises on her arms, blood along her legs, and a something strangely carved into her chest," explained Tim.

My heart dropped down into my stomach. I couldn't believe what I was hearing, though I knew it was true. The beings of Mary Sullivan and Annie Slocum were merging into one. Though they lived separate lives, their deaths were integrally fused by the taut yoke of a cotton cord, the ominous quietus that had taken their young lives, and the emblem of mystery—the strange symbol carved into their delicate skin.

I am discovering that if I am to be realistic about helping uncover who has done this vile and monstrous deed, I must do so with a platinum heart and not allow bad news to tarnish it with brutal facts or miserable developments—study it all with the mind and not the heart, deprive it of color, withdraw compassion, and above all detach it from intimacy and emotion.

"Does Samuel know all this?" I asked.

"We talked about it this morning," replied Tim.

"What are we going to do about it—should we not go to the police?"

"This is bigger than the police, Amy," declared Tim. "Both dead girls worked for wealthy and powerful men. Josh advised that I let it be. People like the Sanfords are governed by a different law. That is why we were sacked from our posts on the steamer ... not because we did not do our jobs well, but for what we knew about Mary Sullivan. When the captain of the steamer let us go he did so with a cautionary warning."

"Warning," repeated Amy. "What sort of warning?"

"Just that, if Josh and me broke the jar of silence we could be next."

"My Lord. I never!"

"We must keep our heads and investigate this quietly," I maintained. "No one must know what information we hold or what we plan to do about it. For Josh's sake, I, for one, cannot let these murders go unsolved."

"Oh, Emmie, I'm afraid," moaned Amy. "Here! You hold onto this." She held the pendant with the tip of two fingers as if it held some sort of malady. I took the charm in hand and admired it. It was precious—a jewel of great value. But its worth to me was not a monetary one, but a clue to a tragic, unsolved puzzle.

"Here comes Sam now," said Tim. "Must get below and finish my work."

Amy placed her hand on his arm as he began to walk away—thought twice about it, then quickly removed it. She gazed at him, a tinge of fear mingled with a subtle desire. "Will it be all right, Tim?" she asked.

He smiled and winked. "If not we will make it right," he declared, getting up to leave.

"You know Emmie, I think it's a locket," she said. "Look!" She plucked the gold heart-shaped jewel and studied every facade of its surface. "See that little bump on the seam?" I reached out and examined it. "Try poking between it and see if you can wedge it open."

I ran my fingernail around the edge of the charm and tried wedging it open. "I don't think so, Amy. If it was a locket it should have a hinge on one side."

"You are familiar with cheap store-bought lockets. This was delicately crafted and specially made. If so, the hinge would be on the inside. Believe me, I know jewelry."

I tried again. "Nope, it will not open!"

"Give it here and let me try it."

I handed her the pendant. With a determined tongue pinched between nacreous teeth, she crammed her fingernail along the charm. While she worked at manipulating the pendant, I noticed Moses wandering around the *Nimrod's* deck looking busy but not getting much done. Billy Cain loitered along the whaleship's rail and stared over at us. Hosea Sanford was one of the few boat owners who would hire Old Moses, since he was yet to discover what all the other whaling masters already knew—that it took old Moses a week to do a day's work.

"I got it!" cried Amy.

She was about to open it. She stopped. Squinting over at me she grimaced and bit her lip. "I'm afraid to look," she announced.

"Give it here!"

I took the piece in my hand and without looking spread it open. We peered at one another, wavering, afraid to see what we would discover. Amy looked first.

"Oh ... my ... God!" She snatched the charm from my hand. Her mouth plopped open and her eyes blazed like two sparkling, blue marbles in a pool of milk.

"What? Tell me. I don't want to look."

"It's a portrait."

"Yes, yes, a portrait of who?"

"A portrait of ... of ..."

I took the locket from her hand. Words melted on my lips.

"David Sanford!"

Chapter 16:

Gracelessly, I carried two chairs, one under each arm, down Point Road toward the fishing dock. Grandmamma tottered behind lugging a large bag of healing medicines. We were on our way to a celebration down by the waterfront. There had been much talk this year about canceling the Fisherman's Festival since Jacob Briggs and Aaron Gifford, two boys from the Village, went south to fight in the war. But Mr. Briggs, Jacob's father, would not hear of it and rallied the Giffords and others in the Village to carry on with the festivities.

Fisherman's Festival in Westport had started four years previous—a token of appreciation by town merchants, and an observance of fishermen, whalers, and the bountiful harvest gathered over the previous year. After all, it was the fishing fleet that kept tiny Point Village and most of Westport prosperous—though many of the town's farmers would graciously beg to differ. As Grandmamma astutely observed, *Man cannot live by fish alone.* That's what she said. That's Grandmamma!

During the festival, everyone at Point Village participated. It was one joyful family, with a sprinkle of new faces from near and far, working together to make certain everyone had a grand time. Tables and chairs lined the wharf as every household contributed what they could to seat participants and make those who came comfortable. More happy people could not be found seated at one table anywhere.

I stopped walking and plopped down the chairs. "Are you all right, Grandmamma?"

"Carrying this bag, it's a longer walk than I remembered," she remarked. She stopped to catch her breath.

"Why don't you wait here?" I placed a chair in front of her. "Here, sit and I'll carry your bag of potions down to the dock and come back for you."

"I'm afraid if I sit, child, I'll never get up. No, no, you go on ahead. There's not very far to go."

Just that moment, Ian, Louisa's younger brother, came running up the road. "Emmie, Emmie, look, an infantryman," he said, holding up a new toy soldier. He handed me the carved figurine to examine.

"A new one, I see? You must have an entire battalion by now."

He's carrying a rifle," chirped the boy, jumping in place with enthusiasm. "Mr. Moses just finished carving it for me."

"He did, did he?" I asked, examining the whittled figure. "Is your sister down by the water?"

"Uh-huh!"

I handed the wooden doll back to him. Suddenly, someone clutched my arm from behind. A cold tinge of foreboding creeped over me, and my skin crawled as the callused, icy fingers squeezed my elbow. I jumped.

"Jamboree is well underway, Miss White," croaked the raspy voice.

Speak of the devil. There stood Moses, grinning. It was like he materialized out of nowhere. Though it was a hot day, he wore the same old torn, bulky coat, smeared and blackened by whale oil. Sitting in one of the chairs, he wiped his face with a sullied handkerchief. Moses Reyals never failed to unhinge my spirit. I just didn't trust the man. Especially with that snarly squint he carried in one eye. He had a nasty habit of rubbing his hands together and grinding his teeth when he wanted something. His jaw swayed and quivered—virescent teeth quaked like grinding, dueling files—a muffled gnashing that was only a little less disturbing then his odorous scent. It is hard to believe that he was once captain of a whaler and commanded his own ship.

"Here, Ian. You take your soldier and tell Louisa I'll be down shortly," I said.

"Thanks, Mr. Moses," shouted Ian as he ran off.

The grizzly sailor ignored the boy. With limited wit, he focused all his attention on Grandmamma. "Come, come, sit by me, Charlotte. We'll chew the fat."

"I will sit when it is polite to do so," said Grandmamma.

He ignored the hint. "Oh, it's gonna be a grand celebration, I tell ya, grand."

I clutched his chair from behind and began to lift it. He leaped to his feet.

"Need some help with tat, Miss White?" he asked, unconvincingly.

"I'll manage," I countered, pulling both chairs away.

"Ah … see ya have ya bag of panacea, Charlotte," he declared.

I stood behind him and shook my head, warning Grandmamma not to engage in idle talk with the man.

"How's that hip been feeling?" asked Grandmamma.

"Oh, poorly, m'lady, poorly." He ran his hand up and down his leg, walking to and fro, moaning. Suddenly, he developed a clumsy limp. "As ya can see, dear lady, it pains me tremendously."

"I have just what you need," she said, rummaging through her wicker bag.

He reached inside it just as she slapped his hand.

"Don't be a beggar," snapped Grandmamma.

"I was just try'n ta help," he whimpered, pulling his hand away and holding it under his arm as if she just broke it.

"If I need your help, I'll ask for it," declared Grandmamma, rummaging through the sack.

Not unlike a salivating, craving dog, Moses wiped his mouth with a grubby, tattered sleeve. A repugnant chill permeated and filtered up my spine. He stood there, pathetically, waiting with extended hand, as Grandmamma handed him a small corked bottle.

"Now here! Take a mouth full of this whenever you ail. Wait an hour. If you still hurt then, take another."

He quickly clutched the vessel from her hand—afraid she would change her mind. "How can ah repay ya, dear lady? Ya'r a saint, ah tell ya, a saint."

"Just return the bottle when you're done. Now off with you!"

He hugged the flask of coffee colored liquid tightly to his vest and snailed away through the alley behind the carpentry shop. There I noticed Billy Cain loitering around the corner. The old sailor placed his arm around the younger man's neck and laughed. They both vanished behind the building with their liquid prize. With any luck they would not be seen again for the rest of the afternoon.

"Oh, Grandmamma, must you?" I grumbled, disappointed by the gift she gave the old whaler.

"He would allow me no rest if I didn't give him a bottle."

"What was in it?" I asked, "Looked like black coffee."

"Pure sour mash, black tea leaves for color, and a touch of laudanum. I made it especially for him. He'll be asleep before nightfall," she said, smiling and shaking her head, all the while knowing the joke was on old Moses. She wagged her finger. "Out of my hair, makes me happy and fair, I always say. He'll empty that bottle before sunset and sleep like a babe till tomorrow."

I placed aside the chairs and insisted on helping her with her bag. Though she fussed, I would not hear any of it. "I'll carry the bag, Grandmamma. I can come back for the chairs directly."

I took the heavy bag from her hand. Though she pretended to object, she offered not a word. Relieved, she threaded her arm through mine and we slowly made our way down to the waterfront.

I set up the small table, which I had brought down earlier in the day, at the head of Lee's Wharf. Any one who came and went would pass this way. Here Grandmamma sat and displayed her nostrum and potions which she sold for a modest sum. I helped empty her bag, lining the bottles along the table. Fever elixirs and headache extracts in round bottles—seasick nips in small square ones. Old tobacco tins, which she painted and labeled, were filled with an aloe vera paste, a mixture of flour and ground up leaves from the aloe vera plant—a panacea for burns, scrapes, and bruises. Grandmamma even extolled its merits as a beauty ointment to keep the skin supple and new—a contrivance which she claimed would remove the wrinkles of time, and that makes young housewives her best customers. Whether it does or does not do what she professes, I can't say. The success of Grandmamma's creation must hold some truth or customers would not continue to buy them.

I must say, her medicines weren't the most attractive looking mixtures. One bottle contained a leafy wine-colored soup, while another a thick syrupy, brownish-green liquid.

"Ugh! Grandmamma! What's this used for?" I picked up a bottle and inspected the glutinous concoction.

"Ah, that's a new remedy of mine."

"What's in it?"

"A secret formula," she whispered. "Perry Davis and I have been working on it together."

"What are those green bits floating around in it?"

She looked over her shoulder, making certain no one was listening. "Kale and spinach, or whatever is available."

I tore the cork off the bottle and sniffed. "Oh, Grandmamma, it stings my nose."

"It's for your stomach not your nose, dear," she chuckled. She took the bottle from my hand and put the cork back in place. She picked up another bottle. "This one I made especially for Mr. Cornell of Adamsville. If it doesn't bite he doesn't think it's medicinal. Makes a fuss. Well this batch should bite and bite good."

"What's the reddish liquid in this bottle, Grandmamma?"

She snatched it from my hand and placed it back on the table. "If you must know, it's for the cure of lumbago ... pepper, pulp of pumpkin, a pinch of salt, extract of opium, and rum ... lots of rum."

"That sounds ghastly."

"Well, to someone who's in lots of pain it's a godsend. I told Perry that it was too thick and soupy. He claimed that if we included some red pepper pulp it would be readily acceptable as a medicine and not used for evening nips."

"It doesn't look appetizing. I can tell you that."

"It's not supposed to, dear. It's medicine. Still, I should place some of these remedies into colored glass to make them less repulsive to the eye, but you know Perry Davis. Clear glass is cheaper than colored."

"Come now, Grandmamma. You know that it's the rum in all your medicines that makes people feel less pain. Once the effects of the liquor wear off the pain returns."

"And they come back for more. You see?"

"Grandmamma!"

"Shh, child, someone's coming."

"It's Lulu!"

"Over here, Louisa,"

Louisa ambled over with Ian by the hand. "Hello, Miss White. Nice to see you again."

"Good evening, Louisa," said Grandmamma. "How's your father?"

"Oh you know Father," she replied.

"No, I don't, dear. Why don't you tell me?"

Grandmamma looked at me and winked. Poor Louisa. She was never really good at small talk—particularly with grownups. She frowned, as if the chore of giving a reply weighed heavy on her innocent brain.

"Ah, the little boy with the toy figurine," said Grandmamma.

"It's a soldier," he boasted, holding it up for us to see.

"Oh, that's not a soldier," declared Grandmamma. "It's a hunter."

Bewildered, Ian scrutinized the tiny carved pine figure and looked up at his sister. "Is it really a hunter, Louisa?" he asked, in dismay.

"Why don't you go and play with your friends," suggested Louisa, pushing him along.

He held the wood carving high above his head. "He's a soldier!" he proclaimed, defiantly.

Louisa gave him a stern glance and he scurried off. Grandmamma laughed and shook her head.

"As I get older I have less tolerance for children," sighed Louisa, "Look, they're all around us, running, hooting, and howling. Children!"

"It is a family event, Louisa," I reminded her.

Still, Louisa was right. Mischievous youths were everywhere. A little boy ran by us clutching a sand crab in his outstretched hand while chasing a group of screaming girls. Along the water children climbed over and along the wharf, kicked sand, or threw spinachy seaweed at one another.

The little scamps were indeed all around us. Why, the Giffords alone have twelve, not including Aaron, their oldest, who was sent to Virginia to fight in the war.

Screaming and yelling was the order of the day. Younger children were given jaunts on the rigging of whalers and swung out over the water on the end of weathered spars. Older boys participated in rowing contests between Lee's Wharf and Fishing Rock. The festival had more to do with the celebration of offspring then that of whalers.

But it was not just about children. Behind Cory's store, farmers and whalemen played a carefree game of horseshoes, while their wives busily set up tables for the communal meal. Along the shore, those that had them took pleasure vessels out for a leisurely sail. Drifting to the tide, gaffed wrinkled canvas swayed like rust stained wash in a late morning, fluttering breeze.

Down by the shore, men covered a pit with rockweed, in preparation for the main event—the Indian Clambake. This is how it was done. Dig a large hole in the sandy beach and line it with large stones. The hole is filled with wood and a fire started until the rocks practically glow. Once this is done, fishermen pile on soft-shell clams, and fresh cod, while farmers fill the cavity with corn, potatoes, onions, and carrots. Some of the fishermen even include lobster. Not everyone eats the lobster. I don't. Sea creatures that look like enormous insects are not my dish of pudding. Ultimately, the pit is covered with rockweed and an old discarded sail canvas, which is dipped in the river. The buried bounty is then left to bake beneath the smoky wet cloth.

Grandmamma arranged little slips of paper displaying the price for each of her remedies. Simple medications for headaches or back pain—twenty cents. Those which cured more serious ailments were twenty-five cents.

"Why don't you girls go off and search for husbands," proposed Grandmamma. "There are eligible bachelors here from all over the countryside."

"Why, Miss White!" cried Louisa, "I'm saving myself for a capable university gentleman."

"Well, you won't find him here, dear, unless he has a hoe or a fishing rod in his hand."

"Is Amy here yet, Louisa?" I asked.

"Oh, she's on the schooner with Tim." She examined a bottle of potion. "You know, something's up with those two." She popped the cork on a green bottle and took a whiff. She winced.

I laughed at the expression on her face as she struggled to insert the cork. "Oh, that smells ghastly," she whimpered.

"Who else is here?" I asked, taking the bottle from her hand and putting it away.

"Oh, there's this handsome young doctor talking to Sam." Her eyes sparkled.

"See," said Grandmamma. "You found him already."

Louisa rolled her eyes, laughing nervously. "Miss White, you should have been a matchmaker."

"I am. And I have just the tonic for it."

Louisa squinted and bunched her brow. She gave Grandmamma's declaration painful thought.

"Come Louisa," I said, threading my arm around hers. "You stay out of the sun, Grandmamma," I cried, towing Louisa on our way down to the schooner.

"I'm old enough to take care of myself!" she yelled.

"Goodbye, Miss White!" hollered Louisa.

"Enjoy yourself! Don't worry about me. I'll send for you if need be."

"Don't give Moses any more medicine!" I shouted.

The *Sphinx* looked graceful as ever, with its iconic reflection mirrored on the still harbor waters. Banners and flags fluttered from the rope rigging and Old Glory gently swayed on a pole over the stern. On the deck Eli and Samuel worked with a block and tackle lowering Tim Cadman from the top of the mast.

"Hello, girls," shouted Tim.

"I didn't think you were coming, Emily," said Samuel.

"I had to help Grandmamma set up her table of medicines."

"What are you fellas doing?" asked Louisa.

"We're stringing lanterns in the rigging," replied Samuel. "When it gets dark, the *Sphinx* will be lit with a necklace of luminary magnificence. She'll be as bright as the Big Dipper on a crystal clear night."

"I can't wait," she replied.

"Come aboard!"

"Where's Amy?" I asked, holding the hem of my dress above my boots as I climbed over a pile of rope.

"Below—helping tidy the salon for visitors," said Samuel.

"Tidying?" replied Louisa, somewhat incredulously.

"Yes, tidying."

"We don't picture Amy ... well, tidying anything, when she can have others do it for her," I added.

Samuel laughed—leaned over and whispered.

"I think she's trying to impress Tim."

As I stepped onto the deck, a lusty orotund voice, one spoken in broken English, rang out in melodic cadence from inside the cabin below.

"Do you wish I open the hatches, *Capitaine?*"

"Yes, do that," said Samuel, "and then come up on deck. There are some ladies I would like you to meet."

"Ladies!" parroted the familiar voice. The tone of desirable intuition echoed in a distinct French accent. Before I knew it, there stood Marcus Theroux.

"Ah, yes, come over, Marcus. I want you to meet someone," said Samuel.

"My, he's handsome," whispered Louisa, leaning over my shoulder.

"Marcus. You know Miss White."

"Yes! Wonderful to see you again, Mademoiselle." He took my hand and faintly kissed it. A shiver ran up my arm and to my shoulders. Continental tradition, French formality, or European custom—call it what you like—it was delicious and, dare I say, wicked. Louisa stood, eagerly waiting her turn.

"And this is Miss Louisa Macomber," announced Samuel.

Louisa, her eyes, crystal blue spheres the size of two tumescent grapes, curtsied. The Frenchman gave a ritualistic bow.

"Please allow me to introduce Doctor Marcus Theroux," trumpeted Samuel, an artful smile on his lips.

"Pleasure to make your acquaintance, Doctor," remarked Louisa.

"Ah, Louisa! Charming name—very *romantique,*" declared the Frenchman, holding her hand.

"You are very young to be a doctor, Mr. Theroux," Louisa said.

"I am still in training, you see. I am hoping to travel south to le war where *docteurs* are needed. I can attain much experience there."

"Oh my, not the war!" said Louisa. "Do you think that is a good move, Mr. Theroux?"

"Perhaps not, Mademoiselle, but it will be an *honneur* that I can do some good."

"I understand," said Louisa, her eyes fixed on the charming doctor.

It was very unlike Louisa, the way she looked at him. Why, we were gentle ladies, maidens of virtuous moral fiber and exemplary principle. I can understand Marcus Theroux looking at her the way he did. After all, he was just a man. A creature saddled with blatant, superficial affliction and an uncontrollable, if not blameless, desire to gawk at the fairer sex. What was Louisa's rationale? The way she stared at Marcus compromised a lady's ethics and brought the social standing of righteous females into question. There they stood—googly-eyed. This affair went on for what appeared to be ages. It was wicked … wicked I tell you. Oh, I am not condemning her for it, you understand. On the contrary. I wish I had it in me to be so bold.

Covertly, I tugged on Louisa's sleeve. She waved me away as if I were a fly. Amusingly, Samuel rubbed the tip of his nose. A smug silly smirk simmered on his face.

"Samuel! Do something!"

He adoringly placed his arm around me. "Let's get below and give Amy a hand."

The *Sphinx's* rigging glinted in a darkened sky, like a towering pyramid lined with lanterns. Comparing her to his beloved Paris, Marcus Theroux described the schooner—calling her the ship of light. As the night unfolded and the eastern moon ascended, families started for home.

Though she was a picky eater, Grandmamma devoured two dishes of corn, lobster, and soft shell clams. It was nice to see she had a hardy appetite, always a good sign. Now it was time to head back to the cottage.

On the way home, Grandmamma recounted how her people, the Wampanoag Indians, taught colonists to cook the traditional clam meal the way it was prepared on the beach. They also taught settlers how to fish and hunt and plant corn, customs and skills town people take for granted and long forgotten how they acquired them. *We Indian people taught town-folk everything they needed to live in this bountiful land,* she often said. *Once the music has been taken from the virtuoso, the melody changes its tone and is no longer his. Sadly, Metacomet's rebellion and the Indian war is what everyone chooses to remember.*

Grandmamma had proclaimed the celebrations a delightful success. She looked quite happy carrying her empty medicine bag. It was nice to see her joyful. *Enjoy your happiness, always, for it is often brief and suffering everlasting,* she always tells me. And this day was a happy one for certain.

After walking Grandmamma home, the girls helped me carry the small table and chairs we set up at the festival back to the house. There was a full moon and the street was bright as a well-lit bushel. While Louisa and Amy carried the chairs, I carried the small side table. On the trek up Point Road, all Amy and I heard from Louisa was how wonderful Doctor Marcus Theroux was. Lulu had fallen in love.

"Just what do you mean, love at first sight?" declared Amy. "I never heard of such a thing. Who feels that way, Lulu? Nobody!"

The thought of love on the first sight of someone was just a foreign concept to Amy. At least that is what she implied. For if it were to happen to her, not only would she not tell you, she probably would not admit it to herself.

"Amy Chaloner! I've seen the way you behave around Tim. Don't think I haven't," Louisa reminded her.

"I don't know what you are talking about," chided Amy. She rushed ahead, dragging the chair along the ground.

"Amy, I wish you wouldn't carry the chair that way," I protested. "You're going to wear out the legs."

"Carry it this way," said Louisa, the thatched seat of the chair resting atop her head.

"It's unladylike," she maintained. "Besides, I don't want to mess my hair." She proceeded to carry the chair in front of her, holding it by its rails, as if she was about to help seat someone at a table.

"Your arms will tire if you carry it that way," proclaimed Louisa.

"I'll carry it any way I like," groused Amy, lifting her nose and walking faster.

"So, you seem very fond of Marcus, Louisa," I said, changing the topic.

"Isn't he splendid?" sung Louisa. She put the chair down and sat. "You know, I think he loves me as much as I do him."

"You can't love someone in one night, Lulu," growled Amy. "It takes forethought, judicious planning … one must exercise prudence and common sense, and that comes with time, Lulu … weeks even. Not a few hours."

"Emmie, don't you believe in love at first sight?"

"I suppose."

"See! Emmie believes me!"

"When, Emmie?" implored Amy. "Give me an instance of love at first sight."

I placed the table by the side of the road, leaned against it, and gave it some thought. Amy put down the chair and sat.

"Let me think. There was the time that snowy owl landed on the grape arbor by the side of the house. And when I discovered that newborn fawn behind the woodshed waiting for its mother while it nestled between the logs. And then there was that rainy day when …"

"Come now, Emmie. You're evading the question," alleged Amy, "I'm talking about love between a boy and a girl."

"There are many ways to fall in love, Amy. I venture to say as many as there are people."

"See!" said Louisa. "And I am one of those people?"

"Oh, Emmie!" Frustrated, Amy picked up her chair and walked ahead. "You are just as difficult as Lulu," she said, dragging the chair along the ground.

I picked up the small table I was carrying and followed. It did not take long before we were home.

"Are you sure about this, Louisa?" I asked, opening the cottage door.

Amy plopped her chair down. "Where did this fellow come from?" she asked. "I have never seen him around the Point before."

"Samuel hasn't told you?" I replied.

"No! He just introduced us, that was all. He's just a stranger as far as I'm concerned. He said very little to me and I had nothing to say to him."

"When we get back to the ship I'll let Samuel tell you all about him."

When we arrived back at the waterfront, most of the townspeople were gone. Only a handful of men could be seen loading equipment onto the whaler *Nimrod*, which was preparing to leave soon on its maiden whaling expedition in northern waters. As we boarded the ship, Amy led the way down the companionway and ladder. Louisa followed as if the world awaited her, a dreamy expression poised on her face. When we approached, cheers were heard from the cabin. It sounded to me like someone had a little too much punch at the festival. Just before going below, I noticed a dark figure leaning on the rail at the bow of the ship. Up in the rigging the lanterns swung and flickered, casting an orange, nebulous light onto the darkened deck. It was a gibbous moon. The white light it cast illuminated the man's flaxen hair, as the curly strands danced in a twilight breeze. I turned and walked up the deck toward him. His arms were crossed in front of him as he leaned over the side and studied the black waters below. By his side sat the all too familiar bamboo cane.

"Samuel?"

Startled, he looked over then turned away. I noticed him wipe his cheek. Having little desire to embarrass him, I remained in the shadow cast by the mast. "What are you doing out here?"

"Emily!"

He wiped his cheek with his cuff. "I didn't hear you coming."

"Can you not hear that racket they are making below?"

"I have a way of shutting those things out."

I walked over and leaned on the rail with him. "What a wonderful day it was," I said. "Don't you think?"

"Yes. And a glorious night to go with it," he added, looking up at the stars.

We were silent for a moment as we stared down into the shimmery dark water. In the distance, on the other side of grassy knolls just across the river, a gentle surf was heard plowing onto the vast shores of Horseneck Point and its sandy beach. On the *Nimrod*, tied to an adjacent wharf, someone whistled a lonesome tune. Just below the bow of our ship, small minnows leaped and plunged, chased by bigger prey. They swashed and splashed as they sprung out of the water to escape their predator.

"You appear saddened, Samuel. Everything all right?" I asked.

"It's the war you see. While I am merrymaking my comrades are dying in the South."

"You shouldn't think like that. You have done your best."

He took a deep breath and slowly exhaled. "I received news today about a battle which happened in Virginia."

"I understand. It's terrible. The war has been all over the papers."

"This news didn't come to me from a newspaper. I heard it from Marcus Theroux."

"Marcus?"

"It appears he has family living in Virginia."

"I don't understand."

"He received a letter from his cousin giving him news about his uncle."

"And?"

"Pierre Gustave Beauregard, a Confederate general and Louisiana gentleman. I remember him from West Point—a proper and austere officer … very popular with his men. He's General of the Confederate army now."

"Oh, I see."

"It appears that the North attacked a southern strong hold at Manassas Junction in Virginia. The war has started in earnest."

"Virginia is with the South?" I asked, abashed by my lack of knowledge of current news.

"Not all of Virginia," Samuel said. "It appears the western portion of the state broke off and is now calling itself West Virginia."

"Does that mean there's a new state?"

"Appears that way. It's now a border state."

"What does that mean?" I was hesitant to ask.

"They still believe in slavery but they will not fight the Union."

"Oh, my, I just realized. Aaron Gifford's in Virginia!"

"He could very well be. One never knows what orders one may receive in a time of war. News circulates like molasses. Marcus said five thousand soldiers were killed, wounded, or missing at Manassas alone—a place called Bull Run." Samuel slammed the heel of his fist on the gunwale rail. "And here I sit on this magnificent ship, in celebration … having a fabulous time, when I should be down there with Aaron doing my duty."

"Oh Samuel, you can't look at it that way."

He clutched his cane and walked to the other side of the ship. I followed. He looked up at the sky. The pallid moonlight reflected off his face, highlighting his damp cheek and strong chin. His eyes sparkled as he held back tears. Biting his lip, he rubbed his injured knee. The pain was not in his leg, but in his heart—as an officer not allowed to perform his obligations.

Below our feet, muffled laughter and banter echoed as the girls and crew entertained one another. Samuel smiled. I rested my hand on his.

"They sound like they are having a good time," I said.

"Father's below telling old sea stories."

"I love your father."

"Everyone loves Father."

"Yes, and everyone loves you, Samuel." I got closer. "I love you, Samuel."

I gazed up into his forlorn blue eyes. They were distant and melancholy. He looked down at me. I felt like a puppy begging for a treat. I reached up and wiped an evaporated tear from his cheek. Our faces got closer. A serene smile bloomed on his ripened lips, calling down to mine. Not wishing to appear wanting, I closed my eyes and waited—craving, yearning, for their warmth. It felt like an eternity, but well worth the anticipation, as tumid, intoxicating lips rested onto mine. I swooned, knees weakened, and every care I ever had left my inner most being. Like tepid, polished marbles, his teeth came to rest on my upper lip. I licked them one by one while the coarse edges scuffed my tongue. He inhaled me into his mouth and tenderly kissed me. I opened my eyes and looked up at his mouth, moon lit and desirable. He wrapped his strong arms around me and held me firmly. Standing on my toes, my calf muscles went limp. I allowed him to hold me up, my torso tightly against his, as he explored my gaze in search of comfort. I was willing to bathe him in it and much more. As he was about to kiss me, a sudden loud shriek and honking laughter, not unlike that of a tickled mule, rang throughout the harbor. It was Amy. Apparently having a grand time. Samuel threw his head back and laughed. The muscles in my legs stiffened as my feet found the deck. I helped Samuel stay on his as we laughed uncontrollably. The moment, once tender and adoring, had evaporated. Samuel gave me one final heartfelt embrace and stung my forehead with a prickly kiss.

"Shall we get down below and participate in the fun?"

"Yes, we may as well." I replied, somewhat pleasantly deflated.

With his arm around my shoulder we strolled down the deck to join in the hysteria. Though I wished I could have spent the entire night in his arms, I was content that he appeared happier now. For that I would give up all the kisses the world had to offer.

———✈———

Chapter 17:

After the festival was over, I teetered down the gangplank and off the ship. Louisa's father waited in the carriage. I can tell you he looked quite vexed. Captain Seabury Cory escorted Louisa across the wharf to the awaiting buggy. He spoke with Mr. Macomber assuring him, though it was late, his daughter was well taken care of. A somber and somewhat subdued Louisa sat by her father as the carriage waggled up Point Road and into a moonlit night. Keeping a reserved composure, she never turned to wave goodnight.

The day following, I awoke with a faint headache. Perhaps it was the punch. Then again, I often get headaches the next morning when I get to bed late. At least that is a vindication if not a solemn defense. The night before we all spent the evening drinking fruited punch and telling stories. Though the refreshment was expressively made by Mary Ann Cory, Samuel's aunt, and did not contain any spirits, it is my cynical opinion that someone added some. I had my suspicions who. The more I drank the tastier it became. Nevertheless, I kept drinking. I should have known better. Perhaps I did. When it was time to leave the ship, I recall doing so on three legs—the third imperceptible limb stumbled the other two all the way home. I told Grandmamma that it was the heat of night that caused my lightheadedness and funny walk. She knew better. I could hear her say. *Pickle your liver and fry your brain, to stranger and friend, you only bring shame.*

I was reluctant to leave the house since Grandmamma was feeling poorly. A trace of guilt nibbled at my better judgment of leaving her alone. She would not hear of it and insisted I go on with my day. After having breakfast, she retired for a lay down. I left and softly closed the door.

Seabury Cory knelt, tending his garden when I walked by his house.
"Good morning, Mr. Cory," I hailed.
"Top of the day to ya, Emmie—or what's left of it."

"What do you mean? It's only eight o'clock."

"If the day were a bottle it would be half empty," he lectured. "Ya should have been down by the water at daybreak. Ya missed all the hoopla."

"I did?"

"The *Kate Cory* sailed out under full canvas." He stood, and with a small spade shovel in hand, wiped his brow with his sleeve. "Noble vessel, she is. There's a northeast puff—enough to drive her right past the Knubble and into open water. Aye, it was a majestic sight, I tell ya, a majestic sight indeed. I never tire of it."

"The way you tell it, I'm sorry I missed it."

"Young Samuel went down to the schooner 'bout dawn. Told me to tell ya he'd be waiting."

"I'm on my way there now."

"Don't know why the boy even comes home." He nodded his head. "Spends more time on that ship, I tell ya."

"It's a wonderful vessel, Mr. Cory."

"Aye, that it is, that it is. And Samuel's a wonderful boy." He pointed his garden spade at me and winked. "A better companion couldn't be found if ya sailed the seven seas for the remainder of yar life looking for one."

I blushed. "None better."

"Seize the day, young lady, seize the day before it sails on ya." He fell to one knee and returned to his gardening.

"So long, Mr. Cory." Without looking back, he held up his digging paddle and waved.

I was strolling down the road when a familiar voice called out from behind.

"Out of the way, lady. You're impeding traffic!" It was Amy driving a buggy with Louisa by her side. The horse shuffled its legs as it tottered and came to a sudden halt.

"Amy Chaloner! You treat that animal awful," I complained.

"I do not. He loves a frisky charge every once in a while. How's your constitution this morning?"

"You know! I think someone poured spirits into that punch last night."

"I wonder who would do such a thing," she said, flaunting a malevolent smile.

"You didn't!"

"She sure did," replied Louisa.

"Oh, come now. It was trivial fun, I thought."

"It was wicked," I declared, "but I forgive you." I continued my walk down to the waterfront.

"Would you like to get in? We have room for one more," she asked. The carriage moved slowly down the road keeping pace with my stride.

"I feel a little stiff this morning. A good walk will work out some of the knots."

"It was the punch!" confessed Louisa.

"We've already concluded that, Lulu," said Amy, sneeringly.

"Was Father cross with you for staying out late, Louisa?" I asked.

"Oh, you know Father," she said, obliquely. "Thinks I'm still a little girl. It's just the way fathers are, I suppose."

"I suppose."

"Do you know why Samuel called a meeting this morning?" asked Amy.

"No. Just that he would like us all down at the schooner this morning."

"Will Marcus be there?" inquired Louisa. The tone of her voice climbed an octave or two as the words dripped off her lips.

"That's all she talks about," moaned Amy, frowning.

"I suppose he will."

"Oh, Emmie! Is he not wonderful?"

Before I could say a word, Amy snapped the reins and the horse galloped away down the road—a befuddled Louisa held onto her hat, looked back, and waved. "See you there," she yelled.

Up in the rigging, two men performed their trapeze act swinging from spar to shroud, taking down the lanterns left over from the previous day's celebration. The girls were boarding the ship just as I approached. Before going up on deck, I noticed some sort of object just beneath the ship's narrow gangplank. The weathered catwalk pumped to-and-fro with the movement of the ship, its heel end grating over the wharf's granite seawall. I carefully reached under it. It was one of Ian's toy soldiers. I closely studied the wood carved sculpture. Its head was missing. It appeared as if someone had snapped it off, leaving a pointy, splintered butt. I looked around for the severed cranium. It was nowhere to be found. Thinking nothing more of it, I placed the tortured toy figure into my pocket and boarded the ship.

"Hurry, Emmie, hurry!" begged Louisa, leaning over the rail and beckoning me with her hand.

"I'm coming," I hollered. "You wouldn't want me to fall now, would you?"

"He's here, he's here!" she whispered, ebulliently spewing her words into my ear as I stepped onto the ship.

"Who's here?" I said, as if I didn't know.

"Why, Marcus, silly." She spied over her shoulder making certain no one was there.

"I'm happy for you, Louisa."

She took my hand and walked me along the deck. Just before going below she stopped me. "I'll go first," she whispered, nervously tugging on my sleeve. "You follow!"

"Sounds like a plan to me."

"No, no, you go first."

"Are you sure?"

"No! I will."

She bit her nails and thought about it. I crossed my arms and waited. She just stood there fidgeting. She crinkled her face as she wrestled with benign incertitude. I never gave much thought to how pretty Louisa was—when she wasn't making a face. She peeked into the cabin below, turned to me, and smiled. The orangy morning sunlight illuminated her face. Her lips glistened moist in the virgin sunlight. Her eyes radiated, swollen with jumbled excitement. With cherry cheeks and a turned-up nose, not unlike a roused bunny, her face spoke to irreproachability, but one that was friendly and inviting, tamed by kindness and innocence. Sprinkle Louisa with accolades and she is forever grateful. Unlike Amy, flattery with Louisa will get you everywhere. Everyone loved Lulu. She was a child in a grownup frame. She could be so adolescent at times ... like at this very moment.

I took her firmly by the shoulders and pushed ahead. "We will both go," I said, "together. Don't worry, I'm right behind you."

"Oh, Emmie," she wailed, a poignant, mousy smile on her face.

Once we entered the ship's salon, Louisa became a model of poise and tranquility. A minute earlier she was a nervous bowl of fish. Now she conducted herself without the slightest hint of restlessness. It was all an act, of course. Though to be totally honest, I am uncertain as to who the real actor could be—the now affable and uninhibited Miss Macomber, or the faint-hearted schoolgirl, Lulu, who couldn't get out of her own way and decide whether to take the lead or follow. We discovered Samuel sitting at the salon table with Tim and Marcus, while Amy pretended to be toiling away at the galley stove, heating water for tea.

Louisa greeted everyone, with musical resonance. "Hello, everybody, we're here,"

Amy gave her an apathetic, limp clap of the hands. "Lulu, I don't know what we'd do without you," she said, mundanely.

Louisa glared at her. Her shoulders drooped and her face melted into a petulant frown. Straightaway, a confident if not ambiguous Miss Macomber went into hiding and the reserve, shy schoolgirl reappeared.

"Hello *A-mee*," she snarled.

Marcus leaped to his feet. "Ah! Mademoiselle Louisa!"

"Oh, I was unaware you would be here, Mr. Theroux!" said a less-than-forthright Louisa.

Amy walked over, poked me in the arm, and rolled her eyes.

"But, of course," replied the young doctor. "I have been *residant* here on la *navier*. Ah, forgive me. I mean living on la ship for the next few days."

Distinguished doctor and virginal ingénue stood gawking at one another. The ship became a chasm of silence.

Samuel looked over to me and grinned. "Shall we all sit?"

I sat by Louisa where I could keep a maternal eye on her. I kept my foot primed and ready to kick her in the shin if she should say anything compromising or embarrass herself before the French doctor. Meanwhile, Amy continued fiddling with the galley stove in a futile endeavor to make it work. I was eager do discover why we were all brought together.

"Well, we're all here Samuel. What did you want to see us about?"

"A very crucial and delicate matter," said Samuel. He got up to help Amy light the stove.

He poked at the logs in the stove's belly and adjusted the iron flue in the chimney. A flame flared and came alive. Relived, Amy put the kettle on and took her place by Tim's side at the galley table. She reached over and swept his long wilting bangs away from his face and onto his head. Blushing, Tim clutched her hand and tossed it aside. She slapped him on the arm.

"Let's get started," said Samuel. "Shall we?"

"Anytime you are," I said.

"It appears that we are deep into the death of these two servant girls. I'm certain that you all agree that we have too much emotional investment into their demise to allow it to be forgotten or go unforgiven."

"I agree, Samuel. Something is very wrong and we must get to the bottom of it," I said. "We owe it to those two poor girls."

"Tim told me what had occurred by the shores of the Great Watuppa Lake, over on the Sanford property," said Samuel. "That is, the hanging of Mary Sullivan."

"I must add, Sam, I am certain that Annie's hanging, along with that of Mary Sullivan, are connected in more ways than one," said Tim.

"Oh, my!" cried Louisa, clutching me tightly by the arm.

"As you all must have heard by now, Emily and I met Doctor Theroux here at a physician's office in Fall River where he is an intern in practice," said Samuel. "The good doctor here has been gracious in offering his assistance to our investigation of these two girls."

"How can you help, Doctor?" asked Amy.

"Please, Madame, address me as Marcus. I have yet to secure le title of *docteur*. But to reply to your question, I helped diagnoses la body of the young African girl. There was, how do you say, evidence of wrong-doing."

Marcus and his accent captivated Louisa, who sat with an elbow on the table, a chin in her hand, and displaying her heart on her sleeve.

"What sort of evidence?" Amy asked.

"In my examination of Mademoiselle Annie, I discovered a total collapse of the trachea, along with contusions around her arms and back of neck. Also, she had an injury and a cut to her upper bust area," said Marcus.

"Couldn't such injuries be the result of the cord tightening around her neck when she … when she fell?" I asked.

"Yes, but I do not think so in this case. Le cord did compress la larynx and injury to la epiglottis, but the marks I speak of are much lower and segregated portion of la girl's lower neck—along with what appears to be finger-like injuries, bruises, in la back portion of la neck. At la tips of these were superficial punches, like those that may have been made by long nails on a hand, probably from an index finger."

"What Marcus is trying to say is that the injury to her lower neck was probably done by thumbs, since the back side of her lower neck is where the bruising in the pattern of fingers was discovered," said Samuel.

"What does it all mean?" asked a startled Louisa.

"Marcus thinks it is unlikely that Annie Slocum died by hanging, instead she was strangled by someone."

Louisa leaned on my arm and pulled me closer. The fear she felt reverberated down her limb and onto mine. I gave her hand an encouraging squeeze. "Oh, Emmie," she whispered. "It sounds all so terrible!"

I gave her a sympathetic smile.

"I'd like to say something," said Tim.

"By all means, Mr. Cadman," replied Samuel, "please do."

Tim pulled the two cords from his pocket and placed them carefully on the table. "This long one is the one that Joshua Collins took from the Sanford Sawmill. It's the cord that was discovered around Mary Sullivan's neck."

Marcus Theroux inspected it, massaging the thick ribbon like material between his delicate fingers. "*Coton* weave," he affirmed.

"The shorter one is a piece of the cord which was around Annie Slocum's neck," said Tim. He stretched out the cord on the table, this one is very similar to the longer one and probably supplied by the same person.

We all reached out and inspected the lines—running them between our fingers, pulling on them, smelling them. One would think that these common objects had fallen to earth from the moon.

"They look exactly the same," declared Louisa.

"They have the same rust staining," I added.

"Right down to the same defect in the material," declared Tim. "If you look at the longer cord, the one from the Sanford sawmill, it has a couple of loose strands and a nick every nine or ten inches along its length. Now look at the shorter cord, the one used to hang Annie Slocum."

I examined the cord more closely. "Why, it's identical."

"The same fraying," said Amy.

"Taken from the same bundle, more than likely," said Samuel.

"And belonging to one person," concluded Louisa. "What do you suppose the cord was used for? I mean other than …"

"My guess is for bundling cotton," explained Samuel. "Raw cotton, from down South, shipped to the textile mills in Fall River and New Bedford."

"Wait, I would like to show you something," said Tim. He reached for the longer of the two cords. "Can I demonstrate, Sam?"

"By all means. That is what we are here for."

Tim opened a hatch on the cabin ceiling. He proceeded to place a loop in the cord, which he tied securely around his wrist. He gave it a couple of yanks and made certain the knot was tied firmly. Giving Amy a wink, he jumped up and pulled himself up through the hatch and onto the deck above. We looked over at one another bemused as Tim fiddled up on deck. I could see him through the open hatch tying the loose end of the cord onto the brass hinge on the open hatch.

"Now watch," he shouted, looking down through the hatch.

"What are you doing, Tim?" yelled Amy.

There was no reply. Instead, he sat motionless on deck along the edge of the small rectangular passageway. We waited patiently. I gave Samuel a skeptical glance. He just shook his head and shrugged his shoulders. At that very moment Tim tumbled down through the hatch. Clutching the cord with both hands, he hung there for a fraction of a second before the cord parted, sending him flat onto his back on the hard cabin floor. Louisa screamed.

Amy tossed herself to her knees by Tim's side. "Oh, Timothy, are you all right?" she cried.

"Quite the performance, Tim," said Samuel, unimpressed.

"Sam, do something, he's hurt," cried Amy.

"I'm fine," said Tim, loosening the cord, which strangled his wrist. Above him, the other end of the ragged line hung down through the hatch.

Amy stroked his hair, sweeping it up and away from his face. "Are you sure?"

Samuel extended a hand and helped Tim as he leaped to his feet. "Now, can you explain your little spectacle?"

"The cord ... how easily it broke," replied Tim.

"It sure did," I said, chuckling anxiously.

"Yes, yes, I see." said Marcus. "If Mademoiselle Annie jump off le loft, her body would have broken le cord with ease."

"Tim, you weigh much more than Annie," said Amy.

"True! But that makes little difference. I tied the cord to the hatch hinge. I didn't jump, I wasn't pushed. When I fell through the hatch there was very little downward momentum, you see. I only had three or four inches of cord between me and the tie at the hinge. On my descent, the cord was already taut and it still easily separated. Mary Sullivan had four to five feet between her and the beam where the line was tied and Annie not much less. The driving force of her body alone, even though she may have weighed half my weight, would have severed that cord like button thread."

"He's right," agreed Samuel, inspecting the frayed end of the line hanging from the hatch. "I'm surprised that it could hold Annie's dead weight at all, let alone weight at a flying start."

"It broke right where the fiber was frayed, at the nick," I added.

Something to think about," said Tim.

"Good job, Tim, my boy."

"Thanks, Sam," replied Tim, gushing with pride. Amy leaned over and proudly kissed him on the cheek. He grimaced.

"That is what Doctor Dwelly had mentioned about Annie. That the height between the loft in the barn and the ground should have certainly broken her neck," I said.

"Yes," said Marcus. "With that observation I must concur that Marie and Annie's necks should have been broken with le descent. They were not."

"How do you know about Mary Sullivan, Mr. Theroux?"

"Ah, Mademoiselle Amy. I had been in medical school in Boston at le time of Marie Sullivan's death. *Docteur* Dwelly—he performed le examination of the body of Marie. I arrived at his home for my duties on the very day. Mademoiselle Marie was my first *autopsie* lesson outside of medical school, you see."

"You were there, then," I said.

"Yes! At le *autopsie*. I have seen notes on le case of Marie Sullivan. *Docteur* Dwelly's notes. And police records. You see ... *Docteur* Dwelly is a careful man. His hands are shaky, his eyesight is failing, and his dignity has been questioned over and over by many who do not know le man. And I must admit, his ambitions have faded with age. But he is a good *docteur.* That is why I have trained with him. And as Mr. Tim has demonstrated for us … when I read le venerable *docteur's* papers, I discovered les injuries Mr. Tim's friend found on Marie Sullivan were on Mademoiselle Annie also."

"He's right, Sam," agreed Tim. "Josh described Mary's injuries. They were the same."

"And both women had the same ominous symbol carved into their skin," said Samuel. "The figuration we discovered on Annie was just as Joshua Collins described it to Tim. When I first discovered it I thought it was some sort of ceremonial motif, like some natives of Africa cut into their bodies, and that perhaps Annie had placed it there herself. But Mary had the same exact branding. It can only mean that it was placed there by someone … and that someone is guilty of murder."

"Murder?" said Louisa, biting her nails.

"Yes! Murder," blustered Tim.

"Oh, my!" Louisa snagged my arm.

"There is more," declared Samuel. "Something so diabolical, I'm afraid to mention it,"

I held my breath and waited. Louisa drew closer. Was he really going to tell everyone? Louisa, for one, was not ready to hear anymore sinister descriptions of transgression.

I had no choice but to question him. "Samuel! Do you really think it's necessary?"

He thought carefully about what to say and how to say it. "No. I suppose it's not that important. Why don't we take a break? Emily, you and the girls go up on deck for some air. It's getting hot and stuffy in here. We men will sort this thing out some."

"No, I want to stay," I insisted.

"You said there was more," inquired Amy. "I want to hear it."

Louisa clung tightly to my arm. Her stubby round nails, like dull butter knives, dug into my skin. Marcus could sense the tension and terror Louisa was feeling and came up with a plan to liberate the poor innocent from her anxiety.

"Will you escort me for a walk on deck, Mademoiselle Louisa?" He offered his hand. "I would like to learn more about the waters around le Westport *harbour.*"

"Oh, I would!" she said, abandoning my arm for his.

It was wicked. I never witnessed anyone alter moods and jump at bait as quickly as Louisa did. Gleefully accepting the doctor's offer, she exercised very little in the way of judicious modesty as consternation instantly wilted away.

"I don't know about everyone else," declared Amy. "I could do with some air."

"Now there's a plan. We'll all take a break," suggested Tim.

Marcus led Louisa out onto the deck. Amy followed, towing Tim by the arm.

"I'll make us some cocoa. It will be ready in a couple of minutes," announced Samuel.

"I'll make it." I got up just as the water was coming to a boil. After making the drinks I brought some out for the two couples. I returned to the cabin where I drank mine with Samuel at the salon table. Strangely, at that very moment I became aware of the absence of stale cheroot.

"Where's Eli?"

"Oh, I sent him over to the city for some supplies," replied Samuel.

"You said there was something more frightening, Samuel. What were you going to tell us?"

"This is a messy business, Emily. I decided I would not say much more while the girls were here."

"Yes, of course. I knew you were going to describe some heinous detail. Louisa gets so emotional. I'm sure you could sense her anxiety."

"Yes. Lulu's a fragile girl. And what I was going to disclose was just plain abhorrent—details, reprehensible. I'm glad I did not."

"Tell me!"

"No, I really shouldn't. It's not the sort of thing you talk about with a girl or in polite company."

"I need to know. How else can I help solve this terrible quandary?"

He sat quietly and looked up through the open hatch above. Bloated cylindrical clouds hovered in a radiant cobalt sky. Out on deck I could hear a jovial Tim speaking with some whalemen along the wharf. Further in the distance came the sound of giddy Louisa, giggling as Marcus peppered her with compliments. Across the table from me Samuel sat quietly.

"It's all right, Samuel. You can tell me. How much worse can this tale get."

He looked down into his cup of cocoa as if a solution could be found there. The wispy steam from the hot brew rose and moistened his face. He stirred the frothy beverage with the tip of a finger. The hot brew burned his digit. He winched, licked it, and took a sip. I reached out and erased the traces of chocolate left at the corner of his lips with my handkerchief. He smiled. The smile quickly dissolved into a mournful frown. Placing down the cup he took a deep breath and exhaled an endless sigh. "They were assaulted," he said, disgustingly. "A bestial attack of a carnal nature."

"You mean …"

"Yes, Emily! They were raped."

"Those poor girls!"

I was dumbfounded by his revelation … horrified and distressed. How does such a thing occur? Who, why? Are there really such people in the world? Whether I wanted to admit it or not, I knew such offenses befall woman everyday. Even though the cog of life in Point Village appears to turn fluently, still, who knows what transpires behind a locked door. *A latch and door easily obscure the transgressions of perceived innocence and conceal the wickedness of the dammed*, Grandmamma often said. Now, I think I understand more easily what she meant.

"How do you know this, Samuel?"

"Tim's friend Josh had mentioned it to him and Marcus verified it in his medical examination. Everything is recorded in Dwelly's personal notes and his own examination of both girls. Dwelly and Marcus believe that the series of bruises on the back of the neck on Annie and Mary were probably left there by the fingers on large hands, and the bruise at the base of the throat inflicted by a pair of thumbs, which pressed their life into oblivion."

"And the cords?"

"A cloak to blind us! After the girls were murdered, they were hung like game awaiting slaughter. Only the butchery had already been accomplished. The two cords in Tim's possession definitely connect the two crimes. As for the marking on their chests … well there is no doubt it was done by the same person. An African servant girl living on an island and an Irish maid residing miles away. One girl having nothing to do with the other, but dying in the same manner."

"Someone has linked both servant girls—someone depraved and despicable," I added. "Unrelated worlds merged through a common villain."

"A common villain who most likely has a connection to both worlds."

"Both girls were domestics and worked for wealthy and powerful men," I said. "In addition, Mr. Flint and Mr. Sanford are in the textile business. And if that cord is in fact used to bale cotton it may connect them."

"Yes! We can't ignore the cord, Emily. It may hold a key. Then again, it may not. As of now, it is one of the few tangible clues that we can hold in our hands."

"The most diabolical clue is the markings on the girl's bodies."

"Yes, you're right," said Samuel, in bitter agreement. "If we can just discover it's meaning."

"And don't forget the locket," I said.

"I don't even want to think about what the meaning behind it could be," replied Samuel.

"What opinion did Marcus express, if any, on the markings he found on Annie?"

"Curious, really."

"How so?"

"Well, Dwelly sketched the symbol found on Mary Sullivan in his autopsy notes. Marcus copied it and drew it for me. I have it. It's in the desk in my cabin. I'll get it."

I waited for Samuel to return. Meanwhile, I peered out on deck. Marcus Theroux and Louisa sat by the starboard rail where he covertly held her hand. To tell you the truth I was afraid for Louisa. She was such an innocent. It left me to speculate about this 'love at first sight' business. Though I must confess that I often romanticized about it. Most women do, I suppose. I was not certain such a concept was prudent or a real working theory at all. I must agree with Amy's summation on the matter as a more likely scenario and that love, like a hardened steel sword, must be tempered. And that takes lots of work and time. For one must anneal the heart and not allow it to flare like the powder in a reckless gun, firing all its affection in one quick succession. Must give the matter more consideration. For now, there are other pots-a-boiling.

"Here it is," announced Samuel. He unfolded the parchment. "There! What do you make of it?"

I studied the image. "Hmm? You say Marcus drew it?"

"Marcus copied it from the old doctor's notes."

"It's an odd-looking design and at the same time somehow familiar."

"Familiar?"

"I don't know. This impression varies from the one we saw on Annie."

"Just a little?"

"The shape is more like a strawberry or a heart!" I said. "The one on Annie was more oval. Perhaps the killer was crossing out her heart in anger—made advances to her and when they were rejected, he became angry."

"Could be, Emily. Or just the workings of a madman."

"No wait!" I spun the paper around. "If you hold it this way, it's a cross."

"You mean like a cross on a church?"

"Yes!"

"I see."

"A cross superimposed onto the image of a ... heart?"

"Puzzling!"

"We are looking at the work of a monster, Samuel, a monster."

I got up and paced the floor. As I often did, I let my legs do the thinking. When my limbs moved so did notions and theories. It was a habit I had acquired since childhood. "What else did Marcus uncover?" I asked.

"That both Annie and Mary were strangled then hanged to make it look like it was self-inflicted and to cover up any improprieties. Especially since Mary Sullivan was with ..." He suddenly stopped talking.

"What is it, Samuel?"

"Nothing," he said, folding the paper on the table and putting it away.

"You said Mary was with what?"

Looking uneasy, he ignored me. He moved to the galley and emptied his cup. "Would anyone like more drink?" he shouted to those on deck.

"I still have mine," Amy yelled.

"All's fine up here," hollered Tim.

He stirred the embers in the iron stove and the flame flared. He placed fresh water in the kettle. "Would you like more cocoa, Emily?"

"No. You never finished what you were saying. What about Mary?"

He looked over to me, then down at the floor. He shook his head and grimaced. "Mary Sullivan was with child!"

My mouth slumped open and my eyes jounced, while my mind disengaged like an exploding clock spring, startling my womanhood. I could not comprehend what I just heard, or lend an ounce of rational thinking to such an unofficial disclosure. I felt horrible.

"Perhaps I should not have told you."

"You had to," I insisted, "I need to know the truth."

I moved over to the companionway for some air.

"Are you alright?"

"Yes, yes ..." I said, trying to look calm instead of what I really felt, dismay for my fellow man. I have lived more years than I wish to admit, and in that short time, I have only witnessed good people—a village community full of kindness, caring, and thoughtfulness—be it family, friend or stranger. I keep telling myself that if I am to survive the evolution of these cruel and savage crimes I must harden my soul and fortify my resolve ... stomp instead of tiptoe—grit teeth, instead of shed tears and, foremost, understand that there are all sorts in the world, good and bad, for what we are uncovering is an ugly affair. Though I may not have the cognitive ability to compute such a felonious misdeed, I must concede that such depraved miscreants exist. As Grandmamma always insisted, *Just because your apple is shiny and rosy does not mean a grungy old worm doesn't reside inside.*

"I know I planned this little session to inform everyone of everything we know about this matter, but I have decided not to disclose the … well, carnal details to the girls. There's no gainful reason to."

"Yes, Samuel, I agree."

"Though I am certain of much of the information we've uncovered, we must be careful not to let abhorrent details enter the rumor mill in town."

"We must tell no one of this despicable development. Samuel! It just hit me!"

"What?"

"The father of the child. Could it be …"

"We don't know. Let's not think of that right now and concentrate on the actual crime."

I picked up the drawing and studied it. "A circle or heart with the letter X or a cross … where did I see that before? Wait! Why didn't it come to me earlier? Yes! Of course, that's it!"

"What!"

"Oh my Lord! The markings we found on Annie. It's not a circle with an X. It's a heart! A heart with a cross in the center!"

"You think?"

"Yes! I'm certain of it. Amy has possession of it."

"Amy has what?" he cried, somewhat befuddled.

"The heart with the cross! Amy is holding it for safe keeping."

"I don't understand, Emily?"

"You will in a moment." I shouted out an open port, "Amy, will you come down, please."

Tim swooped down the companionway ladder with uncontrollable laughter. He vaulted all five steps in one sweeping leap landing gracefully on his feet. With a swift gait Amy rushed behind, inelegantly but carefully giving each step its rightful respect. With the last stair still under foot she reached out and slapped Tim hard on the arm.

"Timothy Cadman, if you ever do that again!" she bellowed.

Tim laughed. "Couldn't help myself," he sniggered.

"What did he do, now?" I asked.

"He pinched me! On, on … the backside!"

"Come now. It was just a little pinch," he declared.

"Timothy Cadman, sometimes you just tie me in knots," she pouted.

Tim kept laughing. She slapped him again, this time closed fist.

"Hey! That's not funny," he said, rubbing his arm in feeble resistance.

"Why would you do such a thing?" she asked.

"It's just that you have so much of it, I thought I would pinch some."

With a determined stiff lip, she walloped him some more.

"All right you two—stop your foolishness. We have something very important to discuss."

Tim plopped himself in a chair by the table.

Amy sat away from him. He looked over at her, then at me and winked. I just shook my head and smiled. "Amy. Do you have the pendant?" I asked.

"Of course. I have not let it out of my sight."

"Let's see it."

She reached into her dress pocket and revealed the locket. The image that was once hewed into Mary Sullivan's fair skin and incised into Annie's delicate frame swung from Amy's fingers like an allegoric revelation. Samuel quickly seized the telling charm. His eyes widened and his jaw slackened. He was astonished.

"Where did you get this?" he said.

"It's evidence," she asserted, "and I am the evidence keeper."

"Sorry, Samuel. I forgot to tell you about it," said Tim. "It belonged to Mary Sullivan. My friend Joshua Collins had it when he died. He came upon it when we took Mary down from the rafters in the Sanford mill."

Samuel fiddled with the pendant. "A heart and cross!" He quickly discovered the jewel's secret compartment. He sprung it open. To his bewilderment the image of a man looked up at him—not just any man.

"I didn't know it was a locket," said Tim.

"I'm the one who discovered it was a locket," boasted Amy.

"My, oh, my!" exclaimed Samuel.

"What is it, Sam?"

He held the locket up for us to see. Tim jumped to his feet to take a look. "Why … it's …"

"David Sanford," observed Amy. "What do you make of that?"

Seeing the portrait once again, my heart skipped a beat. A locket with a photograph of David Sanford found in Mary Sullivan's possession unwraps an entire new bundle of questions.

"Yes. This makes a little more sense now," said Samuel.

"What do you mean, Sam?" Tim asked.

"Oh, nothing. It's quite an expensive piece. It's doubtful a servant girl could afford such an indulgence. It must have been given to her."

"Not by David," remarked Amy, disbelievingly.

"Then by who?" I said.

"She stole it."

"Amy! No."

Though I repudiated what Amy just implied, it left me in dire speculation. How did she acquire the charm and why was there a photograph of David in it? Could it be possible that he gifted it to her … a servant? And how about the icon on the pendant's face? What was its significance? And if so, how was it associated with the markings found on the dead girls? We had lots more questions then answers.

Taking the image Marcus had drawn, Samuel compared the two. "The similarity is undeniable."

"What does it all mean?" I wondered.

"This investigation business is very exciting," crowed Amy. "Like a game of chess, only using real people as chess pieces."

"Except in a chess game of murder, moves are everlasting and one may not be spared to play another day," I cautioned.

"David Sanford has just become chess piece number one," announced Tim. "We can't ignore the image on the face of the locket, who it belonged to, and the image of the man in it."

"Tim's right," affirmed Samuel. "It's the only piece to the enigma we have right now."

Though to those who don't know him, David Sanford appears quite capable of committing such a crime. But I have always known David to be a squall within a vacuum. I can't believe he would harm anyone.

Samuel held the locket up to the light that entered the ship's port window and studied it closely.

Tim looked over his shoulders. "What are you thinking, Sam?"

"Can't deny the similarity between this trinket, the drawing, and what we discovered about Annie. I know David is capable of many things. But this?"

"It must be just a remarkable happenstance … you know, a coincidence of sorts," I insisted. "There must a logical explanation—more we don't know."

"I, for one, would not put anything past the man," prompted Amy.

I had to come to David Sanford's defense. I had known him too long not to. We all had. David was a spoiled child. As a youth, he was the master of misconduct—as an adult, a nettlesome stone in the shoe of those around him, but not a murderer. He was too tenuous and fearful for that. Though he rebelled against the world, ferocity and violence were not part of his nature. In Amy's game of chess, David Sanford had become a new chess piece—not king, rook, or bishop, but villain. To me he was just a pawn.

"Oh, Amy, you mustn't think that," I said. "David has always been mischievous, yes, but a murderer?"

Samuel secured the locket and placed it on the table. "If we are to investigate this vicious perplexity we must do it responsibly," he advised. "Now listen up. All theories must stand up to vigorous examination, before we begin to fire off presumptions and assert accusations. Assumptions and declarations are not the same. It is fine to air on the side of conjecture but to do so with a closed mind would not only be unfair to David, but to ourselves. After all, is it not the truth that we seek? So, let's all sit and chew over our thoughts on the matter, shall we? And discuss this sensibly."

We did as Samuel instructed. All anyone contributed was silence. We each waited for the other to provide a clue. Tim rapped his fingers on the table. Amy brushed her long blond hair in an unintentional air of dismissal—displaying a pensive stare and remaining distant and uninspiring, which for Amy was infrequent. All I could hear was the perfect rhythm of Tim's fingernails rapping the table. It had a methodical cadence, like that of a clock's swinging pendulum, exaggerating the soundlessness in the room and reminding me that time was short. The silence was sprinkled by the distant clanging of a ship's bell out in the harbor, and the faint conversation of Louisa and Marcus up on deck. Samuel examined the locket, turning it over every which way, springing it open and closed, hoping it would reveal some additional hidden clue or transcendent revelation.

"Any ideas, anyone?" inquired Samuel.

There weren't any.

"Well then, allow me to play devil's advocate. Mary Sullivan was servant to the Sanford family where she lived in the same household as David Sanford. Consider also that David was on Cuttyhunk Island the day the *Nimrod* was stranded on the reef—the same day we discovered Annie Slocum ... dead."

"Your point?" I remarked, somewhat surprised by the stance Samuel seem to be taking.

"So far, he is the only likely suspect, Emily, whether we like it or not."

"Go ahead, Sam, say it," groaned Tim. "You think he's guilty."

"Where you going with this, Sam?" asked Amy. "I thought you wanted us to consider David innocent?"

"He is, thus far. Simply put, it is my supposition that David Sanford may have violated and killed both girls. I say may have."

Was Samuel's accusation a hook to get the conversation going, or a viable presumption? Did he really mean what he said? I, for one, don't think so. At least I hope he didn't. Nevertheless, his approach worked and Amy offered a piece of her mind.

"I always said he killed that horse," she added. "Who knows how many cats and dogs?"

"No!" I shouted. "Yes, David is unruly and defiant. I would even call him a menace. In the end, he's a harmless mamma's boy. Once you challenge his insubordination he retreats. After all, being a bully does not make one a murderer."

"We have not concluded that David is the killer, at least not yet. For the time being, he stands where the proof is taking us," Samuel suggested.

"If he really is guilty, there will be more proof to come," said Tim, leaning back in his chair, his hands resting behind his head.

"Such as?" said Samuel.

"Those two straps," replied Tim.

"They are common ties," I said. "Every textile mill must have heaps of it lying around. Anyone could have possession of them."

"She's right," said Samuel. "Mill workers have been known to weave rugs from it. However, the defect in this particular cord is uncommon."

"That should be something to go on," declared Tim. "If only we could find some in David Sanford's possession."

Samuel picked up the longer, cotton cord and held it out for Tim to see. "Did you tamper with the knot on this noose?"

"It was on there when I took it from Josh. Why?"

"It's a bowline, like the one found on the cord around Annie's Slocum's neck."

"What's a bowline?" I asked.

"It's a knot used by sailors," explained Samuel. "It's very doubtful that Mary or Annie would know how to tie one."

"You think David would know how to tie a bowline?" I asked.

"He should. It's the first knot a sailor learns to tie," replied Tim.

I took the cord and inspected the knot. "That means that the killer would be someone connected with the sea."

"Could be. And we have two links here," explained Samuel. "Someone who is familiar with tying a nautical knot and who has access to common mill ties."

"We need to find out which mill received the bails of cotton wrapped with that particular cord," I noted. "That may help."

"It was used on Mary on the Sanford property. Is that not sufficient to determine it came from one of Sanford's mills?" declared Amy.

"Not good enough," said Samuel. "We already know it was found on the Sanford property, but it could have nothing to do with the Sanfords. Could be the killer carried some in his pocket and brought it with him."

"If some cord was found on Cuttyhunk, would it not make sense that it was brought there by someone on Sanford's ship?" Amy suggested.

Samuel conceded. "Possibility, yes."

"What if we found some of the cord on the *Nimrod*. That would really narrow down the suspect list to someone on that ship."

"You're right, Emmie," chirped Amy, "including David Sanford."

"Wait! I think I saw something like it tied around some rope when I was working on the *Nimrod*," remarked Tim.

"You certain?" I asked.

"Yes. There were coils of lines stacked along a bulkhead and they were tied with cord of some type. I remember. It may have been cotton bale cord."

"So, all we need to do is board the ship ... perhaps at night when no one's around and see if the cords tied around those lines are the same," said Amy.

"Yes, that should be easy," I said, "We played on the ships when we were children. No one would really question us too sternly if they discovered us snooping. Then we could be sure that we're on the right track."

"That, in fact, David Sanford is the guilty party."

"No, that's not what I said, Amy. There's an entire crew of fishermen on that vessel. It could be anyone of them."

"Oh, believe me. He did it all right," she maintained.

"Whoa, whoa!" implored Samuel. "We don't want to go trespassing."

"I think I should be the one to go," sounded Tim, as if Samuel never spoke. "After all, I have worked that ship. They wouldn't question me."

"Is the *Nimrod* not leaving in the morning?" asked Amy. "If David Sanford will be on it, we may not see him for years!"

"No! Listen! I don't want anyone boarding that ship," asserted Samuel. "There are men preparing her as we speak. We must not give ourselves away."

"Then, where do we go from here?" I inquired.

"I don't know."

"Why don't we just directly confront David about it," suggested Amy.

"If we show our hand he may run," said Samuel. "We may never see him again. Besides we don't know if the particulars of this cotton mill cord will prove anything. Perhaps we are making too much of it."

"He's going to get away!" chanted an emphatic Amy.

"This is awful," I said. "We have accused and practically convicted the man and we have no solid proof."

"I bet there's proof somewhere on that ship," claimed Amy. "I know it."

"Look! The day is passing us by and we're getting nowhere," claimed Samuel. "Let's all just call it a day. Sleep on it. Perhaps one of us will come up with some new ideas tomorrow."

"Not likely," murmured Amy. "Tomorrow David will be gone."

"Well, it's just a chance we'll have to take. We have no proof and we don't want to stir up the village by trying to discover some. Let's meet on the *Sphinx* in a day or two. We will all have a better perspective after we give our brains a rest."

"I agree, Samuel," I said.

"He will have gotten away," sung Amy, with a moue of discontent.

We had done our best. This murder enterprise was bigger than all of us put together. We felt like helpless seadogs lacking all sight of land. Though I cannot deny the evidence we had uncovered, the problem was what do we do with it?

We all marched up on deck with Samuel in the lead. Amy followed close behind me with Tim on her heels. Grumbling, she turned and slapped him on the hand as he pretended to pinch her on the behind. Just as he stepped on deck, Samuel looked back at us with a dumbstruck expression. With a finger to his lips he signaled us to be quiet. What we witnessed tickled and delighted me.

Amy's jaw dropped. "Well, I'll be," she uttered.

We stood staring in speechless enchantment. At the bow of the ship stood Louisa—her limber body swaddled in the arms of the debonair French doctor, their arms tenderly tethered around one another—lips intertwined in solicitous desire.

We broke into carousing applause. The lovers broke embrace. Louisa backed away in gleeful sheepishness, while Marcus nervously brushed at his clothing in segregated composure as if the moment never happened. It was wicked! I looked over to Louisa and winked. *Good for you, Lulu.*

—◦◦◦—

Chapter 18:

Life is a halo, Grandmamma often said. *You begin at one point of a circle and around you go, until you return to where you began. It's a riddle never achieved, and one is never entitled to continue the journey the second time around to solve it. And after we have gone, though we go on living in the memories of our loved ones, eternity leaves us unaware.*

Now, you may give this polite pause, if not curious introspection. You may even interpret or appreciate what it all means. If you do, respectfully inform me. For though I am not sallow, neither am I an oracle or seer with keys to the everlasting, or a philosopher who can easily surmise Grandmamma's riddle. At times, I think that even Grandmamma doesn't know the significance of her somewhat spiritual advice.

All talk aside; I must confess I am worried about her still once again. The beginning of summer uncovered Grandmamma in improving health. She was feeling strong and doing so well, especially at the fishermen's bake. I'm afraid, as summer wears on she has begun to feel weak and lethargic. I'm hoping it's the summer heat. What worries me the most is that she has not been eating, as she should, or sleeping well. I have opened her bedroom window so the night sea breeze can comfort her. It has not been much help since the nights have been so hot.

"Grandmamma, I made you some toast," I said, handing her a small plate of scorched bread sprinkled with raisins.

She sat up in bed. "Thank you, dear." She looked out the window to the river and field behind our cottage. "Look how the warm breezes play in the willow trees down by the water. Such marvelous living things, trees! When I die, I would like to be buried between those willows, where their roots can embrace me and keep me warm in the winter blow."

"Oh, Grandmamma, stop saying such things. No one is going to die. I won't let you."

"Of course you won't, dear," she said taking a bite of toast.

I thought about the silly suggestions she made, and how my declaration was just as preposterous. Two girls I knew well had died and there was not a thing I could do to prevent it. I find myself questioning about where they are now—if Mary and Annie have gone to a better place, as Reverend Brightman often quotes. Why should we lament? "Wipe those tears but cry again," he often said, "and this time cry tears of joy for our beloved now stand in paradise." I do not desire to question my faith, but how do we compose ourselves to do such a thing? What sort of paradise is he talking about … a place in the afterlife, a state of mind? I don't understand. I don't understand it at all.

I carried a chair from the kitchen into the bedroom, sat, and had breakfast with Grandmamma. Her shimmering eyes twinkled as she took a mousy nibble of toast and observed the sloping landscape out the window as if for the first time. She munched and chewed and munched some more. The scorched bread thundered and chattered between her long, fragile teeth.

"You look like you are having a difficult time eating. Is the toast too hard, Grandmamma? I burnt it like you told me to."

"Fine, dear, fine. You know, I never had enough to eat when I was a little girl, so I chew my food over and over. When I am done swallowing it feels like I have had a lot more than what little was actually on my plate."

I laughed. "Oh, Grandmamma, you say the funniest things."

She picked a raisin off the bread and held it to the light.

"Born so ripe, moist, and stout. How we age and wither."

"I know what you mean. Why just the other day I discovered two white hairs atop my head." I thought I would cheer her up by letting her know that she was not alone. "And my knees, Grandmamma, they make a raisin look like a new laid egg."

"Nonsense, my dear. You have lovely knees. Men have proposed marriage upon the sight of such knees."

I lifted my dress and took a peek. "I never thought of a girl employing her knees to snag a husband. How would a gentleman ever see a woman's knees, Grandmamma, unless she was already married?"

"There are ways," she said, squinting one eye.

"Oh, Grandmamma, you are funning me." I took another look at my knees.

"Knees are very essential to life. Even in marriage. Whether they be man or woman's."

"How?" I dared to ask.

"How do you think one first gets around in the first year of life? On their hands and knees! How would you tend a garden or hem a dress without them?"

"You know? You're right, Grandmamma. How would I scrub the floors if I had no knees?" I laughed.

She stared out the window to the distant river just beyond the two large willows. A lowly fisherman in a small skiff drifted with the tide. He lay on his back, his pole like a flagless staff trailing a line along the glassy river surface.

"Most importantly, dear, your knees are your podium for asking the Lord for forgiveness or by which you thank Him." She sat back in her bed and made herself comfortable. "And the day your future husband falls onto one of his to propose marriage, you will never see a knee the same way again."

I looked down at mine and thought pleasantly of all that was said—tidbits of humorous wisdom and likely truths. Grandmamma closed her eyes and began to breathe unvaryingly, if not peacefully. Out on the river, a wonted flock of vagrant mallards swooped down behind the floating skiff in an audible drove of wagging feathers and honking beaks. Their distant quacking and protest percolate up the rolling, grassy shore, piercing the wavy window glass of Grandmamma's room. Faraway toots mingled with faint and immediate snoring.

"Grandmamma! Grandmamma!"

She was asleep.

I was expected at the Macomber house and hurried up Drift Road. It was another hot but splendid summer day. The faster my legs moved the more swiftly my thoughts filtered through my busy brain. It had been two days since our little gathering on the *Sphinx* to discuss the fates of poor Mary and Annie, and still no new development. Though, I don't know what it is that I expected. To tell you the truth, if the killer turned himself into the authorities it would redeem a sliver of faith in this affair, and alleviate the sudden disillusionment I have been feeling for the human race. I am certain that he, whoever he could be, has little regard for virtue and truth. Integrity eludes him and rectitude and culpability are as foreign as a distant star. How are we to solve such a crime if my reasoning and understanding of what makes such a person function is beyond my comprehension? What sort of barbarian commits such an inhumane act?

And to think how this all started—that the Drift River Readers Club wanted to investigate and solve the distant-past death of Sarah Cornell. What was I thinking? How were we expected to solve a thirty-year stale mystery without having the faintest idea of how to solve a fresh one? There is so much that is unknown to me in this world, so much I still need to learn. One truth is that death does not always come peacefully and uneventfully. There was Mr. Mosher last year. He was adjusting the bridle on his plow horse when the animal suddenly charged, sending the blade of the plow over him and killing him instantly. And the unapproachable death of fishermen—those who never returned and for whom we are never certain have died, leaving widows mourning in perpetuity—a prolonged and everlasting death.

Though I am left weary and dismayed with news of such passing, the death of Mary and Annie is something else altogether … the random taking of another life. Yes, I know. There is war—a time when men mindlessly kill and are killed. In battle, you can see the enemy coming. One knows death is a possibility. The motives are plain. You are prepared to do your duty. Though there is a twisted sense of honor, there are objectives and goals. Though I find it far from being natural or civil behavior, it is there to be understood, and almost accepted as a historical necessity. But to absorb death by clandestine hands and to have life taken away by a deranged individual—to be unaware and innocent, is most disturbing. Why, it could happen to anyone of us, at anytime, for any undetermined reason.

As I approached the Macomber homestead, I could hear the ominous plodding of feet behind me. An unexpected tinge of apprehension clamped my spine. I was afraid to look back. As the sound got closer, my uneasiness turned to trepidation. The follower gruffly cleared his throat and spat. I walked faster. The footsteps were gaining. Trying not to panic, I fell into a trot until the stumping of feet behind me became more distant. Approaching the front gate of the Macomber residence, I nervously fiddled with the rope lasso that held the picket fence gate closed, still not daring to look behind. The rope was snagged on a nail. The baleful footsteps were closer once again. Swiftly, I freed the fastener from its catch, flung open the gate, and sprinted toward the house. Surprisingly, the sinister plodding did not follow and instead continued on by. Gulping a mouthful of air, I turned to look.

I can be so silly at times. No one was following me at all. It was just Mr. Cuffe who lived across the way taking his morning walk. He tipped his hat and smiled. I was uncertain whether it was a friendly smile or one of amused bewilderment, considering my peculiar behavior. My thoughts had entertained my fears and thus invented a chasing villain—in the middle of the day, no less. How silly.

Louisa met me at the door. "Why were you running and what took you so long to unfasten the gate?"

"Oh, a … a bee was chasing me," I said.

"You can blame Mother for that," prattled Louisa. "Look at this place. There are flower gardens everywhere. It's bumblebee heaven here."

"Oh! But it is so beautiful, Louisa."

"I suppose. I'm happy you're here. I didn't think anyone was coming."

"Why? Is Amy not here yet?"

"No. You know Amy. She comes and goes as she pleases with little regard for others."

"Well, we all know that. But she is never late for the Readers Club."

"Come on out back. I have refreshments. We may as well enjoy the day while we patiently wait for the queen mother to get here."

We circled the house where I sat myself down comfortably in a large wicker chair on the back porch.

"Lemonade?" she asked, lifting the pitcher of drink.

"Please."

It was a gorgeous day. Then again this is Westport. Every day here is gorgeous—well, not every day. If I must be honest I will admit that even the rainy raw ones contain some sort of contorted value. How else would I be sitting amongst this varicolored landscape if not for rainy days? Green things need plenty of water. Everywhere you look there are garnished flowers and shrubbery, surrounded by a manicured, emerald green, carpeted lawn, all overlooking a waterway swollen by spring rainwater. The Drift River flowed like Prussian blue lava, meandering in swirling eddies and caressing tides, encircling passive stones that protrude from the shimmering surface like monumental sentinels, organizing muddled currents and errant drifts. Of course, when it came to the grounds, I am more than certain that Mrs. Macomber had everything to do with it. Staring out into this tranquil Eden made lemonade taste that much better.

"Please, Emmie, have a cookie," said Louisa, extending the tray.

"Oatmeal! My favorite."

"Oh, no. Here comes my little brother."

"Hi, Emmie!" yelled Ian. He ran over from across the yard.

"Hello, little man." I reached into my pocket to retrieve the toy soldier with the severed head. I thought twice about it. "Where's your new toy soldier?" I asked.

"I gave it back to Mr. Moses. It didn't look like a soldier. He said he would fix it for me."

With glimmering eyes, he stood waiting. "Do you have something for me?" He looked down at my hand in my pocket.

"Yes, this," I replied, embracing him and giving him a kiss instead.

He wiped his cheek and grimaced.

"Go play," ordered Louisa. "We are talking about important matters here."

"Oh, all right," he said, running off.

"So! What shall we talk about?" she asked.

"Marcus Theroux," I hinted.

There was silence. I dare say that the color of Louisa's cheeks rivaled those in the rose garden.

"What about Mr. Theroux?" she chirped, dismissively.

"Oh, I don't know. It appears you two have become quite friendly."

"Yes, friendly. After all, it is the way a lady and gentleman should behave, would you not say?"

"Why, of course."

"Good! I'm glad we agree."

"But, Louisa, friends do not kiss in locked embrace."

She thought very hard about what I said. "Well, I suppose you can say that we are friends with … with elevated enhancements. Here, have some more lemonade." She lifted the heavy glass pitcher and overfilled my cup. Spilled drink splashed all over the oak wicker table.

I laughed, "What in the world does that mean? Oh, Louisa, think about what you just said."

She quickly wiped the minty, yellow spill with the tablecloth. "Oh, Emmie! Look what you made me do."

"It wasn't me. It was Marcus."

A worried look quickly occupied her face. "Oh, Emmie, I am so happy. He's so wonderful."

"So what's with the glum expression?"

"It's a tightrope and I do so wish to make every footfall count."

"And you are. You shouldn't worry so much about being yourself, Louisa."

"Do you realize how many men like Marcus exist in Westport? Why none! Most of the boys are either pushing plows or pulling nets. Not that there is anything wrong with those occupations, you see. Marcus is nothing like them. He is refined, educated, and on his way to exploit and adventure. He talks of distant places—Quebec, Madagascar, bridges over the River Seine. And he's such a gentleman. His continental charm so compliments my needs."

"And what needs are those?"

"You know, lifting you up onto a carriage, carrying you over a muddy puddle, holding your hand to protect you from a full moon."

"You need protection from the moon, do you?"

"You know what I mean."

And, yes, I did. Little did she realize how much so. I did not agree with her cursory assessment of the eligible bachelors of Westport, I must add.

Though most never had formal schooling, many were trained at home and could match wits and academic skills with the best university alumnus. There is Terrance Borden, who not only pushes a plow, but can recite every country in the Eastern Hemisphere, along with their capitols, with proficiency. And Andy Winslow, who is just as proficient with a fishing net as he is with a sonnet. After all, just because learning and scholarship are not accomplished formally does not mean one cannot acquire skill and knowledge on your own.

"I'm very happy for you, Louisa. May I put forward some personal observation?"

"Like what?"

"Don't weave your web too tight. Do so just enough to coax his admiration and emotional affections. You don't want to appear unscrupulous."

"Oh, Emmie! I so hunger for advice in the custom of courtship."

"All I can tell you is what Grandmamma has always advised. Her guidance is sugared with both honey and vinegar."

"Tell me, tell me," she pleaded.

"The first thing you must do is give less."

"Give? Give what?" she said, bewilderingly.

"You know … of yourself … kisses and all that."

"I don't know what you mean?"

"Let's say he wants to hold your hand. That's acceptable. But never let him rest it on you knee."

"I never!" she added, with a somewhat peccant smile.

"The less you give, the more he will want. If his intentions are sincere he will wait."

"Hmm." She gave my suggestion the entire weigh of wisdom and frowned.

"How do you keep a man interested if you don't … don't …"

"Don't what?" I asked, baiting her inquiry.

"Never mind. What other advice did Charlotte have?"

"You may feel you must let them lick the sugar on the cookie. Never let them take a bite."

She looked down on the tray of sugar cookies, shot me an expression of passionate arousal and blushed. "Oh, Emmie! Just what do you mean?"

"If you don't know, I cannot not tell you."

"So, is kissing all right?"

"Yes and no."

She picked up a cookie, looked it over, and dropped it back onto the tray. "I never realized that love could be so precarious."

"Look at it this way. If you should find …"

"Shh! Mother's coming."

Mrs. Macomber appeared at the back door, embroidery hoop and needle in hand. "Louisa! Mr. Chaloner is out front. He's looking for Amy."

"Amy's not here yet," replied Louisa.

"That's strange!" I added. "Let's go talk to him."

We met Mr. Chaloner who was sitting in a buggy, stroking his chin, looking worried.

"Good morning, Mr. Chaloner," cried Louisa, in her usual cheerful tone.

"Have you seen Amy? I can't find her anywhere. She didn't come home last night. Did she stay with you, Louisa?"

"You mean here? No, sir."

"I know she's been staying at our cottage on Point Road, but it was her brother's birthday yesterday and she would not have missed it."

"I have not seen her for a couple of days, Mr. Chaloner," I said. "She is usually with us when she is not at the cottage."

"I'm going back there and wait," he said.

"Would you like me to come with you, sir?"

"Yes," he replied, shuffling himself over on the buggy seat.

"Please let me know what unfolds," begged Louisa. She rested her hand on my arm. A concerned expression puckered her face.

I leaned over and tucked a loose strand of hair behind her ear. "I will, dear, I will."

Back at Point Road, Mr. Chaloner and I searched the small cottage for any clues to Amy's disappearance. It took all of ten minutes. Nothing was disturbed. During our cursory search, I was never certain what we were looking for. Though I call the cottage small, it is twice as large as the house Grandmamma and I live in. Why, the upper level alone had three bedrooms. Two of these were furnished with carts or bunks, which folded down and hung from the wall by rope, similar to those on whaling ships. Here the Chaloner clan slept—girls in one, boys in the other. It was a roomy arrangement, stark but cozy. Though some would consider it cramped quarters when compared to the bedroom accommodation Amy and her siblings occupied in the city. I searched the bigger room, the one that contained a proper bed. It was where Amy's parents slept and the one Amy occupied when she stayed at the cottage. The bed was neatly made with no signs that Amy had slept in it the night before. Nothing was discovered which would tell us about Amy's whereabouts. Cornelius Chaloner inspected the icebox in the kitchen.

"I have already looked," I said. "There's been no ice delivery."

"Amy always insists on having a cold glass of milk in the morning," he said, slamming the ice chest's lid.

"I know. I have never seen the chest without ice."

"When did you see her last?" asked a flustered Cornelius.

"Two days ago on the *Sphinx*."

"*Sphinx*?"

"Yes, Samuel Cory's schooner."

"Of course. You were with her?"

"Yes, most of that morning. Me, Timothy Cadman, Samuel Cory, Louisa Macomber, and a doctor friend of ours."

"Perhaps one of the others may know where she's gone."

"I'll make certain to ask, sir."

"Where did she go after she left the ship?"

"I suppose she came here. Sometimes she will go for a walk down the lane and field behind my place. When she does she usually cuts through our yard and will knock on the door and ask me to come along. I can ask some of the fishermen down by the docks if they've seen her."

"Already done that, I'm afraid."

"Oh."

"Some lads thought they saw her down by the wharf speaking with young Sanford but they weren't certain."

"Who, David Sanford?"

"Yes."

"David and the *Nimrod* left a day ago on a whaling expedition," I said.

"I know, I know. There is no asking the man about her now."

"No, there is not."

He threw his weary body into a chair. "Well, I suppose I will wait here," he uttered.

I started for the door. He sat in a corner chair and stared down at the floor—miserable and dejected. Finely dressed as always, he looked out of place in the old dusty cottage, sitting in a black, single-breasted waistcoat, paisley cravat, and gibus opera hat. He was always impeccably dressed, as was his daughter.

"I'm going down to the waterfront, Mr. Chaloner. I'm certain she will turn up soon. Nonetheless, I will continue my search, all day if need be."

He looked up and pried a smile. "Thank you, little Emily," he said.

Oddly he hadn't called me little Emily since I was a youngster. His thoughts were wandering—meandering back to the past, to this little cottage where he and his family had once lived. Amy was his favorite child. They had an exceptional bond. She always addressed him as Cornelius instead of Dad or Papa, unlike the rest of her siblings. She had called him that since she was a baby. Cornelius Chaloner had found humor in it, never correcting or admonishing her. It carried on. To this day she still calls him by his familiar name. Yes, they had a special bond. I hated leaving the poor fellow in despair.

I decided to wander down by the docks and look around. Along the shore I discovered a small clan of boys engaged in horseplay—running, throwing stones into the river. An older boy, fishing, yelled to the others to stop flinging stones and scaring the fish.

"Hello, Miss White," the fishing lad said, as he pulled his line out of the water.

"Hello, Tommy. Have you seen Miss Chaloner?"

"You mean the woman that dresses queer."

"That's her."

"She carries a funny looking umbrella," said one of the other boys.

"Umbrella, not umbrella. And it's not an umbrella, it's a parasol," I said. "Have you boys seen her?"

"A couple of days ago, I think," said Tommy, wrapping the wet fishing twine around a stick. At the other end of the line was a bent nail fettered with some red yarn that he used as bait. He inspected the spiky hook, testing the pointy tip with his finger. At his feet sat a bucket with his single catch of the day. The small flatfish leaped and quivered as one of the boys poked it with a stick.

"Where did you see her?" I said.

"See who?" asked Tommy.

"Miss Chaloner!"

"Oh. She was standing over there." He pointed to where the *Nimrod* was once docked.

Interviewing small children is like opening one of those new tricky tin food cans. You need to keep poking the lid with a sharp object before you can pry it open. With children, a direct reply was always fragmented and uncertain.

"Was she alone, Tommy?"

"No." He knelt and sharpened the point of the rusty nail hook on the granite wharf wall. "Go away!" he shouted to the boy prodding the fish in the pail. "I'm fishing here."

The youngster ran off making faces.

"Who was she with?"

"Talking to that mean Mr. Sanford."

"Which one? The old one or the young one?"

He looked up at me as if the question made little sense. "They're both old."

"Just tell me which," I snapped, becoming impatient.

He looked up at me, bewildered by my annoyance. "The younger one. The one that's always chasing us away from the wharf."

"You mean David."

"Yeah, that's him. Dave the knave."

"Now that's not nice, Tommy. You must show more respect for your elders."

"Sorry, Miss White," he uttered, "but he's mean. He took my coil of fishing string and threw it into the river. It was the other boys calling him names, not me!"

I looked over at the barren water where the *Nimrod* once docked. The gangplank now lay on the wharf precariously hanging over the edge of the granite slab wall. A chill ran down to the pit of my stomach as I pondered Amy's disappearance.

"Can I go now?" begged the boy picking up the pail with one fish.

Ignoring him, I raised my hand and waved him off.

It was a beautiful afternoon. One could not have asked for a nicer day. But there was a gloom in the air. It appeared to surround only me. The sun was hot, yet I felt a chill. I walked down to where the *Nimrod* was once docked. The only thing in the water was the old skiff, which Moses often slept beneath. It was tied to the pier with an old slimy rope. Seaweed hung from the droopy, twisted cable like furry, green wash on a boggy clothesline. With its stringers and bench submerged, the small boat barely floated. At the end of the wharf a seagull stood atop a pyramid of whale oil barrels squawking out in a high-pitched warning. In its own language, it appeared to be crying the words, "murder, murder." I looked down at the partially submerged skiff and shook my head vigorously in an attempt at jarring my thoughts. Suddenly, I noticed something shining up at me from the belly of the swamped vessel. Was it a silvery minnow? It glimmered in the wavy water like a newly minted silver dollar. I called for one of the boys.

"Joey! Come here!"

Humming, the barefoot boy skipped over. "I didn't do nothin'," he cried.

"If you do something for me I'll give you a half dime."

"A whole half dime," he repeated, in gleeful animation.

"Yes. You see that shiny object at the bottom of that small boat?"

"Yeah! I see it."

"Roll up the cuffs of your trousers and get it for me."

"Sure!"

"Don't get wet now."

"Oh, I don't care," he said, climbing down the stacked granite wall. He jumped into the skiff and soon had the item in hand. He looked closely at it. "It's beautiful, Miss White. Did you drop it?"

"Here, hand it up to me, hurry."

I fell to my knees and reached out. He proudly placed the shimmering article in my hand and climbed back up onto the wall. I tried swallowing. My throat constricted and the chill I felt earlier caused me to shiver. I stared down at the lustrous object as the entire world around me faded into a silent and distant vacuum. The loitering seagull loutishly continued his ominous shrill. The object in my hand spoke to me. Its language was unclear. It had plenty to say, but what—why? Amy would never have been so reckless as to lose it.

"Miss, Miss White!"

"Yes. What is it?" I replied, tangled in thought.

"You said you were going to give me a half dime."

"Of course I did." I handed him the coin. "Here. You're a darling."

"Oh wow! A whole dime!" He trumpeted. "Thanks, Miss White."

The boy quickly ran up Point Road leaving me standing to ponder the treasure I held in my hand. Mary Sullivan's locket! How could it come to be that it lay discarded in the river? Amy was much more trustworthy than to recklessly lose such precious evidence. I ran my fingers over the wet charm. The thin gold chain was tied into knots. I tried untying it but the tiny manacles were locked tightly around one another. I sprung the silver and gold pendant open. It cried seawater. A salty David Sanford smiled up at me. I wiped his face dry with my handkerchief. I looked out toward the Knubble, the narrow passageway that channeled countless ships in and out of our little village and snapped the locket closed. Clutching it tightly in my hand I asked.

"Amy Chaloner. Where are you?"

※

Chapter 19:

I scurried up the schooner's gangplank and in my hurry had not noticed Seabury Cory disembarking. We collided. He held onto me as I lost my footing, almost tumbling over the side.

"Whoa there, young lady! What's the rush?"

"Oh! Mr. Cory … sorry! I need to talk to Samuel. Is he here?"

"He's below with Eli making repairs to the rudder. Everything all right?"

"Why, yes! Why would you ask?"

Seabury Cory had a right to ask. I looked worried. Amy's disappearance was taking a toll as unexplained developments unfolded. I had questions and no concrete explanations. For the past several days, like a fish in a waterless bucket, thoughts thrashed about in my head. Seabury stooped down and looked me in the eyes. I could not make contact with his without telling the truth. I looked away.

"Are ya sure nothing is wrong, child?"

"Wrong? Why, no, nothing's wrong. I just need to see Samuel, that's all." Of course, something was indeed wrong—two women were dead, Amy was missing, and I didn't know what to do about it. "I need to talk to Samuel," I cried, gently pulling away.

"By all means!" he said, loosening his embrace.

"Sorry, Mr. Cory. Don't mean to be rude." I turned and ran along the deck.

"Not at all, lass. I'm certain Samuel will be happy to see ya. Watch yar footing now." He shook his head and with a muddled smile continued down the gangplank.

I stopped and looked back toward the venerable sailor, fretting about my behavior. "Have a good day, Mr. Cory," I yelled.

With his back to me, he continued on his way, a hand high in the air, waving.

Once below, I discovered Eli, kneeling and handing a wrench down an open hatch in the ship's floor.

"I need something bigger," came a distant, muffled voice.

"Ah! Good morning, Miss Emily," cried an exuberant Eli. A familiar hand extended from the bilge to accept the larger implement. Always the accomplished gentleman, Eli jumped to his feet and extended his hand to greet me. "Sorry for the mess, Miss Emily." He quickly pulled his hand away and wiped it on his trousers. "My apology. I'm afraid my hands are quite soiled."

"That's all right."

"The captain and I are quite preoccupied at the moment."

"Whatever are you doing?"

"We are tightening the rudder's mechanism and tarring some seams in the planking," he reported.

"That will do it, Mr. Monroe," shouted the faraway voice. "Almost done!"

"We have company, sir," announced Eli.

Seconds later, a grease-faced Samuel emerged from the hatch in the floor like a jack-in-the-box. "That's not company, Mr. Monroe. That, my good man, is an eyeful of loveliness."

"And as always, she brings comfort and joy, sir," remarked Eli.

My worry over Amy's disappearance precluded any appreciation to Samuel's flattering accolade. "Not really," I said, struggling with a smile.

"What's wrong?" asked Samuel, climbing out of the bilge and looking concerned.

"We need to do something about Amy, Samuel!"

"I know. What can we do? We have all looked everywhere."

"It's been days since her disappearance."

"I know. Tim is beside himself. Everyday he rides into the city with hopes of finding her."

"It must have something to do with our investigation of the hangings, I just know it."

Samuel and Eli looked at one another, both men lost for words.

"I'd like to talk about it," I said.

"Yes, sure." Samuel reached into his pocket and handed Eli some money. "Go up to Cory's store and get another bundle of oakum and a small barrel of pine tar. Get yourself some dinner with the leftover change. I'll meet you back here some time this afternoon."

"Should I bring the goods right away, sir?"

"Have your dinner first. Miss White and I have business to conduct. Just get to Cory's before they lock up for the day."

"Aye, aye, Captain."

After Eli had gone, Samuel washed his hands and placed a pot of water on the stove.

"I have a fire going. Would you like some tea, cocoa, perhaps?"

I wiped a smudge of grease from his cheek with my thumb. Blushing, he quickly did the same with the sleeve of his shirt. I backed away and smiled. "Cocoa or tea will be fine," I said. I sat at the salon table and pulled out Mary Sullivan's gold and silver locket.

"I thought Amy was keeping the locket," he said, sitting down.

"That's what I want to talk to you about."

"Oh?"

"That's just it, Samuel. You know that old skiff that was tied to the pier by the *Nimrod*?"

"The one that's swamped."

"Yes. The locket was sitting in the bilge, just sitting at the bottom of the skiff, submerged."

"You don't say! She must have dropped it and not noticed."

"I don't think so." I held the locket up to the light.

Samuel took it from my hand. "How did it get all those knots in the chain?"

"That's one of the things I want to talk to you about."

"Yes. They can be very difficult to get out. It's simple, really. You need to knead it, work it between the palm of your hands to loosen the tie."

"No, that's not it," I said.

"Sure it is. Watch how I do it."

"Samuel. You're not listening. I'm not concerned about taking the knots out of the chain." I took the charm from his hand. "How many knots do you see in it?"

"Oh, four … five?"

"Exactly! One knot could be an accident. But someone intentionally tied those knots in this chain."

"Alright. What are you trying to say?"

"Amy placed them there."

"Well, if you didn't do it, she must have."

"Don't you see? She didn't lose the locket at all. She left it behind. The knots are a clue. She is reaching out to us."

He squinted as he wrestled with the inkling. "Why would she just toss it in the river?"

"Hoping one of us would find it."

"That's taking a chance. Anyone could have found it."

"Yes. But they didn't. I did. I think David has something to do with her disappearance and this is her way of telling us. I'm certain of it."

"Oh Emily, we have no evidence that …"

"No, wait! Hear me out. Every time Amy became upset with David she would say that he tied her in knots."

"And?"

"I think she was kidnapped and the knots in the locket's chain is Amy's way of letting us know it was David. He always had this fetish for her. There's only so much rejection a man can take."

"Fetish, yes, but kidnapping?"

"Yes. He always expressed the compulsion that they would be together some day."

"Just talk on David's part."

"Listen! Growing up, David always felt rejected by his father, right? He inherited a compelling need for approval laced with a compulsion for rejection. After a while, rejection became a banner of sorts—a battle cry. In time, he learned how to feed off repudiation. It became his companion. As the years went by his father's regard meant nothing. What you or I think of him meant nothing. And if we spoke ill of him he took it as a compliment."

"You're right there. He doesn't care what anyone thinks."

"Yes, that's right. No one. Except those he loved."

"Emily, David only loves himself."

"You shouldn't underestimate the power of love, Samuel."

"And you believe that he is attracted to Amy."

"Amy's rejection may have triggered some sort of peculiar if not bizarre charisma for her. The more she rejected him, the more he felt she wanted him. In time, he interpreted an outright rebuff for passion. A mechanism of his disease."

"My dear Emily, where in the world did you ever sort out such a diagnosis?"

"One reads books."

"Books?" he snickered. "Do you acquire all your knowledge from books?"

"Anything and everything one needs to know has been recorded in books."

"Yes, I'm sure. But your assessment ... It all sounds a bit presumptuous."

"Well ... to tell you the truth, my assessment was taken from personal experience."

"Oh?"

"Yes. Remember Elbert Sisson?"

"Elbie! Why yes. Always thought he was God's gift to the ladies—got married to a woman thirty years his senior and migrated out West ... oh, must have been five years now—California, I think."

"When I was fourteen I was in love with him. At least I thought I was."

"Elbie Sisson?"

"Of course, he was much older and took little interest in me. I would look upon him with puppy eyes when we were in church. He would get very annoyed. Still, the more he rejected me, the more I felt he desired me. I was convinced that it was just a matter of time. We would marry. We were meant to be together. I had no idea what love was, of course."

"I would say not," burped Samuel, in a somewhat jealous tone.

His off the cuff utterance flattered me. "And what does that have to do with David Sanford and Amy? Don't you see, Samuel? David feels as I once did. I believe he really thinks that he and Amy belong together—that her rejection, like his father's, is a substitute for love."

"The man would be mad to think so."

"You may be right there. Have you never heard the phrase, 'madly in love'?"

I took the locket and caressed it, running the tip of my finger along the image of the heart and cross on its face. I sprung it open. Gazing up at me was the vain, water-wrinkled image of David Sanford. "He must have given this to Mary Sullivan. She must have meant something more to him than just a servant."

"We don't know how she came to have it, or if it was given to her in the first place."

"I suppose you're right."

The pot on the stove boiled and spilled. A plume of steam hissed and filled the ship's salon. Samuel rushed to remove it from the flame. He yelped, burning a finger on the pot's searing iron handle.

"Tea or cocoa?" he mumbled, a singed finger in his mouth.

"There is more, Samuel," I said disregarding his offer. "David may have had something to do with the murder of Mary Sullivan."

"Now you are really reaching, Emily. I thought you had faith in the man's innocence?"

"I don't mean directly. You have that paper … the one with the symbol Marcus drew?"

He slid open the salon table drawer and revealed the drawing. I placed the locket over it.

"Now, it is my belief that we are looking at the image of a heart and a cross on that drawing. Would you not say it is what Marcus drew?"

"We had agreed that it probably was."

I picked up the locket. "That is what's on this locket. Don't you see? A heart and cross. But they are not exactly the same."

"No, they're really not!" Samuel said. He walked back to the stove to make the drinks. "On the locket the cross is over the heart. In the drawing, and from what we witnessed that day on Annie, the cross extends inside the heart."

I studied the two images. The examination had placed doubt in my mind; doubt that the two images were related, and proof that David Sanford had no connection to the murders. I was not so sure. One thing I was very sure about. "Amy is on the ship," I proclaimed.

"What!"

"I said, Amy is on the *Nimrod*."

"Unlikely. The *Nimrod* has sailed. It will be gone for a year or more."

"Oh, Samuel, I know it. David sailed off and took her with him. Why else would the locket's chain braid be tied in knots? Why would it be in the water where the *Nimrod* once docked? Amy's on that ship, I tell you."

"You really believe that?"

"I do. No one has seen her since *Nimrod* sailed."

Samuel placed two steaming cups of cocoa on the table. "Careful, it's hot," he said.

I continued to study the locket and the symbol on its face. This entire affair seemed so strange to me—unreal. Phantasmagoric confusion. Now, there's a word I did find in a book. A fat book at that—one written by a gentleman named Noah ... Noah Webster. Yes, that's the fellow—the *American Dictionary of the English Language*. Now, the same word I discovered in Mr. Webster's book can avail itself to describe this mysterious dilemma.

Phantasmagoric!

Out in the harbor a Buzzard's Bay breeze swept up the river, rippling the placid water. It gently rocked the schooner like a floating baby cradle. I shut my eyes and my mind drifted—nowhere in particular, you see, just away from heavy thoughts. It appears the human brain has a way of diverting its function when the task at hand is not understood or safely unraveled, or when the chore of doing so becomes unbearable.

"Well, Samuel, what do we do?"

"About?"

"Amy being on that whaler!"

He placed his cup of cocoa on the table and stared at me. "You're a bag of nerves, Emily. Can't you relax just a little?"

"How?"

"Come!"

Without warning, he took my hand and led me to the aft portion of the ship and his private cabin. Once inside he closed the door. Unaware and unprepared, calming lips solaced my face. I closed my eyes as his nose grazed my cheek, coming to rest upon mine. My body became lissome. I shivered with serenity and glee. Immediately, all stained and blemished thoughts dissolved. His gentle finger delicately cradled my chin as he pressed his face against mine. I weaved my fingers through his hair and around the back of his head, holding him there, making certain he did not pull away. All the while, I drank from his ardor and passion as our lips fondled and our noses tussled. If I had ever felt a feeling of well-being, it was this very moment. It was cleansing. I was left with a butterfly tummy and puppy nose desire. I must give admission to my heart and confess. How do I find the words to express to you how I felt for him? What was the phrase I used earlier? Oh yes, *'madly in love.'*

That very unfortunate instant I heard the gangplank outside the ship rumble to footsteps. Our kiss was fractured as we looked at one another. With pellucid blue eyes he embraced my face, nose, mouth, chin, while I did the same, tingling with his every glance. Footsteps outside the ship became louder.

"Permission to come aboard," a voice called out. Suddenly there was a face looking in the cabin port window.

"Disruption comes-a-knocking," declared Samuel.

"Leave a marker on the page," I proposed, "and we'll finish the chapter later."

Samuel lowered his head with a regrettable smile and nodded. He left the cabin while I arranged my hair and straightened my dress.

"Come on down, Tim," cried Samuel. "I'm making some cocoa."

Tim sat himself at the table, took a photograph from his shirt pocket, and dropped it on the table. "People are mad," he said, "just mad."

"How so?" asked Samuel, stirring a drink.

I walked out from the master's cabin. The warm fervor I felt just moments ago was still waning.

"Oh, hi, Emmie."

"Hello, Timothy. What were you saying about madness?"

"I've been on Main Street in the city showing the picture of Amy you gave me to pedestrians, you know, to see if anyone had seen her."

"No success?" I said.

"None," he replied. "Some of the men I showed the picture to wanted to know if it was for sale, or if I would part with it. One even proposed marriage to it."

"What in the world for?" I asked.

"City people," chimed Samuel, placing a hot cocoa in Tim's hand. "City people are just too busy to help."

I thought about what Samuel said, how isolated we all are living in our little Eden by the sea, and how differently, if not mistakenly, we can perceive the city and those who live there.

Tim sat quietly staring down at the photograph of Amy and running his finger along the image on the stiff engraved card. With eyebrows furrowed and biting his lip, he nodded with discouragement.

"Where are you, Amy?" he said.

"Emily has a notion, Tim."

"Oh? What is it, Emmie?"

I looked over at Samuel, waiting for him to furnish it for me.

He took a pencil from the table, along with a scrap piece of paper, and began to write. "I want you to go back into the city, Tim. Take my wagon and get these provisions."

"Sure thing, Sam! I wish you had told me earlier when I was there. I hate going into Fall River twice in one day."

"Go to New Bedford instead."

"From the pan into the fire? No thanks."

We sat in silence as Samuel scribbled across the paper.

"That's a lot of stuff, Sam. One would think you were planning a voyage."

Samuel looked over to me and winked. "I am, Tim."

"No kidding. Where to?"

"As I said, old man. Emily has a notion."

"So what is it, Emmie? I'm game—anything that will lead to finding Amy."

With a raised eyebrow, I looked over at Samuel. Though I was almost certain Amy was kidnapped, I was not sure how Tim would take the news.

"Tell him, Emily."

"I believe that Amy is on the *Nimrod*."

"What!"

Samuel handed him the long list of goods. "Get the crew together, Tim. We are heading north."

"I have no idea what you two are up to," declared Tim. He folded the paper and stuffed it in his shirt. "But I'm with you."

"We are going after the *Nimrod*," announced Samuel.

I jumped up and clapped. Throwing my arms around Samuel I gave him an unyielding kiss. He tried pulling away. I held his lips firmly to mine.

Tim turned to leave. "That's what I thought you two were doing when I first got here. Carry on."

"Oh, thank you, Samuel, thank you!" I cried.

"You are coming, are you not?"

"Oh, yes! After all you will need me. I hear it gets cold at night out at sea."

I rested my head on his firm, pillowy shoulder. Looking down at the salon table, the photo of Amy looked back up at me. Her glamorous face, her Mona Lisa smile, and aristocratic gaze only said one thing. "Help!"

Chapter 20:

Glancing out the wavy glass of my bedroom window, I noticed the new day was a breezy one. The awaiting sun was still below the horizon, primed to introduce itself to a blushing, silk sky. Across the street the spindly branches of the old elm in widow Mosher's front yard curtsied obediently to the sporadic air. An undulating, weathered slab of wood, once used as a swing seat, dangled from a scraggly limb. One of the two ropes that cradled it was long gone. I couldn't count how many times the four Mosher girls and I played on it when we were children. And although three of them have married and moved away, and one had died, still here I stand … and there it sways—the old swing and a wistful reminder of joys past and pangs forgotten.

I remember Lilly Mosher, the oldest of the Mosher girls. I was only nine. She was all of thirteen. We rode the swing and Lilly did the pushing. Then she became ill and died. I remember at the time asking Grandmamma about it. I'll never forget what she said. *Emily, life is like a swing. We all fly high and low, high and low. The secret is to try not to fall off and to have a friend who will give us a push. Sometimes the tree is weak or old and a limb breaks. When those times come there is nothing one can do. We must find a new tree or a new friend to give us a push.*

Behind the house, our trusty rooster tossed his lusty prologue to the creeping dawn, reminding me that it was getting late. I dressed swiftly. Wrapping a waxed canvas cape around my shoulders, I smothered the flame to the oil lamp and rushed down the stairs, dragging my potbellied sea bag with its obligatory cache of wrinkled clothing and personal toiletries. I must confess to stuffing a book or two between my winter brocade dress and my new plaid Mackintosh jacket. I would like to have brought along my blue tea gown or red striped print dress to wear on evenings. But I was preparing for sea, not idle pleasure. Under a starlit night, on a spray-swamped ship, far out to sea, how would one appreciate such attire?

Trying to look fashionable and stay warm can sometimes be a

challenge. Samuel insisted that everyone dress accordingly for the upcoming voyage. Though it's the peak of summer, it gets cold out at sea, especially in northern climes. And I was advised to think cold and bring lots of warm things to wear.

We were all instructed to be on the ship by sunrise and I, for one, intended not to be late. The canvas baggage bounced from step to step as I lugged it down the hollow-cupped stairs. I propped it by the front door. I was concerned about making noise and awakening Grandmamma, but discovered she was already up when I entered the kitchen.

"Morning, Grandmamma!"

"Good morning, child. I thought I heard you stirring upstairs."

Coughing, I fanned the air with one hand and held my nose with the other. Simmering on the stove was a cast iron kettle and pot. On the table sat an assortment of small, slim bottles, each with its own cork and ready to be filled and sealed.

"What in the world are you cooking, Grandmamma?"

"Seaweed, dear, seaweed."

"What in the world for?"

"A new medicine I'm making. To alleviate stomach aliment."

"Stomach aliment?"

"Kelp elixir. I've yet to prefect it or discover which stomach aliment it will cure."

"You're funny, Grandmamma!" I said, laughing. I lifted the lid on one of the steaming pots. "Looks like pea soup."

"That's because it is pea soup," she replied. "The seaweed elixir is stewing in the kettle." On the shelf above the sink were two pickle jars filled and sealed tightly. She took one in each hand and held them up. "This one contains vegetable soup and this one your favorite … chicken corn soup. The pea soup is nearly ready. Now hand me another pickle jar from under the sink."

"What are you going to do with all that soup?"

"To take on your trip, of course. You didn't think Grandmamma would forget, did you?" She placed the two jars on the table. "Now take these and stuff them carefully in your bag."

"Grandmamma, you must have been up for hours." I handed her an empty glass jar and lifted the lid on the black tubby kettle. The biting steam nipped at my face. "Oh, Grandmamma, what in the world is in this?" I rubbed my nose with the back of my hand and dropped the lid.

"Seaweed and sea grass, dear. Burnt pepper and a touch of vinegar is what you smell." She lifted the lid to the kettle, scooped a spoonful, and tasted. She grimaced. "Not sweet enough. Needs a little more molasses.

Hand me that jug, dear, will you?" she said pointing up at the shelf behind the stove.

I gave her the brown clay vessel and she poured some of the sugary liquid into the bubbling, iron kettle. A flare of steam rose to the ceiling.

She stirred it a while then covered it with the lid. "Must be careful not to make it too thick," she said. "Now, dear, what would you like for breakfast?"

"I'm not having any, Grandmamma. I need to get going."

She pulled out a chair, clutched me by the elbow, and sat me down. "Nonsense. It takes all of two or three minutes to make some toast and spread some jam. Now sit!"

Opening the oven, she pulled out two loaves of freshly baked bread. She cut two slices off one and placed the thin slabs on the stove. I poured myself a cup of tea.

"You baked two loaves, Grandmamma?"

"You will need some bread to go with your soups." She reached up on the shelf for a plate.

I walked over and embraced her, resting my chin on her shoulder. "You are a wonderful and mindful mother."

Lovingly, she leaned her head back and kissed me on the cheek. "Grandmamma loves you dear, and we always feed those we love, now don't we? After all, you will be away for quite a while and soup will keep you warm on those chilly nights."

I walked back to the table and sat down. I wondered whether I should go on the trip at all. Samuel had said that we would be gone for weeks, perhaps months. To be away from Grandmamma for any length of time worried me. I questioned what was more important. Finding Amy or not leaving Grandmamma on her own?

I had to confess. We had no idea where Amy had gone or whether she was even on the *Nimrod*. We were setting sail on a hunch and a prayer, or perhaps reckless intuition. But we had to do something. And Samuel has been gracious in entertaining the glimmering clue that I suggested and that Amy was, in fact, kidnapped. Was I doing the right thing? After all, I have never been away from home for more than a night or two, let alone on a ship sailing into the void of the open sea.

I slouched in my chair, elbows on the table, and my chin in my hands— thinking. "I'm not sure whether I'm doing the right thing, Grandmamma."

"What do you mean, dear?" She cut more bread and placed it on the stove to toast.

"This voyage I'm taking."

She moved to the sink window and stared out over the dark flowered field behind the house without saying a word. Down by the river the gray shadows of the Two Sisters took shape in the early morning light. She just stood there, quietly staring, like the sky was about to fall.

"Grandmamma?"

"The willows are so beautiful," she declared, "graceful, like the flowing locks of a Wampanoag princess—strong as a heart of a Narragansett brave."

"You love those trees, don't you, Grandmamma?"

"I was told by an old Wampanoag sachem once that they were but a twig in the ground when I was born. Said one could measure the length of a man's life by them. We have witnessed many changes, those trees and I. Sadly, their time is nearly up. Every year a new branch breaks away and the willowy leaves lose more and more of their pigment—not quite green, not quite brown. They are like the gray hairs on my head."

"Oh, they will be there forever, Grandmamma. They always have."

"Father taught us all about trees. The maple can live to be a hundred-and-fifty years old. Why, the elm in the Mosher yard across the way has been reported to be over two hundred. But willow trees are lucky to remain standing after only sixty or seventy. Yes, child, I love those trees. They speak of soil and water, of sun and rain, wind and snow, of life and ...."

A hidden tear grew in her eye. The bread on the stove began to burn. The iron lid over the simmering seaweed clattered.

"I'm thinking of staying home, Grandmamma, not going on this voyage. I'm afraid ...."

She turned quickly and cried. "No! You mustn't forgo commitment to friendship. Nor should you cuddle asylum and reject adventure. And what greater reason can one have to confront a crisis if not to rush to the call of a confidante in need."

"You are my ultimate confidante, Grandmamma, and I must think of your needs also."

She walked over and cradled my chin in her hand. "Oh, child, a cup of tea in the morning is all I need ... burnt toast, a soft-boiled egg, a warm blanket on cold evenings, soft bed at night, and to awaken to the sight of my lovely willows. Those are my needs. And I could do without any one of them. Most of all I need you to be happy, dear. And I know you never will if you don't go to the aid of your friend. At the moment, my need is your need. And you need to find her."

I lightly rested my hand on hers. "Thanks, Grandmamma."

She kissed me on the head and moved over to the stove. "It is settled then. Adventure and rescue calls your name."

"I suppose I am worried if something should happen to me. We would never see one another again."

"You mustn't think like that." She pulled the pot of pea soup off the stove. Taking a wood ladle, she filled the glass pickle jar with the thick porridge-like broth and sealed it tightly. "Now this is very hot and you must be careful." She wrapped the jar with a towel. "Stuff it into your bag along with the other two and don't drop them."

"Thanks, Grandmamma. I promise to store them on the ship as soon as I board." I took the jars of soup along with a loaf of bread and packed them carefully into my seabag.

Suddenly there was a soft knock at the front door. I opened it. "Samuel!"

"I saw a light on and thought I would help you with your luggage."

"Sorry. I know. I'm running late."

"Not at all. I miscalculated the tide. We have another hour before the ship can leave the wharf."

"Are you talking to me?" asked Grandmamma, as she hobbled over. "Oh! Good morning, Samuel. Would you like to come in?"

"Morning, Charlotte. No, thanks. I have come to fetch Emily."

"You are just in time. She and I were talking about how vital it is that she help search for her friend. She can't wait to be on her way."

I looked over to Grandmamma and smiled. "You sure you'll be all right, Grandmamma?"

"Sure she will," added Samuel. "I've arranged for Mrs. Davis to pay a visit every morning and every evening. And Father is right next door. He will make certain that all Charlotte's needs are attended to."

"Oh, don't make a fuss," insisted Grandmamma. "Now, take your things and be on your way."

I displayed a stiff upper lip. "Love you, Grandmamma." I gave her a long warm embrace. I was about to release her when she drew me in tighter.

"I love you too, dear. When you get back from your adventure, you will write a book instead of always reading one. And it will be the most exciting book I will ever read."

Her declaration gave me consent to cry.

Samuel threw the seabag over his shoulder. A genial and supportive smile graced his face. "I'll take good care of her, Charlotte," he said as we walked away.

"I know you will, dear, I know you will."

Samuel and I started down Point Road toward the ship. I turned to find Grandmamma waving. I waved in return. The further away we got the smaller she became. Growing up, I always thought of her as bigger than life itself—self-made and capable of handling any obstacle that was flung her way. Now, and from this distance, she looked tiny and frail.

Just as we arrived at the wharf, I peered up Point Road one last time. The door to the small cottage was shut and Grandmamma no longer there. I was torn between the mission at hand and the gnawing notion that something would change. And though life carried on making revisions at will, to predict or worry about its outcome made for a fruitless existence. In more ways than one, life was beyond our control. Still, I could not shake the perpetual vexation that I would never see Westport or Grandmamma again. Samuel could sense my fear. He stopped and took my hand.

"You don't need to do this, Emily," he said, looking me straight in the eyes. "I'll still do my best to find her. I know you and Amy are good friends. She's my friend also."

"I want to come Samuel. I need to be there for her."

"Are you sure?"

"I'm sure."

"There's always some misgivings or foreboding when a sailor sets out to sea. It's normal to feel the way you do. Even I sense the same at times. Once you are away and on the roaring waters, the open sea will be all that matters."

"I suppose you're right."

"Sure I am."

I glanced back up Point Road. As was common, a wagon on the way to market rambled along, carrying a pyramid of casks filled with whale oil. It rattled and clattered as it made its way, obstructing the view of my little white cottage. My heart skipped a beat. Off to my right, the creaking door to the carpentry shop swung open. Antonio the cooper propped it back with a stick. He looked over and waved. I smiled and looked away. Fuffy the cat followed, meowing attention. A feeble sun broke over a crusty horizon warming one side of my face. The crisp morning air flushed my senses, distilling all thought, and left my head barren as a surf-washed, sandy beach.

"It will all work out," Samuel said, throwing an arm around me. "You'll see. We'll find Amy and bring her home safely."

"What will I do if a tree limb breaks while I'm gone?" I muttered.

"What do you mean?"

"Nothing ... nothing at all."

—◦/◦/◦—

Chapter 21:

The schooner plowed the foamy sea half-way up the Nova Scotia coast. It was a brilliant, misty dawn as a truculent sun battled to perforate a thick shroud of soggy haze. Samuel had enlisted the same African crew that was with us on our Cuttyhunk voyage after he made the men a wage offer they could not refuse. They were familiar with the workings of the *Sphinx,* thus the expense well worth it.

With Eli Monroe at the wheel the crew made certain to spend all their time up on deck. Since that sorrowful journey to Cuttyhunk Island, the men still insisted on sleeping nights on deck, refusing to go down into the cabin at night or near the forecastle where Annie Slocum's body once lay. One man even swore he saw Annie standing by the wheel steering the ship. The macabre apparition he claimed to have seen only inoculated the fear his African comrades felt.

On a pleasure craft such as the *Sphinx,* one can never have enough capable crew. So Marcus Theroux was asked, and graciously agreed, to come along, leaving a trepidatious Louisa ashore. Though not a fully capable seaman, Marcus had other worthy skills apart from doctoring, which would prove indispensable on a sailing vessel. He and Tim sat on the quarterdeck savoring a new rising sun. Tim whittled away at a piece of oak. Eli steered the ship while making love to his fusty cheroot.

I leaned on the fore-rail, nearby, sipping my hot drink and enjoying the blistering but tranquil bow waves that spanked the ships planking. Every once in a while, a whiff of café noir permeated the moist air, mingling with the briny sea breeze, and eclipsing the sweet scent of cocoa in my cup. Now, I have nothing against the smell of freshly brewed coffee, but I need to be in an agreeable mood to enjoy the bitter taste and smell of it. Nevertheless, out on the open sea, even the noxious scent of Eli's stogie pleasantly stirred the senses.

Though the sun was hidden in a steamy haze, I could make it out low on the horizon rising like a pastel cantaloupe on a beaming, white canvas.

In the distance, a small pod of whales breached the surface, with gusts of air, in an undulated ballet. The fragrance of the open sea sanitized my perception of the world and made me forget those ills I cannot change. Every day I am away from terra firma is like a life reborn. And for those who have no inkling of what I mean, you must take a long sea voyage. And all it would take is one stiff gale to whisk the consciousness, stiffen the spirit, and leave you a new person.

Samuel sauntered up the starboard deck and leaned on the rail beside me. He no longer used a cane. And though he walks with a limp and a painful knee, every step is well placed and stable. He pointed toward the horizon.

"Whales!"

"Yes, I have been watching them," I said. "What kind of whales are they, Samuel?"

"Right whales. You can tell by the white bump on its head."

"White bump?"

"Yes, callosities. Calcified skin."

"Oh, look!" I cried, tearing at his arm.

A pair of the giant mammals ruptured the surface of the water, yards from the schooner—a mother and her calf. Their simmering bodies surged and curled just above the surface as they gingerly plunged in a collective dive. Their bat-like tails waved and lingered, eventually plunging below the rippled water.

"I have never been this close to a whale!"

"Don't you remember the one that washed up at Horseneck, on the beach a couple of years ago?"

"Not alive and breathing," I reminded him.

A school of dolphins crisscrossed the ship's bow. Tim ran over and shuffled out to the tip of the bowsprit like a barefoot, nautical cowboy. He sat with legs dangling, riding the protruding sprit like it was a pelagic bronco. He whistled between split fingers down at the frolicsome porpoises. A distance behind the ship another whale surfaced with blustering breath.

"How delightful! To think that I have never witnessed such a sight," I said.

"It's a common occurrence out on the open water," replied Samuel. "Dolphins and whales together. Now that's an uncommon sight."

"How can they do it ... how?"

"Do what?"

"Kill such majestic animals."

"It's life, I suppose. One of the most beneficial animals we have. They're just big cows."

"That's not good enough. They should let them be."

"How would we light the lanterns in our homes if not for whale oil? And there is the making of candles, soap, and fasteners for clothes … even women's corsets. They're like any other animal man consumes."

"Man consumes? I don't understand it."

"What is there to understand?"

"Why God made the order of things the way He did."

"Hmm?"

"You remember Mr. Franklin when we were children?" I asked.

"Should I?"

"Yes, that little piglet in the pen down Point Road—by the church. Amy had named him after Benjamin Franklin. We would feed him on the way back from Sunday service. He was so adorable. Then he grew bigger and bigger. Still he would lumber over every time he saw us and stick his twitching, button snout through the fence—begging for a snack."

"Of course, Mr. Franklin. I remember now."

"Then he was mated with Martha, Martha Washington. She loved rolling in the mud."

"You're right," he said, laughing. "She had an ear-splitting squeal."

"And screeched bloody murder every time she saw us children feed Mr. Franklin."

"Mr. Franklin and Martha Washington. What funny names for pigs."

"Then he was donated to the church for the spring picnic roast. I cried and cried. It was terrible. I was only ten or eleven at the time. I just didn't understand how people could … could—well, eat Mr. Franklin."

Samuel grinned and nodded his head. He found humor in the way I told it. "It's just the order of life, Emily—the way things were intended," he explained.

"You mean the way man intended it," I said. "I will never understand the computation of things. It just doesn't add up. To this day I don't think I have ever had pork … not since the last time I saw poor Mr. Franklin."

"Well, be assured," he said, throwing his sturdy arm around me, "on this trip it is snapper, cod, rice, and plenty of vegetables. When Tim takes over the wheel, Eli will go down into the galley and make us the best Bermudian fish chowder you ever tasted. You will think you have died and gone to heaven—it's that good."

"Died and gone to heaven? Really?"

"Well, think of it this way. When you do get to heaven I am certain you will find a happy Mr. Franklin there waiting to be fed."

I smiled at his witty remark and rested my head on his shoulder. A pod of dolphins surfaced by the side of the ship, weaving themselves in and out the waves. I could practically reach out and touch them. Ahead, another group crossed over from the port side intersecting the bow in playful daring. With long, slender muzzles, they stitched themselves through the water, heaving; cutting swells with a magic thread of wonder.

We watched with delight as the *Sphinx* swept along supporting acres of bellowing sheets—stiffened canvas—mainsails, foresails, topsails, jibs, magically thrusting us into aqueous bliss. The schooner glided effortlessly and proud, skipping from one dilated swell to the next, not unlike a sure-footed prima ballerina leaping across a liquid stage. I stood there enjoying the scenery, my drink, and especially Samuel. He is an elixir for the eyes. Though, at the moment, he suddenly looked worried. He became quiet. I could tell something weighed heavily on his mind.

"What is it, Samuel?" I laid my hand on his arm.

He rested his over mine and smiled. "You know, Emily, not to disappoint you, but this is bound to be a fruitless mission. It's a big ocean. The chances of us finding the *Nimrod* are unlikely."

I pulled my hand away and thought about what he said. I brought the cup of cocoa to my mouth and took a slurpy sip. The steamy brew warmed my nose and watered my eyes. Suddenly I wasn't enjoying my drink as much. "At least I feel like we are doing something!"

"I know, I know … that's why we are out here. Even if we do find David and the ship, there's no confirmation that Amy is even on it. We are out here on a hunch."

"You don't think there's a chance we will find her, do you?"

"I don't know. It's better than sitting at home not doing anything, I suppose. I've provisioned the ship for two months. All we can do is crisscross this vast ocean, cross our fingers, and beg the Almighty that we find David and his ship and that Amy is safe."

"You think we'll be out looking that long?"

"Can't really say. We will give it a good shot, though. I did talk to a few whaling captains in the village and I have an idea of the route the *Nimrod* is taking."

"That's something, no?"

He threw an arm around me and gave me a quick squeeze. "Yes, Emily, it is."

Thinking about Amy and what could have happened to her turned my stomach sour. My mind kept meandering back to Annie Slocum and Mary

Sullivan. I tried not connecting Amy to them but it was of no use. She was. We all were. I emptied my drink into the sea. The playful porpoises had vanished. The whales could no longer be seen. What was once a magical moment had turned pungent with doubt.

"Don't worry so much, Emily," said Samuel. "Alexander Cory said that the *Nimrod* and its crew were headed toward the south tip of Greenland. They are planning to stay close to the Labrador coast until St. Johns while they break in the new ship. What we sailors call a shake down. From there it's onto Greenland and the bountiful waters of Baffin Bay. Reports have it that bowhead whales are plentiful along Greenland's west coast. Hopefully the *Nimrod* will not venture into Hudson Bay."

"How will we know if they do?"

"We won't. All we can do is pray and hope the ice is not too far south."

"Oh, Samuel, it sounds so hopeless."

"We will keep moving. The *Sphinx* is fast. We can cover a lot of ocean. If the icebergs have moved south early this year, it could complicate things. This vessel is not made to take a hit from a berg like those old whaling hulks."

"What will we do then?"

"Not to worry. We slow down at night and place a man in the crow's nest by day. I'm certain we will be all right."

I leaned over and kissed him. "We will," I agreed. "But will Amy?"

It had been five days and five nights since we rounded Nantucket Shoals. We were twenty miles off the coast of Nova Scotia. Mahone Bay was just abeam. This was the first sailing trip I had taken in which land was not seen for days—not that I have done much sailing at all. Out at sea there is a tranquility that can be experienced nowhere else. No matter how many worries you may have, there is an emptiness that drowns one's troubles—a fullness, which brims with inevitable serenity. Fear is but a temporary ambiance and once its trepidation has passed, contentment immerses the psyche, and the existence of this watery domain commands one to enjoy the moment. Here the salted air is an intoxicant, which flushes one's desires and aspirations and relegates them to a world gladly left behind. You should try it sometime—to sail into the void, run with the wind, chase an unattainable horizon, watch the emerging sun germinate at the break of dawn, and escalade up an early morning apricot sky. At least that is what I am enjoying on this seafaring adventure. I'm saddened that Amy and Louisa are not here to feel it—a voyage into nowhere, in search of it all. You should try it sometime.

A shout came from a lookout standing high in the crow's nest. He hung tightly—one arm scarfed around the mast and the other extended and pointing.

"Sighting to starboard at two o'clock!" he hollered.

Tim stood up at the head of the bowsprit. "Over there!" he shouted. "Looks like a ship."

"Get my spyglass, will you?" said Samuel to one of the crewmen.

"She looks like a brig, sir!" shouted the man atop the mast.

"Could it be David's ship, Samuel?" I asked.

"We'll soon find out. Don't get your hopes up. There are many ships out here."

"I haven't seen one since we lost sight of land."

"They're out there, Emily. We just don't see them. It's a vast sea."

Marcus Theroux came over carrying a chart. "Pray it is not a Confedeate warship," he said, with a nervous French accent.

"We'll soon find out," said Samuel. "Mr. Theroux. You said you knew how to use a sextant?"

"But of course. I am French, am I not?"

"Good! I surrender my navigational duties to you, sir. This haze is beginning to lift. As soon as you can, take the sextant, shoot the sun, and find our exact location. You will find the sextant and nautical tables in the desk in my quarters."

"With pleasure, *Capitaine.*"

I crossed my fingers, closed my eyes, and said a prayer. It was a remote speck of hope on the far-off horizon. It appeared then disappeared as the cresting swells hid it from sight. Tabeu handed Samuel the spyglass.

"Heave to, Mr. Monroe!" ordered the captain.

"Heaving to!" announced Eli.

Eli quickly spun the large wooden wheel to starboard. The ship immediately stood up and straight as the canvas slackened. The hanging cloth flapped in the wind like giant flags of surrender. The ship's bow rolled through the eye of the wind, left to right. Suddenly the canvas stiffened once again and the vessel fell onto a port tack. Eli quickly spun the wheel back to port. With the sails backfilled, the vessel came to an unexpected halt. It was an ingenious method sailors had of stopping a ship mid-ocean, without taking down canvas, and allowing it to hold its position.

"We stopped moving," I said, surprisingly.

"She's in irons," declared Eli, smiling proudly.

"The sails don't look right. They look twisted, or something," I said.

"That's how it's done," he explained. "You maneuver the ship from one tack to another without trimming the sails for the new tack. It locks the ship in place on the water. We'll make very little headway now."

"It feels like the seas have calmed."

"That's the idea," he said.

"There's so much to learn about sailing a ship."

"It's a brig, all right," reported Samuel, studying the speck on the horizon. He collapsed the eyepiece.

Tim came running up the deck. "I wonder where she's from," he said.

"It looks like the *Elizabeth Shaw* out of Fairhaven," said Samuel.

"So it's not the *Nimrod*," I said.

"I recognize the familiar mizzen sail on the *Elizabeth Shaw*. It's black. It's the only black sail they carry."

"Oh," I uttered. "I was hoping that ..."

"Mr. Monroe. Take her out of irons," ordered Samuel. "Steer a new course ninety degrees to compass."

"Aye, aye, Captain!"

"Tabeu! Get those sheets trimmed. Flatten the jibs once we get on the new course." Samuel cupped his hands together and yelled up the mast. "Admon come on down and tend the topping lifts," he ordered.

The barefoot crew scurried, pulling lines and tugging sails. Up in the rigging, Admon wrapped his legs around a rope and with hand over hand, slid down from high on the mast. His sweat sponged, ebony skin shimmered, reflecting a dazzling regal image against a white glaring sky.

The sea wore an unruffled swell. The water's glassy surface heaved and tumbled to the waning breeze. The schooner's bow cut a reverent path through abiding waves with ease, as if the Almighty himself was at the wheel commanding the waters. On the naked horizon, the whaler's ominous black sail was now evident, as the voluminous ship loomed closer.

"We are losing the wind, Samuel," said Tim, looking up at the sails.

"Are you going to try and approach her?" I asked.

"It's not a matter of trying," said Samuel. "It's a matter of doing."

It took us a while. We soon approached the lumbering whaler as it floundered in a tame, playful breeze. Its hollow black sail swayed to and fro, guided by its gray weathered spar, twisting and whipping to the undulating motion of the drifting ship in a futile attempt at finding useful wind. Though there was not enough air to push the hulking whaler along, the *Sphinx* ghosted easily, like an immense, nautical snail. A glaring white-blue sky illuminated my cheeks, making it difficult to see. *Always wear a hat*, Grandmamma would advise. *You never know if you will need it in a driving rain, or a blinding sun, or just to hide from a cloudy day.* I should have listened. Out here, even when a brilliant haze hides a soaring sun, the glistening sky can make it very difficult on the eyes. I saluted, my hand acting as an awning above my brow, and inspected the loitering crew of the *Elizabeth Shaw*. Clutching onto a rope shroud, Samuel climbed up onto the ship's bulwark rail, cupped one hand, and called out to the wallowing whaler.

"Might you be the captain?" he yelled to the one-armed man smoking a pipe.

"Aye! Where do you hail?" asked the crippled man.

"Westport!" replied Samuel. "This is the vessel *Sphinx*. Is that you, Captain Shaw?"

The old captain gave no reply. Instead, he studied the schooner, looking her over from its waterline to its crow's nest. He took several puffs from his curly pipe. Sparse blue smoke sputtered past gritting teeth. Even with his disability, the ancient sailor looked proud and strong, his clothing neat and orderly, his beard smartly trimmed, the sleeve and cuff of his missing limb aptly tucked beneath his left armpit. He struck the pipe on the boat's rail and emptied it. Revealing a small tobacco pouch, he held it with his teeth as he stuffed fresh brown tobacco into his pipe. One of the crew struck a match and lit it for him. He puffed and puffed until the virgin smoke spewed from his lips in unbroken whispy plumes, like steam between the iron wheels of a locomotive.

"Bristol craft, lad," he hollered. "Who may you be, sir?"

"Samuel Cory! Point Village, Westport!"

"May you be Seabury's boy?" he hollered.

"Yes, one and the same!"

"How may I accommodate you, young Cory?"

"Can we gam, Captain?"

The man nodded and walked away. The schooner turned slowly and glided away from the drifting fishing vessel. I walked along the deck to get a better view of the men and ship. The ragged crew of the *Elizabeth Shaw* lined along its rail in undernourished curiosity. Suddenly, one of the men noticed me. He whistled obscenely while his companions howled like begging dogs. Others laughed. I ran over to be by Samuel's side.

"Tim! Get the small boat overboard," commanded Samuel. "We are going over for a talk with the whaler."

"Ship full of rascals," I said, a bit disturbed.

"Not like the whaling fleet in Westport, are they?" said Samuel, smiling.

"Have they not seen a lady before?"

"Not out here," he replied. Samuel rushed back to the wheel and gave Eli Monroe new orders. "Place her in irons, Mr. Monroe."

"What are you going to do, Samuel?" I asked, scurrying behind.

"Have a chat with the captain of that ship."

The wind had all but died. Sloping sea swells heaved and rolled like bloated mounds over a glazy field. Even the nimble *Sphinx* had lost all headway, drifting just yards from the whaling vessel. If not for the squeaking of blocks and incessant slapping of sails, the silence would be deafening. I hid between Eli and Marcus as Samuel, Tim, and a couple of crewmembers rowed out to the awaiting whaler. The rhythmic, creaky cadence of the oars against the gunwale of the small rowboat echoed loudly between the two ships as it quickly drove away.

"Not a solitary choirboy on the entire tub," declared Eli, pointing to the whaler with the chewed end of his cheroot.

When speaking with Eli I always made certain to be down wind of him when he smoked. The spiraling, cloud from his cigar stung my eyes and stogie scent lingered in my hair. In this fluky air, attempts to escape the expelled exhaust were futile.

"Where are all those men from?" I asked, waving my hand in front of my face.

"Desolation, my dear lady," he replied. "Lands of poverty. Looking for a better life."

"If I were looking for a better life I don't think I would look for it on a whaling vessel," I said.

"They are not all looking for rudimentary solutions, Miss White," said Marcus. "Some are wanderers, dreamers, even writers." He practiced taking sites with the bronze sextant, holding the intricate tool to his eye and swinging its complex mechanisms.

"One may even discover a felon or two," touted Eli.

"You mean criminals?"

"He is just bantering, Mademoiselle Emily," said Marcus. "What Mr. Monroe says may be true, but most of them are good men. Some may come from the slums of Liverpool, the humble Portuguese Azores, or from some scenic palm island out in the Pacific, where survival is your brother and hunger your sister. For the most part, they are hardworking, honest men."

"This I can say, Miss White," added Eli. "Though they may appear offensive, each one of them would lay down his life to protect the honor of a lady."

Listening to Marcus Theroux's exotic French accent and Eli Monroe's dignified Bermudian dialect made me feel like I was truly out in the real world, thousands of miles from home and in some foreign sea. Floating just yards away was a tiny continent onto itself, with many nationalities, but one governing body—its captain.

The sheeny waves puckered as the wind began to pick up. The sails hardened and the ship began to list. Eli ordered the crew to take in sail as the *Sphinx* began to move. Flinging the stub of his cigar overboard, he rushed to tend to the wheel. Once again we slowly circled the heavy whaler. Not long after, the small delegation dispatched from the *Sphinx* rowed back.

The captain of the *Elizabeth Shaw* yelled out. "Heed the devil's minion, Captain! Ye be warned!"

Lines were sent over the side to retrieve the small vessel as the breeze blew harder. I hurried over to greet them. Tim was the first onboard, closely followed by Samuel. Marcus reached out and helped him up on deck.

"What warning, Samuel?" I asked.

"Nothing for us to worry about," he replied.

"Something about heeding the devil," I said. "I heard him."

"They thought they saw a Confederate frigate sailing west," explained Tim.

"Out here?"

"I wouldn't worry about it, Emily," added Samuel. "It's doubtful they would venture this far north."

A block and tackle was flung over the side and attached to the small skiff. Samuel gave the order and it was hauled aboard.

"Did you find anything out, Samuel?" I asked.

"I sure did," he replied, clutching his injured knee and hoping I would not notice.

"Would you like me to examine that leg, *Capitaine*?" asked Marcus.

"I'm all right, Mr. Theroux."

"Are you certain?"

"Yes, Doctor!" said Samuel, walking quickly toward the helm. "Mr. Monroe steer us on new compass course, west!"

"Heading, Captain?"

"Two-hundred-and-sixty degrees. Destination, Halifax."

"Halifax?" I said, chasing after him as he rushed along the deck.

"Yes. Let's get down below. I have news."

Though the waves were choppy, the schooner's ride was surprisingly a smooth one. The wind was now a fresh breeze as the *Sphinx* sailed along at a comfortable rate on a heading toward Halifax, Nova Scotia. Without hesitation, Samuel took advantage of the easy ride to finish making coffee. Marcus, Tim, and I sat at the salon table and waited eagerly to hear what he had to say. I for one could not wait any longer.

"Tell me, Samuel, please. What did you discover on the *Elizabeth Shaw*?"

"That Captain Shaw is quite the fellow," declared Tim. "He opened one of his best bottles of rum and insisted we have a drink before any discussion could be had."

Samuel poured himself a tin cup of hot coffee and laughed. "Yes, he's quite the man. Grew up by an exuberant waterfront in New Bedford, a rough-and-tumble sort of fellow."

"Most New Bedford captains are," added Tim.

Samuel threw a handful of sugar cubes into his coffee and stirred. "This is what we uncovered," he said. "The *Elizabeth Shaw* left Halifax two days previous. Captain Shaw had stopped there to pick up a passenger … a Mr. Melville, a close acquaintance of his."

"A writer," said Tim.

"I have heard of him," said Marcus. "He writes books about the sea … the South Pacific."

"Right, Mr. Theroux," said Samuel.

"*The Whale*," I cried. "He is the writer of *The Whale*! Is he not?"

"The one and the same," said Samuel. "He is compiling material for a story about the war between the North and the South."

"Out here?" I asked.

"Apparently. Northern whalers are being boarded and commandeered by Confederate war ships and he is hoping to experience such a raid first hand so he can write about it."

Amused, Tim nodded his head. "The man is mad."

"You said you had some news, Samuel," I pleaded.

"Mr. Melville was on his way back to the States from a visit to Liverpool. On his way home he disembarked in Halifax where he wired home his intentions to write a story about the war. It just happened that his good friend, Captain Shaw, was setting north, out to sea. He begged to go along. He's an experienced whaleman himself, as you may well know."

"You spoke to Mister Melville!" I inquired.

"No, not really."

"He was in his cabin with a bout of seasickness," laughed Tim.

"So the *Elizabeth Shaw* put in at Halifax," said Marcus.

"What does that have to do with anything, Samuel?" I asked.

"Captain Shaw said that while Melville was waiting for passage, he spent most of his time wandering the docks, talking to sailors."

"Ahh! Looking for *materiel* for his next book," declared Marcus. "Continue, *s'il vous plaît*."

"About three days ago he saw an American whaleboat anchor out in port. At first he did not pay it much mind, but there was a big commotion when a young man was brought ashore, on a cart … injured. When he asked who it was, someone said the captain of the whaleship, *Nimrod*."

"David!" I cried.

"Maybe," replied Samuel. "But the *Nimrod* left before the *Elizabeth Shaw* arrived. Supposedly, David was not on it."

Marcus looked over the chart laying on the table. "If we can carry speed, *Capitaine*, we will be in Halifax in thirty-six hours," he announced.

Samuel looked over at me with sad countenance. I could easily read what his expression was trying to convey.

"I know," I said. "Doesn't mean that Amy was on the *Nimrod*. But it is something to go on. We are closer to the whaleship—closer to finding Amy!"

—⚭—

Chapter 22:

Uncertain of my surroundings, I endeavored to open my eyes and labored to chase away the sleepies. Before consciousness could reason with bearings, the pungent smell of beached seaweed sifted through my nose. Suddenly, I heard the screeching protest of a restless seagull cawing right outside my port window. His yells were interrupted by the sound of a blaring steam horn. I jumped! My eyes sprung open! *Oh, yes, I remember now. I'm on a ship and we are out at sea.*

I sat up in my bunk and looked out the tiny cabin window. A flutter of red, white, and blue filled the sky. It was the largest Union Jack I had ever seen. A British frigate was passing. I swiftly dressed, placing my nightwear under my pillow. When I opened the door to the private cabin, a whiff of cooked ham and eggs teased my appetite. Eli Monroe stood by the stove flinging a spatula and fork. A pleased smile graced his face.

"Ah, morning, Miss White. I trust you had a satisfying night's rest."

It was much too early for words. I just smiled. Looking out one of the ports across the cabin I could make out a lighthouse meandering by.

"You are just in time for breakfast," said Eli.

"I'll just have some tea."

"At seven this morning the captain knocked on your cabin as we entered harbor. You must have been sleeping like a baby."

"Where are we, Mr. Monroe?"

"British territory, Miss! Is it not wonderful?" He raised his spatula high in the air. "God bless the Queen!"

A shout came from up on deck. "The Kerosene Lighthouse to starboard," roared the crier.

"What, is that land over there?" I asked, peering out the port window.

"McNabs Island. And that's the Maugher Point Light just off Hangman's Beach."

I wrinkled my brow and grimaced, making sure not to ask why it was called Hangman's Beach. "Never heard of such places, Mr. Monroe. What are these waters?"

"Halifax Harbor," he made clear. "Been here many times when I was in the Royal Navy."

I walked over to the companionway. Still half asleep, the early morning light watered my eyes. I gazed out the rear of the ship, past the large star and stripes that hung majestically over the stern. The British frigate had passed and was now a long way behind us as we moved by a lighthouse on a strip of beach out in the middle of the bay, the gateway to Halifax.

Samuel was at the wheel and the open ocean well behind us. He smiled. "Good morning sleepy-head," he sang.

The sight of him stirred me. In my tummy, butterflies fluttered. A warm rush of elation blossomed throughout my shoulders. I'm not certain whether it was the effects of the clean sea air, the entailment from viewing boundless sunrises and sunsets, or a simple result from experiencing the tranquility and peace offered when sailing far from land, but just seeing Samuel whisked a passionate exuberance. Seeing him from below, he looked ten feet tall—legs spread, arms apart, and gripping the wheel. He was steering the world ... my world.

"We're entering Halifax. You are missing some beautiful sights," he declared.

I climbed out and rushed to his side.

"Here ... take the helm," he said, resting my hands on the polished mahogany wheel. He walked away.

"No, Samuel, I can't. Wait, wait! Samuel!"

"I'll be back!" he yelled. "Just steer it in the direction it's going. You'll be all right. I need to help the crew with the anchor."

All I did was hold the steerer tightly. The ship drove itself. I was pleasantly surprised how easy it was. With the air hitting the port rear quarter, the *Sphinx* sailed pretty much upright. Steering the ship through these waters was much easier than driving a horse through the center of a big city. There was no stubborn animal to wheedle and master, no children to meander around, no dogs to chase the horse—only a polite breeze. I'm certain it would be another matter if we were out in the open sea and a gale was blowing. For now we drifted with a tranquil tide. The gentle wind cradled us from behind, not unlike a doting mother escorting her child through its first steps. And like a starched collar on a well-tailored shirt, rigid sails hung majestically, transfixed and proud. The acre of brilliant woven material reflected a glaring, rising sun as the tepid, white orb hovered just above the eastern treed horizon.

We approached the tiny town of Dartmouth. In the distance, straight ahead, stood Halifax Harbor; speckled with moored craft—a watery quagmire of crucifix masts and spars, a leafless woodland draped with lines and folded canvas over spars and decks. My fists were welded to the tapered pegs of the tilling wheel. I could hear the waves fizzing past the ship's hull—the planking tenderly caressed by billowing crests of parting water. Maneuvering and commanding such an immense mass of complexity and blunt weight was a heavenly experience, one usually reserved or practiced by the Almighty.

A coal barge passed on our port side. I felt like a duchess or an aristocratic countess directing the ship while my husband, the Earl, tended to more pressing matters. The crew of the flat ship looked over in wonder at the mild-mannered lady mastering the schooner's helm as it sailed by. The choppy wake left by the overloaded transport scow, gushed steep rolling waves beneath our bow. The graceful *Sphinx* cut through the tall placid surge, its bow slightly rising and plunging like a baby falling onto a feathered pillow. She slowed for a moment while its sails flopped, then immediately stiffened giving us speed once again. It was a glorious ride—that is—until the anchored ships, which lay in harbor appeared. The nails in my fingers gripped securely to the varnished wheel as I shepherded the ship along.

"Samuel!" I shouted. "There are ships up ahead!"

Steer to the right of George's Island," he calmly yelled, "that lump of land straight ahead. You'll be all right."

I piloted the ship carefully, veering it a little to starboard. The ship went into a slight lean as a puff of air appeared from nowhere. Samuel stood at the bow without a worry, instructing the crew on the proper way to deploy anchor. The African crew circled him, intense expressions of learning on their dark faces. My hands trembled as we sailed precariously close to a large steamer anchored between George's Island and the mainland. Trees on the nearby island interrupted the wind. One of the jibs collapsed, losing air, then whipped itself back into place with the sound of a buffered bullwhip. I tried looking sure of myself as we squeezed by the passing ship and land.

"Samuel, I need you here!" I shouted.

"Hold firm, my darling, hold firm!"

The *Sphinx* passed George's Island and entered the main anchoring field. I was worried more than ever.

Samuel lifted a hatch and shouted for Eli. "Mr. Monroe, take the wheel from Miss White, if you please, and bring us into the breeze on my orders."

He looked back at me and smiled. Another ship, this one moving quickly, crept up on me from behind. He was getting close when Eli Monroe suddenly appeared.

"Here, Miss, I'll take the wheel. You go below and make sure the onions don't burn. Fair trade?"

"Fair trade," I said, relieved.

"Be careful of the vessel behind us!" Eli smiled and nodded. The old Bermudian seaman took the schooner past George's Island. Upon a command from the captain, he spun the wheel hard to port. The ship listed and accelerated as the wind gripped, pushed, and pulled on the sails. We were now moving at twice the speed, between moored craft and right toward the mainland. As we got closer to shore, Eli turned the wheel once again, placing the nose of the schooner into the eye of the wind. The ship stood up onto its feet and all the canvas went limp. We were at an instantaneous standstill.

"Hold her there, Mr. Monroe," cried the captain. "Deploy the anchor, men!"

Admon smited the capstan brake with a long-handled hammer. The chain grumbled and thundered as the hulking iron weight went over the side. Abruptly, the noise stopped as the plunging hook hit the seabed.

"Back her down, Mr. Monroe," ordered Samuel.

"Back the foresail, men, on the quick!" yelled Eli.

The crew rushed to man block and tackle. Some pulled lines while others pushed the enormous boom spar in an attempt to catch the wind with the main sail and push the ship aft. I peeked out the main hatch. The *Sphinx* drifted backwards, as the anchor cable clamored, reverberating throughout the ship, paying out in spurts until the captain was satisfied we were safely tethered to the bottom. The capstan was locked in place, the rode secured, and all sails dropped and stored away. This place was to be our home for the next day or two.

After we had anchored, it could not have been more than a minute before we drew the attention of the harbor authorities. The crewmen, including Eli and Marc Theroux, lined up along the rail, military style. Tim slumped by the rail, arms crossed, and looking relaxed.

"Come, Tim," commanded the captain. "Fall in place, here by me."

Tim sauntered over and slouched himself into line. The British contingent rowed out to greet us while I sat by the wheel and watched. Samuel addressed the crew.

"Now, listen up. No one is to speak unless you are spoken to. I will do all the talking. Is that understood?"

"Right you are, Sam," blurted Tim.

A patchy reply of, "aye, aye, Captain" was uttered by the crew. Marcus Theroux snickered and nodded his impertinent approval.

"Be brave, Doctor," quipped Samuel. "They're only British."

"Prepare to be boarded," came the austere command from the water below. The small pilot boat slammed against the hull. Samuel tossed it a line and dispatched the rope ladder. Before we knew it, four delegates stood stiffly onboard—two officers and two recruits.

"I am Commodore Nelson Lodge of the British Royal Navy," roared one of the men, "and this is my first, Captain Thomas Raymond." The man saluted.

"Lieutenant Samuel Cory, Massachusetts Sixth Militia Infantry Regiment … ah, retired, sir."

"Is this a military vessel, Captain?" asked the officer.

"No, sir," replied Samuel, handing the man the ship's papers.

"You are captain of the vessel," said the Commodore, studying the document.

"Allow me to correct myself, Commodore. Currently, I am captain of this vessel. The private schooner *Sphinx*."

"Have you any weapons aboard, Captain?"

"No sir."

"And you have come here for …?" The Commodore raised an eyebrow.

"On a personal matter, sir."

"How long do you expect you will need to conduct this—personal matter?"

"We hope no more than a day or two, Commodore," replied Samuel.

"Is this your cargo?" the Officer asked, pointing to the crew.

"Other than provisions for me and my men, there is no cargo, sir."

The British officer looked over the crewmen. "Are any of you men enslaved on this ship?" he asked.

The African crew looked at one another. Too frightened to speak.

"Come, come, now, don't be afraid! I am here to help you."

"Just a moment!" cried Samuel. "You are addressing legitimate crew members, every one of them a free man. Their names are there, in my papers."

The Commodore squinted, examining each of the crewmen as he walked up and down the deck. His subordinate followed, hands folded behind his back. "You, sir! Where did you get that medal?" asked the Commodore, pinching the ribbon hanging on Eli's chest.

"It was given to my father by Queen Victoria, sir," replied Eli, proudly.

"This is the Distinguished Conduct medal."

"Yes, it is, sir."

"What is your name?" asked the British officer.

"Second Lieutenant, British Royal Navy, Elisha Benjamin Tyler Monroe … retired, sir."

"You are a negro."

"Bermudian, sir."

"I see. Where did you serve?"

"Bermudian Garrison—Royal Naval dockyard."

"You were assigned?"

"Yes, sir, the *HMS Venture*, sir."

The Commodore closely inspected the medal caressing it between his fingers. "And your father?" he asked.

"The Anglo-Ashanti campaign! He served with General Garnet Wolseley, sir."

"Ah yes, Wolseley. I hear that he has taken leave and is in the Americas working with your General Lee."

"I wouldn't know, sir," replied Eli. "Lee is not my general."

The Commodore narrowed his eyes and delivered an admonishing squint. "What is your rank on this ship, Mr. Monroe?"

"Ah ... second in command, sir." He glanced over at Samuel for approval. Samuel smiled and nodded.

"And all these colored?"

"This is our honored crew, sir; friends, some relatives. They were freed by Captain Cory in a midnight raid in the deep South, and aboard this very vessel."

"Is that true, Captain?"

"There is truth to it, yes," replied Samuel.

I could tell that Samuel had had enough, but he held his tongue well, allowing the old Commodore to flex some diplomatic muscle.

"And you, sir. What is your post on this vessel?"

"He is the ship's doctor," Samuel replied, quickly.

Marcus Theroux displayed a smirk of disdain, as he stood in place bouncing on his heels. He kept his silence.

The Commodore studied the smartly-dressed doctor from his brass-buckled shoes to his ruffled white shirt. "Have you nothing to say for yourself, Doctor?" asked the British Officer.

"Now listen here, Commodore," said Samuel.

"Do not worry, *Capitaine*. Le admiral is just performing his duty," sounded Marcus, disdainfully. "Is that not right, Admiral?"

Samuel peered over at the miffed doctor and covertly shook his head, warning Marcus to say no more. I got up and walked over, not to interfere you see, but to give Samuel some moral support. I discovered early in life that a man's demeanor changes when there's a woman around. The Commodore did not expect me.

"Is everything alright, Samuel?" I interrupted.

"Ah, a lady," said the Commodore, quite surprised. He removed his hat.

"Is there a problem, Commodore?" I inquired.

"No problem, just protocol, madam."

"White, Miss Emily White."

"Welcome to British Nova Scotia, Miss White. If I can be of any assistance, please let me know."

"Thank you, Commodore. It is very kind of you."

"Nelson Lodge, Miss, at your service. I must offer you an apology for the delay. You see, we are experiencing an international incident here in Halifax, one of a very delicate nature. Two of your American warships have entered the harbor against our better judgment, and violated British sovereignty, to say nothing of international decree. They are here for the steamer *Chesapeake*, which was previously confiscated. We were holding the *Chesapeake* pending further orders from London."

"Confiscated by who, Mr. Commodore?" I asked.

"Marauders! Your fellow countrymen to the south, Miss," he replied.

"The Commodore is talking about the new Confederate Navy. Are you not, Commodore?" said Samuel.

"Yes, one cannot be too careful, Captain. I feel I best warn you. These waters are swarming with hostile foreign vessels. Vessels from your southern states are attacking northern ones, including whalers and commercial vessels. You are lucky you made it to Halifax safely."

"And what is your stand on the matter, Commodore?" asked Samuel.

"When it comes to such circumstance what I think does not matter. All that is significant is that we keep the peace here in Halifax. The Crown is neutral on such issues. It is between you and your southern brothers, Captain. Now you say you are here on private business. What sort of business?"

"We are looking for a missing girl," I quickly said.

"Missing girl?" repeated the Commodore.

"Yes. We believe she may have been on the American whaler, *Nimrod*," I said. "It may have stopped here."

"You are correct, Miss White. We boarded the *Nimrod*." The Commodore turned to his second in command. "When would you say that was, Captain Raymond?"

"Last Tuesday, sir," said the subordinate. "She was here for only a day, but we did not see any woman on the ship when we boarded her, sir."

"What was the purpose for their visit, if I may inquire, Commodore?" Samuel asked.

"You will have to take that up with the captain of the *Nimrod*," said the

Commodore. "You will find him at the infirmary in Halifax."

"David is here?" I cried.

"Are we cleared, Commodore?" asked Samuel.

The British officer handed Samuel the ship's papers. "Welcome to the British Maritimes, Captain Cory," said a much friendlier Commodore. "I trust you will keep the law. And I advise you to stay clear of the American naval ships. You will only be dragged into an unfortunate affair. We wouldn't want to impound your vessel as well, now, would we?"

"Who do we see about the missing girl?" I asked. "She could have been let off on shore."

"See the Chief Major Constable at the stationhouse in town. Percy Lodge. He's my brother. Tell him I sent you. He will assist you comfortably."

"Thank you, Commodore," I said.

Samuel saluted.

With two men waiting in the small pilot boat, the two officers and two naval midshipmen climbed down the rope ladder and took their leave.

I tugged on Samuel's sleeve as he watched them go. "David is here," I whispered.

"Looks that way," muttered Samuel, somewhat still annoyed.

"Mr. Monroe! Tim, Miss White, and myself are going ashore," declared Samuel, "You are in command."

"Yes, sir!" said a delighted Eli.

"Care to come along, Mr. Theroux?" asked Samuel.

"Why, of course," replied Marcus. "For a Frenchman, a little tussle with the British always makes for good fun."

At the bottom of Prince Street was the Harbor Stationhouse, responsible for policing the waterfront. It was recommended by the Commodore that we check in there before migrating into town. We had very little choice but to do so, since any information we could discover about *Nimrod* was paramount. Tim, Marcus, Samuel, and I entered the small inconspicuous stationhouse. Manning the desk, a young police cadet greeted us. I discovered that he knew very little about harbor activity, and I was left with the impression that his duties were mainly to tidy the desk and empty the dustbin. Chief Percy Lodge was the man to see, he told us, but he was called away on an emergency—we were to wait.

And wait we did.

Samuel walked over and stared out the window. Threading my arm through his, I did the same.

"That must be the *Chesapeake*," he said, pointing with his nose at the steamer along the docks. "The one with all the naval personnel on it."

"I wonder what occurred?" I asked.

"I count five American frigates," said Samuel "Two by the *Chesapeake* and three just outside the harbor. They are acting as a blockade. I was surprised we were not stopped by them when sailing in. They must have seen Old Glory streaming off our stern."

"I suppose it not the best time for us to be here," I said.

"The American Navy is not going to make it any easier for us, that's for certain."

Marcus walked over and whispered over Samuel's shoulder. "You know *Capitaine*, these British are, how you say … *collaborateurs* with le Confederate."

"You very well may be right. They have been helping the South. They're probably not very happy that the North has come to rescue the *Chesapeake*."

"We French have had many dealings with these British. They will try and profit any way they can from both le North and le South of your country."

"Is that true?" I asked.

"Well, whether it is or not, it is none of our concern," said Samuel. "It is not what we are here for. We have come to discover the whereabouts of a friend. We must not involve ourselves in this conflict—not here on foreign shores. The Commodore was right. The matter with the *Chesapeake* is not our affair. If we step wrongly we may give them an excuse to impound the *Sphinx*. If that were to happen the search for Amy would be over. We must be careful what we say and do."

The door to the station burst open just as Samuel issued his warning. A big man with bushy eyebrows and a Quaker beard rushed in shouting instructions. Behind him, two men carried a cot, which looked to me to contain a body. The face was covered. I immediately concluded that the individual was dead.

"Make way, please, make way!" shouted the bearded man.

We moved.

"This way, gentlemen, this way," he instructed, leading his companions to a room in the back of the station house.

Shuffling their feet, the two men struggled with the stretcher's dead weight, nearly pushing us over. As the stretcher went by, the arm of the poor soul beneath the sheet swung over and rubbed against my leg. It was a woman's arm. I jumped and clutched onto Samuel. Looking down upon what was most likely a corpse, I received the shock of my life when my thoughts took me by surprise. This could be Amy! Before I could reason what was going on, everything faded to black. The next thing I knew, I was lying on a bench with Samuel holding onto my hand. I looked up as a host of faces appraised me.

"She's fine," said the bearded man.

"She just needs to find her land legs after a long voyage." Marcus held the back of his hand to my forehead.

"No fever," he concluded.

"What happened? Where am I?"

"Halifax … the harbor police station," replied Samuel.

"Halifax?" I rubbed my eyes, still unsure. A scraggy beard and dancing eyebrows circled my face.

"Sorry, Miss. If I knew there was a lady present I would have used the back door," said the friendly face.

"You fainted, Emily," said Samuel.

"Amy!" I tried getting to my feet. "Was it Amy?"

"Do not get up, Mademoiselle Emily. Rest for a moment," instructed Marcus.

"Did you not see it? It hung over the side of the cot," I said, "dragging along the floor."

"What?" inquired Samuel, tenderly caressing my face.

"The body they brought in. Where is it? Where is it?"

"They took it away, Emily," replied Samuel.

"I saw it too," chimed Tim. "The line dragging along the floor."

"It was the cotton cord!" I exclaimed, clutching Samuel. Tears swelled up. "Oh, Samuel, it's her, it's her!"

"Whatever is she talking about?" inquired Percy Lodge.

"A line or rope that was dragging behind the body they brought in," declared Tim. "Now that I think of it, it did look like the same cord, Sam."

"Cord?" said the official.

Tim dug in his pocket and retrieved the cotton ribbon that he removed from Annie's body and showed it to the Chief Major Constable.

"No, No!" I cried. Tears finally escaped and rolled down my face.

"Rest, Emily," insisted Samuel. "Let me see what I can uncover." He rested his hand on Tim Cadman's shoulder. "Sit with her, will you, Tim? I'm going to have a word with the Chief."

Samuel pulled the station officer aside and the two men moved across the room. I could do nothing but sit and wait. Tim appeared worried. He sat with his legs spread and elbows resting on his knees. With one leg bouncing off his toes, he folded his hands tightly together and gazed down at the floor.

Marcus stared out the window at activities along the docks. In the short time, I have known him, I found him to be unruffled and unfazed by the stresses of the world around him. I anxiously looked over at Samuel as he and the Chief spoke quietly. He stole a glance my way and winked, just before he and the Chief disappeared into the back room. I rested my hand on Tim's arm. He gave me a despairing smile.

"Are you all right, Tim?" I asked.

"Yeah, sure," he said, looking up at the ceiling. He took a deep breath.

"I am too," I tried assuring him.

We sat silently waiting for the door to the back room to open. Suddenly, it did.

"Doctor Theroux, can you please join us?" summoned the chief.

Escorted by the kindly officer, Marcus entered the room as the door shut behind them.

A steam whistle sounded from the harbor just outside the window. Someone yelled, "Let her go." On the wall above the desk a dusty banjo clock, topped with a tarnished brass eagle, *tick'd* and *tock'd*. It supported the insufferable silence that accompanied the uncertainty of events in the back room. Off to one corner, the young police cadet, the one who first met us when we entered the station, sat polishing the chief's boots.

"What do you suppose is happening back there, Tim?"

"Don't know."

Looking frustrated, he leapt to his feet and moved to the window. Across the room the young cadet spat on the footwear he was scouring and shining away. Though Samuel and Marcus were just in another room and Tim a few feet away by the window, I never felt more alone. I walked over to Tim.

"It's really a beautiful place, isn't it?" I said, looking out the soil blemished glass.

"What place is that?" he replied, his mind miles away.

"I said, it's beautiful here. Don't you think?"

"It should be," he mumbled. "I just can't wait to get back to the ship."

"I know how you feel. The *Sphinx* has an air about her. She's home. To sail across the world and take that home with you is a magical experience. Is it not?"

It was obvious. Tim was not engaging in chitchat. We stood silently studying the busy activities along the docks. A group of naval personnel tied the *Chesapeake* to another vessel as it was carefully moved to a more secure location. Tim looked over at me.

"How you feeling?" he asked. A serene empathetic smile finally flowered on his face.

"Fine, I suppose," I wiped a dried tear from my cheek.

"Yeah, me too."

"You're thinking of Amy, aren't you?"

He nodded and continued staring out the window.

"That body they just brought in, and the cord dragging along the floor. Do you think …"

"I'm not thinking anything!" He snarled.

I rested my hand on his shoulder before walking away. I started to pace, once again, letting my legs do the thinking.

Waiting for Samuel was becoming unbearable. I hadn't lied when I told Tim I was feeling fine. I had to work quite hard at doing so. From across the room, the young policeman spit on the footwear he was scrubbing. I walked over and began to weed his brain.

"Have you worked here long?" I asked him.

"I'm new, Miss," he replied, "I joined a week ago."

"Do you know anything about the body they carried into the back room?" I asked.

"I wouldn't know," he said nervously, "I only do what I'm told."

"I'm sure you do fine," I said.

"Yes, Miss," he replied, running the soiled cloth up and down the gleaming leather boot.

Unexpectedly, the back door opened and all three men came walking out. A somber Samuel shook the Chief's hand. Both men looked stone-faced and dour. Uncertain of what was uncovered, I became faint. I hung onto Tim's arm and braced myself. He placed his hand around me in support. Marcus glanced over at me. He wrinkled his brow and stiffly curled his lips, shaking his head—a sign that I should not embrace any deep concern. We listened as the Chief and Samuel spoke.

"The dead girl is proving to be a bit of a conundrum," said the Chief. "We were leaning toward suicide, though after the diagnosis of the good doctor here, findings refuted such an outcome."

"My condolences to the young lady's family, if you can find them, Mr. Lodge," said Samuel. "We are grateful for your time."

"Sorry your visit to Nova Scotia was not governed by much happier circumstances, Captain. At least it was not the missing girl you are searching for. Though that sword cuts both ways. You still need to find your friend."

It was not Amy after all! Though I felt a measure of relief, the affair was a sad one nonetheless.

"We'll be on our way," declared Samuel. "Thanks for everything."

"Oh! A word of warning," said the Chief, clearing his throat. "You seem like nice people on a virtuous mission. And it is with a friendly yardstick that I tell you this. I have it on reliable account that there is a Confederate warship on the prowl off our coast."

"We have heard rumors for quite a while that there would be," Samuel said.

"No, you don't understand, Captain. This ship was just launched a month previous. Built in Liverpool it is speculated that it is one of the most advanced and fastest warships commissioned by the John Laird Shipyard. I know. My son is a naval engineer there. She may be practicing maneuvers in friendly waters just off the Nova Scotia shore. I suggest once you leave that you hug the mainland."

"What is la *nom* of this ship?" Marcus asked.

"It was launched as the *Enrica*. But I hear the name will be changed once she arrives on the east coast of the Americas."

"Thank you, Chief Major Percy Lodge. We appreciate your honesty," said Samuel. "Consider us forewarned." Samuel shook the man's hand one last time.

With his arm around me, Samuel and I walked out together. I looked back at the brick station house and past the large multi-pane window. The youthful, police cadet held up a freshly-polished pair of boots. The amiable Chief Percy Lodge inspected them, patting the young man on the back.

—◦◦◦—

Chapter 23:

We walked the short distance to the Halifax infirmary where David Sanford was being cared for. Samuel and I led the way, with Marcus and Tim not far behind. On our stroll, we discussed new findings. I had countless questions. Though I dreaded asking, they needed to be addressed.

"Samuel, about that body, what …"

"It wasn't Amy," he confirmed. "It was a barmaid from a tavern up the street. She was discovered in a liquor shed behind the building where she worked."

"What happened to her?"

"They thought that she hanged herself. The tavern owner also reported several crates of liquor missing and the door locked from the outside. Marcus inspected the body."

"I saw it … the cord!"

"Yes. Very disturbing. It was the same one used on Annie and Mary."

"Oh, no!"

"And there's more." We stopped walking. He held me by the arms. "Emily. Her dress was torn. She exhibited the same … the same symbol on her skin as Annie and Mary. A cross within a heart."

"Oh! Samuel, no!"

"This means our search has been narrowed to someone on the *Nimrod*."

"David!"

"I don't think so. They took David off the ship on a stretcher. Hopefully, he can shed some light as to what's going on." Samuel put his arm around me and we started to walk.

"It's all so unreal—the hangings, this trip, Amy's disappearance. The Readers Club should have minded their own affairs. Instead, look what we have been drawn into. A frightful mess."

"You had no way of knowing this was going to happen."

"That dear girl. Her poor parents. I wonder who she was?"

"They have no real identification for her; just a name. Ettie Becker. An immigrant girl from Germany. The constable said that many of the girls that work the saloons don't give a real name. It's doubtful her parents will ever realize what happened to her."

"Annie and Mary both had no link to their parents either," I added.

"Mary too?" said Samuel.

"Mrs. Sanford said that she ran away from home and came to America. And with all the Sullivans in Ireland, they would never find them."

"And Annie?"

"From what I uncovered, Annie's mother and father were separated, sold in the slave trade. The slave owner who purchased her and her mother had a son. The son married and moved away. When he did, his father gave him a handful of slaves as a gift to take with him. Annie was one of them. She was separated from her mother ... never saw her again."

"So these girls had no one who cared for them?"

"But they do," I said.

"Oh?"

"Us."

With his arm snugly around me he tucked me in. I looked up at him with calf eyes. He kissed me on the forehead.

"Well, this must be the place," he said, directing me to a large oak door.

The hospital was housed in an unassuming two-story stone building. By the side of the front door was a small wood placard. *Halifax Infirmary.* We entered and inquired at a small counter where we were instructed to wait and that the doctor would soon speak to us.

I had never been in a genuine hospital before. Off to one corner was what appeared like a waiting area. I took a chair and sat down. It was a busy place with people scurrying all about. When you think about it, it cannot be a good thing. All that hurrying meant urgency—all those ill souls. Then again, Halifax was a big city—over twice the size of Fall River and New Bedford, the two cities which sandwiched the tiny town of Westport where I lived. With it busy port and bustling streets, I expect that there are plenty of people in Halifax who need medical care.

I was unsure whether I wanted to stay or do my waiting outdoors. The longer I sat, the more uncomfortable I became. One thing that did not settle well with me was the smell of the place—difficult to describe. I can safely say it was not a pleasant scent. Marcus described it as the sugary scent of ether and laudanum, mingled with the tangy odor of spent plasma. I describe it as bilious.

After waiting for what seemed an eternity, a tall, lanky gentleman with wired spectacles perched on the tip of his nose, introduced himself as the hospital's administrative physician. He carried a stack of papers and a well-used stubby pencil. The physician placed the graphite stick behind his ear and shook Samuel's hand. Both men walked across the room and spoke privately. The doctor glanced at us over Samuel's shoulder, nodded, and walked away. Samuel walked over looking somber and glum.

"What did he say?" I asked.

"David has sustained a serious injury to his head. His prognosis is uncertain. The doctor wants that he should rest."

"Prognosis uncertain. What does that mean?" I inquired.

"What happened?" Tim asked.

"He fell from the rigging onto the deck shortly after leaving the mainland."

"Can we see le man?"

"Yes. I was instructed—no more than two of us at a time. He's just down the hall—a room to the left, just off the primary ward."

"Oh, poor David," I said.

"Where is the *Nimrod*?"

"I don't know, Tim," replied Samuel.

"Why would la ship just *disparaitre*?"

"A whaling expedition is bigger than any man on a ship—even the captain. It must have continued on its whaling voyage. There's lots of money and people's welfare tied to such an enterprise."

"We must find out if Amy was on that ship," I said.

"Tim! You and Marcus go back to the *Sphinx* and wait. I'll signal the ship when Emily and I are ready to return. Keep a lookout."

"What are you going to do?" asked the young carpenter.

"Going to see David and try to make sense of all this."

After Tim and the doctor left, Samuel and I started for David's room. The passage took us down a dark corridor. This opened onto a ward of perhaps twenty beds with almost as many windows. I looked down at my feet as I walked down a center aisle, trying not to notice which bed was moaning. The hospital odor was now rampant, with the smell of stale urine, buttered by retching and haunting wails, sounds that begged for the pain to stop. At the end of the room was a door within a short hallway.

"Where are we going?" I asked.

"The doctor said they ran out of beds so they placed David in his private quarters."

"Hand it to David to opt for the best seat in the house," I said.

Samuel softly rapped on the polished oak door.

No reply. He tried again.

"Perhaps it's the wrong room," I said.

Samuel carefully twisted the ornate brass knob and the door gently creaked open. He peeked inside.

"Is he there?" I whispered.

"Yes. He's asleep. Let's go inside."

"Do you think we should?"

"We're in a hospital. It's perfectly fine." Samuel stepped aside and escorted me in.

"Who's there?" came a raspy voice.

"It's me Davy, Emily ... Emily White," I said, taking my place by the side of the bed.

He had bandages wrapped around his head and the side of his face was swollen. The sheets were drawn mid-chest and his arms dormant by his side. He lay there quietly for a few seconds, as if falling back to sleep. Finally, he turned his head my way and, with catty eyes, peered past me.

"How nice of you to come all this way to see me, Whitie," he uttered smugly. He slurred his words as he spoke—his eyes barely open. "I knew you couldn't stay away."

"Nice to see you, Davy," I said. I leaned over and kissed his cheek.

He shuddered.

It felt peculiar. David and I were never close enough to even warrant a handshake, let alone a kiss. But in this distant land, amongst all these strangers, he felt almost like family.

"How are you feeling Dave?" Samuel asked.

David Sanford squinted and cocked his head as if a voice flourished out of thin air. "My, my. If it isn't Sammy Boy," he muttered. "The entire village of Westport has come to pay homage to the lowly captain of the *Nimrod*."

Samuel looked over at me, uncertain. "Dave! What happened to you? How did you come to be here?"

"Well, Sammy Boy, you will need to ask my parents that question. The details are sketchy. It happened a long time ago. Something that usually occurs to married people."

Even in ill state, David Sanford could not help but be brash and impertinent. Sunlight drenched the room. A ray of light fell directly on his placid face. He stretched out his hand as if reaching for something he couldn't see.

"How are you ... Captain?" David said.

Samuel shook it. It was disturbing to see such a young, capable man lie there helpless—even David Sanford.

315

Samuel pulled up a chair for me and I sat by the bed. "Tell us what happened, Dave."

"Yes, please tell us," I chimed.

"Have that scrumptious little diary you always carry, do you, Whitie?" he sneered. "Perhaps you would like to write it all down."

"I haven't carried my diary since I was a child."

"We are concerned, Dave ... Emily especially."

"Sorry. Concern is of little help to me at the moment. Unless you have completed your tenure at a medical alma mater, your sympathy is of little use to me."

I have always known David Sanford to be self-assured, arrogant, and dismissive strangers and friends alike. If he did not feel like telling you something, he would not. When he did, he always looked you in the eye when delivering such assertiveness. This signature practice appeared lacking. He never once looked directly at us. It took several minutes before the realization of what was wrong took me by surprise.

I raised my hand and waved it in front of his face. His crystal blue eyes never reciprocated. I looked over at Samuel in dreadful dismay. He placed his finger over his lips and shook his head.

"You haven't told us what happened," inquired Samuel.

"I was demonstrating to some of the greenhorns on the ship how a master climbs ratline. Unfortunately, I inadvertently instructed them on how not to do it—twenty feet off the deck."

"Oh, Davy, that's terrible," I cried.

"Where's the *Nimrod* now?" asked Samuel.

"I sent it along on its mission. Wouldn't want to impede Father's enterprise."

"David, I know this may not be a good time, but we have some questions. Perhaps you can help us."

"All this way for questions. And all this time I thought this was a benevolent quest to inquire about my health. My, my!"

I felt badly for poor David. Yes, he was haughty and proud, but he was part of my world. He was a friend though many would not agree. Some felt strongly that David Sanford had no understanding to the concept of friendship. But I have always believed that even nasty friends have merits worth preserving. Grandmamma put it well. *A nasty friend is just a cub with a thorn in his paw. Remove it and gently nurture the wound, and you will snare their respect.* I dare confess, it's been a while. I am still working on removing that thorn.

"If you don't feel like talking, we can come back another time," I said.

"No, no! I suppose you came all this way and whatever it is must be urgent. Let me guess. You are looking for angel face."

"Who?" exclaimed Samuel.

"Amy Chaloner!"

"Oh yes, yes, Davy!" I cried. "Where is she? Where is Amy?"

"Somewhere on shore, I suppose. Before I left the ship, I instructed Moses to give her fare for the trip back home."

"Is she in Halifax?" asked Samuel.

David gawked in Samuel's direction. "I'm blind you know, Sam," he said nonchalantly. "If I could see, I would tell you."

I placed my hand on his. "Oh, Davy! I'm so sorry," I cried.

He pulled his hand away as if I had bitten it.

Dejected, I lowered my head.

Samuel tenderly and silently rested his hand on my shoulder.

Unexpectedly, David reached out and gripped my fingers tightly. His body heaved as he began to cry. It was the first reaction to emotion I had ever witnessed from him. With a shameful arm over his eyes, he sobbed like a broken child. Watching a man of such proud resolve lose all dauntlessness and utter composure, throwing all humiliation and prized self-regard into one's lap, is a humbling experience.

He tried pulling his hand away. I clutched it firmly and held on. I too began to cry. I could sense his pain drain through his trembling limb. I went to pull my hand away. He held onto it tightly. Finally—I had pulled the thorn.

"The doctor says it may not be permanent, David," said Samuel. "They can't find anything wrong with your eyes. It may just be a condition caused by enlarged brain tissue when you struck your head. When the swelling goes down your sight should return."

"At least I don't have to see your pathetic faces," he declared, chuckling. He wiped his eyes with the heel of his hand. As quickly as he had broken down, he recovered. There was a moment of silence.

"You say Amy was given some money. Did you see her leave the ship?" Samuel asked, pretending the man's display of emotion never occurred.

"No. But she should have."

"How did Amy get on the ship in the first place?" I asked.

"I'd like to say that she finally decided to run away with me. I discovered her in my cabin ... in the liquor compartment. She hid there—said she wanted to see the inside of the ship before it sailed, but got scared when she heard someone coming and hid in the liquor locker. The latch must have locked on the outside when she closed the compartment door. That night, while making ready for bed, I heard crying. I thought a cat had gotten on board ... foolish girl! She was in there for quite some time. She must have gotten thirsty and drank some of the rum stored there and it put her to sleep. By that time the *Nimrod* was much too far from shore to return to Westport. Provincetown town was well behind us. We would have had to beat back with the wind on our nose if we tried to return. It would mean losing two or three days. I decided we would continue north and let Miss Chaloner off at Nova Scotia."

"Oh, Samuel, we must look for her!"

"I told her as soon as she was ashore she must check in with police. They would help her secure safe passage home."

"The Chief Major at the station house said he hadn't heard of any girl being put ashore," said Samuel.

"That girl always had a mind of her own," said David. "A little too brash for her own good. A bit like me, I suppose."

As David spoke, I became more anxious with every word. I stood up and moved to a window. Out in the street, men were loading a wagon with coils of line from the rope factory across the way. The sign on the ramshackle building read *Nova Scotia Line and Twine*. Hints to the hangings were all around me. My thoughts wandered to the lace cord found around Annie Slocum's neck. I was now doubly worried about Amy's welfare. Perchance she was already on her way home, and I fretted for no reason whatsoever. Perhaps I shouldn't look for peril where none existed. I had one vital question I felt I had to ask. I needed to know. Besides … an inner voice nagged at me, telling me that all was not good. I continued looking out the window while letting my voice wander loudly across the room.

"Did you kill Annie Slocum?" I asked.

There was no reply. Instead Samuel shouted out my name.

I marched toward the bed.

Samuel jumped out of the way.

"I asked you a question, David Sanford, did you kill Annie Slocum!"

"Who in hell is Annie Slocum?"

"You know full well who she is!"

"Listen to you," he jeered, "the dove, turned into a lion. Bravo!"

"Answer me!"

"Why would you ask such a preposterous question?" he whimpered.

"You were on Cuttyhunk the day Annie was discovered dead," said Samuel, accusingly.

"Oh, I see where this is going now. So that was her name? Yes, I was on Cuttyhunk that day. But I did not kill this Annie person."

"Tell us. What did happen?" inquired Samuel.

"Well, let's just say it was a delicate matter. After Father banished me from the ship, I decided I would look for a place to spend the night. I went up to the Flint place. I knew it was vacant. I had planned to sleep the night there. When I arrived, the door to the shed was slamming with the wind. I thought that someone was in there. I went over and … that is when I saw her. This Annie. I never knew her name. I had seen her at Cory's store once or twice and knew her as the Flint maid."

"You mean that …" he continued before I could finish my inquiry.

"She … she was just hanging … hanging from the rafters … like game waiting to be skinned. I panicked. I lifted the brace on the inside of the shed door so that when I slammed it shut the lever would fall into place and lock from the inside. Then I ran off."

"Why, Davy, why?" I said.

"I … I don't know. I was frightened. I thought that she would follow when I left … that someone would place the blame on me, I don't know!"

"Who would follow?" inquired Samuel.

"The black servant girl," he said, making little sense. He shook his head as his eyes watered. "He just hanged her there. Hanged her, like … like he did Mary Sullivan."

David Sanford's bewildering admission to what had happened to Annie and Mary fell on me like a phantom weight. Stunned, Samuel and I looked at one another.

"Mary Sullivan did not return to Ireland, did she, Davy?" I asked, already knowing the truth.

"No."

He held his head in his hand and cradled the heavy guilt he felt. Or perhaps it was just a misplaced display of regret. Whatever he sensed, it was an awareness that even David Sanford could not endure without revealing some emotion.

"I know you all think I'm a pampered cad. I have no problem with that. Never did. But, I am not harmful or depraved. I had nothing to do with what happened to the black girl or Mary."

"No one said you did," I assured him. If he only knew!

"Tell it to the village," he jeered.

I sat back down in the chair by the bed. I did not want to miss anything more he had to say. "You said that he just hanged her there like he did Mary. Who hanged her there?"

"I can't really say. I have no proof. I refuse to implicate or slander someone just because I sense the truth."

I tried to sound more conciliatory, lowering my voice—spicing the words with concern.

"I can respect that, Davy," I said. "Can you please tell us what you think happened to them? What happened to Mary?"

"I saw Mary in the sawmill on our property. Tim Cadman had summoned Father to the waterfront. I followed. When we arrived at the mill she had already been cut down. One of the crew from the *Enterprise* was with her. Father immediately sent me away ... said she had hanged herself. I didn't believe it. She was in love, happy, alive. All I know is what Father told me. His instructions were firm and final. He would take care of things. He knew people. For all intents and purposes, Mary Sullivan returned to Ireland."

"He said he knew people. What sort of people?" I asked. "For what purpose?"

He shook his head. "You know, I loved that girl ... even though she was a servant. Perhaps I loved her a little too much. She was always kind to me. With time, we became close ... too close. When father discovered that she was with child he lost all civility."

I was shocked by David's candid revelation. He lay there quietly, slushy eyed, staring into space. A soft smile crept across his unshaven face.

"She sure was a pretty thing," he said. "Adorable smile, silky chestnut hair, velvety soft skin. She never complained, and in her own gentle way, praised every insult I bestowed upon her. She reminded me a little of you, Whitie."

A subtle smile danced on my face, even if he did call me Whitie.

"Tell me more about these so-called people," I implored.

He spoke in riddles, though Samuel understood just what he meant. "Father would never accept the child or let it be born. He should have never trusted the man. He said that he knew a woman who could take care of such problems. Father agreed and assured me that it was a simple procedure and that we would all be the happier for it. But something went terribly wrong. Mary paid for it with her life."

"Who did your father hire, Davy?" asked Samuel.

With erratic breathing, he languished in deep thought as he took a respite and gnawed the question. He shook his head and grit his teeth. The contempt he displayed was plain and intense. Though he appeared furious, one could easily discern sentiments of betrayal and disbelief in the way his seething expression melted into sadness. "Moses Reyals!" he said with scorn. "He said he knew a woman who ... who ..."

"Who what?" I pleaded.

"What do you think?" he quipped. "The sad affair was Father thought he was protecting me. Ha, as if I needed it! I was well-prepared to face up to my responsibilities. He insisted that it was out of the question ... family honor, and all ... that a wrong needed to be made right."

Samuel glanced over at me and shook his head.

I choked on the questions I wanted to ask, gasping at the implication and admission of what had actually happened to Mary—the unnatural cessation of life, the dissolution and inconceivable measures taken to amend the transgressions of the untutored, and carried out by those who are evil and immoral—the corrupt and their sinful actions and distorted panaceas. That the conception of life could be nothing more than a worry, a bane nuisance which had to be stamped out, plucked, and strewed by sinister minds—minds which occupy the dark, rogue fringes of humanity, was all quite disturbing. Such depraved ethics are nothing less than criminal.

"What did they do to her?" I asked, timorously.

He continued with the lurid account. "While their feeble attempts unfolded, something went terribly wrong. Things went from bad to worse. The way Moses tells it, a sincere effort was made to stop the bleeding and save Mary's life. It was all for naught. They sent the woman who performed the deed away. I never knew her name. Afraid of the implications behind their actions, he and that madman Billy Cain hung her from the rafters and faked a suicide. Father, in turn, covered up the truth. The family name was in question. He was not about to let that happen. God knows what else Moses and Cain had done to Mary before she took her last breath."

I stroked my troubled brow. My overloaded brain felt like it was about to burst. "How do you know all this?" I asked.

"I overheard Moses and Father talking."

Sensing my anxiety, Samuel ran his hand along my back, kneading away some of the tension. Still, I felt lightheaded and ill to my stomach. I was unsure how much more I could take. More was to come whether I liked it or not, and take it I did.

"To this day, I don't think there was a woman," said David.

"What do you mean?" I asked.

"I believe that Moses and Billy Cain hurt that girl. The woman who performed the deed more than likely never existed."

"What are you saying, David?" said Samuel.

"It's a gut feeling. I have no proof. But I don't trust those two. Especially that Cain fellow. I wouldn't put anything past him."

I opened my mouth to speak. The words evaporated on my tongue. I could hear no more. I needed time—time to digest the entire tale.

"Where is Moses now?" inquired Samuel.

"He's commanding the *Nimrod*," David said. He chuckled. "Did you know that the man is actually an excellent seaman when he's not drinking … was captain and owner of his own vessel at one time."

"What route is the *Nimrod* taking, David?" asked Samuel.

"I instructed that they were not to go any further than Nuuk and to return after a couple of months when I have recovered."

I looked up at Samuel. "Nuuk?"

"Region in Greenland," he said.

The entire affair was becoming more complicated. I couldn't stop thinking about Amy. I rummaged through my pocket for the locket. "Davy, what do you know about this?" I asked, dangling the charm from my hand.

He just sat there looking right past me. "I'm afraid I can't see what you mean," he replied.

Samuel tapped me on the shoulder, reminding me that he had lost his sight.

"It's a gold locket," I said, "It has a photograph of you on the inside."

Suddenly, he sat up in bed and threw out his hand. "Give it here!" he cried, "give it here!"

I cradled my fingers around his and gave him the charm. Like a wild beast stealing prey from another, he clutched the locket with expectancy, tucking the gold and silver jewel up against his breast.

"Where did you get this?" he demanded. He caressed the polished charm as if it were an amulet containing mysterious secrets.

"I found it." I said.

"Where!"

"By the shore."

"Where by the shore?"

"Close by where the *Nimrod* was docked. It was lying at the bottom of an old derelict skiff, half sunk in the river." I was reluctant to tell him the entire truth and how Timothy's friend, Josh, actually had possession of it. That wasn't important.

"He must have taken it from her," he scowled, "the dirty swine."

Samuel looked over to me and shook his head.

"Taken it from whom, Davy?" I inquired, knowing whom he meant.

"Nobody," he said.

"We know who the locket belonged to," Samuel confessed.

"You know nothing," flouted David. He held the locket close to his vest.

"It belonged to Mary Sullivan, didn't it?" said Samuel.

There was a long pause. He rocked his torso to and fro. "What if it did?" he murmured.

"We are curious about the symbol on the face of the locket," I said.

"Poor Mary. She was such a pretty thing," he mumbled.

He sprung the locket and felt for the photo inside. With a finger, he plucked out the picture. He handed me the charm. "Read it," he said.

Inside the lid where the photograph once lay was an inscription engraved into the gold lid. It read, "Hope sure and steadfast is the anchor of the soul." Samuel took the locket and examined the writing.

"Why, that's lovely, Davy," I said.

"If you know the Good Book you will recognize it as Hebrews, 6:19," he said.

"I didn't know you were fond of bible verse," I said.

"I'm not. It was Mother's. I gave it to her when I was just a boy."

"How does a boy afford such a thing?" I asked.

He hesitated before telling us. "It once belonged to Moses Reyals. He gave it to me so I could give it to Mother on her birthday … said it use to belong to his wife … had no use for it any longer."

"Moses Reyals was married?" asked Samuel.

"Yes. His wife died when he was a young man. Shortly after he had taken on a new wife, along with a mistress. One was the sea … the other a bottle."

"How did Mary come to have it?" I asked.

"I gave it to her."

"You gave a servant girl your Mother's locket?" I said.

"Mary had taken it. Mother didn't even know it was gone. In any event, she had plenty of trinkets. When I found Mary with the locket she begged for forgiveness. Ultimately, I let her have it. I even had it engraved with her initials."

"That was very kind of you," I told him.

"Kindness had nothing to do with it. Mary and I made a deal. She would get the locket and I would … I would get a little bit of flesh."

I couldn't believe what I had just heard, though such a bargain and the person offering it was befitting. Why was David telling us this— implicating himself? Why would he reveal such a ploy and extortion?

"In the end it would prove to be Mary's misfortune," he added, "and in many respects mine. I lost her. I thought I was getting the better part of the deal. A tender morsel for a trivial ingot. With time I never expected that I would pay with what little heart I could muster. I loved that girl. She was an innocent angel."

His admission of genuine endearment for the servant girl surprised me. On the other hand, not as much as some would have expected. I had always maintained that David Sanford was not the evil person everyone made him out to be. I suppose that we can become the scoundrel others make of us, simply because it is easier than working to gain their trust.

I put a crucial question to him. "Davy, what does the symbol on the face of the locket represent—the heart and cross?"

"I suppose it looks like a cross, but it's really an anchor and a heart. A whaler's token of good luck. Moses brought it back from Portugal. The symbol meant a lot to him ... an emblem of his allegiance to the woman he loved and to a sea that had brought him much fortune." A smile fell upon David's face; distant and sad. "You know, he used to whittle little toy soldiers for me when I was a child. He always carved that symbol of the anchor and heart into the base of the stick figurine."

I held my breath. Carefully I rummaged through my pocket. There it was. The headless toy soldier I found by the wharf. I turned it over and examined the base. A rush of dread swelled in my heart. I had given several of the small figurines to Louisa's little brother and never noticed the carving at the base of the toy—the heart and cross, carved just the way we found it on Annie Slocum's bosom. Now I knew why Louisa found the symbol so familiar but could not quite place it. I handed the toy carving to Samuel. His eyes widened as the symbol looked up at him. It was all coming together, now. He pulled the piece of flat cord from his pocket—the one used on Mary Sullivan.

"What do you know about this?" Samuel took David's hand and gave him the short length of line.

"What is it?"

"You tell me what you think it is," said Samuel.

David ran the cord hand over his hand—from finger to finger. "Yes, I know what this is. It's tie cord. Father uses it at the mill, to tie cloth and the like. We have plenty of it on the *Nimrod*. It's used for countless purposes. Why do you want to know?"

Samuel took the line from his hand. "We must get going, Emily," he declared urgently. He thrust the broken toy and line into his pocket.

"If you must." said David, shaking off Samuel's announcement.

"Forgive us, but we need to find Amy," I said. "As soon as we do we will return. Perhaps by then you will be feeling better." We started for the door. Poor David. He just lay there staring and not seeing. "Goodbye, Davy."

"Take care of yourself, Dave," chimed Samuel.

"Wait!"

"Yes," I said, turning just before walking out the door.

"Listen. Please. Find that silly girl. If she did not secure passage it could be that she never left the ship."

"We'll find her," declared Samuel. "You can count on that."

"Sam!" he shouted. He paused, just laying there scanning the room with unsighted eyes. "You must do what I did not have wit to achieve," he affirmed. "Stop him."

The fear I felt for Amy's safety was now dire. We walked quickly and silently through the tunneled ward. A medley of moans and grunts reflected from the iron-framed beds all around me. The odor of stale perspiration and putrid bedpans filled the air. My knees weakened and my stomach quivered. I was becoming ill. Holding my hand to my mouth, I left Samuel behind and ran down the long, dim hallway, through the reception area, and out the door. Once outside I drank a lung full of fresh-scented air. Still, the infirmary's fetor and sounds stained my nostrils and echoed in my ears. Never would I have imagined the noises and smells of big city commerce could strike me as so inviting. I braced myself around a lightpost purging the distasteful experience.

"Are you all right, Emily?" Samuel asked. He cradled my chin with his finger and lifted my head. His crystal eyes, like two blue lanterns, illuminated my aspirations and desires. It did not take long before my ambition and hope was revived.

"Oh, Samuel! I'm so afraid for Amy," I cried, throwing my arms around his neck.

He embraced me tightly. "It will all turn out fine," he said. "You will see." He gingerly kissed me on the head, as he often did. "We must get going," he insisted.

"Yes," I agreed. "Where should we start searching first?"

"We'll go by the stationhouse, give them our departure notice, then it's right off to the *Sphinx*."

"Shouldn't we start looking for Amy first?"

"No! We are leaving Halifax, immediately."

"Leaving Halifax. Why?"

"We are going after that ship."

"What about Amy? How will we find her?"

"If she's indeed on shore, then she's probably safe. But if she's still on that ship!"

"You think she …"

"If my hunch is right, that is where she is. On the *Nimrod*."

—◦◦◦—

Chapter 24:

We prepared to leave Halifax harbor without delay. If Amy had indeed been placed ashore we would certainly have heard about it. None of the authorities had seen her. After receiving a departure confirmation from the chief at the harbor station, we flagged the *Sphinx* and Tim Cadman rowed ashore to retrieve us. It was vital that we not waste one solitary moment. If Amy was indeed on the *Nimrod*, every minute was one of danger. Once we were back on the schooner, Samuel gave immediate orders to set sail.

"I want two men on those halyards," he yelled. "Mr. Monroe, work that helm, make certain we have steerage and let's harvest that wind."

"Right away, sir!"

"Come men! Hank that main, quickly! We need all the drive she can muster."

"Anchor aweigh!" came the call from the bow.

As the forward and aft mainsails bellowed, a gentle southeasterly breeze nudged the *Sphinx* hard over on a twenty-degree starboard tack. Eli Monroe steered the clipper bow east, toward the harbor inlet. Our Canadian sojourn came to an abrupt and cheerless conclusion. Though not uneventful, my first trip to a foreign land was not a pleasant one. It was with mixed regret that I watched as Halifax receded in the distance, taking with it mixed emotions and David Sanford. For some unexplained reason, I was left with the nagging accord that I would never see him again.

"Mr. Monroe, take us out in a straight line, twenty miles offshore," commanded the captain, "then we will turn her north. Destination, Greenland waters."

"Aye, aye, sir."

"Mr. Theroux. Go below and map out the coordinates for the southern tip of Greenland."

"As you wish, *Capitaine*."

I sat in my usual comfortable bench just behind the helm, where I could easily observe all the rampant activity. On the port deck, Samuel stood bristling with authority, keeping vigil, and making certain that everything went well. With legs spread, like two unmovable dock pilings, he stood encouraging the busy crew and dispatching critical instruction. The injury he sustained to his limb when in the military was healing and he was getting stronger every day. All around me crew scurried like frantic farmhands chasing a drove of frightened piglets. Anticipation and eager enthusiasm exhibited on their faces and they performed their duty in good order. After all, they loved their captain and he them.

Though Samuel's brisk commands sounded harsh and somewhat dictatorial, it was warranted, if not expected, when a captain did not want to be misunderstood. Miscommunication was the difference between soaring up an open tributary or colliding with a flagrant shoal. I have come to understand that shouting is a constant on a sailing vessel—more so on a ship full of apprentices or greenhorns, as Seabury calls them. Even though, on the *Sphinx* all tasks were performed with a lively gallop and an obedient smile.

Above my head more canvas sprouted out from the deck. Unfurled, chalky cloth, angrily flapped in the blue heavens, like the swollen lips of a fiery preacher. One after another jibs came to attention, stiffening to the twisted sheets that tethered their tails to deck blocks and winches. Once all sail was aloft, the *Sphinx* glided along swiftly and proudly, skimming the furrowed wavelets with wonted ease. We were one happy crew. I just wished Amy were with us. That would have made all the difference in the world.

"Did you say Greenland, Samuel?" I asked.

"Yes we need to follow the whales. Where there are whales there will be whalers. And Greenland is where they all are, at the moment."

"You really think Amy is on the *Nimrod*?"

"I do."

"Do you think? I mean ..."

"Amy may be a bit impetuous, but she is a resourceful girl. I don't think they would treat her in the same manner they did Mary or Annie. The name Chaloner carries weight. If it is exposed that they have harmed her, there will be hellish consequences. Her father would make certain of that."

"I can't believe that Moses could think he would get away with doing her any harm."

"No, but that Billy Cain fellow may. He's deranged."

"Don't say that, Samuel. You're frightening me."

He threw his arm around me and smiled. "Isn't she glorious?" he said, in an attempt to betray all ill thought. "Optimism is resuscitated every time the *Sphinx* is unbound, her canvas is flown high, and she's running like a carefree child."

"I'm so happy to see you in good spirits, Samuel. I can't stop worrying about Amy."

He sat down beside me. With his hands draped over his knees, he scrutinized the busy crew, keeping an eye on all the sailors, like a father over offspring. "They're a great bunch of lads," he declared. "They have come a long way. Once scared and timid slaves, now brave and noble seamen."

"Yes. It pleasure's me also to see everyone happy, to see you happy."

I studied his handsome face. His eyes danced from spar to rigging, and from line to sail, examining every functioning portion of the ship. I could only make a meager attempt at stealing the moment away from his wooden mistress. I leaned in and kissed him on the cheek. He smiled and threw his arm around me.

"Everything will work out for the good, Miss White. You'll see."

"Oh, Samuel, it will be so perfect when this is all over and Amy is safely aboard."

His swooshing smile faded to a slight somber curl. "Yes. You are right there. Finding Amy is the spirit of this voyage. And we are fortunate to have the *Sphinx* to help us."

"I suppose you're right. You really think Amy is on that ship, huh? We never really looked for her in Halifax."

"If she were in Halifax someone would have seen her. Amy's not the sort of girl that goes unnoticed. If she is in fact on shore, then our worries are unwarranted and this voyage just a minor inconvenience. If she is not, then every minute we spend at sea is a vital one."

"How long do you suppose it will take before we can expect to come upon the whaler?"

"If we ever come upon it, you mean."

"Oh Samuel! What are our chances?"

"Well, a wise man once said, 'Searching for the obscure is like searching for a needle in an open meadow.'"

"We must, we must find that needle."

"We are not exactly sailing without a plan. David has given us the course the whaler was ordered to take and the *Sphinx* is much faster than the *Nimrod.* There's no doubt that we will catch up with her. She will stop many times along the way to hunt every time they come upon a pod of whales. Once we find whales, that's when we look out for the whaler."

"What if we overtake them and not even know it?"

"We can only do our best. Before leaving Westport, I made certain to collect all the coordinates for whaling habitats in the Northern Atlantic. Once we are well offshore I will have a man in the crow's nest, at all times. Everyone will need to don an eagle eye. I have offered a bottle of rum to the first man who sights the *Nimrod*."

"Oh, Samuel, I told you that David was innocent. I knew he would never hurt anyone."

"You're quite the gal, Emily. David is lucky to know someone like you. Heck! I am lucky to know someone like you!"

He made certain no one was watching and softly kissed me on the lips. His warm spongy mouth pressed firmly on mine. He gently engulfed my heart with his supple heavenly advance, running his moist tongue along my parched sea lips. Wetting them, he kissed me a second time.

"I love you, Emily White," he said.

It was the first time I had ever heard the words. "I love you Emily White." No man had ever spoken those words to me. At least not the way he said it. My tongue tripped over my teeth as the sound of his placid voice and what it just reveled reverberated in my head. Before I could tell him how I felt, he quickly backed away, changing the moment as if it never occurred.

"Well, there's no way David could have killed that girl in Halifax. But it is a certainty that the killer came from his ship."

He pulled the little figurine soldier from his pocket and examined the motif at its base. My head was still spinning and my heart shouting declarations of devotion and yearning. I was just about to express my sentiments when the ship hit a rogue wave, practically jarring us off our seats.

"Ease off the fore-main, gentlemen, and spill some air!" yelled Samuel. "Steady course, Mr. Monroe. Keep your eye on that sail trim."

"Aye, aye, Captain," bellowed Eli with a culpable grin.

Samuel handed me the toy soldier. "No, you hold onto it, please. It is frightening to me now," I said.

"I am almost certain that the pattern on the bottom of this toy was carved by the killer of Annie Slocum."

"I don't know what to think. At first we had no leads. Now we entertain several."

"Notice how different the design is on this toy, Emily. You can plainly see the anchor and heart. Just like the one on the locket—but not as similar to the one on Annie's skin."

"Can we be wrong, Samuel? Could it in fact be Moses who committed such a crime?"

"Either he or that Billy Cain fellow. They were both on the *Nimrod* the day it was stranded on the shoals off Cuttyhunk Island. And by David Sanford's account, Moses was one of the last people to see Mary Sullivan alive."

"And the poor girl in Halifax. The *Nimrod* shows up and another hanging is discovered."

"Astonishing! David verified that the type of cord used to hang Mary and Annie was used by the Sanford business and stored on the *Nimrod*."

"What are we going to do if we find the whaler? What if Amy is not on it?"

"Let's worry about that when we know for certain and not anguish over a scenario that may not exist."

"I suppose you're right," I conceded.

One day effortlessly dispersed into the next, with the common thread of urgent expectancy. Though I have come to love ocean sailing, this voyage, unlike any other, was punishingly arduous. Sunrise to sunset—none were exceptional. Instead, I could easily attest to the fact that they were wistfully unappreciated, at least for me. All I could think of was Amy—her presumptuous catty smile, turned up spouty nose, and her dismissive and dauntless beryl eyes. If anyone could use these attributes to a positive conclusion it was Amy Chaloner. That was in a rational world. A whaling ship is anything but—especially one unknowingly harboring a madman.

A week into our voyage the weather changed. Nights became bitterly cold and days damp and raw. As was common every morning, I was usually the last one on deck. This day was noteworthy in that I was one of the first to awaken. Climbing up on deck, I encountered one crew on watch and Eli at the wheel.

"Good morning, dear lady," he said. "You are just in time to see nature at its finest."

Though it was somewhat still dark, the sky was a fiery red like an open wound. I had never witnessed the heavens so ominous—but beautiful. It looked more like dusk than dawn.

"Oh, Mr. Monroe, its so eerie out here," I said. "In a beautiful way."

"The Good Lord is working his palette and brush."

"The clouds look so forbidding and alluring."

"Storm is coming."

"How can you tell?"

He smiled, held his head up proudly, and recited a bible verse. "'It will be foul weather today for the sky is red and lowering. O ye hypocrites, ye can discern the face of the sky, yet can ye not discern the signs of the times?' The Good Lord said those words, Himself."

"Is that true, Mr. Monroe … a storm is coming?"

"Even as we speak, the ocean is becoming enraged," he said. "By the end of the day we will be in full gale, my lady. You can be certain of it."

As the day wore on, I started to question Eli's weather assessment. By afternoon, a damp, smoggy shroud settled upon us. The pendulous *Sphinx* moved at a sluggard pace, adrift in an unhallowed, vaporous troposphere. We were blindfolded. With elbows resting on the bow rail, Tim, Marcus, and I gazed out onto the water and into a ghostly mist.

"It's getting stormy," said Tim, "It is rare to see the sea kick up this way with this much fog."

"I know we get fog in Westport, but this is unlike anything I have ever seen," I remarked. "I can touch it … run it through my fingers."

"*Pacifique*, is it not," observed a carefree Marcus. "*Merveilleux*! We do not get climate such as this in France."

"I love foggy mornings," I declared. "It can be so cleansing, or as you say Doctor, *pacifique*. But out here it feels threatening, unfriendly, like it is concealing something that can hurt you."

"I remember a time in France. I was a boy. I awoke to a day such as this. I thought I had died and gone to, how you say, paradise. *Ma mere* had to comfort me."

"That is daft," said Tim, laughing.

"Most little boys are," agreed Marcus.

"Even some grown men," I added.

We all laughed.

The fog was so thick that we could not see the bow as we stood near the stern. A ghostly figure floated up the deck. The image seeped from out of the mist, as if materializing out of thin air or stepping down from a cloud. It was Samuel, looking somewhat worried.

"Sam! What do you make of it?" Tim inquired.

"We're in strange waters," he replied. "I haven't experienced strong winds like this with such heavy fog in all my day's sailing."

"What's with that drumming down below? Sounds like the boys are stirring up some sort of ceremony?" asked Tim.

"A couple of the lads are thumping the side of the hull. There are whales all around us. We want to make certain they see us."

"A collision with le whale would not be a good thing, eh *Capitaine*?"

"No, it would not."

Far off in the distance we could hear the booming sound of what sounded like thunder.

"Sounds like rain," I said.

Samuel listened carefully. The distant rumble sounded once again. "I don't think so."

"If not, *Capitaine*, what could it be?"

Samuel looked over the side of the ship, ignoring Marcus's inquiry. "Keep your eyes to the water," he ordered. "Yell if you see any ice, a ship, anything. I'm going to take another look over the bow."

As he walked away the drizzled mist folded in on him, until he completely vanished into the smoky veil.

Suddenly, Tim sounded the alarm. "Whales, two points off the starboard bow," he hollered, his hands cupped to his mouth.

"Whales off the starboard stern," echoed another call, this one from the crow's nest above.

The fog had lifted some when, suddenly, there they were. Shimmering, black, polished frames, arching in and out of wandering swells, like prowling vagabonds, sweeping the vast ocean for a day's meal.

"Whales to port aft quarter, Captain," announced Eli.

They were all around us. I dare say, I had counted ten. The bow of the *Sphinx* climbed high on the steep swells, plunging and plowing the fractured, rippled waters. The behemoth titans swam by, grazing alongside. It was almost certain that they could see us and chose to accompany the ship on their docile and gentle ramblings. Such benign looking creatures! How anyone could hunt these lenient giants, these stolid sheep of the sea, was beyond tutored understanding. Grandmamma always taught me, and rightfully so, that the world's animals were a bounty placed here by the Lord and for the good of humanity—to expend as they see fit. Though this may be a valid explanation, I cannot accept such conjecture as pure truth. Especially now, observing such magnificent animals as these. For it does nothing to feed or make right my inquisitive and bewildered understanding of it all—no matter how hard I try.

The seas were now angrier than ever—the wind gustier than before— the fog less dense then when it first started. An unexpected and sudden squall hit the port beam. The *Sphinx* surrendered, falling onto her starboard rail. Before we knew it, it was blowing a full gale. We all retreated to the safety of the quarterdeck at the rear of the ship.

"All men to your stations," commanded Samuel. "Down with the aft main. You two men take in the Yankee jib!"

"Whales all around, Captain," shouted the man high in the crow's nest. "Even more in the distance."

Samuel ordered the man back on deck. It was too stormy to have someone aloft. "This is strange. I have never seen so many animals clustered so close to a ship before."

"Samuel, I'm frightened," I confessed. The distant crashing booms we heard earlier were now closer. "Are you sure that's not thunder?"

"Cannon fire," he replied, staring out in the direction of the noise.

"You sure, Sam?"

"I'm a military man, Mr. Cadman," he said, sternly. "Don't you think I know artillery when I hear it?"

I had never heard Samuel address Tim so harshly. He was wrought with concern. His military training bubbled to the surface.

"Mr. Cadman, get below and batten down all hatches," ordered the captain. "Mr. Monroe take us in the direction of that noise."

"Aye, aye, Captain. What compass heading did you say?"

"Did I give you a compass direction, Mr. Monroe?" he replied gruffly. "No, I did not. Steer in the direction of that noise."

"Samuel! Why are you being so overbearing?" I asked.

He remained silent for a moment. "Sorry, Mr. Monroe. I must keep in mind that this is a civilian craft, not a military ship. This weather worries me. Add the cannon fire to it and ..."

"You do not need to apologize, Captain. I too was a military man at one time. I understand. I am here to take orders."

"Take her in the approximate direction of the noise."

"With pleasure, sir!"

Eli was about to turn the wheel when there was a sudden thumping crash. The *Sphinx* heaved, falling over onto her side. Its stern lifted several feet above the water. The wheel whirled uncontrollably, tossing Eli across the deck. I held on to a cleat for dear life, my feet dangling over the side of the ship. The vessel had listed almost ninety degrees, her sails kissing the waves. Samuel reached out, clutched me by the hand, and pulled me aboard.

"We've hit, we've hit!" someone shouted.

"Make fast to the ship!" yelled Samuel, taking hold of the wheel.

Just as quickly, as the vessel went up and over, she briskly settled back down and onto her feet. The sails whipped violently in the strong breeze as the schooner sprung up and floundered. At the stern of the ship, I caught a glimpse of a mammoth white-winged tail as it emerged from the churning waters. It plunged, slapping the waves and sending gallons of seawater onto the deck. It was a massive blue whale and he had just gone under the stern of the ship.

The mammal swam away, its massive black-blue, shimmering frame burst and coiled through the muddled, frothy swell. It was as if it just wanted to toy with the ship. Suddenly, it turned and swam back toward the schooner, this time diving beneath our bow and lifting it twenty feet into the air. When he dove, this gargantuan, white-winged tail rose high into the spray-filled air just above the foredeck. Its flukes must have been over twenty-five feet across and that much higher out of the water. As the whale plunged its immense torso deep into the sea, the ship was eased back down onto the surface of the tossing waves. Its enormous glistening tail hung high in the sea-tossed air. Just when it appeared that it would pummel the side of the ship, it slowly slithered back into the water and vanished below a whirl of salty foam water. Everyone aboard froze, awaiting another assault. None materialized. The sails caught the howling wind and the ship was pushed over onto its beam. Samuel returned it to its course.

Eli rested against the cabin doghouse, looking tired and beaten.

"Eli! You alright?" I cried.

Clutching his chest, he labored to breathe. "I think so," he muttered. "I must have had the wind knocked out of me."

"Are you hurt, old man?" asked Samuel. "It looks like you've banged your head."

"The wheel ripped from my hand, sir. There was nothing I could do."

"Did you see that?" howled Tim, as he emerged from the cabin below. "A blue whale with a massive white tail!"

"Tim! Take the wheel!" commanded Samuel. "I want to inspect Mr. Monroe's injuries. Admon! Go below and check the bilges for any excess water."

"That was frightening!" I cried. "Will it be back?"

"Let's hope not," said Samuel, inspecting the bump on Eli's head. "I'm worried about this failing weather. It's deteriorating by the minute."

"That was the biggest whale I have ever seen!" declared Tim.

"Never mind the whale. We have steerage?"

"Aye, Sam, she appears to be responding nicely." He tested the wheel, turning it left then right.

"Good. If he had damaged the rudder we could be dead to drift these waters for months."

"Bilge is dry, sir," reported Admon.

"Are all hands on board?" inquired the captain.

"Everyone's where they should be, Sam," replied Tim.

The fog had diminished, making the seas look more intimidating. Like a peachy bruise in a clearing sky, the sun bravely battled to break through the migrating mist. All around the blowing of whales could be heard as they rose to the surface and exhaled the briny sea from their ballooning lungs. The wind had picked up to an alarming state and the swells became short and choppy. Still, the graceful *Sphinx* seem to be taking it all in stride.

"Heave to, Tim. Let's take a breather while I try and sort things out."

"Aye, aye, sir."

With the sails backfilled, the *Sphinx* drifted calmly.

"Whoo-ei! That was some fish," wailed Tim, tying down the helm.

"How are you feeling, Mr. Monroe?" I asked, as the doctor examined him.

"A little wobbly. I'll be fine." He took out a stogie from his pocket while Marcus appraised the bump on his head.

"Nothing serious. You should recover, Monsieur Monroe."

Eli lit a match to his stogie, and flung the tiny flame overboard. "I just couldn't hold her."

"It couldn't be helped, Mr. Monroe. The important thing is that you are not seriously hurt and that there is no damage to the ship."

"The whales are still around us," I said, looking over the side.

"Yes, they're feeding. These waters must be saturated with krill," Samuel said.

"Krill?" I said.

"Small shrimp-like crustaceans."

"Sounds very un-appetizing."

"The cannon fire has stopped, Sam," declared Tim. "We still can't see much."

"Keep her hove-to."

"Aye, aye, Sam."

After a short while, Eli insisted he was feeling well enough to take the helm. Samuel, Tim, and the doctor went below to surmise the events that just occurred and what we should do next. I followed.

"It's unusual to see this many whales so close to a ship," declared Samuel.

"Nothing about these waters are usual," chimed Tim.

"Who do you suppose were firing those guns?" I asked.

"American navy, no doubt," said Samuel. "I can't imagine what they were shooting at."

"What's our next move, Sam?"

"Well, Tim, we are in the Labrador Sea, somewhere between the Labrador coast and Greenland. We will need to wait for this fog to clear before we can take a sun sight and get a more precise location."

"How will we find la whaling ship in le fog?"

"We can only do our best," said the captain. "We have provisions for another six weeks. We will just keep looking. It's all we can do."

"I am so grateful to you, Samuel," I said.

"Amy's my friend also, Emily." He unrolled a chart on the salon table. "We are here," he said pointing with a pencil, "just off the Labrador shelf."

"Looks like you circled the area at an earlier time," I said.

"Yes, this is one of the whaling fields mentioned by the Westport whalers. It is the first place we will look. The whale sightings are a good sign. If whales are here, chances are so are the Northern whaling fleet."

Eli appeared at the cabin entrance. "Captain! I think you should come up on deck and see this."

"What is it, Mr. Monroe?"

"Fog is lifting, sir!"

"I'm sure we are all happy about that, Eli. Carry on."

"No, sir! You don't understand. There is smoke on the horizon."

"Smoke!"

"Yes, Captain. A ship."

"Meeting adjourned!" announced Samuel.

—⟨⟩⟨⟩⟨⟩—

Chapter 25:

The fog had not so much lifted, as it was left behind us. Suddenly I could see the late day sun as it settled over the western horizon. To the east was a small black speck where a milky blue sky met a blueberry sea. I prayed that it was the whaler and that Amy was safe.

"Retrieve the sight glass for me, will you, Tim?"

"Will do, Sam."

"Do you think it's the *Nimrod*?" I asked of Samuel.

"We will soon find out."

"There are two ships, *Capitaine*," trumpeted the eagle-eyed Frenchman.

"Take us in the direction of that sighting, Mr. Monroe."

"Aye, aye, Captain."

"Here it is, Sam," said Tim, handing him the scope. As he peered through the glass, a blithesome smile blossomed on his face.

"What do you see, Samuel, what do you see?" I cried.

"Well, well. I think we found them. There are two vessels. One is definitely a whaler. Not sure about the other."

Samuel handed Tim the glass. "Here. You have younger eyes. Tell me what you see."

Tim Cadman carefully studied the horizon through the tunneled aperture.

I held my breath waiting for good news.

"It's the *Nimrod* alright," he confirmed.

"Are you sure?" I asked.

"Yep! And another ship just the other side of her."

"Oh, Samuel, we have found her!" I clutched him by the arm.

"Emily, don't get your hopes too high. We have yet to confirm that Amy is even on that vessel."

"Oh, I know she is. I can feel it," I declared, leaning over the rail and gazing out in the direction of the distant ships.

"The other vessel is lowering her flag," announced Tim.

"What sort of flag?" Samuel asked.

"Couldn't tell. It's running up another … the Stars and Stripes. There are gun ports along her bulwark, Sam."

"Let me see," said Samuel, taking the scope from Tim's eye. "It's Old Glory all right … an American warship. It's got a smokestack—looks like one of those new class steam driven vessels."

"The other ship is certainly the *Nimrod*," verified Tim. "I can tell by its mizzen. When we installed it, we raked it forward twenty degrees so she could carry more canvas. You don't see that on other whalers."

"I wonder why we heard cannon fire?" said a worried Samuel. "Why would an American ship fire upon an American whaling vessel?"

"We will be losing light in a couple of *heures Capitaine*. Do you think we have enough time to approach?"

"If it gets too dark, Mr. Theroux, we will hold off and ghost them till morning."

While the next wearisome hour unfolded, I spent most of my time below deck in an endeavor to stay warm and dry. Up on deck the weather had taken a turn for the worst. The swells had become enormous as the ship lifted and crashed down upon them. Everywhere there was spray and the sound of the wind through the ship's rigging produced a deafening roar. I lay in my bunk managing an unexpected bout of seasickness. Samuel had warned me about this ancient malady and the three terrible trappings that it embodied—vomiting, vomiting, and more vomiting. On most of this trip I have been fortunate and none of it has befallen me. Until now, I have suffered only the slightest affliction, with a modest tempest of the stomach.

Outside the port window over my bunk a demented sea came at us from all directions. When the ship was built, the window was installed just below deck level on the hull of the ship. It was the only source of light for the small cabin. When the ship dipped its rail below the surface of the sea the port was submerged and water would seep around the glass and into the ship, dripping down the planking and into the bilge. Though the glass was well bedded in puttied tar, it was a thoughtless place to put a window, according to Samuel. I, for one, was happy it was there. What marvelous views one received when the hull of the ship was under water!

The *Sphinx's* bow continued to crash down from swell to trough with ear splitting thuds. I tried to nap but it was just not to be. My twirling tummy would not allow it. Instead, I rested and listened to the queer and curious sounds which can only be heard deep in the bilges of a sailing vessel, far out at sea.

Without warning, the ship's movement suddenly became less violent, the sea less stormy. The ship's violent hurdling became a slushy roll. It was then that I first heard it. The sound was faint—muffled—a wailing or shrieking trill. I held my ear firmly to the ship's hewed timbers and listened. It became louder, closer. The long, screeching fusions were just the other side of the vessel's planking—a vibrating harmony—like a pack of lamenting baby wolves, howling, weeping beneath the muted water. This was followed by a series of crisp clacking and snapping ticks mingled with shadowy warbles.

Then it came to me. I knew what it was I was listening to. It was the mandible, lullaby chorus and chanting hymn of the venerable whale. Strangely, their eerie song eased my pounding head and quieted my churning belly. I sprung up and looked out the port window. The ship was moving at an accelerated speed, its port deck partially submerged. There they were; a nautical parade of leviathans—a consort of Goliaths followed by more diminutive companions, all swimming in unison.

Suddenly, as the ship leaned to the fresh breeze, my view was blotted out and everything out the port window became black. It took me a moment to realize what had happened. When I finally did, I found myself staring into one breathtaking, humongous eye. I jerked backwards. The glazed image filled the cabin's entire port window, staring back at me—one immense eyeball. My mouth dangled open as the curious eye continued to peer. As quick as it appeared it vanished. I rushed back to the window just in time to witness its enormous white tale as curling flukes plunged into a turbulent, turquoise sea behind the ship. I rushed up and onto the sloping deck.

"Anyone see that? Anyone see it?" I shouted.

"Les whales? Yes. They have returned," acknowledged Marcus.

"No! The blue whale—the one with the white flukes. I saw him again."

"Oh! Splendid!" moaned Eli.

"I saw him again, Samuel! The giant whale with the white flukes."

"Thar she blows!" shouted Tim, holding the spyglass and pointing ahead. A spew of spray shot high into the air. "It's the whale that swam under the ship! He's heading toward the *Nimrod*."

"Let's hope it doesn't come back," declared a worried Eli.

Holding onto the ship with both hands, I stretched my neck for a better look.

"Where did he go? I don't see him." I yelled.

"He's gone under," replied Tim.

"We are closing in quickly on the *Nimrod*, Captain."

"Steady as she goes, Mr. Monroe." Samuel looked over at me and smiled. "Feeling better?" he asked.

"Yes, a little."

"We should be approaching the two ships shortly. When we get within hailing distance, we will soon know if Amy is on that *Nimrod*. For now, we need to be certain as to what it is the war sloop is doing. Until then, I am keeping distance between us."

"I understand," I sighed. "I know Amy's on that ship. Unless ..."

Images of what could have happened to poor Amy percolated in my head. The more I thought about it, the worse the sequence of possibilities became. Perhaps she had fallen overboard and drowned trying to get away, or molested by some carnal delinquent, unable to control his erotic and depraved desires. Or worse, left hanging in the shallow reaches of a whaling ship's hold, deep in its putrid bowels, where severed slabs of putrefied whale blubber are contained, hanging by her neck like a prized, licentious trophy, waiting to be immersed in the blazing boiler vat and dried out, poached, and reduced with the paunchy blubber of industrial necessity. I hid may face. I did not want anyone to witness my weakness. A tear trickled down my cheek.

The *Sphinx* got closer to the two floundering ships dancing on the choppy swell. Tim examined them closely through the sight glass.

"*Nimrod* has harpooned a whale, Sam," he announced.

"Where!" shouted Samuel, through a shrieking wind.

"Tied alongside. And it looks like there are two others low in the water. Sharks are feasting on them."

"I'll take the helm now, Mr. Monroe."

"Aye, aye, Captain." The first mate gladly surrendered the wheel.

"Tim! Take your place at the bow and keep watch," ordered Samuel.

Tim folded the sight glass.

"Can I have the telescope, Timothy?" I asked.

"What are your plans, *Capitaine*?"

"I'm not sure what's going on with those two ships. Something is not right, Mr. Theroux. For now, we will keep our distance and make certain that the *Nimrod* is kept between us and that war cruiser. Mr. Monroe, run Old Glory up the aft mast."

"Which one, sir?"

"The largest one we have. I want no mistake to be made by that navy ship. He must be sure that we are an American sailing vessel and mean no harm."

"Aye, sir."

We continued our snail-like approach. I threaded my arm around the ship's rigging, gave myself sure footing, and examined the two ships through the telescope. The waters around the *Nimrod* were crimson red, cloaked with an oily layer of blood. I could see a congress of sharks circling the hulking torn body of a dead whale tied to the side of the ship. The waters were churning and boiling with frenzied attacks by the savage finned sea beasts. I diverted my attention to the navy ship. The Stars and Bars streamed from its backstay. Along its rail was a series of cannons. Naval troops lined up along its bulwark, guns in hand, as if waiting to do battle. On the *Nimrod*, I could make out a contingent of at least three naval personnel. The crew of the *Nimrod* sat on deck, all gathered in one place sitting with their hands folded atop their heads.

"Samuel! The crew of the *Nimrod* are being held prisoners."

"I saw them," he confessed. "I can't imagine what they could have done to be boarded and detained in that manner. Mr. Theroux, take the glass. Keep an eye on that warship. Report to me any developments."

"Yes, *Capitaine*."

I handed Marcus the spyglass.

"Ah, *probleme, probleme!*" He recited, looking through the glass and shaking his head.

As we got closer to the whaler the ocean picked up and became rough. It was then that I noticed the whales had all vanished. When they followed the ship, their enormous bodies acted as a breakwater, giving us a satisfying ride. Now that they were gone, the sea was free to have its way with us once again.

Tim bravely perched himself at the tip of the protracted bowsprit, straddling the tapered timber, and looking like a seafaring, Michelangelo's David, keeping watch for danger ahead.

"Do you see any sign of Amy?" I yelled to him.

He looked back and shook his head.

I was becoming frantic with expectancy. Impatience and restlessness were now my intimate companions. "What do you see, Marcus?" I begged as he spied through the scope.

He slapped his tongue on the roof of his mouth. "Ah, Mademoiselle, it does not look good."

"Prepare to come about," shouted the captain.

The *Sphinx's* bow turned through the eye of the wind. The sails lost their fuel, shivered, then congealed once again, as the ship tacked gracefully. We were in retreat.

"Are we not approaching them, Captain?" Eli inquired.

"No. We will keep our distance and study the situation. Besides, a quick approach may be misunderstood for hostility."

"I think they are signaling us, *Capitaine*," announced Marcus.

"A flashing light from the war ship," yelled Tim from the bow.

"Take the wheel Mr. Monroe," ordered Samuel.

Marcus handed Samuel the scope.

In the distance, I could make out a series of flashes from a lantern on the war ship. A sparkling language that only a naval military man would understand.

"What does it mean, Samuel?" I asked.

"From what little I can read, it looks like they are asking us to strike our colors," he said peering through the glass.

"I don't understand."

"Neither do I," he replied.

"What do you mean, by strike our colors?"

"Asking us to stand down—surrender."

"Surrender what, Captain?" inquired Eli, "We're an American vessel. We have nothing to surrender."

Samuel continued looking through the scope. "Something makes no sense here," he said.

"They're running up a white flag, Sam," yelled Tim.

"They must want to parley, Captain," added Eli.

"Just a ploy, Mr. Monroe." said the captain, examining the ship through the glass. "What in God's name ..."

"What ... what is it Samuel?" I cried.

"I can't believe it!" he howled, looking through the scope. He clenched his teeth. "Bulloch is on that warship!"

"Who?"

"James Dunwoody Bulloch. The man that tried taking the *Sphinx* away from me in Baltimore. He's standing on the quarterdeck. He must be commanding that warship."

"You must be mistaken," I cried. "You said he was a Confederate. Perhaps it's just someone that looks like him."

"I had a bad feeling about that vessel. And if I'm right—it will do anything and everything in its power to take the *Sphinx* into its custody. We must not let that happen. Emily, get down below."

"No!" I said.

He folded the glass and handed it to me. "Please! Take this with you and do as I say. It's for your own safety, girl."

"I want to stay here, on deck, with you! Please Samuel, don't make me disobey an order."

He gave me an endearing look and nodded his head. "Always the adventurer," he chided.

Samuel worked the helm as the crew of the *Sphinx* hung by the starboard rail watching events unfold. We quickly sailed away from the other two ships.

"Are you sure it's this fellow, Bulloch?" inquired Eli.

"Positive! I know that flowing beard and mustache anywhere."

"What do you think they want, Captain?"

"This ship, Mr. Monroe, they want this ship."

I staggered up the deck to the bow for a better look. Perhaps I would see Amy and assure myself that she was safe—even though there was no promise that she was on the *Nimrod*.

Samuel shouted, commanding me to return.

I could not. I hung on precariously as the *Sphinx* hobby-horsed to the steep churning swells. A fractured wave washed over me. The water felt raw and wintery. Its brine stung my eyes and tingled my lips. I could hear Grandmamma cry, *Wear your Macintoch and Wellingtons, dear. It's going to rain today.* I was never one for wearing slickers or rain shoes.

Once at the bow, I knelt along the wave-swept deck, extended the spyglass over the side rail, and peered through the spray-spewed scope. A deckhand jumped over me while performing his duty tending the jib sails. The ship leapt from one wave to another, in a hellish, balletic promenade.

At the helm, the captain gave orders for more sail, more speed. I wiped the salt-encrusted spyglass on my sleeve and took another look. It was then that the horrors on the *Nimrod* transpired before of my very eyes. One man was being lashed while the others sat along the deck reluctantly watching. I held the instrument tightly to my eye as it shook violently in my hand. Suddenly I observed a familiar likeness—two white limbs, waving frantically toward the rear of the ship.

A large wave crashed over me. I was drenched. I wiped the glass best I could and quickly looked again. The fuzzy image with the beckoning arms blurred and disappeared as the ship descended into a trough. By the time it scaled the crest of the succeeding wave, the image had vanished. I stared through the glass. And stared some more. The waving arms were gone. I was certain I saw it—a woman. Samuel cried out my name through the howling wind. Before I had a chance to get to my feet, there he was standing over me.

"I saw her, Samuel, I saw her! It was Amy!" I cried. My clothing was completely drenched. I knelt there convulsing.

"Emily! Look at you! You're soaked," he sighed. Though it was an angry sigh, it was laced with compassion and concern. "You have to get below. I will not hear any more complaints. Get into some dry clothes." He helped me to my feet as Tim rushed over.

"Are you sure it was her?" said Tim.

"Yes!"

The *Sphinx* climbed a monster swell, crashing down the other side, and nearly sending all three of us over the rail. Samuel placed his arm around me and escorted me to the aft deck. Tim followed close behind. I was sodden and shivering—there was not one square inch of dry patch of clothing between us.

Samuel took the spyglass from my hand and gave it back to Marcus. "Place your eye on that whaling vessel, Mr. Theroux. Let me know if you see a woman."

"*Femme*! It is what I do best," declared the French doctor.

"Look, Sam!" said Tim, "the warship. It's lowering the Stars and Stripes and raising another flag."

Samuel looked back over his shoulder at the naval cruiser as we sailed away. "Can you see what it is Tim?"

"A blue flag. It has something on it! I can't make out what it is from this distance."

"What flag are they raising on that war sloop, Mr. Theroux?" inquired Samuel.

"It is *bleu*," said the doctor studying the ship through the spyglass. He counted to himself, "*une, deux, trios, sept*, how you say, seven stars in a circle at le *centre*."

"A Confederate naval ensign," sniveled Samuel, angrily. "I knew it!"

"Cannon smoke!" warned Marcus.

I had gone below to change out of my wet clothing. When I returned, I heard a loud distant rumble. The Confederate ship had set off its guns. The iron shot fell well behind us as we continued sailing away.

"What was that?" I cried.

"Cannon shot," said Samuel. "They are firing at us. After they lowered Old Glory, the deception was over. We need to keep our distance from that warship. We will circle and maneuver so the *Nimrod* is between us and that warship. The Confederates have at least three men on that whaler. They will not want to risk injury to them by firing over or around them."

"Oh, Samuel, what will we do?"

"Yes, yes, I see her!" cried the even-tempered Marcus. It was the first sign of excitement I heard in his voice.

"Where, Marcus, where?" I pleaded.

"She is hiding behind les barrels."

"It's Amy!" I cried.

Samuel gritted his teeth with grim and determined demeanor. "Mr. Monroe!" he bellowed.

"Yes, Captain!"

"I want every man on this ship to arm himself with whatever weapon they can find. Do I make myself clear?"

"Aye, aye, sir," saluted Eli.

"Do you have something to protect yourself with, Tim?" asked the captain.

With a decisive smile, Tim Cadman raised his muscular arms and wiggled his fingers.

"Very well, my friend. Take your place at the bow and prepare for hostilities."

The *Sphinx* spun its bow through the eye of a gale-swept breeze with a nimble pirouette. The ship heeled over treacherously as Samuel turned onto a new course directly into the teeth of peril. The fluttering canvas swung gracefully from starboard to port, drinking gusty air and submerging the rail in sizzling froth. A carbonated sea swamped and engulfed the decks. The *Sphinx* quickly railed and recovered, thrusting forward while snagging the sea-drenched wind. We were heading back toward the two ships a quarter mile away, and at full gallop. The captain kept the *Nimrod* between the schooner and the Confederate vessel, using the whaler as an obstacle to the war sloop's line of fire. Around me, crewmen grabbed anything they could find to defend themselves—chains, oars, belaying pin. Eli had acquired a toggle harpoon that hung in the cabin below while Marcus retrieved his doctor's bag.

"You can run someone through terribly with that instrument, Mr. Monroe," said Samuel.

"I have been out at sea and free much too long to allow some slave-lover to take me south again," he declared.

"And you, Mr. Theroux, have you not armed yourself?"

The doctor shook his head and held up his physician's bag. "I give life, *Capitaine*" he said, calmly, "not *retirer* it."

"Let's hope it doesn't come to that, Doctor, shall we?"

"In any case, I am ready with le tools of my occupation."

"Very well, Mr. Theroux. Why don't you get down below with Emily and look after her. Keep her safe. I will call on you if needed."

"No!" I snapped. "My place is by your side, Samuel!"

"Emily, we may be boarded. You may get hurt."

"I can take care of myself," I insisted.

Preoccupied with unfolding events, the captain was in no mood to argue. I used his lack of appetite to quarrel to my advantage and remained on deck. Though I had planned on being resolute in my insistence, at some

345

time his suggestion that I get below will probably need to be realized. For now, I was just one of the boys.

"What are we going to do, Captain?" said Eli, resting on his spade.

"If need be, we will ram her, Mr. Monroe."

"Ram who?"

"That warship."

"Ram her, sir! She's over twice our size. Would that not be insanity?"

"Aye, Mr. Monroe. A good choice of words. The *Sphinx's* sprit is eighteen inches in diameter, ten feet long along the deck, and nineteen over the water. That gives us a twenty-nine-foot battering ram. We will ram her aft quarter where her hull is vulnerable. If they want the *Sphinx* they can have her. But not before I send that war sloop to the bottom."

"Will we really ram her, Samuel?" I asked, a tinge of fear in my heart.

"Our mission is to get Amy off that whaler," he said. "I will use the dead whales as a cushion between us and the whaler and come alongside. We will then board her—at which time we will rescue Amy. I am not sure what I will do after that." He reached over to a locker and retrieved a whaler's cutting spade, a ghastly looking cutting tool, and placed it by his side. "First and foremost, let's stand firm and get Amy off that ship."

Tousled sea conditions made it challenging for the Confederate ship to aim her guns and fire them with any success. We were approaching the *Nimrod* as a volley of cannon shot fell well to our port beam and the *Sphinx* continued its breakneck momentum toward its noble appointment with the drifting whaler.

On the *Nimrod* one of the Confederate soldiers fired his rifle at us, while his companions held their weapons on the crew, keeping upwards of fifteen whalemen at bay. Samuel ordered me to my quarters once again. With gunshot whizzing by, I knew it was time to do so. I stooped down on the galley floor behind the cast iron stove. Marcus Theroux sat nearby and watched over me. I heard a bullet strike the hull. Everyone on the *Sphinx* ducked and took cover. Samuel stood firm despite the flying lead, remaining at his station, defiantly brazen and dauntless.

The grand old schooner was now only a couple of hundred yards away from the flailing whaler. The Confederate gunman who was shooting at us panicked and ran down the *Nimrod's* deck, certain the two ships would soon collide. Amy, who had been kept in one of the *Nimrod's* cabins, escaped her captors and hastened along the deck, frantically signaling her presence. The crew on the whaleship cheered, as we got dangerously closer. As for the warship, if anything went in our favor it was the element of surprise.

The order on the *Sphinx* was given. "Prepare to come about."

In the near distance the roar of cannon-fire echoed like looming thunder. The crew scrambled to their stations, manning line and canvas, as cannon ordnance careened by the *Sphinx's* rigging.

I rushed up on deck with a complaining Marcus close behind.

Samuel looked over to me without saying a word. I ran toward the bow.

"Get back here, Emily," shouted Samuel.

Along the side of the *Nimrod* hung the grisly carcass of the dead whale. The whaler floundered in a vast pool of lathered blood. Ravenous sharks circled the ship, trashing about as they clashed for random hunks of ragged whale meat. The scent in the air brought forth memories of the infirmary at Halifax. Though it did not sink in earlier, I now realized that we were in a precarious circumstance. Marcus took me by the arm and I gladly allowed him to escort me to the rear of the ship. We were only thirty yards away from the whaler and traveling at speed. A collision with *Nimrod* was unavoidable. The faces of the men on the whaleship bloomed with horror as the schooner's massive bowsprit bore down on them.

Just when it looked certain that impact was inevitable, Samuel swiftly turned the wheel. The ship immediately wielded to port and slowed, veering as its mammoth bowsprit swept along the side of *Nimrod's* port beam with loud, repulsive grating. The daunting sound, like fingernails filing along a schoolroom blackboard, made me cringe. The schooner's bow rose to a swell and fell, splintering the whaleship's spindled rail. The iron cranes fitting on the tip of the sprit strummed the *Nimrod's* shrouds just above the rigging's dead eyes. One of the shrouds parted. With her sails still pregnant with wind, the *Sphinx* continued its advance along the whaler's hull. Masts shivered and convulsed violently as the ships suddenly collided. The schooner's bowsprit continued along the deck as it thrust forward, shattering deck hatches, shaving off vent cowls, and tearing the lifeboat from its davits. Finally, the battering sprit came to rest over the *Nimrod's* foredeck, wedging itself between the rigging. We were trapped— the ships anchored together.

The *Sphinx* pivoted violently, slamming into the whaler with a grinding, shattering thunder. If not for the mammal's prodigious carcasses that dangled from the side of the *Nimrod*, cushioning the blow, the schooner's elegant hull would have shattered like an egg on the rim of a baker's bowl. With its piked snout firmly pinched over the whaler's foredeck, Tim dashed to the very tip of the oscillating bowsprit, straddled over the *Nimrod's* deck, and scoured the ship for a sight of Amy. Suddenly there she was running toward him.

With an outstretched arm, he urged her to hurry.

A complexion of terror flushed on the faces of the *Sphinx's* crew, as they watched, unsure of what was to come next. The flaming sound of rifle and cannon fire echoed in the wailing wind. Men hollered. The two ships groaned, grated, and splintered. The *Nimrod* rose to the crest of a bloated swell, lifting the bow of the *Sphinx* high above the foamy water. As the enormous seething wave swept by us, both ships plummeted into its bottomless trough, sucked down into a watery abyss with a backbreaking clash. The schooner shuddered and swayed ferociously, like wet, tattered prey in the jaws of a mad dog. Its lightly-built hull was no match for the whaler's hulking construction as timbers cracked, chainplates buckled, and planking exploded their fasteners. This sort of punishment could not go on much longer. In short order, it was certain to sink our floating home.

Amy ran along the frenzied deck, pushing herself past the *Nimrod's* frantic crew as the men fought to free themselves from their Confederate captors. A large wave crashed over the ship, sending Tim to his knees and nearly ripping the clothing off his body. Bare-chested, his torn shirt dangled from his arms like tattered wet sails from a gale swept spar. He continued hollering for Amy to hurry.

Just before she reached him, her foot became entangled in a coil of rope, sending her tumbling to her knees. She struggled to set herself free as the *Sphinx* did the same. Tim immediately jumped onto the whaler's foredeck, ran over, and freed the boot that was wedged by a barb to the coil of line. He climbed back up onto the bowsprit, offering her an outstretched hand. Amy desperately reached for it. Clutched by the wrist she was swept up into his muscular arm. He held her close just as the shattered ships began to pull away from one another. Amy gazed up at her unlikely savior with tears of joy. Tim offered her a sanguine smile.

The *Sphinx* slowly wrestled itself free. As it did, its lovely mahogany rail tore away like bandages on a splintered wound. Its church-white planking sprung free along its bulwark with alarming thunder. The schooner skated sideways as we slowly pulled away into a blowing tempest. A two-inch line from the *Nimrod* raveled itself on the *Sphinx's* Samson post and tethered the two ships together—preventing the schooner from pulling away. The crew hacked at the line with their pocket knives as a relentless sea washed over them. The hull rose to an uneven swell, slamming into the threatening whaler. Just when it appeared hopeless, the line was severed and the *Sphinx* began drifting away. Swollen sails tugged and heaved as Samuel struggled to hold the bucking vessel away from the drifting whaler.

Cannon ordnance suddenly shattered one of the *Nimrod's* upper spars. Splintered timber rained down on us, as the bruised schooner began to draw away. Still, the whaleship shielded us from unrestrained cannon-fire as a second volley of iron pierced the *Nimrod's* stern. Ultimately, the dignified *Sphinx*, now seriously marred and injured, but still afloat, listed heavily to port, and with the help of a stormy breeze, turned tail and sailed away. We were free. More importantly, so was Amy. Yet the danger was far from over.

A storm-kissed ocean heaved, sending a rogue wave showering over Tim and threatening to snatch Amy from his arms. The sturdy bowsprit quaked and shuddered. Its shrouds groaned as it submerged itself deep into an oncoming wave. Nonetheless, the ship continued picking up speed as we left the *Nimrod* behind.

Tim carried Amy along the slippery sprit back to the safety of the ship's deck. With grateful arms flung tightly around his neck, she desperately clung onto her bare-chested rescuer, kissing him profusely.

In the chaos of the moment, the crew of the *Nimrod* had turned on their captors, disarming them and taking back their ship. Eli took the helm while Samuel hobbled forward to lend Tim a hand. In spite of his injured leg, Samuel performed his duty with pluck and determination, as Tim gently handed Amy down into his hands. Gratefully, she bundled her arms around the captain and started to cry. Samuel peered over her shoulder at me and winked. All I could do was stand by in euphoric, silent applause.

"Are you alright? Did anyone hurt you?" Samuel asked, shouting over the howling air.

"No, I'm fine," replied Amy. "Just a little shaken." She looked up at Tim and blew him a kiss.

"It is a pleasure to see you safe, Mademoiselle Amy," said Marcus.

"Mr. Cadman! Cover yourself," commanded Samuel, in a taunting tease. "There are ladies aboard."

We all laughed as the modest carpenter jumped down from his perch on the bow and dauntingly tugged at his drenched, torn shirt. I immediately ran up to Amy and we embraced. She still looked elegant as ever, even if she was drenched to the bone. Only Amy Chaloner could go through such turmoil and mayhem and still retain an air of loveliness.

"Where is Moses and his partner Cain?" I asked.

"On the *Nimrod*, I think," replied Amy.

"Look! They are climbing down the side of the ship," said Tim.

"Where to?" I said.

"I can't tell. The ship is turning. They must have gone down a rope ladder."

"Climbing down into the small boat," added Amy.

"Boat?" said Samuel.

"Yes. The one used to ferry the men from the *Alabama*."

"*Alabama!*" roared Samuel. It was the first time he had heard the name of the Confederate warship.

"Yes. That's the name of the ship that held us hostage," said Amy.

At that very moment a gust of wind hit the schooner dipping the rail into a surge of rushing seawater—knocking us off our feet. We had all we could do to hold on and not be swept over the side. We quickly retreated to the quarterdeck and safety.

With Samuel back at the helm, the *Sphinx* continued to pick up speed and place distance between us and the two fading ships. The seas had grown to enormous heights as blue water washed over the schooner's clipper bow and down its mahogany decks. We were sailing into the mouth of a deafening wind. Behind a veil of cannon smoke, the *Alabama* raised sails.

"Look!" shouted Eli. "Men in the small whaleboat rowing toward the warship."

"It's Moses and his companion," shouted Tim. "They're making an escape toward the Confederate vessel."

"Prepare to come about!"

Without waiting for the crew to take their stations, Samuel turned the ship around. It was not long before we were on a tack back into the jaws of danger. A round of cannon-fire echoed along the horizon.

"What are you doing, *Capitaine*? We will be blown to bits," declared the Doctor.

"Not while she's busy getting up sail, Mr. Theroux. It will take her some time … time we can use to our advantage to take Moses and his companion into custody. Once we do, we will quickly be on our way."

"You forget, Sam. She is steam driven," declared Tim.

"I forget nothing. Get a rope and the gaff hook. We will snag the skiff as we go by it."

"Anything you say, Sam."

Once again, like a recurring bad dream, we were careening backwards, our nose to the wind, in what looked like a futile attempt to apprehend the two escaping men. Tim stood along the beam rail with a gaff hook ready to entrap Moses and Cain before they could get away.

"Oh, Samuel, you think we should?" I said.

"If we don't get them now we may never see them again. If they are indeed awash in guilt, they must be taken to the authorities. Now, you should go below, Emily. Amy needs dry clothing and so do you."

With my best friend safe and sound, I had no reason to disobey his command. We had a full view from the ships cabin ports below. The tiny rowboat looked so far off and the warship so near, though it was more the other way round. The men in the skiff rowed like demons from a crucifix.

As I stared out the port window, two gigantic white flukes burst from the sea behind the small rowboat and quickly vanished. I ran up the companionway, shouting.

"The white flukes," I cried. "I saw him. He's back."

"Emily, get down below!" commanded Samuel, as he fought the wheel in the ferocious gale.

I looked toward the front of the ship just in time to see the heaving hulk weave its shimmering body through the sloping, mountainous ocean swell.

"The white tail monster, Captain!" cried Eli.

"Where?"

"Between us and the skiff."

As we got closer, Samuel battled the rudder as the gale tried to push us back with every gust.

Amy stood by my side and watched. "Look!" she shouted, pointing toward the tiny rowboat. "A giant wave!"

We all watched as the skiff carrying Moses and Cain bobbed in the water. The desperate men looked like feeble beetles rowing a walnut half-shell. They made little headway as the towering swell grew behind them. The mound of water was much more than a simple wave or the sea pumping its tumescent underbelly high into the heavens. In reality, the swell was a bulging profusion of awe and dread, growing higher and higher by the second—surging—moving faster than anything I had ever witnessed on the land or sea. It was then that I realized it was not the sea at all. It was the whale—an angry whale at that.

The surging water billowed, and like a gargantuan inky cork, the gruesome animal exploded to the surface, flinging the wretched occupants of the small rowboat like discarded straw dolls high into the water-swept air. The furious whale's glittering white tail sprouted from the water to impressive heights.

Suddenly, its giant notched flukes descended, violently slamming the surface of the seething sea and shattering the tiny skiff into matchsticks. The terrified men swam franticly toward the *Alabama* as we all watched in horror. With their paddle-limbed arms, they slapped at the sea like drowning dogs. Their meager attempt to escape was all in vain. The shimmering, black monster surfaced one last time, opened its enormous mouth, and ruthlessly swallowed the hopeless swimmers. Amy turned and hid her face. I embraced her and we comforted one another, while trying to blot out the shocking scene we just witnessed.

"Oh, Samuel, is there anything we can do?" I cried.

"I'm afraid there is nothing anyone can do," he replied.

We watched in anticipation, waiting for the men to surface. The whale was now gone and so was all sign of life. We were stunned. The actions Moses and his companion displayed in trying to escape to the Confederate ship had corroborated his guilt and sealed his fate. There was no doubt in my mind that they were responsible for the death of at least three helpless women. The motive to why they committed such crimes was lost in the depths of an unforgiving sea.

"Astonishing," said Samuel. "I never saw a whale attack a human. He just swallowed them whole."

"Poor Moses," I said. "We will never know what happened to Mary and Annie now."

A puff of smoke spewed from the stacks on the warship. All the concern we expressed for the dead men was now focused on the warship.

"Captain," cried Eli. "I believe she has started her engine."

The puff of black exhaust expelled by the warship's chimney was followed by a second, then a third. There was a thunderous rumble as the determined Confederate cruiser fired its guns. A shattering swoosh was heard high up in the schooner's rigging as a cannonball was hurled past us. Amy and I retreated below.

"That was close, Sam," declared Tim.

"All hands to your stations, men," yelled the captain, "Prepare to turn tail and take her downwind."

Unlike a tack, where the ship slices into the eye of the wind, in a downwind course the ship sails in the same direction as the wind. Done well, it is an unruffled, swift, and peaceful maneuver—one which the *Sphinx* excelled in. But this downwind run was anything but peaceful. Samuel had ordered more canvas to be hoisted. Perhaps too much canvas, as the schooner whipped and yawed, and the stern tried to sail faster than the bow. It was not long before we were sliding down fifteen-foot swells at an alarming speed. The gale was now our friend, as the schooner complacently rode the top of ocean breakers with competence and swiftness.

"Do you think we can outrun her?" asked Tim.

"No doubt," said Samuel. "Even at twice our size we can still easily out-sail her. I'm not certain about how fast she is under steam. It will take some time for her to stoke her boiler. It should give us a good head start."

"We will soon *decouvrir*."

"They're underway and picking up speed, Sam," declared Tim.

"They still have a long way to catch us."

"It will be getting dark soon," said Eli. "Perhaps we can lose them then."

"At least they stopped firing their guns," said Tim.

"We're too far off," said Samuel. "The seas are too lumpy to sail and fire guns."

I was curious to know what had happened while Amy was on the whaling ship. When I had asked her about it, she became quiet and begged not to be questioned. I had so many to ask, but the poor girl was tired and wanted to rest. She retired to her tiny room and closed the door. I remained on deck.

While the evening wore on, we were all drowning in somber uncertainty and consternation as we watched the *Alabama* get closer. In the distance, we could make out the *Nimrod* now under full sail as it made its escape. This was the second time that Samuel and the *Sphinx* had saved the whaler from peril. The *Sphinx's* crew sat atop the cabin roof lined up like a tier of dominoes uncertain what would happen next.

Samuel voiced his concern as he watched *Alabama* slowly gaining ground. "Tim, Marcus, will you follow me, please" requested Samuel. "Mr. Monroe, take the helm and keep us on course. Careful with the wheel, she is begging to roundup."

The men all scurried below.

Inquisitive, I followed.

Samuel rummaged through his desk. We all sat around the galley table wondering what it was he wanted to talk to us about. He took out a series of large diagrams, unfolded one, and proceeded to give us all a lesson in naval propulsion.

"That warship's main purpose is to capture or sink us," declared Samuel. "The men on the *Nimrod* were lucky. I'm surprised the Confederates did not stay put long enough to sink her. But that would mean that we could get away. And this ship is too dear a prize for them."

"So what's our next move?" inquired Tim.

"This," he replied, taking a thin volume from his desk.

"A book?"

"It's a book I found in a book store in Boston, when I was away at school."

"*The Art of Naval Propulsion*, by Francis Pettit Smith, I found it very interesting."

He turned to the middle of the text and unfurled a centerfold illustration. It depicted a cross-section of a steam engine deep in the belly of a ship.

"That's all good, Sam," complained Tim. "But do you think now's a good time for a lesson on shipbuilding?"

"Ah, yes! It is a Frederic Sauvage *helice*," said Marcus, pointing at the drawing. "Monsieur Sauvage ... a great French mind."

"Helice?" said Tim. "What is a helice?"

"You know, a *helice*. Ah, how do you say ... rotor?"

"I don't understand," said Tim.

"Doctor Theroux's means a helix ... a corkscrew, you know, a propeller. This fellow Frederic Sauvage was a boatbuilder who experimented with steam-driven ships and steam propulsion."

"Yes. I was there. I saw it, Monsieur Tim ... le bolt propeller."

"All right, you were there. What does this all mean for us now?" inquired an anxious Tim.

"Even at the lightning speed we are doing, it is just a matter of time before the *Alabama's* steam-driven power overtakes us. At which time they will simply move within yards of us and blow us out of the water. We may be left with little choice but surrender."

"Surrender!" howled Tim. "After all that we have been through?"

"We must consider the women on board."

We were all stunned by the captain's dire report. Though there was a good possibility that we would not be able to escape, to hear Samuel announce possible surrender was discouraging and frightening.

"What will they do to us?" I asked.

"Probably leave you and Amy ashore somewhere and take the *Sphinx*. If they discover that I was an officer in the army, they may take me back to Richmond as prisoner."

"Need I remind you, Sam, we have a crew made up of all black men," said Tim.

"I know." Samuel lowered and shook his head. "They would be taken into custody and sold once the *Alabama* returned south. You and Marcus would probably be allowed to go your way."

"I am not worried about myself."

"I know, Mr. Theroux," replied Samuel. "All the same you and ..."

"I don't want to be left ashore," I cried. "I mean ... I want to go ... go with you. We can't let them capture us. Not without a fight."

"I know Emily. I have no intention of letting them take us, or the *Sphinx*. I would just as soon scuttle her. We must consider our options. And they are very few."

"What are we going to do about it?" asked Tim, looking out to the rear of the schooner at the ensuing Confederate ship.

"What do you see, Tim?" I asked.

"Holy hell gaining on us!" he affirmed.

"Listen, Tim. We were supposed to make a delivery of fishing net and rigging line to Gloucester. Remember?"

"Yes. That was last week, Sam. The buyer's probably still waiting for it."

"And all of it is still down in the hold, correct?"

"All half ton of it," confirmed Tim. "In place of some ballast."

"Well, if you look at the illustration in the book, you can see what is labeled as a screw propeller ... here." Samuel pointed with a pencil.

"Yea, shaped like a brass plank screw," said Tim, examining the drawing.

"The propeller spins at a tremendous speed. I watched them test one in Boston Harbor."

"And?"

"Well, they didn't get far before the engine died. It froze. At first they thought the engine had seized. When they pulled the ship out of the water there was a ship's line tangled around the propeller device. When they left the dock, someone had left a line trailing in the water. It slipped under the boat and wrapped itself tightly around the propeller until it stopped the engine. They tried cutting the line but it was so tightly jammed it took a hammer and chisel and all of an hour to cut it away."

"I see what you are planning, *Capitaine*. How will we accomplish such a feat?"

"She's only a couple of thousand yards away, Captain," yelled Eli from the helm. "What are we going to do?"

"What do you propose, Sam? I'm ready for a little action," said Tim.

"It is our only chance. We must try and tangle their propeller."

"It sounds so complicated," I said.

"No more so than fishing off a dock."

"What do you want me to do, Sam?" inquired Tim, looking anxious.

"Take some men and pile every foot of line and net we have below on the aft deck. We're going fishing!"

—◦◦◦—

Chapter 26:

The *Alabama* was closing fast.

"Why are they not firing on us?" I asked.

"No need to," said Samuel. "They are gaining on us. Why waste ordnance and damage your spoils if you don't have to? After all, we are not armed."

"How can they be so fast? We must be doing close to twelve knots," said Tim.

"A steam-driven vessel like the *Alabama* has the capability of doing upwards of fifteen. Besides, it's a new ship, probably of an advanced design. With all the progress made recently with steam propulsion there are no limits to what they may have accomplished when they built her."

"They are getting closer, *Capitaine*," warned Marcus.

"Get the men ready, Tim. Move us to starboard, Eli, so that the cruiser is directly behind us."

"Shouldn't we stay closer this side of her, Sam, when we deploy the nets?"

"Why?"

"Wave and wind … you know, drift."

"Good point, Tim. You're becoming a better sailor than carpenter."

Humble Tim Cadman smiled and scurried off to help deploy the line and netting. The nets paid out quickly, running out over the stern like a dog chasing chickens. Bundle after bundle were sorted out, unraveled, and dumped over the side. Next came coils of snarled rope—unraveled mountains of it, like piles of discarded knitting. It all went over the stern— all but one. A six-hundred-foot long line was left trailing in the water tied to the schooner's stern. We all stood and eagerly watched as discarded webbing sunk and drifted away toward the *Alabama*.

"That's all of it, Sam," declared Tim, "an entire eight-hundred-dollar's worth."

"Keep us in front of her, Mr. Monroe," commanded Samuel. "If the netting doesn't do the trick, we must try to keep the one-inch line we are trailing under her hull. Perhaps that will entangle their prop."

"How will we know it's done its job, Captain?"

"If we snag her propeller it will tear the cleat right off the back of the ship or snap the line. I guarantee it."

"What now?" I said.

"We wait. If she loses steam propulsion, there is no way she can outrun us. She was built for war, very stout and heavy. We may be much smaller but we are definitely faster under canvas."

"Almost dark," Marcus reminded us.

"Looks like we have a full moon rising, Mr. Theroux," said Samuel. "I don't think darkness will help us in our escape."

The next half hour was the longest I had ever experienced. From a distance, the sight of the two vessels, our schooner and the warship, sailing under a full suit of canvas, flying along the top of stormy waves, with amazing agility and quickness, must have been a breathtaking sight to behold. Behind us a cold yellow sun had long disappeared and an enormous dimpled pie moon took its place. It was a luminous sea— beautiful and stunning. But there was nothing beautiful about the events that were evolving—at least not for us. After all, we were just a pleasure craft being aggressively chased by a warship whose intent was to procure or sink us. If there was anything appealing or pleasing to chronicle it was the *Sphinx's* performance, which could only be described as absolute grace under stress.

"She's still gaining, Sam."

"Yes, Tim, she is."

"It appears that le netting did not work, eh?"

"No," said a dejected Samuel. "No it appears it did not. And we are going too fast and at the wrong angle to have the line we are trailing do its job. Cut that cable, Tim. It's only slowing us down."

"She can't be more than five hundred yards off, Captain," declared Eli, looking over his shoulder. "What are we going to do?"

Samuel remained silent. The *Alabama* was gaining and picking up more speed than ever. I could clearly see the enlisted men loading cannon with shot. On the bow one of two men flashed a lantern.

"They are signaling us, *Capitaine*."

"I can see that, Mr. Theroux."

"What does it say, Sam?"

"In one word? Surrender!"

"I'm afraid, Samuel."

He placed his arm around me and kissed me on the head.

"They are loading cannon, Sam," informed Tim.

"I don't think they will fire upon us now," declared Samuel. "They have the upper hand. Besides, they must see that we have women on board."

"What's going to happen now?" I asked.

"They will take the *Sphinx* as a spoil of war. With James Dunwoody Bulloch on that ship, I will be taken prisoner and sent to Richmond. Destroying the *Sphinx* is the last thing he would want to do. He wants to take this ship intact. It would be a trophy for him ... sweet revenge."

"No, Samuel, we can't let them!" I cried. "We must keep going."

Samuel wistfully took me by the arms. He looked me in the eye with a doleful smile. "It's no use, Emily. Know that I love you, and the sacrifice I'm about to make is for your safety ... Amy's safety."

"No, Samuel, the ship, the crew?"

"The crew will understand," he said, turning his back to me. "There is nothing else we can do. If we don't surrender they will fire upon us. It's only a matter of time before they are broadside and have a clear shot to our bow. James Bulloch wants this ship. He has nothing to lose. If he can't have her, he will sink her. We will all die and no one will ever know."

I looked over Samuel's shoulder at the approaching Confederate ship. It was now closer than ever. A white moon would be the only witness to what was about to occur. I was not so worried about what would happen to me. I felt dreadful sorrow for the faith of the *Sphinx*'s African crew and the impending injustice that would surely befall them. After all, they did not need to come on this trip. They did so because they felt a sense of devotion and duty to a captain who helped set them free from injustice, tyranny, and repression.

"There is nowhere to hide them, Emily. I could set them off on our small whaleboat. Even so, in this bright moonlite, they would be discovered and easily captured. Besides, the fate they would endure on a small boat this far out from shore would be worst than anything that awaits them on the *Alabama*."

"We must do something, Samuel. Please!"

He gave me a look of reprimand, compounded by defenseless guilt. "There is nothing I can do, Emily. Don't you understand?" he shouted.

I lowered my head and began to cry.

He brought the heel of his fist down on ship's rail, gritted his teeth, and closed his eyes. He shook his head. "There is nothing that can be done. Absolutely nothing."

Between his vulnerability and the sense of betrayal he felt for his crew, along with my daunting sensitivity, it must have been one of the saddest days of his life. I know it was for me. I started down the deck, leaned over the rail, and watched as the Alabama steamed behind us. One of the crewmen walked over and stood by me. I wanted to apologize. That would only make me feel worse and perhaps him too.

"Are you afraid, Tabue?" I asked.

He rested his elbows on the rail and stared up at the moon. "Yes, Miss. I am afraid. Afraid for you and Miss Amy."

Astonished by his revelation, I opened my mouth, but my words were aborted as he continued to speak.

"There is nothing that they can do to me that I have not been wise to," he said.

"What do you mean?"

"I have been a slave all my life. Freedom to me tastes sweet but I am not allowed to swallow it. You see freedom is a condition of the soul and mind. The body has no say. And though there is no paper that tells me when to come and go any longer, such a paper still lives in the hearts of men. Even up here in the North. I have been grateful to the Captain. I have experienced freedom, been treated like a gentleman, with honor, dignity, and kindness. All thanks to your man. So, if I must be honest and answer your question … No I am not afraid. Come what may."

I lightly rested the tip of my fingers on his forearm. "Hold on to hope, Tabue, hold on to hope."

"Is that an order, Miss?" he said, with grinning moonlit teeth.

I smiled and walked back to the rear of the ship. Above my head a bedsheet-sized American flag flapped in the fresh breeze. Poor Samuel. It was with mixed regret that he was prepared to surrender *Sphinx*. I understood now. We are left with no alternative.

As I watched the cruiser get closer, there was a sudden blaring rumble. The booming blast echoed ominously between the two ships. We all took cover, though there was really nowhere to go. The *Alabama* had fired a volley forward of our starboard bow with their pivoting cannon.

"That's our warning Mr. Monroe." said the captain. "Run up a white flag and hove-to. We will await instructions."

Eli reluctantly prepared to turn the ship around and place her in irons. While he spun the wheel the *Sphinx* suddenly came to an early and unexpected halt. Something had stopped us. The action swept everyone off their feet. Tim was thrown to the deck. I was flung across the quarterdeck coming to rest in Samuel's arms. Marcus Theroux hung onto the ship's gunwale as he dangled over the side. Tim hurried over and gripped the desperate man by the hand.

"Sam, give us a hand!" he shouted, clutching the French doctor's arm.

Samuel grabbed onto Marcus' collar and immediately pulled him up on deck. Suddenly, the vessel heaved and shuddered as the bow rose high out of the water. I clung onto Samuel with fright. The ship climbed higher and higher until the bow dangled twenty feet into the air and listed terribly. Finally, an enormous wave washed beneath the ship and it settled back down, gently gliding into a hilly sea.

"What in God's name just happened?" cried Tim.

"Freak wave," said Samuel.

"Look, Captain!" shouted an alarmed Eli, pointing in the direction of the warship.

"What is it?"

"I see it," echoed Marcus. "Le whale! It must have swum under the ship once again."

A hulking, black dune surfaced as the sea rolled off a shimmering onyx frame. It was unmistakable—the white-fluke whale was back. It dove and surfaced and dove again as it swam speedily away from us and toward the *Alabama*. Its enormous white tale ascended high into the air illuminated by an aberrant, bright moon. We could make out its immense, protracted flukes tangled—wrapped in a heap of rope and netting. It flung a mesh of line high into the air as it tried to free itself. We watched in bewildered amazement as it swam toward the steaming cruiser, trailing an endless slew of snared webbing and tangled rope. With its nose into the wind, the schooner's sails flapped wildly. We all stood frozen with astonishment by what had just happened. Just when it looked like the furious beast would collide with the soaring warship it vanished into the void of an endless sea. Suddenly the *Alabama* heaved and heeled, twisting to a stop as the two-hundred-ton monster lunged beneath the two-hundred-and-twenty-foot war vessel.

A minute later a flurry of sooty smoke fluttered from the *Alabama's* iron stack, rising up into a moonlit sky. Samuel rushed to the rail and gazed out toward the prostrated warship. The Confederate cruiser unexpectedly and abruptly heaved, twisted, and changed direction—its crew in a panic. Another plume of pitch-black smoke spewed from its stack—then nothing. The *Alabama* sat motionless.

"Look, Captain, the warship has changed direction," declared Eli.

"Sam! He looks dead in the water," said Tim.

"He's done it … by God, the whale has done it," uttered Samuel, banging his fist on the rail. "Let's see if you can catch us now, Mr. Bulloch!" He walked away leaving us to stare out at the prostrated *Alabama* and wondered what was next. "Mr. Monroe, take her out of irons! And get this lady underway, now!

"Aye, aye, Captain."

"Steer south by south east, a hundred and forty degrees."

"A hundred and forty degrees, Captain!" replied Eli with a determined grin.

The *Sphinx's* sails hardened as it bore away into the lunar night. On a starboard beam reach, the schooner immediately began picking up speed. The black smoke spewing from the smoke stack on the *Alabama* had ceased and the warship drifted as its crew frantically trimmed sail.

"What's happening?" I asked.

"The white-fluked whale!" declared Samuel, a tenacious flicker in his eye.

"The warship! She's not moving!" announced Tim.

"Let's give them the chase of their short careers, gentlemen, shall we?"

"Why the last-minute decision to run, Sam?"

"Le whale has come to our assistance, Mr. Cadman!"

"Right, Mr. Theroux," exclaimed Samuel. "My guess is when the whale swam under the *Alabama* the netting and rope he was trailing became caught in the war cruiser's propeller."

"Are you certain, Samuel?" I asked.

"The black smoke it ejected from its smokestack … a sign that the engine was struggling. Then when she rounded up and the smoke stopped, I was certain. The white-fluked whale must be tethered to the ship's propeller and dragging her away from us."

"She's floundering, Captain," announced one of the crewmen.

"Looks that way," said an optimistic Samuel. He studied the warship as we quickly made distance.

"We are placing some space between her," announced a cheerful Tim.

"All we need is a small head start," declared Samuel. "Just enough to keep us out of range of their guns. If they can't start their engine, we will surely lose them."

"What about that poor whale?" I asked.

"With any luck, he will set himself free," replied Samuel. "With his size and weight he should easily pull away and part that tackle."

The frosted moon became smaller and higher in the sky. With Tim at the wheel, Eli retreated below deck where he took a well-needed respite. Samuel, Marcus, and I sat with fingers crossed, but there was no sign that the *Alabama* was following. It was now a speck on the horizon. All around us the scintillating crests of effervescent waves reflected its phosphorescent light—tinsel nebulas, dancing off the tops of wheeling swells tumbling like silver surf onto a golden beach. Behind us, our blistered wake fizzed and sparkled in a lustrous turquoise illumination. It faded into the dim moonlight and the black retreating sea as we sailed ahead. The ocean had turned beautiful once again. The Labrador coast receded and the day was quickly becoming nothing but a bad dream … a dream that will reign with my thoughts for as long as I live.

Unexpectedly, Amy made an appearance. "Are we almost home?" she muttered, still half asleep and rubbing her eyes.

We laughed.

"What ship are you on, silly girl! We are still a week away from home," said Tim.

"Stop picking on me," she pouted, like a spoiled child who had just awakened.

Only Amy could have slept through everything we had just been through. Neither whale nor cannon would be allowed to detour her from anything she needed. And at that moment it was rest. She wore a dress I had lent her while her clothing dried. The dress itself never looked so radiant. Though it fit loosely around the hips, her breasts tugged at the buttons, spreading the material along her chest.

"Are my clothes dry yet?" she asked, with a curled petulant lip. She poked the strained fasteners along her bosom, testing their resiliency. "I'm afraid I'm bursting out of place."

"Looks great from here," declared Tim, smacking his lips.

"Oh, stop it!" she griped with a moue.

"I'm afraid they will not be completely dry for a couple of days," said Samuel. "Not in this salty sea air."

"Oh, shoot! This dress is tight on me," she declared. "Don't you have another, Emily."

"Loosen some buttons," urged Tim. "We don't mind."

"Oh, shut up!"

"I prefer you in that dress," said Tim.

"You really think so, Timothy?" she said with a faux shyness.

"You look *marveilleux*, Mademoiselle Amy," proclaimed Marcus.

"Don't worry about the dress. Come sit with us." I implored. "It's a beautiful night."

"Where are the other ships?" she inquired looking around as if asking about the weather. I laughed and gave her a hug.

"Oh, Amy, I love you," I declared. "You are so calming and together."

She shot me a vacuous glance. "I hope I didn't put you all through too much trouble," she said.

"Oh, I wouldn't say you did!" said Samuel.

The men looked at one another. A preposterous countenance danced on their faces.

"No trouble at all," I said laughing.

"I can't tell you how happy I was to see you all," she declared.

"Feel like talking about things?" I asked.

"Oh, it was terrible! Just terrible. I have worn the same dress for over a week."

"Why were you on that ship in the first place?" Samuel asked, somewhat irritatingly.

"Looking for clues."

"And?" I added.

"I don't want to talk about it." She crossed her arms and frowned.

"No one is making you," said Tim. He looked over at me and winked.

Amy gazed over at him as if his remark was rude.

"That's right," I affirmed. "You don't have to tell us or do anything you don't want to."

And indeed, she did not. That should go without mention. Amy had a mind of her own and when she used it, few could tussle with her and claim any success. For now, she would remain a reservoir of treasured enlightenment. And when she was ready she would tell us—in her good time, of course. And that was fine by me. Wicked and fine.

—◦∕◦∕◦—

Chapter 27:

The voyage back to Westport took a little longer than expected. We stopped in Halifax one more time to look in on David and see if he was ready to go home. We found him doing better. He alleged that he was not prepared to go home and instead would remain in Canada awhile … perhaps forever. His sight had returned and like Samuel once did, he used a walking stick. He did look happy. Before we left Canada, he introduced us to a young nurse who was looking after him. He shocked even Samuel to how kind and sweet he was to her. Her name was Mary Sawyer. MS, the same initials as Mary Sullivan. I had noticed that the pendant with the anchor and heart was now around her neck. All bets were off that he would ever return to Westport again.

With the war down South heating up, the world had become a different place. Perhaps it always was. Maybe I had finally realized what was always there. And it was I who had become a different person.

While in Nova Scotia we discovered that Confederate commerce raiders were scouring the coast from Newfoundland to Brazil for whalers and merchant ships from the North. Though it was probably unlikely that we would encounter the *Alabama* again, the *Sphinx* hugged the craggy Maine coast in an attempt to evade another unpleasant confrontation. In doing so, we stopped in some beautiful anchorages, including Eastport, Mt. Desert Island, and Boothbay Harbor. Once we entered Massachusetts' waters, we made a short stop at Gloucester to apologize to the proprietor of all the line and netting we had tossed overboard and to promise him a new shipment if he still needed one—at no charge. It was a small sacrifice and meager expense to save the *Sphinx* from a certain end.

Finally, we made one last overnight stop at Cuttyhunk Harbor. We all deserved it. Samuel spoke to a couple of fishermen who were sailing home to Westport and who were kind enough to spread the word that Amy was safe and that the *Sphinx* was back. We would be in Point Village by noon on the morrow.

The next day, the *Sphinx* started for home just before sunrise. As we sailed into Westport waters, the first sign of light appeared. Above the horizon, the North Star shined brightly, tipping the Big Dipper over on its edge. Just below it, Gooseberry Island was to starboard and Two Mile Rock to port. I could clearly see the scabrous mound we called the Knubble. To the right of it sat the narrow opening and the sandy shores of Horseneck Point. Here we would thread the eye of the needle and enter the safety of the river and Cherry and Webb Harbor.

As the schooner was being tied to Lee's Wharf, a small contingency of spectators had gathered. Jubilant cheers and a frenzy of applause rang out in the early morning sunlight. Amy's father, Louisa, and the staff and proprietors of Cory's store all watched as we prepared to disembark.

Townsfolk lined up to praise and thank the captain of the schooner *Sphinx* for a job well done. Though we told no one of our mission, gossip in little Point Village was alive and thriving.

Tim let down the gangplank and Amy ran into her father's loving arms. Mr. Chaloner thanked Samuel profusely, while Louisa and Amy embraced. Handshakes and pats of the back were extended freely. We had not been home long before we hear the sad rumors that the whaler *Kate Cory* had been sunk by the southern navy. Sad news indeed.

As I greeted Louisa, she peered over my shoulder, eagerly, for sight of her French suitor. She did not have long to wait. Before the good doctor could take his last step, off the ship's gangplank, Lulu ran over to him. Marcus Theroux bowed, and attempted to kiss her hand. Louisa slapped it away and threw herself into his arms. Before we knew it, Marcus was on one knee proposing marriage.

Samuel and I scurried over to congratulate the happy couple.

Louisa beamed as she told us of the happy news. "Marcus and I are getting married!" she announced.

"My, my, that was sudden." I said.

"Congratulations, my good man," said Samuel, shaking the doctor's hand. The elated Frenchman embraced him, kissing Samuel on both cheeks. Samuel blushed.

I smiled.

The happy look on Louisa's face quickly trickled away and she became sullen and foreboding. "Oh, Emily. I'm so happy you are back," she said, embracing me.

"And I'm happy to see you too, Louisa."

"You must tell me all that's happened!"

"Well, I can tell you for certain that the Drift River Readers Club will never investigate another murder, ever!"

Her eyes watered and she embraced me again. "Oh, Emmie!"

"What is it, Louisa? You're crying! I thought you wanted to get married."

"No, it's not that. I … I can't say."

"Can't you?" asked Samuel. "Why not?"

"Your father wants to see you, Sam," said Louisa. "Right away."

"Where is Father?"

"I thought for certain he would be here to greet us," I said.

"He is waiting for you at your place, Emily."

"For me? Is something wrong with Grandmamma!"

"Mrs. Davis has been staying with her. She is not well." Louisa threw her hand over her mouth and sobbed, "I can't say. I just can't!"

I ran up Point Road, leaving everyone behind. I arrived at the bungalow and burst in the front door. Samuel and Marcus were right behind me. Standing by the kitchen door was Seabury Cory. He shook his head while staring down at the floor and placed a forlorn hand on my shoulder as I walked in. Samuel rushed in—Marcus at his heels.

"It is not good, Emily," lamented Seabury. "Her time is coming, I'm afraid. Mrs. Davis is in with her now. She has been caring for Charlotte for the better part of a week now."

"Father, Mr. Theroux is a doctor," said Samuel. "Perhaps there is something he can do for her."

Seabury Cory shook his head. Father and son embraced. "There is nothing anyone can do," he said.

I threw myself into Samuel's arms looking for support and courage before going into the tiny bedroom. "Please come with me, will you Marcus?" I pleaded.

"Why of course, Mademoiselle."

The curtain to the tiny room was pushed aside. Abbie Davis came walking out. She silently took my hand in hers and gently patted my wrist. I thanked her for looking after Grandmamma. She shook her head and offered me a dour smile.

I pulled back the linen curtain, entered the room, and knelt by Grandmamma's side. Marcus examined her. Her breathing was shallow and of brief duration. She looked so old. She had aged considerably in the short month I was away. Guilt and remorse washed over me. While I waited for Marcus' diagnosis, I stood up and looked out the little window above Grandmamma's bed and down at the Two Sisters, the old willow trees by the river's edge. The evening breeze swept their flexing limbs like flowing, green locks of leafy hair. A grousing flock of black crows circled the weeping giants. Their haunting caws echoed up the river valley. Time was passing swiftly. Beyond the cascading trees I could make out the same old lonely fisherman that Grandmamma often watched, drifting down the tributary in his little white skiff, his fishing pole and line draped over the side. I wanted to scream out to him that life was passing by, to ask him, why he dallies without a care in the world … unaware. Then again, perhaps he knew something I did not. As always, the tiny boat was ushered by a regiment of begging mallards following like a string of feathered rosary beads.

Was it I who was unaware?

Three little boys ran, laughing, along the flowered field behind the house, chased by a bumptious, little, golden-haired girl begging kisses. I remember playing the same callow games just yesterday, or at least it seems that way to me. It all went by so quickly. Life! No potion, fame, or riches, could change the order of things—not a single one.

Marcus turned to me and whispered. "She does not have long, Mademoiselle Emily. God speaks to her now."

He lowered his head and disappeared into the kitchen where the somber gathering waited. I was astonished when Marcus' news had not evoked tears. I thought about it. They just were not there. Perhaps it was the shock of the moment. I couldn't say.

On the other side of the curtain I could hear the murmuring drone of voices in purring whispers, as everyone echoed their sentiments. I sat down on the side of the bed and took Grandmamma Charlotte White's sweet hand into mine. It was so delicate and tiny. Hard to believe that these rickety thin fingers, withered and drawn, had scoured floors, toiled gardens, made potions, delivered babies, and mothered countless children—other people's children. Though her limbs looked spindly and haggard, to me they only spoke to tender devotion. I studied her face and called her name. There was no reply, only short, fleeting breaths. Something beckoned me to look over to the curtain, which separated the tiny room from the kitchen. I expected that someone would walk in at any moment. They did. And just as I had anticipated, it was Tim Cadman.

"Can I come in?" he whispered.

"Yes, please."

He meekly walked over and stood over me.

"You need to be here, don't you, Tim?" I said.

He bit his lip and nodded. I knew why he was there. He knew why he was there. He knew much more than anyone could ever know. He had

witnessed it at the Sanford Sawmill, and again on Cuttyhunk Island—
communed with it as it harvested his best friend, Josh. He was not about
to let me greet this tempestuous moment alone. We would stand up to it
together.

He rested a sentient hand on my shoulder. We patiently waited.
Grandmamma's bony hand twitched and quivered as I tenderly held it. She
lightly gripped my fingers as if to say goodbye. Then her hand went limp.
Eerily, I could feel the essence of existence, the wisdom of the soul, and
the cognizant spirit of being, abandon her old frail body. The sensation
pulsated and fluttered up my arm to my shoulder where Tim's big hand
rested. He began to shiver, gripping my shoulder tightly as life dissolved
into eternity before our very eyes. Suddenly the sensation I had felt ceased,
Grandmamma's hand became withered and cold. Tim removed his from
my shoulder and stepped away. She was gone.

I turned and looked back at him. I asked if he was alright. He
nodded and hid his face, smuggling a brave tear with his hand. We had
gone through so much together. Death had taunted us. Still we remained
resistant if not unyielding, resolute if not single minded. Bravery and
prudence had become our edict. We had become its masters. As always,
death had won.

I looked out the window. The day was crisp and the air gusty. A tepid
breeze tunneled up the Westport River. The crying willows were briskly
tousled. It was Grandmamma's perfect kind of weather. Tears finally
ruptured down my face. There will always be tears at times like this.
Grandmamma often said, *We cry for those who left us not because they
have gone, but because we are left alone.*

Wildflowers in the overgrown field behind the house gently swayed
with the taunting breeze. Suddenly, the wavering willow trees waxed
placid and still. I knew Grandmamma was with them.

GLOSSARY OF NAUTICAL TERMS

Aft-main: On a schooner, having two masts, the aft-main pertains to the mainsail on the mast closer to the rear of the ship.

Backstay: Wire or rope that travels between the top of the mast to the transom of the boat and holds the mast up and from falling forward.

Bark: A sailing vessel in which the main mast or the foremast has a square-rigged sail or sails. A ship that has sails that hang perpendicular to the ship and facing forward.

Beam*:* The width of the ship, from side to side.

Belaying pin: A pin or rod, typically made of metal or wood, usually along the rail of a ship where ropes, lines, and sheets can be tied.

Bilge: The inside belly of a ship where the bottom of the hull curves and meets the side of the ship.

Bow: The very front of the ship.

Bowline: A non-binding knot. One which can be easily untied no matter what load is placed upon it.

Bulkhead: Walls inside of a ship that separate compartments and which add strength and rigidity to the hull of the ship.

Cable: On a ship, a cable may refer to wire or rope.

Capstan: A revolving cylinder used on a ship for winding the cable or chain for anchoring a ship.

Chainplate: A strong point or steel plate bolted to the ship's sides, transom, or bow and to which the stays, rope, or wire which hold up the mast(s), are attached.

Come About: To change the ship's direction.

Companionway: The opening in the cabin deck leading to steps or stairs and the ship's interior.

Crans iron or fitting: An iron ring with eyelets. The ring wraps around the tip of the bowsprit and supports the wire or cables, which hold up the mast and support the bowsprit.

Crown and anchor: A simple gambling game of dice, traditionally played by sailors in the Royal Navy or fishing fleet.

Davits: Small crane or superstructure used to suspend or lower small boats.

Deadeye: A circular wooden block with grooves around the circumference to take a lanyard or rope, usually in series, and used to adjust the tension on the shrouds on a ship.

Doghouse: A raised portion of the deck to provide headroom below.

Fairlead: A ring or slot in the side of the ship to guide a rope and keep it from moving about and therefore chaffing.

Flensing: To slice the skin or fat from the carcass of a whale.

Forecastle: The forward part of a ship below deck, traditionally used as the crew's living quarters.

Fore-main: On a schooner, having two masts, the fore main pertains to the sail on the mast closer to the bow of the ship.

Forestay: A stay leading forward and down to support a ship's foremast.

Frigate: A fast naval vessel, generally having a lofty ship rig and armed with guns on one or two decks.

Gaff: A spar or boom rising aft of a main mast and supporting the fore or aft main sail having four sides (gaff sail).

Galley: A kitchen or cooking area on a ship.

Gam: To visit or converse with one another for social or business purposes.

Gangplank: A flat plank or small, movable bridge-like structure for use by persons boarding or leaving a ship at a wharf, dock, or pier.

Gunwale: The upper edge of the side of a vessel at the rail.

Halyard: Any line or tackle for hoisting a spar, sail, or flag.

Hawsepipe: An iron or steel pipe in the stern or bow of a vessel through which an anchor cable passes.

Heave to: To stop a sailing vessel by turning it through the eye of the wind and backfilling the sails without readjusting their sheets or lines.

Hove to: (see heave to)

Hull speed: The maximum speed a sailing vessel can attain, for which is determined by the length of the ship at the water line.

In irons: A ship that has lost its wind and forward motion and has come to a stop or left drifting.

Knots: A unit of speed used by nautical vessels, being one nautical mile (about 1.15 statute miles per hour).

Lanyard: A short rope or wire through a deadeye to hold and make taunt standing rigging.

Lead line: A thin line that is dropped off the side of a vessel to determine the depth of the water.

Loggerhead: A rounded post, in the stern of a whaleboat, around which the harpoon line passes and is controlled.

Masthead: The very top of a ship's mast.

Monkey fist: A ball fashioned into the end of a line to act as a weight for throwing, usually in a decorative weave.

Port: The left side of a ship (as you face forward toward the bow).

Quarterdeck: The part of a ship, usually aft of the main mast, or at the stern or rear of a vessel.

Ratline: A series of small ropes across a ship's shrouds to act like rungs to a ladder and used for climbing the rigging.

Reach: A point of sail in which the wind is within a few points of the side or beam of a ship, or either forward of the beam (called a close reach), directly abeam (called a beam reach) or aft-beam (called a broad reach).

Rigging: The ropes, chains, wire, etc., employed to support the mast, sails, etc.

Rockweed: A seaweed growing on rocks and exposed at low tides, usually having egg-shaped air bladders set in series at regular intervals in the fronds of the plant.

Roundup: When a ship is no longer in control and heads up into the wind or into irons, causing the boat to slow down, stall out, or tack. When the wind overpowers the ability of the rudder to maintain a straight course, the ship is said to be rounding up.

Rudder: A post hanging from the rear of a ship and contains some sort of flap or blade used to steer a ship. The rudder is controlled by a tiller or ship's wheel.

Schooner: A sailing ship with two or more masts, typically with the foremast smaller than the main mast, which is closer to the rear of the ship.

Samson post: A strong pillar fixed to a ship's deck to act as a support for a tackle, anchor chain, or line, or other equipment, with most being located at the bow of the ship.

Sheets: These are the lines that control and tie the ends of the sails to a winch or cleat.

Shroud: A set of ropes or wire forming part of the standing rigging of a sailing vessel and supporting the mast from the sides.

Sloop: Historically, a small square-rigged warship with two or three masts, but in modern times used to describe a single-masted sailboat with one main sail and a jib.

Sounding: The action or process of measuring the depth of the sea or other body of water.

Spar: A thick long pole such as is used for a mast to support the bottom of a main sail and/or the top of a gaff sail. A bowsprit is sometimes referred to as a spar.

Starboard: The right side of the ship (as you face forward toward the bow).

Stay: A rope, wire, or rod used to support a ship's mast, leading from the masthead to another mast or down to the deck at the bow or stern of the ship. Not to be confused with a shroud that supports the mast from the sides.

Stern: The rear portion of a ship, opposite from the bow.

Tack: To maneuver the head of a sailing ship from one side of the wind, into the wind, and onto the opposite side of the wind.

Topping lift: Wire or rope used to support a spar or boom on a main sail or other sails and usually attached to the top of the mast.

Topside: The upper part of a ship above the waterline.

Transom: The flat or rounded surface forming the stern of a ship.

Trying: The process of obtaining whale oil by boiling strips of blubber harvested from a whale.

Try pot: Large tub, pot, or container used to help extract whale oil from blubber.

Tryworks: Location usually aft of the foremast on a whaling ship containing one or two cast iron pots set into a furnace and where whale oil is extracted and cooked from whale blubber.

Whisker stay: A line, wire, or chain usually attached between the sides of the ship at the bow and to the end of an extended boom, pole, or bowsprit, made to hold the spar in place and where a sail can be attached.

Yankee sail: A triangular jib sail usually flown off the tip of the bow or bowsprit and hung high on its stay.

The Whaling Brig Kate Cory at her Home Port in 1862
by John Stobart.

A hearty thanks to Sandy Heaphy of MHP Enterprises, Inc. for her gracious assistance in obtaining the authorization for the use of John Stobart's painting. I would also like to express my heartfelt appreciation to gentleman John Stobart for his kindness in allowing his perfect painting to be used for the cover of this book. Prints of Stobart's works can be purchased through stobart.com.

ACKNOWLEDGEMENTS

I would like to thank my publisher and editor, Stefani Koorey, for her endless assistance in adapting this narrative into print and express my appreciation for her extraordinary talent in constructing and fashioning the cover design for the book.

Thanks also goes to Pat Stafford for her skill in proofreading my drafts. Much gratitude goes to the Westport Historical Society for taking the time to reply to my historical inquiries. And finally, my praise and friendship to furry Onsloe for his patience and calmness and diligently waiting for his walk.

ALSO BY MICHAEL BRIMBAU

*By the Naked Pear Tree: The Trial of Lizzie Borden,
a Play in Verse* (2015)

❦

The Sadness I Take to Sea and Other Poems (2014)

❦

Lizzie Borden: The Girl with the Pansy Pin (2013)

❦

52091928R00227

Made in the USA
Middletown, DE
07 July 2019